STRANDS OF EXISTENCE 3: KING OF NAUGHT

Aino Lahteva

To friends forgotten.

CONTENTS

I

The rooms in the Needle buzzed, hummed, and were a mess of treatises and studies, broken distilling equipment, and other instruments. Only one small, light-filled room under the highest chamber had no trace of the other world or the anxiety that I had felt in the Needle the last time.

And more importantly, it wasn't my old room or a room I had shared with Riestel. It was the only place I could spend the night with Rime. It had simple, light gray furniture and curved walls. The floor was of warm, aged, gray-hued planks. The room was filled with calmness, order, and silence in its entirety.

Rime pulled the sturdy oaken sofa and widened it into a bed. Frazil's servants brought us quilts and pillows. They tried to shoo Rime away from the bed, but he directed them back out with no hesitation and kept making the bed himself.

Now that the city had been taken, it was hard to stay the questions I didn't want to ask. When we had fought Irinda, I still had an ounce of doubt about my feelings, but not anymore. I had no idea how to live without Rime. He had become my missing piece. It was a dreadful feeling, and quite a solid piece of evidence of my stupidity from one life to another.

"Shall this do for the lady?" he asked, pleased. "It's a little cramped, but should work for a few nights."

Rime kicked off his shoes and let himself fall on the bed. It groaned an objection like it had forgotten what it was made for. Rime looked at me and waited.

"What is the matter? Put that pillow down and come to me," he urged.

I fiddled with the corner of the ornamental pillow and laid it down on the chair next to me. I walked over to Rime and sat on the bed. He frowned and raised himself on his elbows.

"Are you afraid to be alone with me, now that you know what I am?"

"I don't know if fear is the right word."

"Uneasiness then? I know I've kept you in the dark on some things. I lied about the letter; I have further secrets too. And now you are here, safe, for the first time in a while. It is natural that you'd question everything. I see it often in soldiers after their first taste of war," Rime told me calmly, turning on his side and taking my hand in his. "And you're a liar too," he noted, smiling. "You kept my father's secret."

"Even?" I suggested.

"I don't think it matters. We did what we did for our life and this city. It couldn't have been helped. There aren't many things that are more important than the welfare of this land."

"You are so committed to this city. I am rather jealous at times. If I were to be truthful from now on, would you do the same?"

"I won't promise that. It's not a useful promise. I pledge you my loyalty. I will never do anything against you, no matter what it might look like. That's more important. Will it be enough?"

"I should think so."

"A hesitant answer. Have I done something to deserve it?"

"No. And you are right. Loyalty is more important. But it cannot be helped that you married an inquisitive woman. If I could, I'd dig out all the mysteries in the world. Maybe I will."

I laid down and pressed myself against him. I was at home with him. Despite knowing now why he calmed me so efficiently. It was strange to think my negative feelings could feed him.

"Strange, isn't it?" I whispered.

"What?"

"This silence. It was only a day ago that you couldn't hear anything but the sounds of battle. Now we are in perfect peace. I can still hear everything in my ears. As if it was still happening."

"The echo lasts for a while, then it becomes a memory," Rime mused.

"Have you experienced it?"

"Many times. I brush it off these days. I can stop the thought before it grows and grows."

Rime stroked my cheek. My whole body tensed up.

"You do feel it?" he breathed. "You are safe. I wouldn't harm you. You know that. I've never laid a finger on you, even when I was dying and it would have saved me, as I needed a soul to heal. Not earlier either, when you were the one ill and defenseless. Why would that change?"

"I know…" I replied. It was the truth. But at the same time, I could see a small stream running from me to him. The stream carried my worries and fears, all that I would give away in a heartbeat. He had never taken any memories and life force that I wouldn't have willingly volunteered.

"You are learning about your powers to keep us safe. I will do the same. There isn't anything we can't solve," he assured me.

"I love how much faith you have. So much that I can't do anything but believe you. Wait, do you remember the time you were unconscious? I thought you didn't know what happened when the arrow hit you?"

"I didn't then. Later I had flashes. The mind takes a while to heal. You made the choice that kept me alive. I had no way to reach the souls myself."

"I didn't know what else I could have done. I… I wasn't about to lose you," I confessed softly and looked away. Rime turned my head back.

"Don't be ashamed of it," he ordered before kissing me. "It kept me here. Do you think I'd rather be dead?"

I closed my eyes as he kissed my neck. Now that I knew it existed, I could feel his shadow around me at all times. It crisscrossed through all that existed in the room. I suppressed my natural fears and pressed closer. We had chosen each other, we broken and created. The worry bowed its heads down only for a moment. His touch was tender and lingered, but Riestel's threats of the fate of our progeny didn't relent. I jumped up.

"What now?" Rime groaned and turned on his back.

"What if I get pregnant? We have been at this for a while, and though I have medicines. They aren't exactly foolproof."

"What of it?"

"What would you… do… if we had twins? Would you do as was done to you?"

"Come here."

"Please, tell me…"

Rime got up on his knees on the bed and grabbed my arm. He pulled me back without yielding one inch.

"Do you understand how unlikely that would be? They aren't just born. They are made with healers. Do you see anyone else here? The only healer close by is Riestel. Do you suppose he would help me knock you up?" Rime laughed grimly.

I shook my head. The mere thought was ludicrous. I cursed Riestel. I had to learn how to guard my feelings and thoughts better. It was silly to allow others to influence them. I laid back on the bed and gazed into Rime's eyes. They looked almost uniformly dark in the dim light. Maybe it was possible to return his soul to a normal soul or to fashion a new one. Anything would be better than just disappearing. If we could do it, everything would be better and these questions wouldn't even exist.

A wonderful lazy pleasure crept into each of my limbs with his touch. I didn't fight it anymore, or, well, just a little for fun.

II

I n the morning, Rime went with his father to inspect the food and seed storages of the Peak and whatever other resources it might offer. I headed to the Needle's main room in my morning robe. It took a lot of effort to maintain the other world in sight, so I always focused on one particular spot and grabbed a hold of what I wanted to examine.

I began to realize that the objects were not in the real Lighter World, but they were in woven pockets between this and it, just as the staircase during my initiation and the tunnel I had jumped through in the battle. They made it possible to travel between locations intact. It was impossible for me to walk in the Lighter World at the same time as in this one. The only person I knew who could was Tammaran.

The stored creatures in the jars were both horrific and beautiful. Six-winged butterflies in the colors of the rainbow, spiders with pulsating, maggot-like behinds. Next to them were notes written with an equally horrid hand than mine. The letters differed greatly from the ones used today, so despite the similarities, I had trouble reading the texts.

Something flashed behind me. I turned and saw the dark figure that once plagued me and stopped me from entering this state while I stayed in Launea's temple. It smirked in an ever-so-familiar manner.

"Do you need help with the handwriting?" it asked, pleased with itself. The dark surface crackled and gave way to a bright blue sun. Then the sun became Riestel.

"Are you fully in the other world?" I guessed, trying not to show any emotions and to seem like I knew the dark figure that taunted me before I had been trained in the Temple had been him.

"No. My body is on its way here."

"On its way? What does that mean?"

"Exactly what I said. Well?"

"Well, what?"

"Can you read her writing? I can help to interpret it. I haven't browsed them much before, but I can read her hand. Istrata mainly spoke of her trials when she needed another point of view. But I suppose we must make an effort to go through them."

"Didn't you even read them after she had died?"

"I said I've browsed some when I've been able to come here unnoticed."

"Just browsed?"

"Do you think it has been easy to spend decades and centuries in this city in the same body? I've had to die and return countless times. It takes time to fight your way back to the Peak after all those who knew me the last time around have gone. I didn't have this kind of access to the Peak before Irinda. She was the first ruler to have the balls to add a consecrator into her entourage. All the good it did her," he snickered. "And after that I was rather busy babysitting her, you, and others like you. And I had my own life, too. This isn't exactly my favorite place in the world."

"How many times have you met me during all of this?"

"Oh, I stopped counting at around twenty. At first, the same semblance of you floated into town each year. I lived in the Harbor at that time. It was convenient, but none of them were viable. It was easier to let you drown than to try to mold something of you," Riestel answered and tilted his head away, frowning.

"You just let me die?"

"If you had seen yourself, you would have chosen it," he sighed, avoiding my gaze. "My body comes."

Two sweaty and out-of-breath servants entered the room carrying Riestel. His manifestation dispersed and entered the body.

"What shall we start on?" he asked once he came to. "Leave us," he ordered the servants and closed to door after them.

"How did you do that?"

"Well, you press the handle and…"

"I hate you," I groaned, though it amused me. "You know perfectly well what I meant."

"So, a lesson instead of studying, fine," he sighed. "When you walked through the wall and into the attic in the temple, you did the same, in a slightly coarser form. Though, you managed to force the transfer of your body thanks to a device and the space Istrata had created and the power that still lingered in them. Going into the true Lighter World... We can only take our consciousness. Taking our bodies is not a safe option at your level. At first, we form something small and simple there to which we can transfer our minds. You will practice moving a fraction of yourself into another body in the Lighter World. A spirit body which you can focus upon and keep intact. You can mold things there as you can in the pockets between. You can create a small vessel to use until you can handle your image. During your time there, your physical body will be useless."

"I'm not sure I understand."

"Not my problem."

"A wonderful lesson; a grand thank you, master."

"You are ever so welcome. I can feel the warmth of your admiration all the way over here," Riestel smirked and smiled with narrowed eyes. "But I offered my assistance in a more important matter. If you don't want it, I have other things to do."

"Alright, help. What do you think we will find in here?"

"Treatises on existence, creation of life, death, souls, and bodies. Whatever subject she may have needed to study to solve the problem. I hope we can get an idea of what she actually did and what went so horribly wrong. Maybe then we can figure out a way to fix the world. And you."

"I don't need to be fixed."

"You don't think so, but the fact that you happily lie with that mongrel of man and beast says otherwise."

"Would a pure monster like yourself be a better option?"

Riestel turned away and drew a book into this world, slamming it on the table.

"Begin with this one before it disappears back," he snapped and headed for the door.

"You can't berate the person I love and get all touchy when I defend him. Don't be such a coward."

Riestel's steps slowed down. He stopped.

"A coward?"

"Did I stutter?" I pressed.

"No," he muttered and turned back. "Fine. At least we have now established you have some backbone."

"What should we look for?" I wondered, ignoring his attempt to annoy me more. I touched the slowly fading book. It solidified again.

"Depends on what question you want an answer to. I do realize I know more of these things than the little lady, but I'm hardly a mind reader."

"How in all the skies can you catch your breath?"

"My breath?" Riestel asked, puzzled.

"I would imagine that amount of self-righteousness would choke anyone."

Riestel slid his tongue over his teeth, trying not to laugh, and drew another book.

"I would advise you to focus on other things than me," he replied, and sat in the only chair in the room. "I'd imagine your husband would appreciate that as well."

"Could you at least answer the question?" I grumbled in frustration, which brought a lovely yet smug glow on to his face.

"The books are color coded by themes. I cannot remember what was what. Let's begin with one color and see if we can find anything resembling proper answers. I presume the most important thing would be to find out how the land can be healed and the primary cause of all this."

"Yes," I agreed. A part of me would be infinitely happier to find a way to build a soul for Rime or even just to stop his body's ability to eat other souls. Of course, I had to ponder if he'd want it. It was impossible to say if empty souls had any part that lingered after death. No one believed they did. They'd just cease to be. A soul cannot manifest itself anywhere but the Lighter World, and they had lost that connection. An alternative was surely worth digging around for.

"If you'd prefer to find a cure for your beloved half breed, you may want to check the animal tests," Riestel remarked when he noticed I was lost in thought. "Though, I warn you, you may spend a lifetime doing so with no success. I have never heard of a way to fix what has been done to them."

I took the red book Riestel had slammed on to the table and sat on the floor.

"What are all those preserved creatures?" I asked while flipping pages that had drawings of plants and lists of their effects and what they contained.

"She was trying to create different and new animals to understand how life and death work. How life evolves here and in the Lighter World, what links them, and how death affects them. What is permanent in what world. Only a few lived for long. Some were moderate successes."

"Is that all you know? You were her lover for years."

"A lover? Could you try to diminish our relationship a little more? Or, well, maybe you don't dare to call things by their correct names."

"A husband, then."

"Indeed. You might not believe it about me... I wasn't studious by nature," Riestel remarked and closed his book for a moment. "I trusted her to solve the issue as she wished. There was no world crisis then. She always explained what she wanted me to know once she had figured something out. I executed what needed to be done. I don't think she ever got far enough in these tests... And... I never asked. I was selfish, thinking that my support and encouragement was all she needed. I brought her food, drinks... supplies... anything and everything, but I never tried to take part. It's a mistake for which I'm paying the price now. If I could have seen all this then, it might have opened my eyes to what too much determination can lead to and what she was truly working on."

"Do you think she wanted help?"

"Absolutely not, but she would have needed it."

"Do you want to help the city now?"

"A dangerous question. It practically exudes that you need a favor."

"I was just thinking about the temple," I mused.

"And how do I come in to it?"

"You know more about us than anyone. You could teach them better than anyone. You could tell us things we haven't known for ages."

"True."

"You once said you would consider helping. Would you?" I requested.

"No."

"Why not?"

"Why would I?"

"Give me a reason."

"You give *me* a reason."

"Because Kerth needs knowledge to survive this. I alone am not enough, neither are you."

"Maybe not. What about it? Do you think I have any desire to play around as an instructor?"

"Just to a few. Just to the former instructors that still live. Teach them to teach others."

"No, thank you," he scoffed and picked up another book.

"Are you truly saying no or just trying to annoy me?"

"Oh, you think in such a limited fashion. It could be both," he answered.

"What would I need to do to make you more amiable to the idea, then?"

"Now you are approaching it from a better angle. Fine. A trade could work. You must help me get to Elona. I do not think I can reach her resting place alone, though I know where to begin."

"To Elona? What would you want with her body?"

"I want to… I need to see if she is dead or still suffers," Riestel explained and cleared his throat. "Wouldn't you want to make sure if someone you loved was at peace?"

"Where would you look for her?"

"Irinda cut off all routes to the chambers below the mountain. They have hundreds of buried kings and their families, but beyond them, there is a… a cemetery of consecrators. A powerful center. If she has been lulled into an almost eternal slumber, that is the place that would keep her. The journey will not take more than a few months, though I'm not sure if it would be into the future or the past. It would only feel like a day or two."

"A few months? Are you mad? I can't just up and leave for months! Aderas and Kerth need us."

"And she does not? I see. I wouldn't suppose you'd feel anything for *your former daughter,* but I think the price is just. As a gesture of good will, I will give you a bit of time to think, and I will go to the trouble of teaching two instructors while waiting. Choose them and set up lodging for them and I will train them."

"You will?"

"I'm not about to repeat myself, but I should think, if your vision was coming true right now, we would have heard about it from the borders or should hear about it in the next few days. If we don't… we may have all the time in the world still. The node may have shown you any time it chose or just mirrored your fears. You can't guide it or ask it things. You are like a child who can see the board but doesn't know the rules.

"Can you use it? Can you check for it?"

"No, we have different gifts. That's not one of mine."

"And what if I don't agree? Will you just stop teaching?"

"I'd like to think you are smarter than that question lets on. Obviously. What kind of trade would it be if you got everything and I nothing?"

"Why would the journey take months? We are already on the mountain," I pondered and looked at the rugged slopes showing from the smaller north window.

"In the light world, there are places where time speeds and where it slows, compared to this one. The Core Chambers is one such place. Time is erratic there. One day may be an hour, a week or a month here. And it can travel both ways, though out here, it only moves forward so when we come back, we may be older or younger. But to get to the burial vault together, you must first learn to travel in the Lighter World as I can. Not completely, but some part of your spirit must do it so we can break the seal of the tomb. With any luck, the lock won't know you are not her."

"You just said you don't want to teach me."

"Did I? I think I answered your query about moving in the Lighter World. The fact that you can't yet do it or understand something doesn't mean I gave a poor answer or that I won't teach you. Our most important goal is to fix this, but it doesn't have to be the only goal. You could try to listen once in a while."

"Then you'd have three students."

"Can I drop one, then? I said I'd train two."

"Don't you dare!"

"Consider my request properly."

"I will."

III

As Rime and Frazil went over the Peak's stores and were more on edge by the day, I devoured books. Riestel had traveled a few days ago to the temple area to talk with Kymenes, and he had done so without attitude. Many consecrators were homeless, as the main temple laid partly in ruins. We had decided to house some of them at the Peak. Riestel, together with Kymenes, prepared them for the move. It wasn't a simple task to relocate dozens of people and their families and possessions here, but having some of Temple's consecrators and administrators and servants here gave us a better chance to sway them to adopt new ways.

Some of the old temple still stood, so temporary walls were built to keep the heat in for those who would remain in the Temple District. Everything worthwhile was being foraged and dug up from the rubble. A new temple or new parts couldn't be built until the spring, and even if the weather permitted it, the funds did not for now. Many were also sent to serve in smaller temples that previously lacked proper staff.

I had gone through the red books. They contained a well of information on nature, plants, and the cycle. Istrata had drawn detailed graphs and noted ways to tally and subtract to find out how much energy and force resided in what plant or how it could be harvested by distilling or destroying it. In some cases, the plants seemed to possess the ability to renew endlessly, even under dire circumstances and allow its life to be harvested bit by bit. Mostly, the greatest benefit to the cycle was destruction.

"Consecratoress," a stuffy sounding Moras greeted me from the doorway. He peered into the room hesitantly, though I had specifically requested his presence.

"Come in. I want to show you something."

"Alright," he muttered and looked around as if something was out to get him. "What is this place? What purpose does it have?"

"Study. You sense the weaved reality, yes? It makes one uneasy at first. Come closer."

Moras frowned but did as I requested. I laid my hand on his forehead to carve a new path in his mind. His first reaction was to pull back, but then he forced himself to remain still. I could extend my ability to see the hidden parts of the room to others this way. But they would have to strengthen the connection by rehearsing to be able to see things without me. His eyes widened, and he reached for the closest hidden object.

"Is this the Lighter World? How can there be things in it?"

"Yes, and no. They have been built from the smallest amount possible and fortify themselves without guidance when pulled into this world. This place is an in-between of two real worlds. You must learn to see it yourself, as our situation is rather dire."

"What situation?"

"My husband has been through the entire Peak. There is no food or anything else to distribute. Irinda contaminated some and burned others before joining the battle. Two-thirds of the city will face famine during the winter. There is nothing we can do to stop it. No matter how well we ration, we cannot guarantee food for all. Therefore, it is vital that as soon as spring comes that we instill faith in the people by showing we can renew the land."

"I will help. Just tell me how," Moras promised, perking up.

"You are different from most of the other Temple's healers. You use poultices and brews, as well as your skills. You count and measure, stir and combine. You use equipment I have never seen others use. I want you to guide us, to come see what must be calculated and how and what good are our talents in the process. I want you to combine the Temple's healers with the folk medics, at least those who can read well enough."

"I would love to. Though I don't quite know why you'd want me to."

"These tomes. You must be able to read them, to copy them," I explained and showed him some of the calculations. "You must pick the plants that will do the most good. Animals too. I have yet to check those books myself. Take this one. This is the most important one, as it contains the formulas. As long as you hold on to it and focus on it, it will stay with you. Let it go, and it will revert back to the higher plane. There's a desk and a quill."

"And when should I gather the other healers?"

"First you must gather what you will teach, then you'll gather the pupils. The language is quite old and some of the terms are not familiar to me. If you cannot interpret something, write it down and I'll ask Riestel when he returns to the Peak. He has a knack for deciphering them. I'll, of course, provide help however I can."

"Right. This is extremely fascinating," he replied, walking towards the chair with his nose so deep in the book he almost walked into the table.

Moras was the first link in my intended chain. A wave of relief washed over me. I would seek help from as many as I could. I would not face this task alone as I did once. I understood some of the formulas but not enough to apply them. Someone like Moras would be much faster and more capable in that and would not have to start at the very basics as I. We read in silence, or, well, Moras read in silence, I read listening to his sighs, grunts, scribbling, and enthusiastic gasps.

"Do we have the equipment mentioned here?" he asked after a long while. His hair was beginning to look like a bird's nest, as he poked it quite often with the quill tangling it up.

"Equipment?" I echoed.

"The ones described here. Distillers and such," he specified and showed the drawing to me.

"Some. Not all. The Queen may have other places such as this. I'll inform you if I find them."

"I'm not sure how I'd make them from scratch if I can't even see broken ones..."

"We will try unless I am able to find them. I've ordered a room to be prepared for you at the base of the Needle. We can gather all we find into that apartment. You will have a private room and five others for experiments and students."

Moras lifted his head and turned in his chair to face me better. He looked quite somber and moved.

"Do you trust me this much?" he asked.

"I've decided to. I see no reason not to," I replied.

Moras took his glasses from his nose and wiped them on his sleeve.

"I thought I would die far from Kerth, on the borders and for naught. Maybe not completely for naught, but I never imagined I would be in the Temple's graces again and that I'd be granted an opportunity to learn new things. Whatever our fate, I'll be forever grateful. I…" he almost continued, but fell silent and lowered his head a bit.

We continued on. The books on animals were, as anticipated, similar to the ones about plants. In some, Istrata had designed new creatures and described how existing ones could be molded into other things with our skills. Their pages contained brief notes about survival times or just the phrase "Failed, find out why."

I stashed away copies that disturbed me. Maybe I could show them to others one day, but now their content was better kept away. It wasn't a matter of good and evil, but such things wouldn't help build trust in me. Istrata's desperation was clear from reading them. All experiments grew darker and required more and more materials.

Among the tomes was one slightly different book, a journal of experiments she had performed on herself. Experiments on how to change herself and how to leave her humanity behind. I hid it away from all the other books.

I retired for the night alone as Rime and Frazil were still arguing over how to best deal with all of it. They didn't agree on much. Frazil couldn't stand that Rime treated him as he had before he became the ruler-to-be, and Rime hated that Frazil thought he should treat him differently. On most occasions, they did manage to write down rules and procedures. The soldiers had been divided between the areas to help with clearing debris and keep peace. Rime pushed Frazil to keep the army in charge for now.

The most important thing was to get the city up and running and to decide on the form of governance. It was their most hotly contested topic. Frazil wanted to give many some modicum of power that would lead to a chain of dozens of decision makers and to set up meeting places for these people to sit on committees to deliberate. Though, he would always hold the last word. Rime felt the country needed a strict and clear ruler, not a watered-down version of a king that would, in time, have no say due to thousands of petty officials blocking all efforts.

Becoming a monarch with ultimate power did, of course, bring with it unique problems, especially due to the city's history. Frazil didn't think Aderas was ready to embrace yet another tyrant, and he wasn't eager to put such a mantle on himself. Still, some of his actions contradicted that claim.

Rime returned in the middle of the night, waking me up.

"Sometimes I just want to punch him," he growled and took off his shirt.

"I doubt that will help," I muttered drowsily. My eyes didn't want to open up, but I forced myself to listen.

"No. But I can't say I didn't enjoy it the first time. I cannot understand why he can't see our situation. For an intelligent man, he is acting like a small child having a tantrum."

"What did you argue over this time?"

"He wished to keep our situation secret from the public. I understand the desire, but why fill their heads with too much hope when it is more than likely he will have to let them down severely?"

"Maybe he has some ideas he hasn't yet shared with you. You know he won't say much until he has it all planned out. Give him a little time."

"I would, if it was mine to give. But think. If he promises the people that he will look after them and provide for them, then he announces we have no water or food to spare and that all must yield theirs for us to ration and settle on whatever we give them back..."

"Many would feel betrayed. It could lead to a mutiny when nothing has been established. The city is already ailing," I guessed.

"Exactly. How can he not see that?"

"He doesn't want to begin his reign with bad news."

"Who would? But it cannot be avoided. Still, it is better for us to see how he would rule now than to see it after the crown has been placed on his head. Never mind. I'll try to reason with him again tomorrow," he sighed and got into bed. "How was your day?"

"Moras arrived. I think he will be helpful in many ways."

"Good. I will not let this city fall due to our actions. Irinda had to be ousted, but I'd hate to think we did it just to hasten our own doom."

"Any news from the Borders?"

"No. I spoke with Veitso about it at length. We decided it was best to withdraw our troops close to the two vasal cities. We will have less ground to cover. We can take the areas back later if some tribe should take it. All soldiers have been ordered to form this new line. We will be able to uphold proper vigil and react quicker should something happen. We still have some scouts circling the old areas, but nothing that you described has been seen yet. Hopefully won't be in the future either."

"I hope that, too."

"The soldiers took the move well. Many wonder why we are withdrawing, but they are happy to return closer to civilization. We'll see how Eladion and Loisto take the news about being a part of the front line."

"How far are the cities?"

"Maybe a ten-day ride, if you have an army horse under you. They are bred to withstand long, hard rides. By carriage, several weeks. We should send the governors official invites to my father's coronation. But their arrival will bring threats and possibilities."

"How much power do they hold?"

"They have a say in their regions, they are Kerth's servants... But it is possible they would seek to take advantage. I would. Especially once they realize how little we have. Frazil has been sending personal messages to them. I haven't been able to intercept any yet. It's disconcerting."

"Maybe he's just making unofficial contacts. Can't we postpone inviting them until the city has recovered a bit more?"

"For a moment. Only until late spring or summer, though, it's not a good idea to stall naming the king. it will give off a weak image and cause its own problems. Once the declaration is made, they must be there. We can polish up places and hide the battle scars on time, but not our weaknesses, should they wish to see them."

I nodded and shuddered as I almost fell asleep mid-thought. Rime looked amused and gently touched the arc of my nose.

"Sleep. I can complain more in the morning," he whispered. "Now, I just want to breathe you in," he added and pulled me closer.

The cool air bothered my toes as I woke up. I drew my leg back into the warmth of the covers. Rime was just getting dressed. The rays of the late morning sun dotted the ceiling and made the room glow in warm tones.

"Aren't you going to get up?" he asked while putting on his cufflinks and taming his hair.

"No," I sighed and pulled the covers tighter.

Rime sat next to me on the bed.

"I was going to take a walk. To explore the Peak a bit. Is that enough to get you out of there?"

"Are you taking the day off?" I asked and sat up. "Finally."

Rime nodded. "Well, sort of. I have the day off, but I'd like to use it for more than sleeping."

I leaned back on my side and drew the cover back over myself.

"What kind of behavior is that?" he laughed and pulled it back down. "I want to spend the day with you, but you know full well it's not in my nature to just *be*."

"I might have noticed," I complained and tried to snatch the cover back from him. "Fine," I laughed and let go. Rime lost his balance just briefly.

"Troublemaker," he accused me and continued getting dressed humming lightly. Then he frowned for the first time today. His boots had a stain. Rime took a cloth from his bag and polished the leather.

"What are you smirking at?" he asked as he noticed I was staring.

"You and your forehead frowns."

"My what?" he scoffed. "I'm not that old."

"Ancient," I giggled and got up. I walked over to the window and cracked it open. It was only slightly frosty. I got dressed and laced my winter boots. Despite my antics, I had no intention of wasting our time together with just slouching about.

The Peak's roads and parks were covered by a soft, fresh blanket of snow. It was mostly untouched and crunched under our feet. Rime studied the Peak's structures and vistas as if he was building a map of everything useful and concerning for the future. We talked about many things but avoided all things related to the future.

We wandered into a small pine thicket near the outer wall of the Peak with a large reservoir next to it. The twisted and curly trees looked as if the wind had first blown them against the ground and once they had reached up, someone had tied them into knots. In their midst, where the ground had a bit more depth before the rock, there were some taller, straighter trees. Rime stopped under one such tree and stared at the city below.

I could feel his thoughts returning to his duties. I was right behind him, so I reached for the pine branch as quietly as I could. Once I got hold of it, I pulled and the light frosty snow fell on him like a storm of flour. Rime turned slowly. His eyebrows were covered with minuscule snowflakes, melting into tiny water beads from his body heat. Before I could escape, I was carried towards a pile of snow. The snow flew up as I went down.

"Help me up", I demanded.

Rime held out his hand and smiled, amused. I brushed the snow off me. Rime stepped closer and wiped my forehead.

"Shall we continue?" he asked.

"I guess," I replied. He turned and took a step forward. I yanked another pine branch.

"Wife…" he growled, but I could tell he was trying hard not to laugh.

"Well, I just really like you in white…"

"Do you hear how that snow bank is calling your name?" he asked, turning around.

"No, I can't hear a thing. Not a peep," I smirked and tugged at the next branch. "You are most definitely imagining it."

The next time I got up from the snow pile, we were both so frostbitten and chilled that we had to return to the Needle. But I had managed to keep him with me and present all day, and that was a victory in itself.

IV

For a few wonderful days, we were able to wake up next to each other and only separate at bedtime. It was a pleasure I easily got used to, though I knew it would be short-lived. Then Frazil announced that he and Rime would go on a tour of the city. The holiday was over and there was no one to complain to.

Frazil had the enormous task of keeping the city unified and under his power while everything reeked of death, all the while life grew more miserable at his command. Most understood that these temporary months of misery would be to sow the seeds of our future once they were told the reasons openly. Rime had been right to trust people.

Everything was soon under rationing. Grains, animals, seeds, root vegetables, wines, beers, fabrics, furs. From the Peak to the Slum's. No one liked it. We didn't either, but there was nothing else to do in order to keep as many as possible alive through the miserable winter. We quietly hoped that the ailing land wouldn't be further burdened yet with more people seeking refuge. If we could have one season of crops with promising results, people would see this wasn't for nothing and that they'd have a reason to hope for the future. They would be hardier with that small light inside them.

I would have gladly gone with them to explore more of the city now that rules about movement between areas were mostly lifted, but I yielded to Frazil's request that consecrators should remain in the shadows for a while and focus on sorting out the main temple's rebuilding. The stories of Irinda's and Riestel's deeds and figures during the battle had spread far and wide. People were uneasy around us. There hadn't been such a show of otherworldly power by a consecrator or a knight of Saraste in generations. People had forgotten we could do more than entertain and heal and that some of us were willing to forgo that conventional role.

Tammaran had moved to one of the floors of the Needle, as Rime wished him to stay close to me when he couldn't. It was a quiet and partial transfer rite to serving the Temple. Riestel would soon be back with the first consecrators. Moras spent most of his time arranging his rooms for his students and trials. Arvida was still with Launea in the Noble's. All sorts of people and things were arriving at the Peak. New servants, superiors, and prisoners.

I touched the node in the White Needle. It was sulking. It didn't want to cooperate. The nexus may have thought I was Istrata at first, but now it had deemed me as a separate creature and didn't yield to my will. I had no intention of giving up, but there was no amount of sheer force to break it, so I left the strange knot in the fabric of the world alone for now. Maybe the last statue would help to unlock it.

I sat by the window in solitude. I reached out my arms, keeping them slightly bent, palms facing each other. I danced using just my fingers and wrists. A gently pulsating wave went back and forth between my palms. The air vibrated. Slowly, the coarser matter pulled back and I could feel my hands slide with my thoughts into another existence. A drop of sweat ran down the side of my nose and broke my concentration. I wiped it and began again. I tried to support my arms better against my body.

As I opened my eyes, I sat in a closed, empty space that was painted by the colors of the deepest, darkest night sky. Between my hands was a small glow which became more and more condensed the more energy I pushed into it. There was about a glassful of the shining material. I turned my left palm upward and swiped the glowing orb with my right index finger. It followed my finger and changed shape according to what I drew. What could I make of it? I put the spring-looking mass down. It didn't vanish right away, even when I let go. It dimmed and started to break down after a while. I placed my hands on both sides of it and pushed more life into it. It shone more steadily again.

My consciousness returned to the Needle as I grew tired. I got up, as focusing again wouldn't be possible before a rest. It would be interesting to see if the object would still be there or the space itself.

I went out to the balcony to cool off. Far away in the south, a carriage that could keep a consecrator in check rolled along the main road. It was bringing Heelis here. I hated that she'd be so close to us. There was no fear, but I disliked being filled with a bitter feeling every time I thought of her.

"Taking a break again," Riestel sighed. He was wearing a temple garment—a long tunic, trousers, and a coat with a belt—all made from three different hues of blue. The red fox fur on his shoulders shimmered and waved in the wind. The bright colors made his skin glassy. His hair was a little longer than it used to be.

"Again. What do you want?"

"Just checking if you've made any progress, but here you are, enjoying the fresh winter air without care and in rather scant clothing. Or were you just thinking about me and needed to cool off?"

"You'll annoy me to an early grave," I scoffed and covered my breasts.

"Maybe," he smiled and leaned on the railing next to me. His icy fingers chimed as they hit the metal.

"Have you given it any thought?" he asked as his eyes narrowed.

"Don't. We can't leave at the moment."

"When?"

"Have I even said I want to follow you anywhere?"

"You don't need to."

"Would you please be bearable just this once?"

"I could try, but what do I get in return?" Riestel asked with a shadow of a smile on his face as he wiped some of the hair strands from covering my neck. I pulled them back. He laughed.

"Besides, I have something for you, so behave," he ordered me softly and put his hand in his inner jacket pocket. He withdrew a small ornamental box. I accepted it hesitantly. The box contained ten seeds.

"For the Needle's glass house. Red irises," Riestel explained and touched a few of the small roundish seeds.

"Red? I didn't know there were red irises. Where are they from?"

"I don't know. People give me all sorts of strange things to buy favor and blessings. I remembered them as my belongings from the Noble's were brought here. I thought you could try to grow them before they spoil."

"I can try. How did things go at the main temple?"

"The cleaning and clearing of rubble are going well. Kymenes has gained much trust among the people, and most accept what must be done. We have drafts of the new curricula. Some of the older consecrators have declined to abide by our rules and will not accept that we want to study the other side. We have given them a period to reflect, but if they do not yield and agree to the new ways, they must depart from the Temple."

"Must we kick them out?"

"Yes. Or do you wish that they stay and whisper poisonous doubts to all ears that will listen? They have no proper reasons, only fear. I have seen a time when the temple folk knew their power and abilities. It should not be feared."

"Are you sure? I was born from that time. This whole catastrophe was."

"I didn't say it's without risk. Istrata's situation became reality, as I wasn't strong enough to stand up to her. No one dared to question her. The whole hierarchy of the temple must be torn apart. Each one must have the courage to point out wrong and dangerous paths and ways. To tell others what they see and experience. Istrata was left alone because she was the peak of it all and everyone wanted her favor. And she wanted to please them and help them. Any doubt that lingered had been hidden behind a smile. Even I."

"Well, politeness certainly hasn't detained you from barking at me."

"One could say we are off to a good start then, couldn't one?"

"I... guess... so?" I sighed and studied the seeds. "I suppose I can't plant them yet. The winter is not even halfway over."

"The glass house won't suffer frost, but there isn't enough light. You can put them in the soil, but don't try to awaken them before the spring."

"I'm sure they will be gorgeous. Thank you."

"Think nothing of it. I can be nice now and then."

"Once a year maybe, don't do it more often. It would be too odd."

"Well, we should talk about the temple more. I want to show in detail what we have planned. Are the governors still out and about?"

"Yes."

"Come dine with me tomorrow evening. We'll eat and chat."

"And the others?"

"Your decision is all we need. I promise I won't do anything uncouth. Don't be so suspicious. Besides, we have the say in these matters, no one else. Or would you rather I come to you?"

"Like I would ever let you in my chambers."

"No? Well, then, show up when it's dinner time."

I knocked my head against the door frame a few times after he left. Still, it was nice that we were on good terms. It was for the benefit of the city. Actually, I was quite elated that the Temple's new course was forming and that Riestel was taking some of the responsibility, despite his muttering. He was even suspiciously helpful.

"Heelis is now in the prison's counter room," Tammaran announced from the door. "She is surprisingly calm. When were you planning on visiting her?"

"I'd rather not."

"And her family? Will you just let them suffer in an eternal state of ignorance?"

"Obviously not."

"I get it. But you were the one who spared her life, so you must decide her fate."

"Stop preaching. Everyone keeps lecturing me," I moaned, annoyed. "I'll go in the morning."

"I have one more issue to press you on, or to preach about."

"Let's have it."

"You promised to return to deal with the bodies after the battle. Now, you have spent half a moon doing many other things. The men await."

"I did. It has been important to get things started here. Changes must be made to the Temple."

"I have no doubts, but people are walking by sky-high piles of cadavers daily in other parts. The piles are not shrinking, though the rats are fat and jolly. It's not good for morale. If you have no intention of returning, they must be transported away. Still, I'd recommend that the good Consecratoress would show the people that she will not just lock herself away in the Needle and leave them behind."

"Frazil is touring for morale and to show support to the people."

"And that is enough? You don't care what happens to the rest of us now that you have the Needle?"

"Did I say that?" I groaned. He was truly starting to get on my nerves.

"No… But it is the picture you are painting."

"Give me two days. I will deal with Heelis in the morning. I have some Temple business in the evening. The next day I'll talk to Moras. Then we can head out to release the dead."

"Good, that's all we wanted."

"We wanted?"

"I talked about it with Rime. He thought it would be wise."

"But Frazil disagrees."

"Perhaps. He didn't mention it."

"They fight constantly. Why didn't he say anything to me about this?"

"They do? No matter. I agree with Rime regarding the things he had spoken to me about. Frazil is the city's government. The Temple brings comfort. We can't let worries darken its reputation. Whether Frazil likes it or not that you'd be seen."

"Tammaran?"

"Yes?"

"Is Rime planning something?"

"Always. But right now, he is thinking of what's best for the city. Frazil worries that you will distract from him. However, it may be a good thing. It will give him the peace and time he needs to focus on important things, though he may lose out on some glory. Everyone in the city whispers about the fire bringer. There are thousands of rumors. Good and bad. If you follow Frazil's advice, you cannot control how the rumors develop. He cannot answer the questions people have on the afterlife or the new Temple."

Tammaran was being ever so annoyingly sensible. I had no option but to yield on all accounts.

"I don't know if I have better answers."

"I believe you have."

"I will blame you if this blows up in our face."

"You go right ahead," he grinned and then vanished.

V

The stairs fashioned straight from the mountain were plain. The walls were rough and unfinished. I froze on the last step. The sliver of the prison lobby in front of me was furnished with simple wooden pieces. After a moment, a reddish, sweaty man in a uniform that had so much starch it could stand on its own peaked into the staircase.

"Consecratoress, I thought I heard steps," he greeted me. "Governor Laukas said you might drop by to meet... what was her name?"

"I should think he meant the Consecratoress of Eru, Heelis Navarran. She was brought here only a while ago."

"A feisty one indeed," he sighed and half tilted and half shook his head. "You'll find her in that corridor. Behind the door on the right. There are no other doors on that side."

"This place is much larger than I would have imagined. Are there a lot of prisoners?"

"Only a few. The predecessor of Laukas wasn't in the habit of capturing people. We didn't see much use."

"Not even with small crimes?"

"There are no small crimes in the Peak. Everything here was deemed as treason. And the punishment for that..."

"Right, I see. What a waste. So, who is here now?"

"I don't know if I'm allowed to disclose prisoner names to anyone but Governor Laukas. Are you looking for someone else too?"

"No, just being endlessly nosy," I remarked with a smile.

He nodded happily and directed me to the correct corridor once more. As I stood at the cell door, I felt it. Something was reaching for my powers very similarly to Rime's hunger but with no discrimination. I opened the door. It was a windowless hole with no amenities. Heelis was sitting on the floor with her back to the door. Her force was draining from her body. Faster than she could muster it.

"Heelis?"

She flinched at my voice and improved her posture but didn't respond.

"I want to have a word with you."

"Speak then," she replied, without turning to face me.

"I will not apologize. You didn't."

"Fine."

"Do you miss your family? You haven't seen them in a while. I can request them a permission to visit from Frazil."

Heelis stood up and walked as close to me as possible. An invisible wall separated us.

"How long will you keep me here before the execution?"

"What execution?"

"I'm a prisoner of war. I acknowledge and admit to my deeds. I'm going insane in this small cage, so get on with it."

"You aren't to be executed. No one has given that order."

"You should then. I will never accept the Temple in your hands. You will ruin all we have built."

"But you have only spread lies. Are they worth your blood?"

"And you are the arbiter of everything that is right and wrong? You don't even know the history of the Temple and what is behind all their decisions."

"I am the history of the Temple!" I snapped. Heelis snorted and stared at me as if I just proved her point. I took a deep breath. I had to keep my emotions out of this.

"Fine. Tell me," I urged.

"Tell you what?"

"What is the power we use for our dance recitals and with which we fix broken things?"

"What do you mean?" she asked, suspiciously.

"Answer the question. What is it? What is it made of?"

"It comes from the gods. How could I know how it is made?"

"And so sayeth the teacher. No, Heelis. You need to know it to pass judgement on me. It comes from living things. Us, our memories, our souls, and life force. Every time you use your skills, you use something of them.

Although everything is rarely spent all at once, it diminishes and changes depending on the action."

"I don't believe you."

"You have every right not to. But the Temple will change. You could have been a part of that."

"If I ever get out, I will come for you."

"You can try if it pleases you... But I don't think you'll be free, even though I will let out of here. I will find you a house from which you can see the entire city and the new temple. Once we get it built."

"What?"

"The house will contain you as this cell does. But you'll have your family."

"You cannot imprison them! They have done nothing!" Heelis exclaimed and touched the scar on her neck.

"They can come and go as they please. The only one tied to the house is you. And every day you can witness how the city and the Temple change. I will send you new inventions and thoughts to read. You have until your move to consider whether you can disarm yourself of the bitterness and be a part of this future."

"Or what?"

"Or you'll die of old age, still confined in that house, even if you change your mind later. I'm offering this mercy just once."

"What kind of threat is that?"

"It's not a threat, just a statement. Offer even. If you cannot trust us, you may live among us and see all the destruction you think we will cause. Or you will have to stare out from the windows each day and see how wrong you were."

"Ridiculous!"

"It might be, but I don't think your children would prefer we hanged you."

Heelis looked away and seemed a little unsettled for the first time.

"Oh, yes," I sighed. "I thank you for that sight of Simew hanging from the wall. You do realize you didn't just kill Launea's husband?"

"Simew was a traitor as you were. He went to war, and war claims its victims."

"He would have been a father soon."

Heelis inhaled sharply and bit her lower lip.

"A father?"

"Launea is pregnant. Congratulations on taking the child's father before the birth."

"You liar."

"Call me whatever you wish. I'm sure she will come by one of these days to thank you."

Heelis tried to summon her powers as a rabid animal, but nothing came of it. After a frustrated scream, she sat back on the floor with her back to me. I supposed the conversation had gone as well as it could with our tempers.

"I'll return at some point. Try not to build up more bile while you wait."

The guard nodded as I left. I would bring Heelis's family here soon, but I'd let her stew for a few days. I didn't want her to be a part of the new Temple, and I wasn't trying to fix our friendship. The relationship might be too damaged even if I wanted to. I wanted to prove she was wrong, and I wanted to make her more humble and more aware of her flaws. However petty and small that made me. And it did, but it had its own satisfaction.

I spent a lot of time focusing on my small, blue space where I had left the forcibly made shape. I could stretch the room further from me and carve out more room to move.

The shape was almost gone when I entered. I painted and strengthened it with my fingers. Once I stopped, it was more solid than before. It was still lifeless and pointless. I couldn't transfer my thoughts or my soul into it. There had been a drawing of a butterfly in Istrata's notes. Could I make one? My fingers were too big for such a delicate job. What about the point of a dagger? One of the corrupted statues had mentioned that some daggers of the goddess were meant to change us. What if this was what it referred to?

I took the lifeless mass and squeezed it into a lump. One chain of matter at a time, carefully, I forced it in to a cylinder that was twice as long as my index finger. I pressed it flat and shaped the tip to the sharpest point I could. The other end I pressed even flatter, to a coin-like shape for balance. It looked boring. I picked out parts from the small disc until it looked like a flower. I opened its structures and poured my life into it. It floated in front of me. It was a part of me. I took it and pushed it into my hair.

As soon as I had left the room, I touched my hair. The tiny dagger had moved with me. It was better made than the crude weapons I fashioned with the force of Simew. Those had been the result of sheer fear and force. The same urge I had healed myself with when Riestel was testing me. They weren't a part of me. They had Simew's power in them. I had experimented with trying to gain access to that power, but I hadn't succeeded yet. Still, it didn't feel like an impossible task.

Riestel tilted his head, and his eyes narrowed.

"Haven't you been productive," he noted from the door.

"Can you see it?"

"It's a part of you, yes. But I can also feel you've made your first room into the between. It has stabilized. The imprint is ever so slightly different from hers."

"You can sense it? Can all consecrators sense it?"

"No. But many more in my time could than now. Most have the potential. It takes a lot of practice and knowledge," Riestel explained and lifted a basket up. "I brought some food."

"You want to eat here?"

"I thought I'd change the plans a bit," he said and spread a soft quilt on the floor. "Sit," he urged as he sat.

I lowered to my knees as Riestel took out drinks and fresh-scented pastries from the basket.

"Is this appropriate?" I asked. "The rationing should apply to all of us."

"I won't tell if you don't. Though, I won't force you to eat either. Wine? Proper wine, not some thinned out muddy water."

"Maybe a little."

The drink was soft and full. And it went well with the flaky pastries and cheese.

"Do you like them?"

I nodded with a slight prick of guilt, my mouth stuffed.

"Good, I made them this morning."

"I do not believe for a moment that you bake."

"Well, suspicion is not a charming look on you. Do you think all I do is kill and annoy you?"

"Oh, please tell me you wore an apron."

"We need not go that far," he laughed. "Obviously, you don't remember. My father was the castle's baker, before the Needle was built. We brought in fresh breads and pastries every morning. That was before my talents became evident. I was allowed to help out in the castle kitchens before that, but after I was declared to be an avatar of Saraste... That life was off limits. I wasn't to speak to such low-classed people anymore."

"You retained some skills."

"Some. Although, I've had a few lives in the lower parts while waiting for you to pick up your pieces. This profession never dies. You once poked about and asked if there was someone who could have made me stop and just give up. There was no one but a certain life. In the Crafter's. I had a small bakery. It was a simple, good life. Rough, but it filled me with an odd sense of serenity. The same routines, the same customers, but there was something so warm about it," he explained. Riestel's whole visage seemed to melt, even his skin tone and eyes seemed brighter and warmer.

"Sounds to me like you were happy for a moment."

"A moment," he replied and took a deep breath. "But each life has its limits. And now, we are here."

"Right… well, what did you want to go over?"

"I've written out some rules with Kymenes for the new Temple. We thought you would like to hear about them."

"Indeed."

"A moment. I need my notes. Fill my glass."

As I poured the wine, Riestel took out a thin folder. He laid the papers in front of me.

"As you can see, we are proposing to abandon the initiation, trial weeks, and limitations on the number of students."

"Won't that exacerbate the lack of balance and speed up our use of souls?" I worried.

"No. The ones the Temple has abandoned before would never have achieved much power, anyway. But why would we not tell them what fuels their minor tricks? When people understand they are using their or their loved one's essence, it will deter them from doing those small amusing magic tricks. This will, of course, mean that we must close most small temples for now. Until we achieve a better balance. Every action that uses the resources must be thought out and weighed."

"And those who turn to the temples for comfort? What if they don't see the miracles they used to? Such things give people hope. This winter will test all. If we rob them of their faith now…"

"I always forget how humans think. We can leave one consecrator to each temple with the permission to perform rites. But just once a week and only to full rooms. Do you think that would be enough?"

"It's better than nothing."

"Good, we'll do that. Then to the students. We used to have a scale for what sort of powers the person had to possess to be truly educated within the main temple and to become a part of the Temple. The rest were given guidance on how they can bestow small blessings and favors."

"What of those who don't want to be educated?"

"There has never been a proper solution for them. If they are left to their own devices, they can form small cults which are in the hands of their local leader. If you execute them... Well... Either way, a lot of lives lost."

"What would you do?"

"The current way of culling is too destructive. But let's not abandon it completely. It should only be used for those who have substantial powers and still refuse to follow us. If they would humble themselves to give us a year to teach them, all problems would be much smaller. We can install much responsibility and understanding in a year. On top of that, we could check up on them. You can see souls. You can see the distortions certain acts leave behind. Thus, they could have their freedom, but we could root out the threats."

"And what would you do with them?"

"I have no faith in redemption after a certain point," Riestel answered with no emotion.

"You'd execute them? I hate to think that would be a part of the rules."

"Perhaps. But it clears things out and lets everyone know when they cross the line. People must know their boundaries."

"But it will only deter if it is used at some point."

"Obviously, once the rules are made, they must be followed. Whatever one consecrator or mage does despite those rests on their shoulders. We do not condemn them to death. They choose it."

"They choose it...?"

"If you know the punishment for a crime before you commit it and still commit it, do you not choose to accept the punishment?"

"I don't think many think about it like that. Though... it is kind of true. Fine, write it down," I agreed, though a part of me tried the best it could to find a reason for mercy.

I watched as Riestel made amendments to the previous texts. His handwriting was controlled and had a lot of sharp angles. It was old fashioned and clean.

"Stop smirking or I'll make you do these notes with your disgraceful scribbles," he threatened with a smile. "I conversed with Kymenes on the fact that many consecrators are sorely lacking in the basics. They should be taught as you were by Frazil on all sorts of subjects. General knowledge is important. You became significantly more tolerable with his help. When they can think and reason better, we can start to dismantle the lies about the gods."

"I've thought about the gods a lot."

"Why?"

"Isn't the thought of them useful? They were designed to control people. And how do we know that's all there is? Maybe real gods exist... creators... somewhere," I mumbled. "Or maybe they can be made..."

"Would you like to keep the lie, then?" Riestel asked, looking serious. "For your own status?"

"No, not exactly. I just mean, I can see the benefit. They bring hope and act as a conscience. Is it a good idea to strip people of them? What would arise in their stead? What did people worship when you lived your first life?"

"People, idols, pointless carnalities... I did not like it. I'm happy you have given this matter your attention. I didn't think you'd see it this way based on your previous attitude, so I was willing to dismantle them."

"Right, at first, I hated them. The lies. And now I'm advocating to keep some of them. But I love the idea of teaching people more and about everything. That's good. Maybe someday we can trust everyone enough or know the true gods, so none of this show is needed."

"Can I interpret that to mean you do not trust people now?"

I hesitated. "Maybe. I trust that all have the potential to improve and do better, but I don't trust that all want to, that everyone would be inclined to do so. I struggle at times to understand others, but I don't know if that's the reason or the result."

Riestel put his pencil down and crossed his arms.

"Are you a human?" he asked.

"Me? A human... How can I answer that? How can I know what that is? I've never been born as they have. Are you a human?"

"I don't think I've been one for a long time. I think... humanity requires a certain perspective only a limited creature can have. I've begun to feel limitless, without or out of time. With no particular beginning or end or location. I don't see the same kind of beauty in them or their lives as I did when I lived it. Not anymore."

"Isn't it sad?"

"It's a wistful feeling."

"Then what are you?"

"Wrong question, dear girl," Riestel answered and smiled. "First, define yourself. Then you can ask me."

We went through many smaller rules and plans for the new building, so everything would be set up once we'd get the permission to start.

In the morning, I exchanged a few words with Moras. The study rooms were ready and the first batches of equipment parts had arrived for the distillers. His student copied the books studiously and measured and wrote down quantities and benefits. Half a moon from now, they'd experiment with seeds and plants. Without telling anyone else, I asked Moras to also find out more about emptied souls and what happened to those souls they ate. I wasn't expecting him to single-handedly find all the answers, but any theories would help.

VI

The battlefield had been cleared out relatively well. A two-man-high pile of bodies stood in front of me as an icy mountain in the dusk and falling snow. The Temple's surviving higher-ranked consecrators had arranged themselves as an arc behind me. Kymenes and Liike were explaining the events to them.

"The bodies have been anointed. You may start," Tammaran told me and stepped aside.

I gathered power from the other side while painting flowery patterns in the air. I felt the Lighter World around me, like water. It flowed and ebbed, following my every move like a wave. Then it rushed inside me. The knowledge of what sparked the fire made these rites more sacred to me. Each unique life was destroyed and transformed into something new, while the greedy flames and sparks looked for more.

I clenched a partially purified soul into my fist. I walked to the students and opened my hand. The bright soul floated comfortably just above my palm.

"Who of you can see it? Or feel it? Raise your hand," I urged. "Touch it. Let it tell you something. Quickly and without hesitation."

Kymenes held out his hand and brushed it lightly. He withdrew his hand as if he had been stung. A few of the younger consecrators followed his lead. Some of them smiled, some grew somber, and some showed disgust, depending on which memory flashed in their mind.

"This is the very essence that grants you the fuel to save lives and make miracles happen. People's very core, and around it the life force and memories. Ultimately, the soul itself, if they possessed one, if you drain it," I told them.

"What right do we have to use them?" Merrie squeaked sadly. Few things could bring her joyous nature down.

"What right does the wolf have to eat?" I asked. "We have no right; we have the ability and the need. Why are we letting the Temple's secrets out now, you might ask? We want to show you the responsibility you all have. We are not here to entertain. Our rites and rituals should be anything but cheap thrills. Every cast, chant, and dance, every expression of power you manifest, comes from a living creature. You must be ready to draw the line. Is it more valuable to heal the child you tend if it requires magic that can only be used by breaking a soul? Or is it more important to save this ridiculously small but eternal distillation of life and will to its next cycle?"

"How can anyone make that decision?" one of Liike's students wondered and took a step back.

"That's our burden. There is much we can do with just the force coursing through nature. But that, too, is life from plants and animals. From thousands of passed creatures. We are a part of the cycle, or perhaps we are parasites. We have used too much considering how slowly it replenishes. That is why all ails. Irinda crushed and destroyed hundreds of souls to keep her throne and this dying land. It is likely they will never be recovered. You, you do not have the power to break souls. You can only use the life force to change its form, whether you handle it directly or through the sand we make together. But even then, you will destroy something forever."

"But if we had the ability, as you do, to break a soul, it would be destroyed?" Liike asked for his students.

"Yes, completely. Some of its power would return to the cycle as it transforms in our hands, but much will be lost and it will take a long time to direct it back into the world. At this time, the destruction of souls is my burden. You can only use the direct life force. You have no ability to break bonds. You should still respect all manifestations of it because all you consume and direct from its original form will be redirected from its natural course. We do not yet know what differentiates one who can break them from another who can use them fully. Once we do, new abilities may open to you."

"If a dead or dying relative gifted their remains to a sick but curable person, would you permit that?" Merrie wondered.

"Perhaps. It is a question of your personal morality. If you ever test yourself. I will stress this one last time to you all. Not everyone has a soul, so even if I am the only one who can break them, you must keep in mind that when you use the life force gathered by a person, you may in fact be erasing all that exists of them."

"It is quite hard to keep the two concepts apart," Kymenes said. "Perhaps we ought to give a proper name to this life force to distinguish it from the soul. Right now, many use them interchangeably."

"I know I sometimes do," I admitted. "Please, gather some suggestions for it."

"What do the gods make of all this?" an older consecrator asked.

"The gods… The gods, as we have been taught, are perhaps not as involved in the goings on of this world," I dodged the actual question. "And they are not as rigidly divided into their roles as they are currently. Many things will change. Many of you must begin your studies anew as our knowledge improves and grows. You can trust that Riestel and Kymenes will share that knowledge with you as truthfully as possible," I promised. I blew the soul off my palm. It bounced around in the air for a moment and then blinked into the Lighter World.

"I'm tired, I wish to continue the journey," I told Tammaran.

"I'll fetch the carriage."

"This destruction is hard to look at," Kymenes noted. He had a nasty looking scar amidst his hair now. It might never get properly covered.

"The whole square looks like a mess," Liike added. "But I believe we have received adequate temporary lodging from the Peak for those who need to get the knowledge first."

"If there are any complaints and lack of space, let me know and I will assist," I promised. "Then in the spring, we will build anew. Do the ones staying here have enough rooms left?"

"Yes, the repairs and new walls were done very fast. We have enough to survive the winter," Liike assured me.

"I look forward to a new Temple," Kymenes sighed.

"How did things go with Riestel?" I asked.

"Great, actually. He has been incredibly helpful, though rude as can be to the students. Well, to everyone. But the amount of knowledge he has… It puts me and my career to shame," Kymenes groaned. "I think of him as my punishment for not challenging the council and their ideas more."

"Don't tell him any of that. He'd only become prouder," I advised. "I don't know if this is any consolation, but you were the one who gave me hope. You understood some of it all. Don't blame yourself too much, Riestel will handle that."

"Isa, the carriage," Tammaran interrupted.

"Are you returning to the Peak?" Kymenes asked.

"No. I'll tour Kerth for a bit. Almost all areas of the city have dead waiting."

"Do you need healers if you are to work with the soul sand?" Liike enquired.

"No, thank you, Riestel will join me in the Noble's. He will do."

"And the Governor?" Kymenes asked. "Are you joining him? He traveled through a few days ago."

"No, this is my little excursion. They... Wait, did you say 'Governor' not 'Governors'? They were supposed to travel together."

"We only saw Governor Laukas," Liike replied.

"Tammaran, where's Rime?"

"He might not be attending the meetings. I think he has business with the military. He has no need to campaign like his father."

"Right... still... Let's go."

I didn't press the matter further in the privacy of the carriage. Rime had wanted me to take this journey against his father's wishes. Thus, I had done so, even if the request had been passed to me through Tammaran. Now Rime was nowhere to be found. I hated not knowing what he had planned.

I studied Tammaran. I liked him, but even though he had asked to serve me, was he really going to be my servant or would he always be Rime's? Did the answer matter?

"What are you thinking?" Tammaran asked.

"Nothing much. The bodies are so plenty, I'm mainly tired."

"Then rest. It will take plenty of time to get to the Noble's. I'll keep you safe. Not that there have been any riots or any bigger resistance here in the upper parts because of the change in power. Traveling should be fine."

"Good," I said and leaned on the padded bench. I trusted Tammaran. He would keep me safe, even at the cost of his life. And I wasn't worried that Rime was in danger, but something was bubbling beneath the surface. Something they didn't wish me to know. Rime wouldn't tell me his plans unless they required it, just like Frazil. It annoyed me, though I understood the reason. Still, now that I knew something was cooking, it would be painful to keep my nose out of it. If that was, in fact, possible.

Rosenrun's yard was clean and the light ice-crystal snow had been swept aside. Barin's voice echoed already from the door as he came to meet us.

"Consecrator Elona! I'm so very glad indeed that we escaped the fighting without issues. I'm so sorry I stood by the Temple. Consecrator Avaras has been lecturing me about my stupidity."

"Let's not talk about it. Just look forward," I requested, knowing full well he would have said the same regardless of who won.

"Such a delightful attitude!" he thanked me with his filed teeth glinting.

"How did Frazil's visit go? You must have heard something? Did the Governor of the Soldier's District accompany him?"

"The Governor of the Soldier's? No, I haven't heard of him. Laukas stayed here a day, at the Maherol estate. They were going to leave the Noble's but now rule it. I think they struck a deal of some sort."

"Well, there goes that plan of starting anew, far away from other nobles for the next generation. Not that I'm surprised," I sighed when I remembered Usko's oath on moving and relinquishing his power to take care of Simew's child. "Are these all the dead?"

"For now," Barin answered.

There were just a few dozen bodies in the Noble's, so the rituals and other mandatory tasks took only half a day. Almost no one came to pay their respects. These weren't their dead. Now we just needed to wait for Riestel and continue.

"Isa!"

A familiar, chirpy voice made me shudder.

"Launea," I acknowledged her and turned. She was dressed in several warm layers, like the nobles, and she was decorated with dozens of jewels. Her belly was showing. Launea tilted her head. I crossed my arms and avoided her embrace and her eyes.

"What... well, how are you? You look so different," Launea said.

"You too. Have the Maherols treated you well?"

"More than well. Simew's mother, Nissa, has been irreplaceable," she answered and had a quaint smile on her lips.

"Good. Why are you here?"

"Oh, you didn't want to see me, I gather."

"I wouldn't go that far, but this doesn't exactly feel relaxed."

"No," she laughed. "But I decided to brave you. Nissa heard that you've arrived to take care of the dead."

"Is Arvida still with you?"

"Yes, though she was hoping to join you soon. I think I can make do without her already."

"I'd like that."

"I thought you would. But I did have a personal matter," Launea confessed and fiddled with her left sleeve. The small silver bells on it chimed gently.

"Tell me."

"What will you do with Heelis?"

"She is a prisoner and will stay that way for now. I see no regret in her yet."

"Can I meet her?"

"Perhaps. Why would you want to?"

"I… I have to. I can't get any peace before I do. Her actions bother me day and night… I came to you for help. That should tell you enough."

"It does. I'll arrange it."

"Promise?"

"I promise."

"Thank you. Maybe that will help quell the nightmares. I'm afraid for my child. I'm on edge and sleep poorly. I bled a little…" she muttered. "I have to rest. I can't lose my child too… I can't," she sighed and covered her mouth. Her eyes watered and flooded. She clenched her hand and wiped her face. I wished she had stayed away from me; this feeling of pity and sympathy was intolerable.

"My tour will last a week or two… But there's a healer at the Peak. He's very good. He uses both our knowledge and ways and the knowledge and ways of the herbalists. Tammaran could escort you there with Arvida. You cannot meet Heelis before I return and grant you the permission, but you'd be getting the best care there is. Maybe that would ease your mind a little."

"You cannot tour Kerth alone," Tammaran reminded me. "It's not safe in the Lowers. Rime would have my head for it."

"Riestel will be here. He can guard me."

"Riestel? Do you trust him that much?" Tammaran asked, looking a bit unhappy.

"No, she doesn't," Riestel remarked behind him. Tammaran jumped a little and turned, confused. At least someone could sneak up on him.

"But she knows our goals are the same, so even if I don't care for you… I'm not a threat to her at the moment," Riestel continued and patted Tammaran on the shoulder, giving a snide smile.

"Fine," Tammaran sighed. "I will take them safely to Moras and jump after you."

"That's fine," I agreed.

"It will take four days at the most. So, you don't need to spend much time with him."

"It's fine. You'll reach us when you can. I can survive a few days without a watchdog."

"I'm not… watching you."

"I think you are," Riestel whispered, smirking and leaning on me. "But why?"

"Stop it," I groaned and pushed him off. "Tammaran, I appreciate your concern, but this is important to me. Help her."

"I will, I will."

"You may take the carriage we used. I can move my luggage to Riestel's."

"Isa, thank you," Launea whispered and drew me a little closer. "You are… a monster, you know that, but maybe it's what we deserve."

She squeezed my hand lightly and smiled. A stinging observation, though offered with kindness. It didn't offend me. I understood the perspective well.

"Can we collect a few things from the Maherols?" Launea asked Tammaran.

"Certainly… It's not like I have anything else to do," he complained but followed her without any further protest.

"Oh, a journey all by our little old selves," Riestel said. "How daring. Are you sure it won't give the wrong impression?"

"I'll leave an impression on your face. Have you ever heard of a thing called trust? I suggest you try it sometime."

"Ha, well, I have heard of it, but I doubt I'll try it ever again. Just look what the first time brought me."

VII

T he Merchant's District did require a long stop. A part from a few localized scraps, the area had been spared of most conflicts and death. It made me happy. It was the first District I had known here, a home of sorts.

We had only been apart for a few days, but I missed Rime as much as I had missed him during those first temple weeks. An unrelenting vortex of worry in the pit of my stomach only calmed in his presence. We should have had more time to live our own lives after the conquest. Just us. But here I was, sitting close to Riestel and far away from Rime. And I couldn't convince myself that we would get any time alone soon. I didn't even know where he was. It gnawed at me more than I was willing to admit. Why was I always left outside all the plans until I was of use? Was I so unreliable? He couldn't have believed that.

"Don't look like a lost kitten. It's highly irritating," Riestel remarked.

"I'm allowed to be sad."

"A waste of time and energy."

"You are so unbelievably cold at times. Still. Why? You have no reason to act out anymore. I'm stable. I'm not a threat to the city like this."

"Perhaps. I just don't have any patience for feelings that serve no purpose."

"Oh, mighty seas! Purpose? What purpose can feelings have but to exist?"

"You are so easy to rile up."

"I should have made you escort Launea."

"You think I would have jumped to your whim?"

"I'm not that foolish."

"Good. Have you thought about what to do now?"

"Now? I don't know. I suppose we heal the city."

"Aren't you missing something?"

"What?" I asked, as if I didn't know what he was referring to.

"The fifth and final statue."

I stayed quiet. I had hoped he wouldn't have brought it up. I wasn't obsessed with the last one. I certainly wasn't keen on venturing to Istrata's daughter's tomb. It felt like a slightly suicidal path. But... it would be a shame to not collect the whole set. And I would regret it for all my days if Aderas would suffer for my cowardice. If I didn't go and collect the last statue and its knowledge, would it take me too long to learn her will and plan? What if the statue had some information that would help?

"What if I don't want to?" I asked.

"Then you don't... It could become a problem."

"What kind of problem?"

"Your kind. You've managed to fuse your past and present admirably well, but your past isn't stable. You know the fragments yearn for each other. What if their influence grows again because you deny them their unification?"

"And what if the last part is what drives me off the edge? Or what if I become her? Why would I chance it?"

"The same reason you took those steps so far. Because you want power and knowledge."

"If I wanted power, I wouldn't have put you and Kymenes at the head of the Temple or help Frazil on the throne without claiming more of a position for myself."

"Don't play stupid, though you do it so naturally. Power over the world, the material. You don't care about these people. You don't want to rule them. It's a burden. You want to create. You want to be more."

"And you want to pressure me to go with you for your own ends."

"Of course. I want to see whether my daughter still suffers. I want to release her or to say my goodbyes. Is that too much to ask after all these lives? Is peace of mind too much to request? I loved that small thing. From her first breath. I always will. I'd trade my life for hers anytime. You can't..." Riestel started, turned his head, and cleared his throat. "No! Stop that this instant," he demanded and buried his face into his hands as my eyes welled as I felt his pain.

"I can't isolate myself from your emotions," I replied, annoyed.

"Then you are weak. I have no time for feelings."

"Liar."

"Shut up."

And there he was, the same broken man I had witnessed at the Northern Shrine when I learned the truth from him. I placed my hand on his. He grasped it. He held it with both hands and stared at the carriage floor.

"Alright, fine," I sighed. "It would be torture to deny you. I'll travel to the grave. You must promise me you will help me stay me."

"Thank you," he whispered and pressed his forehead to my hand.

"But you must allow Rime to decide the timing. He has a plan of sorts; I don't know more. You must get his permission. I cannot abandon him or the city if they need me. Not even for you."

"You couldn't have placed a more loathsome condition on it," Riestel laughed and straightened up. He let go of my hand.

"But I will swallow my pride and talk to him. What if he forbids it?"

"I don't think he will. He... may not be a father yet, but he wants to be."

"That's why you panicked so much when I told you how emptied souls are created."

"You hit a nerve, I'll admit that. Rime isn't as retched as you'd like to think. There is a lot of good in him. If the timing is right, he will allow it."

"You've gifted me a spark of hope... Be careful."

"Should I just watch as you sulk for all eternity?"

"Sulk? I beg your pardon, I don't sulk, I brood in a mysteriously charming way."

"Gods help me, don't kill me with laughter. You are like a little child when you don't get your way."

"You have a lot of bark in you tonight," Riestel noted and burst into a bubbly laugh. He wiped his eyes, amused, and shook his head.

"You have no idea how good it feels to finally have someone in the world who dares to say such things to me."

"Can I ask a favor, then?"

"Fine. What?"

"Well, you spy on everyone always... If you get an inkling of what he is up to..."

"You want to know. Trouble in paradise?"

"No. I knew what I got into. I have no regrets. I'm just tired of being in the dark. I lived several years not knowing all of what was intended. I don't want to just muddle along. I want to know where the river leads."

Riestel smiled lopsidedly and nodded.

"You know… I remember when I saw Elona for the first time. She was so tiny and weight almost nothing. My hands shook when she was handed to me. The little bundle…" he sighed and glanced out. "More beautiful than anything I've created as a consecrator. What?"

"Istrata loved her too. I could feel the endless affection in her."

"And yet…"

"And yet she destroyed her life."

"Yes."

"Why?"

"I don't know. The only thing I know is that she must have thought she had the solution. Nothing else makes sense. No matter how repulsive her deeds were, I know they were based on a desire to do good."

"Do you still despise me?" I asked.

"No, I've never despised you. You were the first whole thing to be born of her… The first to not break from all the agony I unleashed on you… I could have maybe toned it down, but I wanted it to hurt. I needed it to hurt."

"I noticed, thank you."

"You're welcome. This honesty is getting rough. Let's not do this for a while."

"I agree. Maybe you could spend the next moments badmouthing the Merchant's District and its services. Get back into the routine?"

"The routine," he breathed and ran his fingers through his hair.

"Yes, you can continue being a jackass, and I can pretend to not feel anything."

"To not feel anything? What did you mean?"

"Generally. Don't get any ideas," I quickly corrected him, as I could feel my heart jump out of my chest for such a lapsus.

"Ideas of you? Don't be ridiculous. You're about as attractive as a soggy potato."

"See, there we go," I groaned, but we were both smiling.

I was happy to have seen such a sad, emotional side of him. It alleviated my fears. Despite all my worries, he had feelings, and he wanted good things for the city. That was the Riestel I remembered. Remembered. I remembered him. I touched my chest and turned away. How could I ever forgive myself? I had condemned him to a horrid life. The most important person in my life back then. Now, it was Rime. It was all too late. It was a dreadful feeling. To remember something lost so strongly and all that it had meant just to lose it in the same moment of revelation. I understood him so much better now, and all the pain I had wrought on him by becoming me.

"Riestel?" I called.

"Yes?"

"Can we be friends already?"

"I don't know. I'm not necessarily very good at it."

"That's okay, I'm horrible at it."

VIII

There was several times more work in the Soldier's. I stayed in the same room as during the conquest. The door opened after a politely short knock, a perfect union between too loud and too quiet.

"I apologize, I had no idea you had company," Samedi hurried to say when he noticed Riestel and bowed.

"I can't seem to get rid of him," I smirked. Riestel let out an amused breath.

"I can return at a later time," Samedi offered.

"It's as good of a moment as any. What did you want?"

"Well, I'm in charge of the Soldier's, as you know. Rime sent me a message and hoped I would ask you to speak to some of the higher ranking soldiers while you are here."

"Why?" I asked.

"To make them understand what you are doing. Frazil was here and spoke of rebuilding and the future, but his plans are so grand and on such a general level that many cannot imagine them as anything concrete and there's nothing that can be easily turned into action. Many feel unsure what direction the city will take."

"And I'm supposed to tell them?" I checked, shocked.

"Not quite. Rime simply wants to give the commanders and such an opportunity to ask you questions about the Temple. He will provide all other information."

"Why would the military care what the Temple does?" I complained.

"It's a power they do not control," Riestel remarked.

"Alright, fine. If it is necessary," I agreed, though I wasn't happy about it.

"Thank you. I'm sure it will be beneficial. Rime knows you will know what to say."

"Samedi... do you know where Rime is? He was supposed to tour with Frazil, but as far as I know, Frazil has arrived alone to all of his stops."

"I don't, not exactly. From what I understood, something urgent at the Peak required that one of them returned, but Governor Laukas didn't say anything more. They intend to meet again in the Lowers as the districts require more attention to calm things down."

"Right, so how is the Black Guard?"

"We are all split up at the moment. Rime has placed us all in charge of some part of the city and the soldiers there. Though, there is much else to do as well. The army is responsible for discipline, clearing the remaining mess, and rebuilding."

"How do the governors feel about the military taking over?" Riestel asked.

"I wouldn't quite say we've taken over," Samedi retorted. "No one has complained. And most will lose their status anyway due to a new ruler. We cannot let those Irinda favored to continue."

"Of course not," I agreed.

"I will gather the commanders to the meeting room. They stayed for the night after Frazil left, as I told them you might be coming. Will you be down soon?"

I nodded, and Samedi left. Riestel tapped the window glass.

"Your husband is gathering power in the shadows."

"Perhaps. He wants to stabilize the new rule as soon as possible. I don't know how. He said the two governors from the outside cities must be invited to the coronation and that it will bring an outside danger. Whatever he is doing, I don't believe it's against Frazil. At the most, against his pride."

"Likely so. Weakness, presumed or real, will attract trouble."

"Will you come to the meeting?"

"I have no interest in it. But if you want me to come, I'd be willing to inconvenience myself."

"Do as you please. I don't like this. I don't know what they think about me."

"You do know you are a creature with agency? You do not always have to do as he wishes," Riestel proposed with a dangerously silky whisper.

"Don't patronize me. I'm helping him because I want to. If he wished this to be done, there is only one goal: to help the city. Why shouldn't I do it?"

"Just checking," Riestel smirked. "I shall leave you to your responsibilities in that case. I'll work on the soul sand. We can move forward quicker that way."

"Why are you in such a hurry?"

"I like the Crafter's. I haven't been there in a while."

"I'm not sure if I believe you," I sighed.

The hall was mostly as it had been when Frazil used it. Only the maps and plans were gone. A silent group of commanders stood by the negotiation table. Samedi was standing at the very end and gestured me to take his place. I touched my forehead and walked to Samedi without looking anyone else in the eyes. As I sat, Samedi remained behind me as a servant would.

"Consecratoress Elona," all the men around the table greeted me as I raised my eyes.

Samedi introduced them. There were so many names and ranks that I didn't remember even the first one once he was done. The oldest commander took out some notes, as they had drawn up a list of questions. I hid my sweaty palms under the table and tried to hear what they truly wanted to know.

"And the new power structure? Has it been established? Who will ultimately rule all the day-to-day business?" he asked and stopped.

"We are only just forming the new ways. I cannot give very detailed answers."

"Governor Laukas said that as well, but we must have them," they pressured.

"And you will, as soon as they are decided on," I assured. I glanced at Samedi. He nodded encouragingly. I closed my eyes for a moment. A part of me had ruled this kingdom. This should be familiar to me, if I only allowed those parts to arise. When I found the confidence to look, I could see the question they wanted to ask.

"You helped to bring Governor Laukas his victory," I credited them. "You more than me or any others on his side. Without the support Rime gathered from you, this wouldn't have happened. You worry that, despite this, the Temple will outrank you. Will be more important.

The men adjusted their positions. They didn't like what I said.

"I will tell you a secret," I continued. "The Temple, from now on, can only use its skills in the direst needs. We need you. You are the sword and shield of Aderas and Kerth. We cannot protect it with our powers as we used to if we are to survive this famine and lack. Each attack will eat away at the force we need to bring forth life in the soil. It has been depleted faster than decades, centuries' worth of creation. That is the reason for the ailing lands. We can turn it around, but we need a lot of luck and hard work. Without you... there will be no more Aderas. I ask that you will protect the Temple as you protect all else here. I will not grant any of the Temple's affairs, and I will not tolerate any attempts to affect it. You do not understand the cycle, as I don't understand how to calculate the cannon's trajectory. Do not even amuse yourself with the idea of setting out terms for the gods."

The soldiers looked around as if trying to ask each other if what they had heard was right.

"You are our hope," I emphasized. "By ensuring we can work in peace, you will ensure we can recover. I cannot imagine how dark the days will get. I do not want to, if I'm being honest, but I will trust in your help."

"We... must admit, you caught us off guard," their unofficial spokesman admitted and straightened his posture. "The wellbeing of Aderas is our greatest wish. That's why we do what we do. The Temple, the organization itself, has always been a question mark for us. The previous governor of the district itself didn't like us much. The military was just a place to ship off unruly consecrators. They were, of course, welcome, but we never discussed much."

"You are all, I assume, very well aware of the fact that I'm Rime's wife. Based on that alone, you can assume there will be a more open relationship between the two. We will build more trust. Maybe even cooperate properly," I mused and spread out my hands with open palms.

"Cooperation? Truly? Can you elaborate? We've never been given such a proposition."

"The Temple has supported the army with consecrators during hard times and when forced, but how have they and your units worked together? I'm guessing poorly, as neither knows anything of the other. Wouldn't it be better if all the people transferred to you came of their own accord and they would already know more of the army's ways and you of ours? Maybe even a whole unit to train side by side."

"That would be ideal. Would it be possible?"

"I'm not making promises. I'm not going to claim a position at the Temple, and this most definitely isn't Frazil's suggestion. It's purely mine. But I do have sway. The Temple's future leader, Kymenes, is a reasonable man. He will listen when I talk."

"We heard that Consecrator Aravas will hold a prominent position in the future."

"Not for long… He will help us through the reconstruction and then retire, as I. We are not interested in the management side."

"That clears many rumors. There is, if you can still indulge us, one issue we haven't received enough information on. We have been tasked with observing the Borders, but no one told us the reason. Just that the Temple wished it so."

"You can blame that on me. I had a vision in the Needle about a huge growing mass headed towards the city."

"All that for a vision?"

"I can imagine it sounds strange and that Governor Laukas didn't want to tell you exactly because it seems ludicrous to practical people. I'm ashamed I can't tell you more based on what I saw. It was a very powerful glimpse, and should it come true and catch us unprepared, the enemy would drown us. I couldn't keep it to myself just for the fear of being ridiculed."

"I cannot pretend to understand, but any potential threat will be taken seriously. I will not question your talents or the Temple's concerns. We will keep an eye out for as long as you wish, if that helps to build a bridge between our organizations."

"And you have my thanks. Is there anything else?"

"We appreciate your time. Now, we have a clearer grasp of the whole situation and our own goals. This meeting has been a relief, though, darker than with Laukas. He spoke of restoration, not threats. It made us uncomfortable, as the situation is delicate. We are naturally delighted to hear of the grand plans and visions and make them happen, but we felt as if he didn't want to trust us to help. Now, at least, we have peace of mind regarding your Temple."

"You may always reach out to Rime, or me. I know how proud he is of the forces of Aderas and how much he valued your support. We are at your service."

"I don't know of one single man who'd be pining for the previous Governor of the Soldier's. We are all but delighted with the changes in that respect. But, considering these changes, how do you see the inner threats?"

"They are one of the reasons I'm touring. I want to see all the districts so that I'm not solely relying on second-hand information."

"Maybe that's a discussion for a later time, then."

"Yes, but... you must be ready to thwart any insurrections in the city. There will be some. We hope they are small and local. The City Guard is in no shape to take care of things until we have vetted them. I know, from what Rime tells me, that he would see the army taking care of our internal safety for a few years."

"We are fully prepared to do so."

We exchanged a few less severe sentences and opinions until they excused themselves. Samedi sat next to me. He put his feet up on the table and leaned back. It was the most relaxed I had ever seen him.

"You read them well," Samedi remarked. "Can you utilize the Queen's memories when you handle people? I find it hard to believe the experiences you've had solely in this life would have given you so much insight."

"Did Rime tell you about that?"

"Yes, to all of us after the city fell. He thought it was important that we know the whole situation."

The whole situation. So, he entrusted more information to them than me. It hurt, though there was no denying he had known his guards for years longer than he had known me. Of course, he would lean on them.

"Her skills and memories are betwixt my own. At first, they were very separate, but slowly they have become mine. I do not mean that I would be more her or less me. But I have no doubt that they influence my behavior and talents. I'm using her life, but through my perspective. If that makes sense. I'm not her, nor am I becoming her."

"I see. I guess that's why you can stand Riestel better. You share a long past."

"Sort of. It's easier not to get angry at him when I know what drives him. It doesn't make him a nice person or harmless in my eyes. You don't usually pry into personal matters. Are you worried about something?"

"I might be spying for a friend," Samedi sighed. "I apologize. It's none of my business. I know you love him. I have no doubts about that, but he has been my brother for years."

"You are looking out for Rime. I won't harbor ill will because of that. I should return to the dead. We wish to move on tomorrow."

"Of course."

Samedi escorted me out. We didn't speak anymore. The quiet, sad work was a relief after all the talking. With Riestel's help, it was quick and calming. He could guide much force and life to where it was needed. He did it with a steady and precise control, humming and flickering at the edges of the worlds like a pure crystal statue.

I floated off into a dream-like trance as I as made my steps fit his song. The dance didn't require any focus. I could close my eyes and my movements flowed like waves. In that state, the unraveling of lives caused no emotions. All was just as it should be in nature. I opened my eyes after the last life was gone. The skin on my arms shone with a slight golden tint as the last remains went through me into the Lighter World. Some remained in me as a tingle and a shiver, like a feather would have brushed my neck.

IX

I didn't know what to expect in the Crafter's District. I didn't have many memories from there, just that one night when I sought one of the statue heads with Rin. Riestel seemed happy and almost elated when we passed the gate. Marelin would be waiting for us at the very first tower. He held the region through the military's might. The official ruler, Governor Jona, had made no objections on the matter. He hadn't even returned to the area after the change in power. He had scampered to the Peak to his main villa to wait for others to sort things out.

"Consecrators, welcome," Marelin greeted us and gestured us to follow. "You are right behind Frazil. He only departed this morning."

"Whom did he meet here?" I asked.

"Mostly members of the military. We discussed how we will start to deconstruct these temporary holds and how we will move forward after that. Nothing particularly riveting."

"And the locals? Did he contact them in any way?" Riestel asked, as if that mattered to him.

"Not really. There aren't a lot of significant people here," Marelin shrugged.

"Rubbish," Riestel scoffed. "There are always important people in communities this size. You just don't know them."

"Whom should he have met?" Marelin asked, perplexed.

"All those people from whom others seek advice and who influence the district's mood," Riestel said in a harsh and annoyed tone. He shook his head.

"Well, maybe he will do so later at a better time, once the rebuilding is well underway," Marelin guessed.

"Then he would be wrong," Rime said. "The correct time is now."

I turned around. Rime and Tammaran were behind us on horseback. Rime lowered himself off the steed when I hurried to him. Just a few steps before I reached him, I stopped. I glanced at Riestel. He turned his gaze away at that same moment. My happiness underscored all that he had lost. It made me immensely sad. Rime pulled me into his arms in a slightly showy fashion. We breathed each other in for a moment.

"Mare, if my father didn't do so, I would like to."

"I have no idea who those people are," Marelin muttered. "This isn't a familiar place to me."

"Send a few people to ask around. It shouldn't be a hard task. The people will help as long as you are polite," Rime commanded. "Thank you for following my wife instead of Tammaran, Consecrator Aravas. You may now return to the Temple or the Peak."

"No, thank you. I think I'll see this little outing to its end. I haven't toured the city in a while. Besides, you are here on horses… Isa would get bored to tears in the carriage all alone," Riestel pondered with a sly smile. "I shall have a walk about the old neighborhood. Have fun at the meetings. You'll sniff me out when you want to."

"I hope he hasn't been too troublesome," Rime whispered.

"No, surprisingly not," I answered. "Did you see Launea?"

"No. I heard about it from Tammaran. I didn't have time to pay her a visit. But as far as I know, Moras and his flock took her in."

"Good."

"Are you awake enough to meet the locals?" Rime asked.

"Yes… But when are you going to let me in on all of this? Frazil requested that I lie low. He hasn't shared much of anything with anyone either."

"Because he is wrong."

"But he will be king. You can't defy him now."

"It doesn't make him untouchable. Besides, these are just precautions in the shadows. He can keep his desires on the surface. My task is to retain peace and secure the city. If he will reprimand me for doing so, let him. I know what is needed now better than he does. I'm not belittling my father's skills, but the situation is volatile. He is a brilliant tactician when sitting safely in a comfortable chair, playing the long game, but with people… With most of the ordinary people. They are outside his realm of experience; he has no sway or say with them. It's a dangerous time. We can make up the difference. He doesn't even need to know. Or once he does finally hear about our little operations, it will be too late to get mad on that throne of his."

"Aren't you afraid that he will lose faith in you?"

"No. I am the army," Rime whispered in a low, almost purring voice, which made me shiver.

By the evening, Marelin had assembled a group of people of the block elders. Rime greeted them all individually with his best smile and a courteous manner with no falsity or unnecessary pomp.

Rime told them what to expect from the winter and what would have to change during the next growing season for the suffering to end. He didn't spare any words when talking down Irinda or forget to thank his father's actions, or his own, when there was a reason to. People asked a few questions about the Temple from me, though mostly they just wanted to focus on practical issues such as food and firewood.

"If you want to go, you can. It will be a while still," Rime suggested as he leaned closer. "But after that, we could spend some time together."

"Promise?"

"I suggested it."

"Well, you didn't like dancing either and still suggested that."

"Do you need to be put in your place since you are dragging up ancient things?"

"I dare you," I whispered.

The late evening sky was clear. The air carried the scent of smoke and a sweet pastry. There was something familiar about that. It didn't seem to fit in this place and disregarded all of Frazil's restrictions. Riestel. I followed the scent to a slightly larger wooden house. I could hear lively chatting and laughter from inside. I sneaked up a couple of steps to the porch and leaned on the door.

"Sing, sing, a jest!" the people chanted.

"Again? And what would you fine, upstanding lovers of classical culture be happy with?" Riestel asked in his usual snide way. No one took offense. On the contrary, they chuckled merrily. So, there were people in this world that liked him.

"There once was a lady so sweet," Riestel hummed with a light tune. "That all the grains of wheat, she took in her hands, turned into gold sands. Then a fine gentleman entered, and her heart surrendered. They chased each other, what a delightful bother. Soon, spewed forth all the seeds, and her belly was filled with such deeds."

The people inside stomped their feet and giggled. Then it became quiet.

"Well, well. The Consecratoress honors us with her presence," Riestel exclaimed as he yanked the door open. The whole room stared as I stumbled forth. Riestel grabbed my arm and stopped me from falling on my face. I was spun around and stopped an inch from his face. He had flecks of flour on his cheek.

"Shall we offer the Consecratoress a drink and a warm snack?" an older woman asked as I stepped back with flushed cheeks.

"If that is thy will, aunt Ombra," Riestel smiled and put down the pint in his other hand. "But be warned, when one rat comes sniffing, more may follow."

"Is that how you talk to women? Shameful boy," Ombra scolded him and slapped the back of his head. "No wonder you are still unmarried. Osse, make room for the lady."

"Please don't bother... I was just..." I stammered.

"Snooping," Riestel completed the sentence and pressed me to sit on the chair next to the gray-haired and bent, but bright-eyed, Ombra.

"Make a jest of her!" one of the children suggested. People snickered and peered at me to see my reaction.

"I'm sure we aren't so crude as to make a jest of a Temple's representative," Riestel hushed them, turned on his heels, and bowed. "At the door, there was a small rat, a daring little thing at that. Sneaked its way in carefully, nibbled bread to fill its belly. Sniffed around and met another, spread its legs and became a mother."

"Are they all so vulgar?" I groaned as others laughed.

"Well, they either end with sex or death, and I didn't feel like killing you," Riestel responded and gave me an odd look. "They are the only two things this crowd appreciates. Don't be an uptight stick in the mud. You are the one who chose to come here to meet my kin."

"Your kin? But...?"

"No one can do without someone they can trust. I've come here to be born again many times. Of course, I have my own people."

"Well, one would be a right old arse to abandon their own forefather," Ombra laughed. "Welcome, welcome. We haven't seen our father-son for ages. So, you are the fire deity's manifestation that is turning this city upside down? Look all ordinary to me. But I suppose so does Riestel to the human eye."

"I don't know if you can thank or blame me for everything. I think the coup would have happened either way."

"Perhaps, perhaps. People here fear many things. No one has the energy to gossip about governors with a fire god running about."

"I'm nowhere near a god."

"You are no human. Neither is Riestel. I've heard things, you see. Old Ombra has ears and eyes so many, you wouldn't believe. Some whisper that we could save this world by sacrificing others to you. It's a dangerous story to spread and tell, true or not. Who knows what desperate people will think to do?"

"I'm sure no one would think that," I denied. "No one should sacrifice anything to me."

"But you do work on the dead, don't you?" Ombra checked, and her eyes darkened for a moment.

"I... sort of. I can revive the earth with them... But we do not know the whole situation. There is no reason for anything excessive. And we don't know if it's a permanent solution."

"Hey, Mousy, here is your drink," Riestel said, in a mood that was almost too good, and shoved a wooden pint into my hands so fast that some spilled on my sleeve.

"What is it?" I asked after sniffing it. Some of the children snickered and whispered that a mouse would do that when offered food.

"Drink when offered. Don't fret."

I raised the pint to my lips. It was foamy, dark, and sweet. Not quite beer, but not quite mead.

"And some more," Riestel said and took the empty pint. "Just a moment."

"I don't need..."

"But you will."

Ombra leaned closer once Riestel had gone. The whole room was filled with joyous people and merriment.

"You know he fancies you," she whispered. "Be kind."

"You are wrong. And I'm married. There can be nothing here."

"But there is. I know the whole history. And I've never seen him this falsely happy."

I glanced in the direction of the room where Riestel had gone.

"Excuse me," I said.

"Sure, sure."

I went to the kitchen. It was dimly lit. Riestel was crouched over a barrel. He held on to its rim with white knuckles and his head hung down. For a potential god, he was truly very small and sorrowful. I kneeled beside him.

"You are not okay, are you?" I whispered.

"By the sharpest needle, you are perceptive."

"Don't be mean, however natural of a state that is to you."

"It wasn't before," he sighed and got up with me. "This... is much harder than I thought."

"Can I help in some way? Perhaps to get some closure on Istrata?"

"It's not that. I've closed that book. I know she is lost. But... I find I am..." Riestel tried to force the words out as he inched ever closer.

"I'm sorry to interrupt, but there are people asking for the Consecratoress," Ombra said, annoyed from the door. "A serious looking, darker-haired man."

"The mut can smell you from anywhere. Go," Riestel muttered.

"You just cannot help but to insult him."

"Should I kill him instead?"

"The very moment I think there is something good in you, you efficiently prove why I shouldn't spare any thoughts on you. Stew in your own broth."

The infuriating jackass. When was I going to learn? I shut the front door. Rime was standing by the steps.

"What in the high skies were you doing there?" he asked.

"I followed the scent of pastry, and they invited me in."

"I'm surprised anyone has the spirit to celebrate these days. Or that anyone has anything to celebrate with."

"Yes, well. Please, let them carry on. They are having a family meeting."

"Alright. It's comforting that people can still find joy. Come," Rime asked and held out his hand. "We should move on."

"Already? But you said that we'd spent some time together," I wondered and took his hand.

"Tammaran will be here with the carriage in just a moment. I want to catch up to Frazil before he talks to Gramo and the other workers."

"Why?"

"After talking to all the people here, I have my doubts on whether he is doing more damage to his cause than good. I know I promised, but we will have time once we get to him."

"Do people think he is too vague?"

"The workers will appreciate direct answers and clear ones. Frazil is not known for such, though he is an eloquent speaker."

"I can't say I disagree," I said when I remembered his speech in the Merchant's so long ago.

"And here comes the ride. Will you get Riestel if we are to drag him along?"

"Riestel? Right, just a moment," I agreed, a little baffled. How did Rime know he was here, or that I was here? Had someone followed me?

I walked back in. Riestel was sitting next to Ombra. They whispered. She smiled at me and patted him on the shoulder. Riestel glanced at me. There was no warmth or remorse in his eyes. Not that I would have expected any from the stubborn ass.

"The carriage is outside. Rime wishes to carry on. Are you coming or will you head back? You don't need to babysit me if your nerves can't handle it."

Riestel stared at his shoes for a moment.

"That's what you think," he muttered.

"And you know better?"

"We'll see. Let's go," he scoffed and got up. Ombra hugged him for a moment without Riestel making any faces or showing annoyance. There was even a passing moment he looked comfortable and happy. I was of the mind to ask if he had forgotten he disliked people.

Soon, I was again sat in the carriage with Riestel. I had so longed for these uncomfortable moments. Someone knocked on the window. I opened it.

"I thought we might plan for the future, for once," Rime proposed as he straightened to sit in a better pose in the saddle.

"Now?" I asked.

"There isn't much else to do."

"Oh, such passionate words," Riestel smirked.

"I'm glad if an outsider can see that," Rime responded without any chance in his expression. "I can see the future I want the city to have clearly, so I thought we could think about our lives. Where we will live, and all that."

"Really? Are you that confident?" I asked.

"Reasonably."

"Where we would we live... Are you considering leaving the Peak?" I pondered, a little worried. Riestel changed his posture to a more alert one.

"I'm the Governor of the Soldier's still. I don't know how fast the city's development will be and where it will start, so for now, the old structures stand."

"But…"

"You don't want to leave the Needle? I thought it only contained bad memories."

"Yes, but…"

"We have made some good memories there too," Riestel remarked with a half-smile. "Many, many times."

"Choke already," I snapped. "Rime, I'm just beginning. The tower and the palace have so much to explore. All vital. I cannot leave it. Can't Samedi hold the Soldier's well enough according to your commands? Your scribe, Lyri, can help him and guide him."

"Then I'd be a governor in name only."

"Are you saying you'd be ready to leave Frazil alone on the Peak? You keep saying that he cannot see the complete picture and is too gullible regarding the future and that his plans stopped at the conquest."

"No. All of that is true. He goes around only giving good news. He may bring up some minor concerns, but not as honestly as he should. I can't understand how power can change a man that quickly."

"You father is afraid. Anyone would be in his boots. Maybe he cannot see any other way to stabilize things," I suggested.

"Is that what it is?" Rime sighed. "Such fears will have to be chased away and soon. He must be able to function with the same amount of reason as before."

"You cannot help him from the Soldier's."

"He isn't planning on it," Riestel corrected me. "Listen closer. Shouldn't your kind be good listeners?"

"Your arrogant friend is right. I want to relinquish my governorship to Samedi, but it would mean we'd have to stay at the Peak. I wasn't sure you'd like that."

"Are you sure you want to give the title away?" I asked.

"It means nothing to me. There are more important goals. But if you would have wanted, I would have attempted a quieter life," Rime offered.

Riestel groaned, annoyed.

"No, don't think about such things yet," I said and reached my hand out to Rime. "Let's first fix what I broke. Then we can live freely," I suggested as the thought of parting from the Needle stabbed my very flesh with severe pain. It was the key to everything, me and this world. I couldn't live with myself if I just left it.

Rime nodded.

"But what will you do if you yield the title?" I asked.

"We… are in an exceptional situation, legally," Rime mused. "It gives me the opportunity to wield a very certain type of power. My father will hate it, but there is a way I can force him to listen. I'm not sure whether he just didn't plan further than getting to power or whether he cannot make up his mind on what to pursue now that he can no longer work in the shadows. Thus, he must humble himself to take advice from those who can make decisions quicker."

"Are you going to demand the title of war counsel?" Riestel enquired and pretended to flick lint off his trousers. "You will need… Ha. You have placed your men to the highest positions of the districts. You almost have the votes."

"Would one of you explain this to me, too?" I demanded.

"Always in need of schooling, aren't you?" Riestel teased. "The governors have the right to declare a war counsel if the city is in jeopardy and it is generally recognized that the current ruler doesn't have enough experience to guide the country through it. A king wouldn't lose his position, but the counsel has absolute control of the military and the safety arrangements. If the Black Guard doesn't let the old governors back to their positions or a new one in, they may act as a substitute for the area. But they would have to hold their places until after the coronation, and time it so the new king doesn't have the time to name new ones. You cannot do it before everything is official. It is legal, just," Riestel explained. "Maybe I must adjust my insults. The doggy is capable of thought."

"He gave you a very thorough rundown," Rime said, ignoring the insult. "But it is a last resort. I'd like to believe my father will still listen to reason once I urge him enough."

"I think he will," I sighed. "I hope so."

"If I had to go to such lengths, would you condone it?"

"If you see no other way… I like your father, but I'm not his servant."

"Stop with the melodrama," Riestel ordered and pulled the window shut right onto my fingers. "Worry not. I won't say a word to anyone of your little treasonous plot. I mean, to whom would I share it? I have no friends," he noted and chortled as I stared at him angrily and rubbed my fingers.

Once we caught up to Frazil, he was unnervingly kind when he noticed us, though he did express his concerns over my travels. Rime assured him I wasn't out to campaign, just to accompany him and see the city some more. Riestel kept to himself to such an extent Frazil didn't even notice him, so we didn't mention his presence either.

Frazil had invited Gramo and Veitso to discuss the district's future. Rime didn't sit down at the table but remained leaning against the plain wooden wall of the small townhouse. They talked a good while. Gramo insisted on particulars, actions, and promises that they wouldn't be abandoned.

"The reconstruction and all the arrangements will take time," Frazil responded. "I cannot give any guarantees right this moment. We must plan first. This winter may turn out to be as bad as the ones before it, but we will work on bringing change during the summer and fall. I'm drafting a list of all the changes we will strive to bring."

"Look now, I'd just like a promise on the grains not stopping. We got nothing to live on here."

"He isn't lying. The stores are empty and people jittery," Veitso concurred. "We'll see lynchings soon for whatever reason. After that, riots won't be far off."

"We distribute flyers on the future changes," Frazil promised. "Many good things will come once the winter is done."

Gramo folded his arms. Rime placed his hands on Gramo's shoulders and squeezed gently. Gramo turned to him and nodded.

"The Governor forgets that people here cannot read," Rime noted.

"Well, those who can can spread the word," Frazil suggested as he fiddled with his papers. "Will that be possible?"

"Suppose so," Gramo sighed and shook his head.

"And if we encounter outbursts?" Veitso asked. "I guarantee we will. I can't do much about them with these authorizations. Sure, I can smash them down with the army, but the locals don't appreciate that."

"Would the District accept Veitso's command better as a temporary governor? Would that help as you'd be their representative? Rime doesn't need you right now, or do you?" Frazil asked.

"No, I don't. If Veitso wishes to stay and help, I have no objections. People will be more apt to trust him when they see him as someone with a stake in their wellbeing. The Black Guard can wait."

"Good, we will do that. I will send my plans and other notices. You can then lecture about them to the rest. I haven't made up my mind about the next governor, so a temporary one will take some pressure off."

Once Frazil withdrew, Rime exchanged a few quiet words with Gramo and Veitso.

"I can now understand a bit better why you'd make such a plan," I whispered as we left. "This is hardly the time for lists and drafts," I pondered as I walked next to Rime to a small guest room in Gramo's house. It was as simple as the cottage on the island.

"I believe he will turn out to be a good ruler in time, but this pressure and urgency is new to him. He has always had the luxury of time and darkness. He doesn't like that he can't dictate the flow of things and that an error may be all that is remembered in the history books," Rime answered once the door was closed.

"He's as stubborn as you," I remarked.

"It has its dangers."

"What do you think will happen if he finds out?"

"Nothing pleasant, but nothing I'm not prepared to pay. The plan must be in place in case it's needed."

"How can you be so sure your way is the correct way?" I asked as I removed my outer clothing and slipped under the covers.

"I'm not sure. It can be the wrong way. But with everything I've seen and experienced, it is not," Rime answered and yawned. "I have trouble sleeping without you," he said and rubbed his temple.

"Headache?"

"Slight."

"Come here then."

Rime laid on the bed and put his head on my lap. I rubbed the muscles of his forehead and jaw. His breathing relaxed as he closed his eyes.

"Can I just stay here until time ends?" he asked.

"I wouldn't mind if you did."

He breathed heavily and laid on his pillow. He pulled me close and buried his face in my hair. I snuffed the lantern out. It was somehow freeing to be in such a simple place with him. The outside world and our actual life seemed far away. I should talk to him about Riestel's request, but he seemed so peaceful and content in the darkness, I couldn't get the words out.

X

After a few more days into the journey, we passed the Harbor District's gates. The brisk sea wind and the salty air were more noticeable here. I had liked the sea air, but ever since I had nearly drowned it made me a little nauseous. We rolled down to a road that stretched on right beside the harbor's piers. It was a paved road, connected to the wooden maze of piers, and it went on almost for the width of the whole of the city, according to Rime.

The houses were lean and tall. Bright sky-blue and moss-green. A few white ones in the mix. They were the homes of harbor officials. The windows were often small and round or oval. None had curtains. The storms would break larger windows easily, so they weren't in fashion.

"Can we visit a ship?" I asked as we stepped out of the carriage. "Now that I might remember the experience."

"Can do," Rime replied and inhaled deeply. He seemed well rested and composed, like he knew every step on his path to whatever destiny had planned.

The Harbor's Governor, Laki, greeted Frazil and his servants. He led us to a nearby tavern and to its upper floors. The house had come to lean to the right so much over time that we had to hold tightly to the railing in order to not fall on our back into the stairwell.

The whitewashed walls and dark beams made the room seem much lower than it was and slightly oppressive in mood. Laki and the servants went off to get supplies and refreshments. Frazil lifted his document bag on the table. He was frowning.

"What exactly are you doing here?" he asked. "I'd like a more believable answer than the last time I asked."

I glanced at Rime. He shrugged and sat across from his father.

"We? Isa is exploring Kerth, as now is the time for it. And me? You invited me. And of course, I'm going to travel with her every chance I get."

"Should I believe in such a simple motive?" Frazil pondered coldly.

"Have I ever left things unsaid if I disagree? Have I ever falsely supported anything?" Rime enquired.

"No," Frazil sighed and squeezed his bag a little.

"Then… what is the problem? We support you. Isa has toured with a very low profile. She hasn't arranged any large meetings or gatherings anywhere. She has obviously talked to those who have sought her out if word of her presence spread. You can check this from anyone in any region. She has not defied your order to lie low for a moment which, by the way, you cannot suggest to mean that she would have to lock herself in the Needle. People would only gossip more."

Frazil let go of the bag and let out a sigh. His face was still covered in worries.

"I will gladly step out once the meeting starts," I added. "I have no interest in these discussions."

"That's a good idea. I'll come too. Let's head for the ships since I promised to show you one," Rime suggested and turned to his father. "You can then wonder if we have deserved all this suspicion after all we have done for you."

"There's no need for that," Frazil reassured.

"Clearly there is. If you don't trust me enough, do not name Tammaran as the temporary, but keep Laki in his place. There will be trouble if we withdraw the army this early, but if it grants you peace of mind, do so," Rime suggested and got up as Tammaran and Laki returned.

Rime walked over to the men and touched his nose ever so casually as he passed Tammaran, who then brushed his ear lobe. How carefully was this planned? I stared at Rime's face. How many of the things I perceived as coincidences were such and how many were the plots of other people?

"Governor Fall, Consecratoress Elona, will you not stay?" Laki asked, confused. "I'm sure all this applies to you, too."

"My father will fill us in on all that is necessary. He holds the power, after all. Why would we be needed?"

Outside, the locals were quite curious about us and not at all shy when it came to staring. Rime's black and blue military gear differed greatly from their clothes or the clothes of regular army folk who wore brown, simple short jackets and pants. Rime's long coat was lined with fiery colored silk. The bright orange flashed in the darkening evening as his boots kicked the hem forward.

Most we met on our walk had very practical clothes. The fabrics had no jolly colored dyes, but everything was of good quality, much better than in the Crafter's or Worker's. In complete juxtaposition, they had very elaborate, small pieces of jewelry, and a lot of them. All scarves and hats were decorated. Almost all carried a short, brightly painted knife holster on their hip or belt.

"Why is everyone carrying a knife?" I asked Rime, who seemed suspiciously calm.

"It's a tool for most things here. They need it to gut fish, to defend themselves, and to carve parts for the ships."

"It's much calmer here than I thought it would be. Have the riots been contained?"

"For the most part. The Harbor folk are tempestuous. However, they listen to reason after breaking a few things. I wouldn't roam around here alone. The area is quaint but full or criminals. There's no better place for an opportunist than this."

"Tammaran told me awful things about the time he lived here. Are children still used in the workforce and sold?"

"Yes. It's a problem the next ruler should address. Laki is weak, and his relatives are far too corrupt and in the business themselves."

"Does Frazil know that?"

"I'd imagine so. I would be shocked if he didn't. I would assume it would have been one of the very things he used to blackmail Laki to support his own cause. Laki isn't a rebellious man. He won't stand for anything unless he might lose something he values. But… he wouldn't withdraw his support now, even if we would crack down on his relatives once we hold the power. Once the inner walls are down, the Harbor's power and influence will grow as one of the main suppliers of everything. It will give them new opportunities for a better line of work. Look, there is the ship that brought us here. I queried the crew earlier. We can go to the deck. I will check if we can go up now. Wait here."

The ship was impressive. You could have lined up forty horses next to it to match its length. Three shiny, white masts reached up to the clouds. I had only seen wooden hulls, but this was partly made from dark red-painted metal. The stern was decorated with metal flowers and waves painted with a sparkling gold. Why did anyone wish to make a military vessel so beautiful?

I walked quietly on the wooden pier next to the ship. It seemed to sleep. Perhaps it would be better if we didn't board it. I turned to look where Rime was but couldn't see him.

At the very end of the pier, a vast bay opened up. The only way out was through the opening in the middle of the curved, ox-horn-like rocks and cliffs. The sea was still open. The water rippled against the thick wooden pillars. Something dark lingered under the moon-sparkled waters. Lurking, waiting. The sky looked much more hopeful.

Riestel stood at the end of another pier. His eyes were closed. He seemed to speak to himself or recite a silent prayer. Then he crouched and stretched his hand above the water. He opened his fist and a light substance floated to the waves. Ash. I don't know how, but I knew it was all that was left of my... Istrata's wedding dress. The water darkened for a moment, as if the deed made it mad.

"Isa, come," Rime called by the ship. "They are lowering a ramp."

"Just a moment," I replied. Riestel turned to face me and touched his temple with two fingers as a salute of sorts. I lifted my hand just a little before I returned to Rime. He was looking at the hull.

"I think I made an adequate work of it, or they have improved my work after it," he said.

"Governor Fall. This way," a straw-haired man in a thick wooly coat beckoned.

"Thank you, Captain."

"Through here, please."

We followed the man on to a wooden ramp that led to the deck. A dozen men stood on the deck to greet us.

"Most of us were on that trip, the one that brought you here years ago, Consecratoress. We are all glad you made it," the captain said. "The Governor was starting out on his more political career. I wish we'd have known what would become of the city."

"I'm grateful for your help back then," I replied. I instinctively didn't like him.

"It is we who are grateful to have been a part of your journey. Some here believe the gods protect you. That they hoisted you from the seas to help us.

The crew here wishes you might bestow some of that protection on us."

"I'd hardly think my presence here is the work of any gods… The one I serve is not a protector."

"You won't change their minds. Seafarers are a superstitious bunch," Rime whispered. "To a fault. Just shake their hands before we leave. It should be enough for them."

"Well, know this, we do like our rituals when we face waves twice as big as the ships," the captain chuckled and pulled on his collar. "Have a look around as you please."

"I'll have a word with him. You can go ahead," Rime suggested.

I wandered into the ship. A part of me objected to this trip, but I was also fascinated with the place where I had, in a way, been born into the world— or perhaps stabilized was the better word. The ship had a small lobby from which stairs went both up and down to the bridge, and to the cargo deck, and cabins. The air smelled of salt and smoke. All corridors had been painted.

Most cabins were small and had bunkbeds. The flashes I could remember were of a much larger cabin. A more room-like cabin. I found it closer to the bow. The whole room sighed. There were small fragments of some lingering enchantments in its walls. I traced my fingers on the walls and furniture trying to catch them. Whenever I could reach and touch one, short flashes and shreds of feelings of my fake time on the island and of the statue's thoughts during its solitude invaded my head. None of them were enough to form a proper thought.

I rubbed my eyes. It looked as if a few seams in the wall oozed black tar.

"Does it feel odd to be here?" Rime asked as he closed the door.

"That would be an understatement."

"What were you looking at?"

"Nothing," I answered, as I didn't see the drops anymore. "I was just lost in thought. Did I ever tell you that I remember you from here?"

"You do? How? You were conscious only a few moments."

"I still remember you reading to me, telling me stories," I explained as Rime glanced sideways. "I can't believe you're blushing!"

"Don't be mad."

"You are!" I laughed. "What might you have done that I can't remember but you do?"

"You have a dirty mind," he groaned and tugged at his sleeve.

"Oh, do I? But you once said you saw me like this from the start?" I whispered and wrapped my hands around his waist.

"You get far too much enjoyment from teasing others."

"To be fair, mostly you."

"Wife, dear…"

"Yes?"

He pushed me onto the bed.

"Alright, a confession. I did undress you twice, at least," he whispered and bent over me.

"You did not!" I objected.

"Because your wounds needed to be cleaned, you imp," he reminded me and smiled. "Have you seen enough?"

"Maybe," I grinned and pulled him into a kiss by the collar. It pinched. A black film flashed in Rime's eyes.

"Should we go?" I asked as a cold shudder went through me.

"You are the one flirting."

"But we could retire to our proper room," I suggested, a little unsure.

"You'd have me walk several streets over in this condition?" he asked in a low voice, shook his head, and moved my skirts. "I remember you had a bandage here," he whispered and brushed his hand on my inner thigh. I felt his touch with more bite than before.

We kissed again. His dexterous and heavy body pressed on mine, efficiently silencing whatever sense I had left. The bed made a just nearly audible clinking sound against the wall. I bit his shoulder to keep quiet. He pulled my hair and head back. Our eyes met, and I could see his normal, beautiful eyes again. I turned my head. I felt bad for having felt a moment of hesitation, worry even.

As we emerged with the proper amount of bashfulness, there were twenty more men on the deck. The captain greeted us.

"Why are there more here?" Rime asked with a visible change in posture and demeanor.

"Everyone from that journey wanted to greet the Consecratoress. To get her blessing, if possible. It's been a wild ride in the city for the last year. People need hope. We have many dead from hunger and the rebellion."

"I'm sorry, but I'm not a talisman. I do not like this," I added.

"They are only asking for a quick touch," the captain explained and pursed his lips a bit. "They did help to rescue you. We brought you here," he pressured.

"You don't need to," Rime assured me and placed his hand on the hilt.

I glanced around at the crew. This would turn into a huge mess and fast. I suppose it would be a smaller inconvenience to just agree to shake their hands. That way we'd avoid getting a bad reputation. Still, something about the way their eyes gleamed was unnerving.

"Alright, fine, but fast," I promised. The sailors surrounded us. Someone shouted that I had agreed to bless them. More people boarded. Even Rime was so taken aback with the numbers that people managed to push in between us. The first took my hand and stroked it. Several more reached for me.

"Allow me some room," I asked. "There is no need to push and hurry. You will all have your turn."

They didn't seem to hear me, or if they did, they certainly didn't react.

"Stop crowding her!" Rime demanded, but none responded. I could feel someone grab my hair, and I heard a snip. I turned my head. One of them had cut a lock off and was holding it like a trophy.

"Let me go! Rime!"

"Back off! Captain, control them or I will," Rime shouted and drew his weapon.

"But even I could use a little..." the captain mumbled. "We only want a bit of protection. We've lost family and friends... We brought her. We deserve protection. We deserve a reward."

"You will regret this!" Rime cursed as he grabbed ahold of the men between us. He pulled them away with as much force as he could.

Once Rime reached me again, he pulled me to his side. There were dozens around us. Was I imagining it or was there black goo dripping from their eyes? The same as the ship had wept earlier? Rime punched a few of the closest and tried to shield me, but it was difficult to do with them pressing on us more and more.

I almost forgot how to breathe at that point. My muscles tensed and my confidence drained. A paralyzing fear crept in. This was the first time I had ever felt I couldn't defend myself. My whole body trembled and shook. This is what they had done to her. They had tried to chop her up into little pieces for their happiness. Was this how it began for Istrata? I could see my reflection in Rime's eyes. I was supposed to be the grand manifestation of an almost almighty Witch Queen's plans? I who couldn't even cope with past nightmares?

I got so angry at myself the fear begun to wane. As I was about to call the flames, Rime stayed my hand.

"Don't. Fire will call attention," he said. "If we cannot get out before that... I will handle this," he promised grimly.

Rime slapped his hand on the forehead of the nearest intruder as the black mist conquered his eyes. An electrical crackle and a hiss. As if he had opened a pressurized bottle. One life. Distorted and gone from the cycle. I clenched my fist. I didn't want to be the damsel in distress. At other's mercy. I didn't want Rime to have to use his horrible gift for me. Whether it spelled trouble or not.

Before I could act, frozen spears rained down and through the closest men. The rest stopped. None tried to run. They didn't seem to act as humans would. None screamed. They just swayed and stared in silence.

"So, this kind of trouble today," Riestel sighed from the steps above the deck. "Did I call it or what? Let's make some room for you."

Riestel's hand and notes guided the needle-sharp ice to the men who surrounded us. The rest of them finally took a simultaneous step back.

"I would suggest that Isa leaves this the ship at once," Riestel said and secured an icy passage to the boarding plank.

"Take her to safety," Rime ordered. "I have things to clean up."

Rime pushed me to get me to move. Once I was off the ship, we stopped. I didn't turn to look at the deck. I could hear full well what was happening.

"Breathe," Riestel urged coldly. "You must face the past better. You cannot freeze like that. It's too dangerous."

"You are right," I whispered and clung to him. Riestel seemed a little flustered.

"Must you be so jumpy in this life?" he sighed, ever so falsely annoyed but stroked my back gently. "The things I must endure. Do not spoil this coat."

"I wouldn't dream of it," I laughed nervously and wiped my face on the lapel to spite him.

"Why did you come?" I asked as I let go of him.

"Mostly to see what a grand, idiotic mess you'd land in this time. Can't say I'm disappointed. Can you handle yourself for a moment? I'll check what is going on."

"I think so. There's no danger here."

Riestel walked up the ramp halfway and turned his head to me. There was a smidgeon of pity in his eyes. Rime walked into sight. His eyes were pitch black, and he reeked of eaten souls. Riestel stopped him, and they talked quietly. Rime came about slowly. Once he seemed himself, they both came to me. Rime handed me the lock one of the sailors had stolen.

"I didn't want to leave it in their hands," he said.

I nodded and took the hair. I didn't know what to say.

"Burn the ship," Riestel urged me.

"What? And the crew?" I asked.

"Burn the ship. There are no people… nor souls there anymore," Riestel remarked somberly.

"Burn it," Rime repeated his words. "We can't leave the bodies to be examined. We can get out fast enough now. There are no people to stop us."

"Alright…" I yielded and walked to the ship's side. I pressed my palms to it. It felt wrong, but what good was a guilty conscience now when I was ready to burn them just a few moments ago when they were still alive? In self-defense, surely, but still.

"It's an army ship. There will be explosives," Rime remarked. "It should be a sufficient cause, especially if a few blackened glass shards from liquor bottles are found in the remains."

I felt the cargo on the other side, and the spark skipped between the materials. In a blink of an eye, the whole frame shook. We ran along the piers into the dark night. As we looked on from the shadows, the greedy flames engulfed the ship. Once we were sure the fire was hot enough to mask what had happened, we continued our escape.

"We must talk," Riestel said as we reached the inn we had been housed at. People were starting to run past us towards the harbor and to help with putting the fire out. We turned to see the spectacle as if we didn't know what had caused it.

"Tomorrow," Rime answered. "I need rest. I will join you in the carriage when we start our ascent."

"Are we not touring the Slum's?" I asked.

"The area is still on lockdown. We had to destroy all gates leading to it during the attack. They haven't been cleared yet, as there have been reports of a pestilence. We do not want any disease spreading to the rest of the city. We have sent food and medical help over the walls. I must sleep. Come," Rime ordered.

I laid in the bed all night, staring at Rime. Black tentacles surrounded him. They had grown stronger since his near-death. Now they were happy and satiated. If I hadn't been so paralyzed for a moment, he wouldn't have had to use them. I had made things worse with my cowardice. I know he had told me to not act, but that didn't help the way I felt. I had made his condition worse. Or was that true? He was more powerful also, but that was a dreadful thought. The emptiness, whatever it was in the end, should be chained somehow. Maybe to a machine like Irinda had.

I took Rime's hand while he slept. He had never left my side. I would return the favor. Whatever Riestel had to say about my intelligence due to that. I was a little baffled by Riestel's reaction to my fear. It had been a mix of caring and warmth. I shook my head. I shouldn't imagine a connection from a few shows of kindness. There was no reason to assume he was any safer to deal with than before.

Breakfast was just a porridge of seeds and water. We were offered honey but as Frazil declined, we did too. We were surrounded by ordinary people, after all. Every table was buzzing. Everyone had their own theory on the accident. According to the already given official version, it was a rehearsal that had gone wrong. They had decided on this explanation after finding the bottle shards to cover up that their men had been drinking. Many didn't believe it all. Many thought there was too much misfortune in the city and it couldn't just be another unconnected thing.

We left the inn quietly. Tammaran bid us goodbye momentarily, as he was now a temporary governor as Rime had wanted. Tammaran would still return to the Peak after a few days of information gathering. Rime would hold him in the position only in name.

We settled in the carriage and sat in an uncomfortable silence for a good length of the journey's first part. Only once we left the Harbor behind did we start to relax.

"You aren't taking this seriously enough," Riestel admonished us.

"How so?" Rime asked, visibly annoyed.

"The more you eat, the more you crave. And Isa… She is getting emotional spikes that aren't her emotions but a transfer."

Rime glanced at me and I him. We couldn't really argue the matter.

"What do you suggest Isa and I do?"

"First, try to be careful around each other. You cannot sleep together before your hunger is on a leash."

"Can you rein it in?" I asked.

"No. But we may be able to find something in the books," Riestel responded.

"I must confess," Rime interrupted, "I have talked to Moras about the issue. Asked him to research it."

"Is that why you stayed behind in the Peak at first? To talk to him? Why didn't you just say so?" I asked.

"I didn't want to worry you. I was going to talk to you once he had something to work on. I can see my condition gives you anxiety. We wanted to try to find a solution quietly and share knowledge once we had something. I didn't want to burden you or give false hope."

"Burden me? I just sit and read... Don't be so frustratingly chivalrous."

"As much as a fallout between you two might amuse me... you are no innocent, Isa. Since you won't bring it up, I will. I wish to take Isa to the last statue."

"Why?" Rime asked and straightened his back.

"Because it could save her sanity and offer us more knowledge of Istrata's final goal."

"Tell him the whole thing since you started," I urged.

"The statue is in the grave of our daughter. The child may be alive or not."

Rime studied Riestel's face intently for a moment and then sighed.

"Where is the grave?" he asked.

"Close by. But Isa must first learn to walk in the Lighter World. After that, we need a fully safe room, as we will have to travel in another world."

"Your requests are never pleasant," Rime groaned and squeezed my hand. "I'll arrange it."

"Tammaran can watch us. He sees both worlds," I suggested.

"There's no need for that," Riestel assured.

"No, that's a good idea. I do not trust you," Rime said.

"Oh, and how that pains me," Riestel scoffed. "Do try to talk to each other a little. Do not be as dumb as we were."

XI

Each of us seemed to be avoiding someone. I was avoiding Riestel, as he constantly urged me to study the Lighter World when I would have rather gotten to know this one with my husband. I longed for the day Rime could hold his promise and take me to see the apple orchards of his former commander and the precious stone mines. Although, a small melancholy part of me was starting to believe that day was never going to arrive.

Riestel was dodging his students and Moras, as he was tired of their constant enthusiastic questions. Rime was avoiding Frazil as he tried to lessen the strain on their relationship and avoid endless arguments about what he had or had not done. And Frazil was avoiding me, though I had no idea why.

"You are too soft," Rime disapproved of his father, behind the slightly ajar door. I tried my best not to be seen or heard, even if my curiosity drove me to listen. He was arguing with his father, for the second day in a row, about the correct way to handle riots in the Harbor and Worker's and what should be done with the Slum's District where the situation was growing more and more dire.

The disease there spread like wildfire. Kerthians had named it "tar sickness", as those who fell ill bled and oozed a dark, sticky, viscous substance before death. The descriptions of it shook me. I couldn't get those lazy black drops I had seen on the ship out of my mind. The similarity disturbed me, though I couldn't find a connection outside the visuals.

"And your way would create much discomfort and disdain among people," Frazil responded and took a deep breath. "I do not appreciate that I must get involved. The riots cannot be stamped down with threats. You must find another way."

"I'm not planning on threatening them. I'm going to tell them what the end result will be if they mutiny. You cannot give the uprising and negativity a route to burst. It must be stamped out, and yes, with force, if need be, in this situation. You have to lay the ground for the throne before you can sit on it and think you are the king!"

"Think I am the king? You are getting awfully close to slander. I will not tolerate methods that will harm or kill my people at this point. My reign will not start with bloodshed. I will not have it! Are we clear?"

"And that is all the arsenal you think I bring? Do you think I can only solve issues with those methods?"

"No... of course not!" Frazil snapped. "But we must use the least amount of force as possible. Guide them gently."

"And that is your final stance?"

"It is. I may not have all the power of an anointed king yet, but I will not become a tyrant at step one. Do not test me on this. We must arrange the escorts and celebrations for the external governors. That is the top priority. The invitations have been sent. I want all of these issues dealt with by then. With my tactics."

"You can want all you like," Rime groaned as he came out of the room and slammed the door shut. He rubbed his forehead, fixed his collar, and glanced at me sideways. The tension melted from his face.

"You know, for a woman who says she wishes to stay impartial on the matter, you are always handily in the best place to get information."

"You asked me to wait here."

"If I recall correctly, I left you on that couch way over there, not behind this door."

"I was just stretching my legs."

"Right."

"Yes. You'd benefit from doing so too," I said just before I flicked his forehead and started to run through the corridor. Rime waited for a few seconds with a mightily stern expression and then charged after me.

"Don't you dare escape!"

I could hear his steps coming closer. After two corridors and a staircase, his fingers grabbed my wrist. He pulled me with quite a bit of force right in to his direction and I bumped into him. We took a few uneasy steps, slammed into a door that gave away into another hall. We laid on the floor laughing despite of the just acquired bruises.

Rime leaned over me. He brushed a strand of hair off my cheek.

"You're an odd creature," he whispered.

A pair of boots stopped right beside us.

"Did I not tell you to stay away from each other?" Riestel asked with an icy gleam in his eyes and slammed the book he carried shut. "You undisciplined brats. Isa, march to the tower."

"Oh fine," I muttered and got up. Rime followed suit. It was funny to get scolded like school children at our age. But Riestel had a point. We had ignored his warnings to a certain degree. Rime controlled his hunger well during the days. We didn't share a room anymore, as Rime didn't want to take any chances. I simply couldn't get myself to fear him, even if it was the smart thing to do. I did recall what had happened on the ship, but I tried my best to bury those memories with a soft, warm blanket of forgetfulness.

"I'll head to Moras for the rest of the day," Rime said. "He has some ideas."

"He does?" I asked, feeling elated.

"Just ideas, but he was quite keen on explaining his calculations."

"He doesn't get excited for small things," I smiled.

Riestel grabbed my hair and started pulling me towards the tower with a disgruntled sigh.

"I'll try to come by later," Rime promised.

"Wonderful. Now she won't be able to focus on anything. I don't constantly wreck your plans, so must you make my work with this lump of clay even more difficult?" Riestel groaned and pulled me behind the corner. Once out of sight, he let go of my hair.

We sat down in a stable position on the Needle's floor. Riestel could join me in the space I had created now that he knew about it. Riestel gestured me to begin. The turquoise butterfly had been stable for a few days now. But it was lifeless and useless. Like it had died and froze in the air in the middle of its flight.

I focused on it, tried to project myself in it and see what it saw. I felt a small jolt, as if I was fainting. For a moment, my mind whirled in a tunnel. When the movement stopped, I saw my face. I snapped back like a whip.

"Good. You did it," Riestel remarked as the butterfly's wings were in a new position. "You need to build something bigger. And while it stabilizes, you need to practice this. Controlling it. Every day. We will encounter pockets of

Istrata's doing on the way. You should be able to revert to yourself there, as their laws are the same as in your spaces. But for the true Lighter World, you will need a shape. A smaller one you can hold together with your thoughts."

I tried again. I could move the wings for a few rounds, but I needed to catch my breath and returned to my body. It took as much strength to do as creating fire had taken during the fight against Irinda.

"What was the first body you made?" I asked.

"Mmm... What was it? I think it might have been a dawn's bluebird. We had better basic skills and teachers to help shape the bodies, so I didn't need to start with insects."

"How can you not remember that for sure?"

"You try living this long. It's amazing how much you forget. Besides, you are the last person who should be lecturing about memories."

"Well, yes... I'm just frustrated," I admitted and walked out to the balcony.

I leaned on the thin railing of the White Needle. It was my favorite spot these days. The banister had leaf and spiral motifs that glistened in the unforgivably bright late winter sun. The bare metal that was visible in places the coat of paint had flaked off blinded one easily.

The winter had taken a heavy toll on the population of stray animals. And people. I could see carriage after carriage of dead arriving at the Needle's base. I followed their lazy uphill battle. It meant I'd have to do another cleansing prayer in the evening. I would have been much happier without that as my burden, but we couldn't afford to not hasten their journey.

"Quite a lot today," Riestel noted as he leaned next to me.

"Seems like a record since the battles."

"If you want to visit your husband and Moras today, you should go. We have a long night ahead."

"I will stop by quickly. I'll meet you outside."

"I'll go and supervise the unloading. The last time they laid them too close to flammable structures."

Moras's helpers and students were busy buzzing around different glass jars and tubes. They distilled, condensed, and calculated tirelessly each and every outcome. Poor Istrata had tried to do it all by herself. The stupid woman. No wonder she never reached her goals in her lifetime.

I had found some of Istrata's equipment and instruments with their swirly and curious parts from other in-between places. Now that I knew better how her influence felt, I could seek them out. Moras practically purred when he got his hands on them. Currently, they were trying to replicate them into copies that would stay in this reality easier.

I glanced at the notebooks on Moras's table. We had identified a hundred plants that would be helpful. Some used only a little bit of soul sand to produce crops. Some would yield a steady flow of energy to the cycle, and some a significant amount when harvested completely at the peak moment. More than they had required during their growth. They were the first step in reviving the earth. All living things consumed and created during their existence. Some created more than they consumed—but only at very specific moments.

Those studying the phenomena had slowly moved on to animal experiments. The thought brought no one joy. However, it was something that we couldn't ignore. Thankfully, they were nothing like Istrata's trials and attempts to create new things. Moras was fully conscious that no creature should be removed from the cycle without a good reason. They had to conduct most of the experiments on livestock meant for slaughter. There was still plenty to examine in a city this size with these limitations, though it did affect the taste in odd ways at times.

The door to a smaller study was half open. Rime sat at the desk with no shirt. A needle with a tube stuck out from his arm. Moras transferred something through them into Rime. His eyes were coal black, but he remained peaceful, in a trance of sorts.

"What are you up to?" I asked and closed the door behind me.

"Consecratoress," Moras saluted me as he jotted down some observations. "We are studying the hunger reflex and why it grows. We can keep him satiated like this. He doesn't need to kill or feast from a living thing directly, but it's not the best solution."

I waved my hand in front of Rime's face. He didn't respond at all. The tube fed the tar right into him. I hadn't known they were using the substance left by twisted souls to avoid taking from the soul sand and soul stores.

"I've calmed him. Usually, when an emptied soul feeds, there is aggression, so to keep us all safe, we must have him sedated."

"Will it do any permanent damage?"

"Considerably less than the actual state itself. We have been delving into his glove. It contains such magnificently dainty spikes, as thin as a thread in a spider's web. They bite into the skin precisely at the location of the channels. I assume they are what helps to control the flow, even the direction. Irinda was able to use what she ate after all."

"Has Frazil been of any help?"

"Some. He had some old drawings the gloves are based on. I have a hypothesis, by the way. Frazil has never used his abilities without the glove, so he doesn't suffer from the same control or addiction issues. Rime, on the other hand... He has had to use the skill in his line of work by instinct with no mechanical help or regulation. I think that's what causes the difference in their situations. We have made good progress, and my students are hard at work with Irinda's libraries and rooms to find more information. I am cautiously optimistic about getting this under control."

"I know you have a vast amount of work to do. I am ever so grateful you are taking the time to explore this as well," I said.

"The city needs him. You need him. I will require a long vacation once all is done... but until then, we are fully committed to working day in and out. Besides, all of this is truly fascinating. Now that we have the correct equipment, the work progresses better and the results are more stable."

"Will he have to spend all the evening in that state?"

"I'm afraid so. He will stay like that until the morning. Apologies."

"That's fine, I have work as well..."

"There's no shortage of that for a long time. I must confess, I am glad I don't have your part to play," Moras told me surprisingly softly and shook his head.

"You get used to the dead. Not that I ever wanted to feel like that."

"I believe life will be victorious. We will turn this around," he assured me with a confident smile.

"You have a wonderful way of giving me strength," I replied.

"It is, perhaps, the most pleasant of my duties, Consecratoress."

I touched Rime's cheek. If his eyes would be forever covered by this shadow, I wouldn't know what to do. I bent just a little closer and messed up his hair.

"You may expose me as the culprit," I offered.

"Thank you, I believe I may," Moras chuckled.

I stepped out at the base of the White Needle. Riestel was ordering people around. Kymenes and Liike were present and had commenced with the actual burning of the bodies. It was left to me to unravel their lives. The families of the dead had gathered around. Now that the gates were mostly open, many carried and escorted their dead to us. We offered boarding for these somber travelers. Not in the Needle or castle, but in tents with heating erected all the way from here to the gate itself.

I began the dance while Riestel hummed. I didn't really need to dance to deconstruct the matter in the Lighter World, but we had reached the conclusion that it would be comforting if we acted as though this was a mass at a temple. It gave them comfort. The dance was slow and thoughtful, maybe even uplifting. I didn't attempt to scare people or seduce them. There was something deep and holy present. Something even my old teacher, Uudean, might have appreciated had she had the capacity for it anymore.

People rarely spoke to us. They just observed, and sometimes they'd hum along and then fade into the night. From morning till dusk, grieving people came and went. We tried to give each the provisions that would have belonged to the dead to ease their lives for the few weeks the winter still lingered.

I wiped sweat on my hem after the performance. A quiet group of old men and women stood still on the side of the square. They seemed immovable. Usually, people only stayed until they saw their own disappear and join the earth and sky.

"Who are they?" I asked.

"No clue," Riestel sighed. "From the Lower's, by the looks of them."

I walked to them out of curiosity. They huddled together and stared at me expectantly.

"The ceremony is over," I remarked. "You will find places to sleep in by the roads."

"Thank you, we know. We…" an old man started. "We just wanted to see the end. We…"

I studied them a little closer. They were all very old, limping, hunched, and sick. I took a step back.

"Will it hurt?" an old woman asked. "If you perform it on a living soul?" she continued and grabbed my sleeve.

"Do not bother the Consecratoress with such madness!" Riestel scolded them and yanked my sleeve free. "No one will do this to the living. Go back to your families!"

"We meant no offense…" he mumbled and consoled the startled woman. "But why should we be kept alive when we all know we will not live until spring or the summer?"

"What kind of an example would that set?" Riestel asked, annoyed. "Imagine what would happen if the city knew we will kill people for the benefit of others! I believe you are in pain, but this is not the time or the place. Leave, please."

Riestel guided me back to the White Needle.

"Thank you," I whispered.

"For what?"

"I didn't know what to say to them."

"The harder the times are, the stranger the solutions people think of. Not that I blame them for trying. They are all very sick, and they are right about not making it to summer."

"All of them?" I enquired. I was surprised Riestel sounded this compassionate to their plea when he had just refused them so directly.

"Yes. We could try to alleviate their pain for a moment, but the resources are what they are."

"Then... do we have the right to condemn them to suffer?"

"No more than to decide when their lives are over."

"But if it's their wish?" I asked, though I wasn't eager to grant it.

"Do you think life is holy? What is its value?" Riestel countered as he opened the balcony door and the fresh night air flooded in. "Does it have any value in itself? A soul, yes, but just the life force?"

"There are those who don't possess a soul. They cease to exist."

"Indeed. So, is their life more valuable because it is the only manifestation of them that will ever exist?"

"I... I don't know. Maybe. It's odd. Why do some people have a permanent soul and some not?"

"Istrata had a theory on it. I'm not sure if she ever proved it."

"Tell me."

"Well, souls develop through action and desire. A hunger to exist. From life lived. Experiences get distilled and solidified in the Lighter World until they are no longer a part of a singular life or a persona, but their own thing. An eternal spark, a will, built from the foundation of this world."

"So, all who are born could develop a soul?"

"Supposedly, if she was correct. Animals too, though it is rarer."

"If we gave them the change to die gently and without suffering through, would we then rob their chance to get a soul?"

"That's impossible to say. No one knows how it happens. It might have already developed or might have crystallized tomorrow. Maybe others can attain it just before they vanish. Pure, pointless conjecture."

"Not to me," I sighed and leaned on the banister. "To me, it's the most beautiful subject in the world."

"Well, you are a bit damaged anyway," Riestel remarked and smiled merrily as the last slivers of daylight died on the horizon. "What's with that stare?"

"Just thinking..."

"It's something horribly intrusive again, isn't it? Just ask. You won't be able to stop yourself."

"Thank you ever so much for the permission, sire."

"I can withdraw it."

"I just... You, no doubt, have a permanent soul. But around it... there's so much life force that you've accumulated along the years."

"Yes. And?"

"I was just..."

"As the sky is my consort, spit it out before I throw you off this balcony."

"You said you might want to die once all this is over. That you are old and spent. But if all that life force and the memories it contains would be torn away, wouldn't everything be new to you? You wouldn't recall Istrata, not these years, nothing. All the burdens would be gone."

All the color drained from Riestel's face as he stared off into the distance.

"You could do it, couldn't you? Cleanse me of all this."

"I think I could, though, I've never done so to a living person."

"But you cannot fix my age," Riestel noted with a faint smile. "I'd have to start all over again as an adult."

"It's a possibility to continue your life without any of your current agony."

"I don't know if I would give everything up. Or maybe I don't want to give up anything. If we can fix things, remembering these dark days may bring joy. Once you know all this wasn't in vain. On the other hand, the idea that I might wake up without any of these sad thoughts during a better time..."

"I can try it someday if you wish."

"Would you?" Riestel asked, and his head hung a bit. "You wouldn't miss me at all then?" he added and turned closer to me.

"Did I say that? You are such a gloom cloud."

"Why would you? I've been nothing but an annoyance."

"But you are so talented at it."

Riestel tilted his head, and his eyes narrowed. Then he laughed.

"You truly are different than her. She would have apologized and tried to find out how deeply she offended me."

"Well, wasn't that the whole point? To force a change?"

"Yes, and yet... I think I like you better," Riestel whispered and touched my cheek with his icy finger. "Don't panic, for Peak's sake. What a face. I didn't just profess my undying love to you. You are that enchanting. I thank you for the offer, but now is not the time to think about forgetting it all. Ask me again once I know what befell my daughter. I fear I might need more than wine."

"Are you afraid to go there?"

"Am I afraid?" Riestel smirked. "More than anything. But enough. I'm not a project for you to mend. You already have one."

"Good. You're too much work, anyway. I can't do everything."

He nodded and breathed in deep. Then he smiled with an astonishingly serene look. A strange determination shone from him. I caught myself studying his nose, which at first glance was straight, but upon closer inspection, there was a tiny dent on it, just about half way. A warm wave of quiet compassion welled in me. I knew very well his protest had been a lie.

XII

A shaken elderly guard appeared at my doorstep in the early morning hours.

"Consecratoress, I apologize profusely for waking you up. There is an issue in the square."

"What issue?"

"I'd rather not describe it. No one is in danger, but it is not a jolly sight. Bodies."

"Again? I didn't know we were getting carriages in the morning."

I hurried at his heels, pulling my coat on. Tammaran stood some way from the outer door and sent the guard on his way. He escorted me the rest of the corridor in an awkward silence. This couldn't possibly be a normal delivery. As Tammaran opened the door to the square, I saw all the old people from yesterday. In a circle, dead. The only one alive was the woman who had grabbed my sleeve. She swayed among the corpses and cried. For some reason, I felt it was my fault.

"Does Rime know?" I asked.

"Yes, but he and Frazil are busy butting heads, so we came to get you. We can't leave this mess here for long," Tammaran explained, frustrated.

"No... Alright, get Riestel or Liike. We will fix this. The fewer have time to see this, the better. I don't quite know how we could explain this to people."

"Understood," he answered and vanished.

I walked over to the old woman. She didn't make a sound when she noticed me. She was shaking. I took my coat and placed it on her. She flinched.

"Oh, I'm sorry!" she cried. "I didn't have the courage. I was supposed to leave the note, but I didn't dare. And now I'm alone. This wasn't supposed to be the result... We just wanted a painless..."

"You could have waited for a day at least," I sighed. "We would have talked to you," I continued. It wasn't a lie. I hadn't been capable of reacting to the situation as it occurred and had allowed Riestel to lead me away. But there wasn't a moment afterwards that I hadn't thought of their request, and what I truly felt was the right thing.

"We traveled so far on foot. No one could bear the thought of returning. Except me, the coward."

"Do you want to return? We can alleviate your aches and send you home."

"No. No. I already left all I had to my children. I'm just a coward. I couldn't! But I can't go back. Failed at this as well…" she cried and buried her face in her hands, squeezing a small piece of wrinkly and coarse paper.

"This is what you were meant to leave us?"

"Our wills," she said, nodding.

I took the stained paper and rolled it open. They had named all the streets and houses in the Crafter's they came from and where they wanted their souls to feed the earth.

"Do you mean you want to gift your memories and life force to the city?"

"Yes. All of it. Everything we have."

"Do you realize that if I take your life, you may not exist after it? There may be nothing else."

"Nothing else?" she repeated, baffled. "But surely something will make it to the Gods?"

"Not always," I answered, but it was clear she didn't want to hear it.

"It's just days or weeks, anyway. I want to go with my friends," she requested with a cracking voice as she wrapped herself tighter in the coat. "I let them down, but I fear the pain."

I studied her face. The wrinkles were deep grooves and the cheeks hollow. Tired. Not like after a poor night, but hollow like she had been gnawed at for years from the inside.

"Are you absolutely sure?" I asked.

"Of what?"

"That life holds nothing for you? That you don't wish to see even one morning more?"

"I saw one more than I was supposed to and there's no joy in it," she replied and lowered her head.

There were only a few guards in the square. I didn't want to take a life, and yet, this would be the first time I'd take a life because of mercy. It made it a thousand times harder than in battle.

"Look at the sky. It glows so beautifully," I whispered. She furrowed her eyebrows and nodded. She turned her head and her gaze from me to the sky. I twisted her tether around my hand and said a silent prayer to some god somewhere in case they had ever existed. Then I pulled. A deep sigh emanated from her lungs as she hunched on her side. There was no more pain or sorrow on her face.

I sat next to her and stared at the horizon in its glorious dawn ballgown. Did a human do this to a human? Was it a merciful act or a game my powers gave a permission to? I could feel her life coursing through my channels. It warmed me like sugary tea and biscuits. That was perhaps the most worrisome thing about these powers. I was made to do this, and it felt frighteningly good. I understood Istrata's mentality better and better. Who could tear apart their loved ones and friends when it was their time knowing that deep down there was enjoyment in it from the power?

"This is the end you chose," Riestel sighed.

"This."

"Let's clean it up."

"Do you regret last night? That we didn't help them right away? Or give them hope of help?" I asked as I got up.

"No. I'm not responsible for another's life or death. And I will not take that burden on myself willingly again. Unlike some busybodies. And I didn't want to affect your decision, nor let them pressure you to make one."

"Do you think I did wrong?"

"You did as she desired. It was her life. What does my opinion weight in that? You just want to hear me say that you chose right so you can stop thinking about it."

"Perhaps."

"But if it eases you… You did right. You did what you are supposed to do. I didn't see it yesterday as clearly as now. That is your sad destiny. All in this world can pass on only through you. For now. Hopefully not forever."

We began to clear everything up. The shape of the old woman hovered, confused, close to her body. It stared at me. I reached my hand towards it. It came to me with no hesitation. In joy and health. I gathered the life force it had gathered and passed it on to the world. A part of me still loathed this role.

The thought of death at any other moment than some elusive blink of destiny, a moment ordained by something larger, felt unholy. But who was I to say if it was destiny or not?

"Do you want your coat back?" Riestel asked.

"No. I have others."

The door to the square opened. Frazil almost lunged at us. Rime was right behind him, looking more annoyed than ever.

"What in the High Peaks is going on here?" Frazil demanded to know. "These sorts of things cannot happen! Not in any circumstances. This is why I told you and the Temple to lie low at the start of my reign! This is because of your negligence. People outside must not know about this."

"Father, stop. You cannot blame Isa for their choice."

"I will blame you, then! Both of you constantly think you know better than me. We are here because of me," Frazil shouted and hit the ground with his cane.

"You are wrong," Rime said and stepped right next to his father. "You are here because of my army. Do not forget that. Isa, come," he asked and took my hand. It sparked and stung.

"What do you mean by that, exactly?" Frazil hissed. "Fine, go, stay in! Stay there until this stupidity has been reigned in! We will talk about this. Consecrator Aravas, you can clear this up, correct?"

"No, thank you. Here's the list of places to deliver the soul sand to. And do put this coat in the trash. Good day," Riestel told him and followed us to the door.

"But... I," Frazil huffed, confused, and surprised at the lack of impact he had on Riestel.

I followed Rime to our quarters and then sat down. Rime paced in front of me, clearly trying to think of what to say. I wiped a few black tendrils off my wrist.

"So, what were you arguing about this time? Before you came outside."

"Everything we always clash about. Frazil has erected a new tactics table. He had it specifically made to better ponder things. He is neatly placing hundreds of tiny paper bits on it. This thing today, that in a week, to be considered, to be thought about. The piles just grow and nothing is solved. He does everything else except act. He is of the mind that the most important thing to get done in this situation is a governmental renewal. A bureaucratic renewal! Try telling him that it might be more urgent to focus on keeping the city alive, to improve resource distribution, and to draw up plans for spring on how we can get the most out of the growing season," Rime spat out with more passion than normally. An icy breeze welled around him.

"But you can do all that with just your influence? You do not have to ask him for approval to improve such things? I thought the army was already in charge of deliveries."

"It is," Rime groaned and stopped. "It would still be better for everyone if I didn't need to do these things behind his back. The city will soon think it has two rulers. That is not a good thing. Especially now that the governors from outside have been called here for the coronation."

"And your back-up plan?"

"If I go ahead with it... If I steal his power with a stunt, he will become a threat. Even if he is almost paralyzed under all this pressure, it doesn't mean he isn't still smart and capable. That's where he thrives, in the shadows. Would you want him as an opponent and to wait and see what rock he crawls under?"

"No, but what else can you do if you are convinced he is wrong?"

"To keep arguing and keep the appearances as polite as I can. It doesn't amuse me, and it consumes time that we don't necessarily have, but it is still the best option. The city needs the army and his web. They work in such different ways and are suitable for different things."

"Do you think he will be angry at me for long?"

"Possibly, but I will take the blame. You wouldn't have toured the city if I hadn't urged you. We might have avoided this. Clearly, some believe that if we sacrifice to you, we can redeem a better future. Though that is partially true, this is not your doing. Personally, I think you showed compassion."

"Maybe. Honestly, I just didn't see the purpose in arguing with a person who was dying already."

Rime sat next to me on the couch and leaned on me. He took my hand.

"I will begin arrangements for your other journey. This would be a good time if you are going to help Riestel with his child."

"I'm still unsure if I want to go there. The morning practice with the bodies is making me nauseous. I don't know if I'm capable enough yet."

Rime stroked my hand and shook his head a little with a faint smile.

"I don't think you can avoid it. There's a part of you waiting. Whether it is...

Elona? Was that her name? Or an actual part of your former life in the statue."

"Yes. I can't really picture Riestel as a father," I commented, amused.

"I don't think he had much chance to be one if I understood everything correctly."

"Was that a hint of compassion?" I asked and changed my posture. Riestel wasn't a subject I thought we could talk about in this manner.

"Just a bit… I was thinking of us. Our situation. It is… unsustainable. I keep wondering if this is truly the right thing for you," Rime sighed.

"What? What does that mean?" I demanded to know with as carefree of a tone I could muster as I tensed up.

"You are in constant danger. With the glove, I can contain my urges better. But I'm nowhere near stable. Moras believes that the years of instinctual feedings and maintaining a constant flow against Irinda tore the channels open in ways they aren't meant to be used. You fear getting pregnant due to the possible repercussions of this, having a child go through even the basic transformation. I promise I would never curse our children with this unless there was no other way… But… how can I protect you or them?" he agonized, rubbing his forehead. "We shouldn't be alone even now. Especially as I'm getting emotional… This was reckless of me."

"I don't want to be alone all the time. Without you."

"But I cannot offer a future with me anymore," Rime said and got up. "It's too uncertain. I cannot guarantee a cure for this."

I grabbed his hand.

"You can't say that. I'm your wife, like it or not. I can keep a distance, if you insist, but you cannot ask me to abandon you."

"I'm not asking, but I don't know any other way to keep you safe."

"You say it's compassionate when I take a life when they request it, but then say I can't decide what risks to take with mine!" I snapped and pushed him as I stood up.

"Don't," he asked quietly and took my hand. "This is hard enough."

"No. There is nothing hard about this. Yet," I remarked and pushed him again. His back hit the wall. I leaned on him and took my hands to his face. I kissed him. I could feel his arms tense to push me away. I bit his lip and slid my hands down. His breathing became shallower. I opened his belt.

"I fear you not," I whispered.

"You're devious."

"Call me a witch any day. See what happens."

Rime's expression melted a bit.

"You aren't the only one in this room capable of killing," I reminded Rime and took his gloved hand to my bosom.

"I know," he sighed. "But do you understand that if you die because of me, I will die? You are my only weakness. The only weakness I've ever loved."

"I have no desire to live without you," I answered.

"But there's the difference," Rime noted and smiled sadly. "You don't want to, but you can."

I took a step back.

"You don't believe I truly love you. Why?" I asked, annoyed.

Rime stared past me as if someone had been standing behind me, but when I looked, I saw no one.

"Because I know you better than you think," he finally said. "Much better."

"I'm not going to accept that answer. You are the only thing that has kept me alive. I was about to burn myself alive in the temple, but the thought of you stopped me. And only that."

"Really?" Rime asked as though he had just woken up. He looked at me.

"You can't separate yourself from me anymore than I can from you. Yes, you are right, I might not kill myself from grief if you died. That's not who I am, but that doesn't mean I wouldn't be dead. That doesn't mean I wouldn't tear the very fabric of the world if that would return you to me. Haven't you noticed how selfish I am?"

"There's no denying that," Rime replied and smiled.

"Then don't be such a tease."

"A tease?"

"What? You want a welcome sign to find your way in?" I taunted him the best I could to make him forget his overly conscious suggestions.

"You have a very sharp tongue, wife," he almost growled and pulled me close.

He pushed me back towards the couch while our clothing made a path on the floor. The metallic glove was like ice against my skin. It brushed my back like a hard scaled snake, but the rest of him was so warm. As he leaned over me, a shadow creeped over his eyes. I took a hold of his face.

"Just us. Nothing else," I whispered as I felt him. Rime took a deep breath. The shadow flickered and vanished. I hugged him and allowed myself to forget everything else.

We laid against each other sweaty. His head was tucked against my neck as I played with his hair. I wouldn't allow him the opportunity to make a decision that would drive us further apart. Not even if it would kill me, which, of course, could be an even more stupid decision than what Rime was capable of. I'd never let go, not until all hope was lost, and he had better live with that.

"I don't dare and sleep next to you," he said and supported himself with his arms.

"I thought you already were sleeping. You were so quiet."

"Almost. I would rather sleep in your scent than anywhere else. I was silent because I was thinking. I must take some great risks to guarantee a future I want. If we want to be free," he explained while getting dressed. "If I do take the path that could give us our best chance, do you think you can forgive me if it ruins everything?"

"You are talking much too mysteriously."

"There are reasons for it," he whispered.

"Do you think someone listens in on us?" I asked as quietly as I could. "Who? Your father wouldn't be that paranoid, would he?"

"Anything is possible. Let's just say that we have one road that requires no sacrifice and we can live the rest of our lives like this and do what we perhaps can to stall the demise of this world. Then there is another road where we can offer each other up to fate to gain so much…" he mused in a hushed voice. "A road that maybe isn't meant to be walked and that can destroy all… But if it were to succeed, you'd be free of all demands and the burdens my father or your past has laid on you."

"I'm guessing the likelihood of success is pretty tiny."

"Probably around the same as your existence in the first place."

I studied his face. His eyes were brighter than normal and craved for my permission. I nodded.

"Do what you must and what you think will be the best. I will chance it with you," I promised, even if something worried me about his words. Still, I knew he wouldn't tell me no matter how hard I'd press him when he wasn't ready to share this plan. Right now, I was content with him giving up on his foolish idea of distancing himself from me.

Rime pressed his forehead to mine. He laughed nervously and stood up. A strange mix of enthusiasm and nerves.

"Alright, but first Riestel's wish so we can be rid of his sulking."

"Fine. But I don't have to like it."

"No, I'd rather you didn't. But try to make the most of it. I can't guarantee you'll wake to pleasant news," he warned and stopped at the door. "I am sorry for what you will have to go through. A part will probably be my fault, but try to trust me even if I don't always seem to deserve it."

XIII

A part of me was against this meeting, but after all that had happened, I was all burned out of revenge. Heelis could have a lot to give and contribute if something could shake her up from her resistance and make her get past her grudges.

"Thank you for coming," I said as I opened the door.

"Of course. She is my wife," Heelis's husband, Juone, mumbled. "Is there any news of her fate?"

"No. Nothing has changed. She is a liability. I've tried talking to her, but we aren't on the best of terms at the moment. I have promised her that no harm will ever come to you. Not you or the children."

"Then… What do you want from me?"

"I have no wish to keep Heelis as an eternal enemy, though I know this will likely make her mad at me. Again. You know about the secret the Temple held and how it was revealed. Heelis blames us for falsehoods and will not admit to her own mistakes. As long as she cannot face her actions and see that those are also worth scrutiny, she will not hear what I say. She doesn't need to like me. She doesn't need to agree on anything… But…"

"I think I understand. I can't promise anything. She is as stubborn as the sky is blue."

"Believe me, I'm aware. That's why…" I sighed and hesitated.

"What?"

"I know only one way to shake her core enough. I'm just not sure I want to use that knowledge. It might affect your family badly."

"I'm not a stupid man, though I only tended our children while she served the city. This is about our first born, Asana. Am I correct?"

"Yes."

"Was she one of the victims of these initiations I've heard about?" Juone asked and continued as I stayed quiet. "Just be honest."

"Yes."

Juone took a deep breath and hunched over. His slightly red-tinted hair hid his eyes from this angle. He was quiet for a long time, drawing circles on the desk with his finger. I had never looked at Juone in much detail before. He had always just been in the background as a relatively charming, very well-mannered man.

"Well… at least I know for sure now. It was difficult to swallow all of her excuses over the years about why we could never see Asana. I knew it on some level that she must have died. Can I see Heelis now?" Juone asked as he got up. His face was tired and pale, but an ounce of relief shone in his light eyes.

"Of course. And if you survive and stay a family and if she hears reason, you can live as before. Well, not exactly as before. Heelis would be at home. The Temple won't accept her back at the moment, and I'm not sure she'd accept the Temple when she hears what we plan."

"Will you come?"

"No, I have a journey to make. Better that way, you need to settle it between yourselves. At this moment, anything I ask, she'd do the opposite out of sheer spite. We are very much alike in that," I remarked, amused, and missed her peculiar friendship for a moment.

"Alright."

"You may take your children to see her at any time. I arranged all the permits with the guards. You have no limits to your visitation rights."

Juone nodded and left. I changed my ordinary clothes into a white, loose robe that would be as comfortable as possible. I walked towards the Needle. I wasn't ready to do this. The mere thought made me weak in the knees. As though I would have been led to slaughter.

Tammaran, Riestel, and Rime stood in one of the Needle's smaller rooms. I looked at them from the door for a moment. Rime walked over to me.

"I will leave you to their care," he said and embraced me. "Come back."

"Don't you run away while I'm away."

Rime put his hands on my cheeks, pressed our foreheads together, and stayed silent. Then he left.

"Let's begin," Riestel rushed me and sat in a comfortable padded chair in a cross-legged position. That way, the other chair could be placed right in front.

I climbed on the other one and took the same position. Riestel passed me a cord with a loop. I put my hand through it. He did the same with the other end.

"What is that?" Tammaran asked. "It looks like a fasting ribbon for marriage."

"In a way. The ribbon used in that ceremony is a degraded interpretation of this tool. It is a consecrator's precaution. It is easier to establish and upkeep a connection on the other side when it exists here. It will ease my task to keep her from getting lost," Riestel explained. "Take your place. We need silence. Do not let anyone that doesn't need to be here in until we are done."

"I know my duty," Tammaran muttered, locked the door, and set next to it, fading partly into the lighter realm.

"Ready?" Riestel asked.

I shook my head.

"Tough luck then. This promise is something that you aren't allowed to break," he remarked. "We will stop and rest when possible. You will revert to your normal appearance during those moments almost with no effort as we will rest in spaces Istrata created. You will be able to move in them as you do in yours. You just need to reach them intact and not unravel."

"Sound delightfully easy," I sighed.

"Attitude," Riestel scolded me and tsked. "See you on the other side."

Riestel closed his eyes. A saintly, concentrated smile spread across his face. His whole being sighed with serenity. I pressed my hands on my face, but there was naught to do but follow. A promise was a promise. I leaned back and controlled my breathing. As I opened my eyes in the between, Riestel stood waiting, all alight with summer sky blue hues. Tammaran was visible from this side. I waved to him, and he nodded back. He couldn't talk to us.

"Change your shape," Riestel ordered, and a sea-green vortex appeared in the wall of the space.

I replaced and shaped my body into a smaller one. A much smaller one. One that would protect my core being and would be easier for me to control. Riestel crouched down and smirked.

"Well, well, what do you we have here? A little white mouse. Come on then," he said and offered his hand. I ran on his palm. It still felt odd to move with four paws. Riestel lifted me to his face and petted my head. I tried to bite his thumb. He laughed and stepped through the glittered swirl.

A misty scenery of lights and leashes and strands reached out to infinity before us. My body rippled as if something was testing whether it was real or not. Everywhere were stars, glowing, shining, glittering vortexes, dark, deep caverns, shimmering walls. All of which were far and near with distances impossible to measure. A thin strand connected my front paw to Riestel's hand, but I could faintly sense other natural connections too.

"The true world. Do not focus too much on any one thing, it will suck you to it," he reminded me and placed me on his shoulder.

Riestel took no steps and yet we moved, or perhaps the scenery moved as we stood in place. It was impossible to say which was true. I heard him chant the same words over and over. I smelled his sweat from the effort it took to maintain focus in the room our bodies were in. It almost yanked me back to the ordinary world.

When I dared to peek around more, several souls floated around us. Two very tiny specs were right above us. They were mesmerizingly lovely. One the color of a bright mountain brook and the one the color of a hazy dawn cloud in the summer. Further, the deeper we went, I could see darker, frayed shadows and dimming, sickly stars. They seemed distorted and heavy. Like they could fall between the worlds in an instant and tear the very fabric open.

Riestel stopped and raised his hand. A blue, oval swirl opened and allowed us to pass into a small circular space. The walls were like rock someone had painted here from memory. I looked at my hands. I changed instantaneously to myself in here. Although, it felt a smidgen unfamiliar, as the body was built from Istrata's materials.

"The first pocket," Riestel said, breathing heavily. "I haven't done a trip like this in years. I have to sit for a while before we continue. How are you holding up?"

"I'm a little nauseous. My eyes hurt and I see these sparks and flashes."

"Perfectly normal."

"How many of these little spaces are there?"

"One after this one. Then we are there. I can do one more jump before a longer rest. Is that fine with you?"

"I'm just riding along. You may decide all."

"All? Alright, leave him. Now."

"About this journey, don't be a fool."

Riestel smirked mischievously to himself. He closed his eyes. I studied the space and walls. My small room wasn't the worst, but it would take much work to stabilize it as well as this one if I wanted it to last for a century or two.

"Let us go," Riestel ordered after a short rest.

I swayed on his shoulder when he stepped out. The scenery was very different from when we had stepped in. It was made of the same elements, but none were in the same location as when we had gone in. Riestel began his chant and everything was yanked into movement. I only looked forward. The squiggly shapes and lines resembled mountains, trees, sometimes animals, sometimes men. They melted and stretched. Everything went from being ruled by one color to thousands of shining hues in the blink of an eye. I twisted my tail tighter around my body and clenched my small nails into Riestel's coat.

Our speed decreased. Riestel's shape flickered from exhaustion. The skin on his forehead was tight and his eyelids tremored from keeping his concentration. I could see a familiar vortex opening someway from us. In the corner of my eye, I could see more miserable souls. In their midst were red, hot coal-like dots, like eyes. The dark shapes condensed to a more human form and rushed towards us like a wave.

Riestel slammed through the swirling gate just as they reached us. A few tufts of the black mass dropped on the ground as the pocket entrance closed. These weren't things of this world, but they couldn't seem to get out.

"What were those?" I asked.

"The suffering. Distorted souls and lives who have been out of the cycle so long they have begun to rot and focus on only the bad things, their agonies, and disappointments," Riestel answered and dropped to his knees. "For Peak's sake... this is much harder than it was before."

"Well, you aren't exactly younger either," I remarked.

"Well, I do have a one very heavy rat to carry."

"A mouse. Clearly a mouse!"

"Same thing."

"Not."

"Do you really want to start something over this?"

"I might."

Riestel shook his head, smiling, and sat in a more comfortable position.

"Did you know you had mice? When you... she was a child."

"I did?"

"Three. Spotted ones. They'd run amuck around the Peak. They had names too..." Riestel said, trying to remember. "Weedy, Tickler... and Pitterpaw. Your father almost had them killed when they nibbled holes in his cape. You mother wasn't particularly fond of them either once they found her rosewater-scented linens."

"Strange pets for a Witch Queen."

"Long before those days."

"I've been thinking."

"And?"

"Why do her memories contain so little of her, you, the Peak, and the Temple? About her personal life? Wouldn't it make sense to get more personal memories, too?"

"Maybe, I don't know. No one has ever tried this kind of molding of a soul. She might have intentionally removed some, if that's possible. Would you like to remember more?"

"I'm not sure. Perhaps. I could understand this all better."

"Or you could lose the 'you' you are."

"I might. But now that we are alone... I remembered you one day. I remembered us. I know you worried about it, but it didn't mess my head up."

Riestel stared, frozen into the distance. He didn't like the subject, but I wanted to say something, something that was too difficult to say in the real world.

"I'm telling you because... you deserve an apology. A sincere one. I can never repay nor fix your destiny."

"Stop."

"Let me say it."

"Stop!" he groaned and got up. "You have no right to say it. Your apology is just a way to bid farewell. Do not think you will be rid of me that easily."

I closed my mouth. He was right. I wanted to apologize and seal the past to keep it from flooding the present. To keep him away from me and Rime. So, there would be nothing to worm its way between us. A part of me was terrified to see the last statue and Elona.

Riestel oozed anger and hurt. I didn't dare to continue with the subject. He'd leave me here in the middle of this vast realm of possibilities if I'd keep this up. I looked around. The two little souls from earlier hovered next to my hand. They had drifted in with us in all the rush. I poked one with my finger.

It changed position like a small startled bird and slowly returned to the other one. I followed their play as Riestel slept.

A gentle touch woke me up.

"I'm refreshed enough. One more jump. If you see more suffering, do not focus on them. I told you before that the Lighter World does not have dimensions in the same way as us. If you focus on something, you will draw it to you and strengthen it. Try to look and focus on me or should you spot the vortex door, that. It will help us travel faster. The suffering may still be around."

"Can they harm us?"

"Can you harm a soul?"

"Obviously."

"Then don't ask stupid questions."

As I changed into the mouse, I could see the two little sparks of life hiding close to us come closer. They wanted to get out from this artificial place. I didn't know why, but there was something so familiar and fascinating about them. Like I had known them. Riestel glanced at them. A feeling I couldn't categorize at all flashed on his face.

XIV

As we glided onward on the last journey, we reached our destination. It was a vast cavern covered in amethysts and other crystals. It looked so real that I could have never imagined we were still in a created space.

I lit the torches on the walls. The room was filled with rows of statues resembling those we used in worship. They were the size of a person or a little larger. They had been made with respect, love, and fear. Polished a thousand times.

"Who made these? How were they brought here?"

"The most gifted Ado's worshippers shaped them once. Each has been imbued with the manifestations of each time. I did say it was a cemetery of sorts for manifestations."

"I can't see or feel their souls anywhere."

"Of sorts. Do you ever listen? The statues contain their life force just as the statues of Istrata you collected contained hers. It is passed from here to the mask hall by created pathways so the initiates can get a sense of something larger than them, something holy, and a visage of the god. The thought about being chosen, a direct connection to something true. Who would ever doubt it when a god speaks directly to them?"

I walked over to one statue. The more I observed, the more I could tell apart the persona and skills imbued in it. It was almost like a multidimensional painting of the nature of a particular god. In the middle was Saraste. I touched it. Riestel seemed to despise it.

"It's you, right? As the most powerful one. I can sense it."

"Yes. Each new manifestation would charge the statue after these god doctrines were founded. I don't know how many generations did so. The statue is an anchor between worlds. We put a little more of us to them than others."

"Are they a part of the spell? Is this what keeps you alive?"

"They are a part of it. But the length of my existence is another misery altogether. You'll get there eventually if all goes well. Normally, the person's persona and skills are copied here. They are stored for the copy to act and seem genuine. They are layers of your predecessors. Some are weaker than others, so the stronger spirits surface."

"That means I met my old self in the attic."

"It was Istrata's performance of Nef'adhel. When she took on her role, she was able to make hard decisions better. She left herself out of it. I think I once said that she never accepted the gift she had been granted. She hated performing as her. That's why Nef'adhel seems colder and more demanding than she was. Almost as the opposite."

"Noticed. Were you observing the situation even then? When she made me sacrifice something to bless me with fire?"

"I was. But you do already know the gift was in you, blessing or no? It's all a grand show."

"Yes. I'd ask why you didn't help to save Launea when you knew it was just a ceremony, but I guess I know the answer already."

"I don't know if you'll believe me…" Riestel began. "But it wasn't easy. Not once was it easy to kill her. To kill you. To watch you get destroyed."

"Well, you could have fooled me."

"I had to. How else could I have done so if I myself doubted my justification?" Riestel asked and folded his arms, almost to the point of hugging himself.

"Is the last statue one of these?"

"Correct guess," Riestel answered and pointed into the dark.

Right at the back of the cavern was a door almost like the one at the top of the Needle. I felt a deep disdain walking towards it. The same reluctance as I had felt when trying to open the nursery door in my memories. There was no doubt that Elona was behind the door.

"Does it open like the other one?" I asked.

"Not quite. This requires us both at the same time. Do you remember when you visited me and I made a pattern into the glass of fire and ice?"

"Yes."

"The mechanism is of that sort… A little more challenging."

"Are they both behind that door?"

"Yes. This was the only place she trusted back then. No ordinary person can just stumble and find it. And she started to fade this place from the Temple's active use and memory. I suppose that continued after her to the point where they completely abandoned it and almost all other true knowledge. Are you ready?"

"No. But it's why we've come."

We left each row of the statues behind us as mute and oppressive witnesses. I felt a lump in my throat with each swallow. Riestel glanced at me and sighed.

"Give me your hand," he demanded. "You are unbearably nervous."

When I hesitated, he grabbed it and pulled me to his side. There was something painfully familiar there. Despite the icy hand, it calmed me. We stopped. The door surface was a gleaming, mirrorlike metal.

"Press your back into it," Riestel instructed.

"Why?"

"Why? So I can play darts."

I protested with an annoyed stare but positioned myself as requested. Riestel stepped in front of me.

"Lift your arms into a Y shape. As if you were that snowflake in the fire circle. This works the other way, as Istrata wanted to make sure only a true manifestation whom I have accepted in terms of character and power can enter."

Accepted? Riestel's bright eyes were so sincere and honest I couldn't utter a word or protest his orders. Silly as it felt, I lifted my arms. As my back brushed the door in that position, I felt a current running through me. Riestel bowed and placed hands right at the bottom of the door. He drew a circle around me and pressed his hands on mine. The door hummed and buzzed more strongly, and the current circulated in each cell of our bodies. He leaned in closer with his entire body. Our noses almost touching.

"I'd apologize, but I'd be lying," Riestel whispered and leaned on me. "We can go through only if we are one."

"One? Don't you dare to think..." I protested when he kissed me. A treacherous softness dragged memories hungrily to the surface. As our breath combined, the whole door electrified. Everything crackled and sparked and small arches of light appeared between us as when Riestel had helped me to wed Simew and Launea. The air smelled of thunder. I felt the structure of the door change. Each hair on my body stood out as the air vibrated.

A sly smile flashed in Riestel's eyes. He ran his fingers down on my arms to my face. I shook my head as he closed his arms around me. The number of sensations and feelings covered my mind in a brilliant, beautiful fog and, without a thought, I kissed him back. The weakened door cracked to pieces. Riestel let go. I wiped my mouth on the back of my hand.

"You could have warned me. That was wrong," I scolded him as much as myself as the feelings subsided and my thoughts cleared.

"That was the key. Whatever could be wrong with a key?" Riestel mused and tried his best to seem arrogant, but the veins in his thin skin brought up a charming tint of pink on his cheeks.

"Do you think Rime would have approved if he knew?"

"Oh, it's not like there were feelings involved? I'm not as big of a bastard as you take me for. I even talked to him about it. He knows."

"I do not believe you."

"Just ask how much that bothers me."

"You little deceitful…" I began and turned after Riestel who had nonchalantly walked right past me to the room. The statue of Nef'adhel towered as tall as three people. Below it was a small basket with wilted flowers all around it.

We stood side by side just staring at them in silence. Neither could move nor speak. A moment later, Riestel squeezed my hand and walked to the basket. He kneeled beside it. I didn't know if I should follow or not.

"Hi… Hi, little one," he whispered. "Daddy is finally here," he added.

I wiped my face and glanced away. It felt as if I was witnessing something I had no right to see. Riestel picked up the tiny parcel in his arms and held it so very gently.

"I'm sorry it took so long," he said to it.

I turned my back on them and crouched down. I wanted to disappear from the room. Riestel walked to me.

"She lives. I don't know what I'll do," he sighed.

"Lives? But she was so poorly then…" I gasped and got up though I didn't want to. I took a step back when I almost looked at the child.

"Are you afraid of her?" Riestel asked, softly.

I shook my head. I already knew what the child would look like. That wasn't what terrified me. The whole situation was hard to accept. I didn't want these emotions which resided under a carefully constructed dam. Riestel's face was full of sorrow, but every time he looked her way, he conjured a warm, reassuring smile.

"Her soul or life force is still partly glimmering and lovely. It's not twisted, though there are some signs," he said. "Should I ask you to kill her? Could you if I asked for her freedom? You did so to an old woman."

"Is that what you'd want? After all this?"

"No. Of course not. But what else can I do for her? Not here anyway. I don't want to leave her here. I want to take her to the real world if even just for a moment... Aren't you going to even greet her?"

"I can't. I'm sorry. I can't," I refused, as I just heard the ever so quiet, raspy breathing.

Riestel nodded and walked back to the basket. He lowered Elona into it and covered her. He took the basket by the handles and walked back to me. He looked at the statue and took a deep breath.

"Take her knowledge, and bring that mockery down forever if you can. I'll take Elona further away. I cannot get involved, no matter how much I would wish to help."

"Are you really not going to help? Even if it seems I'll die?"

"I... If there is even one true god somewhere in the fabric of this world, I will pray to it. But it is all I can do. If you survive her, there will come a day when I will not hesitate to put my life on the line for yours."

As Riestel walked away with the child, I approached the statue. I hated it. I hated what I had been. Her and her precious pretty empire and her lovely obliging character were all a curse. I placed my right hand on the statue. It burned me. Try and keep me away. This was my right. I pressed my other hand on it and felt a similar wave as in the attic with the statue. The statue became pure power. It shrank down to half the size.

"*Initiate. Welcome,*" it said with a smile.

"I'm not. I am you, and you are out of time."

The statue blinked and stared.

"*I know you,*" it finally said with a cracking voice. "*Are you ready to continue on our path?*"

I nodded. It didn't need to know I loathed everything it stood for. There was a small indent in its chest. A small heart-shaped indent. I took my necklace.

"*Yes. Give it to us... to me...*" the statue sighed, yearning. "*We know what to do.*"

I held the heart in my hand. The statue inched closer to it. I closed my fist and melted the heart. Everything in it charged into me. If her soul were to be made whole, it would be made whole in me for me, not in a stone container made for whatever purpose. My body burned and vibrated. The statue's face distorted. The fragments of the Queen whispered and echoed within me.

"*What did you do? Traitor!*"

"You won't eat me that easily. I'm not you, nor your puppet in this world. If you want to kill me and this eternal spark, you will have to drag yourself to me in flesh."

"*Give me what is mine. I command you, creation.*"

"Oh, believe me, you will get yours," I said and lit up my hands.

"*What do you think that will do?*" the statue laughed. "*You will not conquer me with my weapons,*" it warned and all the walls of the room burned. Her attacks and fire were much more powerful than mine. The ceiling began to drip molten stone and the floor turned to flowing streams of lava. The statue stood in the middle, fiery and made from liquid orange. I couldn't insulate myself from all the heat.

None of my attacks did damage nor slowed it, as our steps and flames mirrored each other. There was nothing I could do to win with my skills, but if I couldn't stand my ground here... I wasn't worth defending. The heat, fire, and molten stone were useless. They only made the room harder for me to survive. The lava was eating its way through everything and destabilizing the room itself.

My skin pricked and my clothes would soon catch fire just from the heat of the air if I lost concentration even for a moment. Then I stopped. This was a made reality in-between true ones. Was I really so silly that I would try to win just by fire in a world where we could mold the world and its possibilities? There were infinite possibilities. This wasn't a battle of strength and fire; this was a battle in my mind. I needed Simew. I halted all movement on the last piece of solid floor.

"Help me," I whispered and summoned the sabers. If there was ever a place pure willpower would allow me to shape things, this was it. I'd still have to sell it to myself to make it.

I took Simew's stance and followed his style and steps just as in the practice hall years ago. Everything in his way and rhythm. I focused on each particle and strand of this reality around me. A strange, different feeling welled up through the sabers. As I let the accumulated power out, a cold breeze raged through the room. It cooled each melted surface and forced the statue back to stone. I just needed to keep focus and believe. The statue's movements became slower and cumbersome. I ran toward it as new fiery lines started to crack open. The statue's limbs began to move again. I threw myself on it and kissed it as all the previous ones.

I opened my eyes, my head ached, and I had dust on my lips. Why was I in the God Cavern? Riestel bent over me.

"Istrae?"

"Eli? What happened?"

"What did you call me?" Riestel asked.

"What do you mean what? It's been your nickname for years," I laughed but felt an uneasy worry. "Don't you like it anymore?"

Riestel kept staring and helped me up. His hand was strangely cold.

"Eli, please. What has happened? I can see you are worried."

"Is it... you?"

"Whom should I be? Eli, you are scaring me."

Riestel took a long breath and shook his head. I felt like we had been separated forever, though that wasn't possible. We just... He did look older, but it was Riestel. I'd know him anywhere. A strong longing welled inside me as if I had waited centuries for him. We looked at each other.

"Please, Eli, touch me. I need your reassurance," I whispered and held out my hand. "Why are you shunning me? Please, what happened?"

After a moment of hesitation, Riestel took my hand and squeezed it. His face was holding back pain.

"So, now you have come?" he sighed, tired and pulled me into his arms.

"Now? Please tell me," I urged and leaned back. I stroked his cheek. Riestel wet his lips and kissed me. A lingering, light as a summer's breeze kiss, but without joy. A salty taste. There was something foreign there. A part of me felt such fulfillment and a part felt terror. Painful waves coursed through me. I touched his lips with my fingers. Riestel's cheek had moist lines. He pushed me away as his face lit up and he smiled.

"No, still not her. You are not her. Gods help me that I rejoice from that knowledge after all this. I am not the one you seek."

"What do you mean?"

"Not that it wouldn't fill a certain longing to... But I've caused enough evil and I will not steal this experience. I know, one day, I will have you and you will love me as I you. Isa."

"Isa? You've never called me that."

"Focus," Riestel demanded and grabbed my arm tight enough to bruise it. "Focus on your core. You are feeling remnants of a past life. Drowning in them. Do not let them overpower you. Do not let her take you. Abandon her. I do not want her back. Isa, I need you, not her."

"What are you talking about? What do you mean I'm not...?" I stuttered as I felt a sharp pain in my stomach as if someone had stabbed me. I felt sick.

"We are not together in this life," Riestel reminded me so gently. "You must return to yourself. Rime is waiting. And... for all that is holy, must you be so blind that I have to tell you this... Your children," Riestel sighed and let go.

"Rime..." I repeated. The name woke me and cleared away illusions.

"Don't worry, he need not know. It wasn't you asking for my affections."

"I'm so sorry," I breathed as I gained control of my thoughts and my body seemed to settle. "You've suffered too much. I know you would have her back," I said as my head cleared and all that had just been said began to disappear from my memory.

"A while back, yes. Not anymore. But you have more urgent problems," Riestel reminded and pointed at my shoulder. I looked. Two bright specs, much brighter than before, were still by my side.

"Your children."

"Two. No... not twins," I prayed as my body convulsed from pain. All what held me together rippled.

"Something is very wrong in the normal world," Riestel noted. "We must haste. Come."

"I can't move. It hurts too much."

Riestel's face paled, and he backed away. He put his hand on his mouth. As I looked at what he saw, I could see the other bright spec turn black and eat the other. The terror froze me in place. Riestel hurried to me.

"This will hurt and you may lose some more recent memories, but you must return now," he said and kneeled. "I will follow as soon as I can without making Elona suffer too much," he promised and slapped my forehead. I blacked out. I could feel myself spinning at a speed through all matter like never before. I snapped into my body as if a catapult had flung me into it.

Tammaran was lying on the floor unconscious. My stomach had been cut open and stitched together hastily. Blood was everywhere. There was a frail body of a newborn next to the chair. It was tiny. I reached out my hand. Her skin was still warm. I recognized her as mine. I kept blacking out and couldn't move or help her. Riestel stepped into the room. He dropped the basket, took his body back, and kneeled.

"You will live, breathe," Riestel ordered calmly. He ran his hands hastily over me and fixed all he could. As the pain subsided, my eyes became heavy. I took Riestel's hand as he stopped humming. It trembled ever so slightly.

XV

I laid in bed for the third day. Rime only left my side briefly to visit Moras. He didn't dare to sleep here with me despite his treatments, or perhaps because of them, so he only rested when he was examined. We had barely spoken. The soulless child slept in a crib next to us. It was a matter of hours or days until it would stop breathing. Due to the hurry they had been in to cut the twins out, a smidgeon of life had been left. Rime stroked my back slowly as he sat on the bed's edge.

"We have some leads," he said. "We will find the child."

"And Tammaran?"

"Showing signs of waking up."

"Did you know about the children?"

"Not before you left. But some days, when I came to visit and see that everything was alright, your body would look very different. Like it was switching between different times it existed."

"So, I'm several months older than when I stepped into the Lighter World," I tallied.

"I guess."

"Am I a horrible person if I can't cry? I didn't even know I was pregnant... I only saw their souls for a moment. I didn't have time to grow fond of them before they... Before I lost them," I pondered and sat up. The scar on my stomach stung even though the healers had done a good job of fixing the damage after Riestel's first aid. The scar wasn't particularly pretty, though it would fade almost completely, they said, but the one inside was raw and red and would take much longer to improve.

I looked at our child. For a creature with no soul nor power, it was lovely. Or as lovely as a small wrinkly creature could be. Rime leaned on his knees.

"Are you sure it can't live?" he asked quietly and touched her fingers.

"Yes. All that would have made it a human is gone. The soul, or just the life force, whichever it was… There isn't enough left, it won't develop. And I can't weave a new one. It's not like the power you amass during your life. No one can create it. It's a spark of a different nature. You can feel it if you use your abilities."

"I know. I don't want to. We are about to bury one and Riestel another alone," Rime lamented. "For the opposite reason… I don't know what to call that," he sighed and rubbed his forehead. Then he stared at me and the child with no emotion.

"But does it have to be that way?" he asked and got up.

"What else can we do?"

"We have a body; he has a soul. We wouldn't be creating anything new, just transferring," Rime pondered and picked the child up. "Then it wouldn't be a complete waste."

I couldn't utter a word.

"Moras… He has done so many tests on me and others. What if he could transplant a soul?"

The proposition was horrendous and fascinating, and exactly as practical as Rime.

"Do you think he could?" I asked.

"I don't know, but wouldn't it be a better option? Instead of just death for both."

I gazed at him, trying to assess his mood. He swayed with the child. It was painful to see.

"I know… it wouldn't be ours anymore," he said. "But at least something good could come of this."

"I thought you hated Riestel."

"What does that have to do with his child?"

I smiled to myself. I didn't know if I could have been as noble and merciful in his shoes. I wanted to give the child a chance, but I knew it had none, not as itself. Not in our hands.

"Take her before I… before I think too long. I'll fetch Riestel," I offered.

"Are you well enough to get up?"

"Are you asking me to stay out of this?"

"I'm not even going to try."

I rushed down the stairs as Rime ran with the nameless to Moras. The nameless. Should we gift her a name before this? Too late, I thought. She was already lost.

I knocked on Riestel's door. A colorless, poorly slept, and stubbled man opened the door.

"You aren't doing that well either, I see," I laughed and got a sharp pain in my pelvis.

"I'm beginning to doubt my own intellect. I should have left her there. Why did I drag her here to suffer?"

"Weren't you going to ask for a mercy killing?"

"I was... but I had to try to resuscitate her. I'm just not having any luck. The body is too... damaged," Riestel sighed and wiped his face and neck. "Is that why you are here? To grant me a way out of this misery."

"Actually, I'm here for Rime."

"What does he want?" Riestel scoffed and tensed up.

"For you to take Elona to Moras. Our child is there already."

"Why? What... use..." Riestel began with a cold, self-conceited note until it hit him. He said nothing, just turned and fetched Elona.

"Are you sure about this?" he asked once we reached Moras's door.

"Absolutely not, but I don't want more death for a moment. We can try to save one."

"I didn't think he'd give me an opportunity like this."

"Not you. Her. You may hate each other quite freely after this, but maybe now you can see why I feel what I feel for him."

Riestel nodded awkwardly, but then a calm smirk appeared.

"You know what?" he asked.

"What?"

"It's fine. He has this life. I have all of eternity," he remarked and opened the door.

"Consecrator Aravas. Come in. Both of you, we cannot wait another moment," Moras hurried us with odd multicolored glasses with exchangeable lenses on his face. "The body will not last long."

Rime placed our daughter on the table and stepped back.

"I never thought I'd give away my child like this," he said.

Riestel froze in place.

"Put her on the table," Rime ordered. "If this sacrifice goes to waste because of your hesitation, I will end you."

I took the basket from Riestel, who seemed too overwhelmed to act. I moved the soft cotton quilt aside and lifted the dry body onto the table. It pained me to look at it. Rime and Moras averted their eyes from Elona.

"I will need your help," Moras said to me. "And you, Consecrator Aravas."

Riestel walked closer, getting control of his nerves. Rime made room and walked to the window. He turned his back to us and lowered his head. I wanted to escape to him and from this room. I perhaps didn't have the capability to grieve this loss in the same way, but I felt what a family would have meant to him. However wrong the moment had been. Continuity meant more to those who had no hope of a next life. The thought felt like a strangle hold on my mind. Three of my family. This was all they had, all we had. All Rime had to share and give unless there was a way to undo the ritual he and the other child had been subjected to.

"Consecratoress," Moras called. "We need you now."

"Right, sorry."

"She was born of you," Moras said. "And even if the soul will, for the most part, be different, I'm sure some of her will live on if we act fast. You must detach the leash of the soul and keep it in control. Consecrator Aravas, your task is to keep the new body alive and calm. I need time to assess where the strand will connect to and to find a combination that seems stable enough. To forge it, I will need the fire of creation," he explained and took out an elaborate, small mirror instrument. "I can observe the unification with this. Please start."

"Isa…" Riestel whispered.

"Do not utter a word. I can do this if you don't."

The nameless slept a labored sleep. It was very weak. I tried not to look at Elona, but it was impossible. The girl's light golden locks shone beside the yellowed bone. The skin was dry and cracked. If I hadn't been able to see her soul, I wouldn't have ever considered her alive.

"Take the leash and pull when I say," Moras instructed.

I wound her soul around my palm. Moras looked for the location of the previous soul tether. Riestel hummed with his hands over the nameless. He kept the body soundly and carefully asleep. Moras kept turning and adjusting the mirrors.

"Please, pull," he asked.

My hand felt so heavy. My whole body was tense. Rime took a few steps toward me and pulled my arm. The soul tore from the body with a sigh. I held on to it with both hands, though it seemed content to just wait. Elona's soul was the color of a sunrise, though partially frayed and dirty. It wasn't like the suffering ones. It wasn't anywhere near lost. Maybe the location Istrata had chosen had kept her safe, or maybe she had trusted her father's promise over all her fears. I definitely would have trusted Riestel more than myself.

"Here. Bring the tether," Moras exclaimed and pointed at the nape of the nameless' neck. "Look," he urged and moved the mirrors so I could see. A light green beginning of a leash and fog which, when looked at closely, was just hovering in the Lighter World. A glittering fog of thousands of small drops.

"Take the tether to that point. Push them together and heat them until they mix and combine. I will say when it happens. After that, the place must be cooled rapidly to prevent it from unfurling."

"How do you know all of this?" I asked.

"My goodness, Consecratoress, this is what you hired me for! I haven't taken one single day off from my studies since I met you," Moras laughed but quickly returned to a more appropriate behavior. "We've worked long and longer days. And I will not rest until we have better answers, all the answers that I can provide. Now! It is in place. Hold it right there and heat the tip. Good. Slide it just a bit further so they mix more. Enough. Consecrator Aravas, place your hand in the exact same position and cool it to stabilize."

"Will this work?" I pondered as I withdrew my hand to make room for Riestel.

"There are no guarantees, but I agree that it is better to try to save one. In the books we have been studying, your predecessor made similar tests but as she only used her powers on animals with no will... the results were never permanent. That is the theory anyway. She was able to use other elements through instruments, but those are always lesser than an actual practitioner in strength. Good, the parts have bonded in place. You may stop. You will have to observe the area and repeat the cooling as needed or, if you prefer, for your peace of mind, at least daily."

Riestel opened his eyes. His normally proud brow was wrinkled with worry. He took a deep breath after forgetting to breathe for a moment.

"Look... How fascinating," Moras sighed. The body of the nameless twitched and flickered, but the child didn't cry. The dark tufts of hair became lighter, and some of her features changed. She opened her eyes. The color morphed from a dark brown to a light blue. The other eye stayed the same. Her skin became a healthy color. She yawned with a little squeal at the end.

"Elona," Riestel whispered. The girl straightened her hand and grabbed Riestel sleeve. He leaned on the table and cried. Then he laughed. And cried.

Rime sneaked a kiss on my head.

"I'm not wanted here," he said quietly. "I'll go and check on Tammaran."

"I want you."

"That's not what I meant, and you know it."

"Still worth saying."

Rime left with Moras. I stood silently next to Riestel.

"You've been holding that in for centuries," I remarked. "But you need to stop and cry later. You don't want to scare her," I recommended to him and touched the child's face. I saw a frightening amount of myself in her.

"Your father is having just a teeny nervous breakdown," I told Elona and picked her up. "Look, this is the world we live in. You'll get to crawl around and explore it now. Maybe you can taste some dirt too," I suggested.

Elona stared at me all sleepy, but her curious nature still shone through.

"I don't know if you remember her. I'm not quite your mother, though I look the part."

"Give her to me," Riestel demanded and held out his arms.

"Oh, he's back to his old self. I guess you can go to him."

"You are getting too much enjoyment from this," Riestel grumbled and took her.

"It's so odd… With everything else," I said and shook my head. I leaned on the table a bit.

"Are you alright?" Riestel asked without a mocking tone.

"Just a little dizzy. I don't know what I should feel or think about all of this."

"And the memories? The last statue?"

"They are starting to settle. I've studied them for several days now while resting…"

"What does that mean?"

"The spell she cast… It was to end all suffering and death, but the thing is, the only way she can achieve that is to… stop progress and life."

Riestel looked at me expressionless and placed his sleepy daughter in the basket.

"Are you saying that her grand plan is to kill us all? All that lives?"

"I'm not saying it was. I'm saying it *is*."

"That makes no sense."

"How so?"

"If she wanted everything to just cease... why would she have escaped death when it was coming for her? Why would she chop up her soul to preserve and mold it for better use?"

"Because then she would have returned to the cycle as all else. She doesn't want to just not exist. She doesn't want to die. She wants the whole world to stop. No real life, no suffering. Sort of. No new suffering anyway."

"Still. Why would she make me guard her soul? Why dissect it and hide it? Why have me mold it with torture?"

"I'm not sure. It's hard looking for answers in her maze of memories. And I don't know which are real and whether I can trust them all. I think I can, but... the simplest explanation could be that she needed time to explore the stasis and how to make the world stop. And..."

"What?"

"I don't think it is possible for a person to kill their own soul. And she would have needed to preserve it in case her plan failed and she couldn't find a way to continue without it. But now it's no longer her soul that is born and carries the flame. Right? It is mine."

Riestel paled and looked as someone had punched the wind out of him.

"I'm sorry but..." I began.

"She used me," he laughed. "I'm a perfect idiot."

"I agree."

"What?"

"Oh, so now you want sympathy?"

"You are hilarious," he muttered.

"I was just checking in the name of self-defense. You have been known to punch me for trying to console you."

"Fine, I grant you permission to be sympathetic."

"I don't know if I feel like it anymore."

"Please, you are itching to fix all of this."

"Are you admitting there's something to fix in you?"

"Now you are definitely pushing it," Riestel scoffed and returned to a more serious tone. "If you are right, she will come for you now that you are whole.

That way, she can break the cycle completely. As long as you exist, the world can recover. If she destroys life, most of it, and then breaks you down to the very soul… you can't be reborn fast enough to seek a new body before the world's planes have been isolated and the routes between them closed. That would stop life and death."

"I think that is the goal. The last statue… Its purpose was to collect the soul from me and keep it for her as a sacrifice, but now… she will have to come for me as you said."

"Have you talked with him about this?"

"Rime? Not yet. I don't know where to start… There's so much to do and so many problems that I just want to curl up and ignore them."

"I'm sorry, whatever that's worth. If I hadn't pressured you to take the journey, you might have carried them normally."

"Maybe is a big word right now. I don't believe it. Someone had prepared for it, planned for it. How would have they done it if I had been in full strength? I could be dead. Elona would be buried and the other child complete lost."

"You are frightfully calm."

"I can't be anything else. And I don't want you to have to pretend you aren't relieved," I said and sat down next to him. "You waited a long time. You fulfilled your promise to her. You saved her. You have the right to be happy."

"You are making this so damn difficult," he breathed and leaned on me.

"What?"

"Not killing your husband," Riestel smirked as he covered whatever was truly on his mind.

"You won't lay a hand on him, no matter what you feel."

"Why not?"

"You are too honorable. Beneath all that suspect stuff."

"Honorable? You have gone mad. Go and sleep so you can think straight."

"Going, daddy dear."

XVI

I stayed by myself for a few days. I hated grievances and pity. Happily, most didn't know what had happened, and those who did knew me well enough to leave those unoffered. Except for Merrie. She was ruthlessly sympathetic when bringing paperwork from the Temple. She even managed to hug me before I could to defend myself. Arvida, whose behavior didn't change one bit after what had happened, almost choked on her quiet amusement.

Rime buried himself in his work. He tried to find out where one of the children had been taken and by whom. Frazil tried to get him to take a bit of time off his duties, but we had talked him out of that idea. Being idle would drive Rime crazy.

When I was alone, I didn't grieve, though I was sad. It was impossible. How could I grieve for something I had never had? But it felt like everyone expected me to cry and be torn apart. Everyone should wail after their own children, right? But I hadn't known them. From my perspective, I hadn't even carried them, I hadn't given birth. I wasn't a mother. Nothing, but I still had a scar on my stomach. What if Rime found what had been taken? Could I love it… her or him?

"You are far away again," Rime remarked from the balcony door.

"How long have you been there?"

"Long enough to know you are agonizing over some problem that is impossible to solve by thinking."

"Maybe I'm just enjoying the scenery."

"You? Enjoying the scenery? Doth the lady understand how impossible that is to believe?" he teased and hugged me from behind. Whenever his hand brushed the scar close to my breast, it made me smile. It always reminded me of that sweet suspense I had felt in the beginning. Though now under it all, there was a small, shameful echo from the memories Riestel had awakened.

"Talk to me," Rime asked. "I can handle it."

"I don't doubt that."

"Then you doubt yourself."

"Must you be so insightful? It's quite annoying," I scolded him and turned around. The lines on Rime's face were a little deeper than when we had met, but not in an unpleasant way. His eyes were as kind as before if one didn't notice the darkness behind them.

"You always said you wanted a family. Now we have a child out there. Am I a bad person if don't feel all that much?"

"Stars and winds with you... You could sometimes try to talk to me before you think yourself into a knot. Do you think I was prepared for it?"

"Well, you at least wanted it."

"In the future, when all is well. Not in the middle of this god-forsaken chaos. But... we can't just leave the child out there somewhere. To be used. And I want to know if it is a she or a he."

"I as well," I answered and considered for a moment to tell him what the souls I had seen were like, but they weren't like that anymore.

"Besides..." Rime started with a mischievous raising of his eyebrows. "Do you think you'd raise the child? Didn't anyone tell you that royalty and nobles have maids for that? You'd barely see the child. And with your manners, you might not be allowed to. Gods know what you'd teach it."

"You say that because you trust I will do the opposite of what I'm told."

"Well, it has worked so far as surely as there are waves in the sea."

It was a relief to hear Rime wasn't painting a nursery. As my mind calmed, I could talk to him about the new memories and knowledge. Contrary to expectation, Rime relaxed once I told him all.

"How can you be so calm?" I asked.

"Why wouldn't I be? Now we know for sure who is behind the waning. We know why and partly how. We know our enemy and what they need. We were fumbling blind. Now we can plan. Isn't that a good thing?"

"I hadn't thought of it that way."

"Of course not. You always withdraw in to your shell and seek help only once you are almost ready to explode from worry. And what, wife, do you notice when you share those worries?"

"That you are there to support me."

"And do you think you could learn something from that?"

"Me? Learn something? Please, don't you recall you diagnosed me as marvelously stupid?"

"It was a theory, but you keep tilting the scale that way certainly," he laughed. "I have to get to work. The Temple and the Noble's have been cleared. The more permanent reconstruction will begin soon. Now we need to focus on the Soldier's and the Crafter's. The governors of the other cities will travel through them once they arrive in the spring. They must look as normal as possible."

"Has Frazil been any easier to deal with?"

"Just about. He is concentrating on family matters and hasn't argued with me for a few days, so I've managed to take care of many things, though he would have preferred to wait for confirmation on some issues. He strangles his reign with hesitation."

"And you'll drive yourself mad if you try to force him to decide on instinct and based on a few bits of information."

"Perhaps. But we both want the best for the city, so I will make an effort to find compromises and challenge him only when I must. Granted that he doesn't need to know absolutely everything that goes on in the regions."

"You are quite fearless."

"Only in certain things. Now is not the time to make amends and hand out privileges. The only thing that matters is that the city remains unified and appears strong."

"Is there anything you wouldn't do for this city of yours?" I muttered.

"No," he replied. "If it comes down to its survival."

"If the city is a priority in all things, shouldn't I be cast out? If I'm right and the Witch Queen is still alive? She will come for me. And I wouldn't be surprised if Irinda had referred to her during the battle."

"Mother Eternity? The title she called out at the end. It would make sense if their goal is a muddy and stale eternal existence. But regarding your question, don't even think about it. Do you think I would take such a risk? If we lose you, we lose the flame. Whatever the battle will be, the city is the best place to defend. What good is an untouched city if the earth is dead? Once Tammaran wakes, you will tour with him. Everywhere in the city. If something is happening because of Irinda or your former life, there must be signs of it. Maybe places where the blight is worse or places that don't respond to the soul sand. Gates between worlds. Or whatever you think she is capable of."

"Maybe… A disease must have symptoms. You are right. If we know what they are and locate them… they can reveal much. Someone must cause them from somewhere."

"Good. Now you understand."

"I don't know if it is possible, but should we try to track Irinda? If she rose from the dead, she is heading to Istrata. I'd assume so, anyway."

"We have tried, but our methods aren't effective enough. The consecrators must find the way, the army will help and support," Rime promised.

"Do you think the Witch Queen is out there somewhere right now?"

"Pondering that doesn't bring us any closer to a solution. We must find out, but before we have any undeniable knowledge, there are other dangerous matters to take care of."

"Need help with anything?"

"Not yet. Just your company at times."

"Reasonable," I smiled. "How goes it with Moras?"

"We are making progress. He is building containers for ill souls. We can collect the distorted ones there. He means to investigate how their power affects the living and how we might heal them or their effects."

"I was thinking of it before. They have been twisted through time, so if we can pass them through the cycle again, could they slowly be cured?" I mused.

"Through something? Like what?"

"I didn't get that far, but you know how metals or distillations are purified. Something like that, but I don't know how you do it to them."

"What if they can't be healed? Would it be better to destroy them out of existence?" Rime asked.

"I suppose so. But that would mean the cycle would be very weak."

"True. But if I would have to use souls, would you not agree that I should use them through this gift or curse instead of the healthy, normal ones?"

"I dislike the whole thought. They are so… dirty. But… if something must be lost to win a battle or for you to get this under control, it is the best option for the city. If you are planning on using them, then please do so only under Moras's supervision," I pleaded. I knew he had already been fed with it. There was no mistaking what was in those black vials, but the less they had to use it, the better.

"Of course not. I'm not excited to have it injected."

"Where are you building this container? I want to see it."

"To the storage room in the second bow. It's largely empty."

"And how will you collect them?"

"There aren't that many options."

"So, it's up to me?"

"Only if you want to."

"Burden me as you wish."

"Well, I know one way I could burden you…" Rime whispered. "But perhaps it is better that you heal wholly first."

I closed my eyes and smiled. If any good had come of all this, it was that he no longer entertained the idea of shielding me by pushing me away.

"Before I forget, I had this made for you some time ago," Rime said and placed a small box on the table as he was leaving.

I picked it up and opened it. There was a small, bright, polished crystal star attached to a hair pin. When raised in front of the sun, it sparked and dotted the room with colorful flecks. There was a delicate inscription "Come what may, remember me."

XVII

T ammaran stared at his brightly colored quilted and checkered blanket. He said nothing to me as I stepped into the room. His forehead furrowed and head lowered. He drew his legs closer to his body.

"How are you?" I asked.

"Too well," he sighed and looked past me as I sat on the bed.

"What happened? I'm sure you told Rime already, but I don't know how much he dares to tell me."

"There honestly isn't much to tell. I opened the door to a healer that had come to check your condition. When I was closing it behind him, he took me into a stranglehold. From the wound on my head, I guess one of them also hit me with something.

"One of them?"

"Another person came in later. I could see it hazily from the Lighter World at that point. I couldn't do anything, as I couldn't connect to my body."

"But you saw their souls?"

"I remember them. I'll know if I see them again. But I doubt they'd linger close by."

"Very likely not. Still, you never know. So, two people all in all?"

"There was a sweet, almost honeyed scent that wafted in with the second person. I can't put my finger on it. I'll let you know if I do."

"Good. We have quite a bit to do."

"I gathered as much. When do we leave?"

"As soon as Moras or one of the other main healers grants permission."

Tammaran picked at his blanket and kept avoiding my eyes.

"I don't know if I should say something," he sighed.

"Don't you dare. This whole mess is ridiculous. Let's just focus on one issue at the time," I denied him the opportunity to express his regrets.

"Thank you."

"For what?"

"For not blaming me more."

"How could I blame you? No one knew I was carrying them when we started. And even if we had known, would we have thought that I was in danger? I don't think so. Your task was to guard our bodies for health issues not a murder attempt or... well, this," I mused, uncomfortably. "I know you. I know what you'd be willing to do. I'll leave you to rest. Don't tell anyone but me and Rime what you remember."

"He said the same thing," Tammaran noted. "I think I got it."

As I left, I took a deep breath. I would have gladly blamed him. It would have been the easiest route to let out this strange, sick feeling. But it would have been so wrong. He hadn't caused it.

As I wandered about, I thought if this could have anything to do with Istrata, but it didn't seem to sit. This had human fingerprints all over it. Could it be that the governors of the other cities had something to do with it? Perhaps Irinda had sought help from whoever remained loyal. Perhaps some of the people in the Temple who were against the changes had planned it. There were many possibilities without my old self.

Whoever it was, they had left me feeling insecure, timid, and annoyed. The one thing I was certain about was that this had been made in the name of gaining influence. The thought came with a creeping suspicion I wasn't ready to deal with.

I walked out to the garden on top of the first bow. The snowy scenery was almost untouched. Only Riestel's footprints and those of a few servants were visible. I hadn't seen him since the operation on Elona. I knocked on the door. I knew he was in, but I wasn't sure if I wanted to see him. Istrata's feelings. The kiss inside the statue hall. They still tickled my skin.

"I have invited none here," Riestel shouted from inside. Annoyed as ever.

"Open up, you insufferable grouch!"

A moment later, the door was ajar. Riestel looked colorless and tired, but in a different manner.

"Isa, I thought you were still in bed, recovering."

"You could have visited."

"I rather think your husband would dislike that," Riestel noted, without any mockery.

"How is Elona?"

"Well, all in all. She sleeps mostly. Moras said it is likely due to the strain on her new body and her soul. We have to wake her up to feed her. Then she nods off again."

"You look like you haven't slept for a few nights."

"I don't dare to sleep for long in case the soul begins to detach. If that happens, I need to take her to Moras. And you aren't exactly the epitome of well-rested yourself," he remarked and let me in from the cold.

"Well, no. Are you planning on taking care of her alone?" I asked as the door closed and I realized I had absolutely no reason to be here and I had to think of something to say. Why on earth had I wandered here?

"Are you offering to help?" he asked with an amused note.

"Not a good idea," I replied and smiled.

"Indeed. And no. I'm in no way qualified to do so, not in character or temper or skills. And I cannot drag her around with me. The problem is… I don't know anyone suitable. Or really that many people to ask anything of."

"Your relatives?" I suggested, though I wanted to say that his character was just fine for the job. I had seen the way he handled the child with so much care and love, but admitting to having noticed it wasn't something I was about to let him on.

"Maybe not the best of ideas, but isn't there anyone remotely suitable among them?" I continued after an awkward silence.

"No. And I'm not ready for a larger family. Would there be anyone in the Temple I could approach? You know them better."

"Are you seriously asking me?"

"You know how to talk to them."

"You could talk to them if you just wanted to be nice."

"If," he stressed, looking all high and mighty.

"Right. Well, maybe. I don't know how she'd react, but I can ask her. At least she'd be good at soothing her."

"You refer to that darkish-haired friend of yours?"

"Arvida. She has no children of her own, and I don't think there will be any in the near future."

"She isn't terribly annoying."

"Ah, yes, that is the most important thing," I smirked.

"Can you ask her?"

"I tell her about the situation, but nothing more."

"Could you do it now?"

"Why?"

"Just asking."

"Why?"

"I can't guard Elona and you at the same time. Or do you want me to carry her into all the messes you are still to cause in this city?"

"That is such an insulting thing to presume, but you are probably right."

Riestel sent a maid to fetch Arvida. I studied the peacefully slumbering child. She seemed content and well. Riestel kept fidgeting in his chair. We didn't really find any natural topics to talk about in her presence. Luckily, Arvida arrived shortly. Her expression remained still as we explained the request. Then she burst into laughter.

"Good skies, well, that was the last thing I expected," she confessed and shook her head so rapidly one bouncy strand of hair fell out of place. Arvida's long, slender fingers tucked it back into her hairdo quickly and flawlessly.

"It was a surprise to me too," I noted.

"Well… it would… be an experience. Can I see her before answering, or will it bother her too much?"

"Of course you can, though I don't know why you'd need to see her."

"I want to see if she'd like me."

"Why wouldn't she?" I asked, confused.

"If you haven't noticed, I'm almost as friendless as you. Especially since you have one of my closest friends under lock and key. And Launea can't manage to talk of anything but her pregnancy."

"Yes, but she is partly mine, and I like you," I reminded her.

"How can you just confess it like that?" Arvida blushed but seemed happy enough to hear it.

"Temporary social inaptitude."

Arvida leaned over Elona's bed. Riestel fiddled with his fingers and bent his wrists by the window, trying not to bother us. His icy hand sounded like a frozen lake when you stepped on the ice.

"Hello, I'm Arvida," she introduced herself, smiling.

Elona opened her eyes just a little. She was so sleepy she didn't manage to look at us for long, but she did make a small squeak, like she was trying to answer her greeting before she yawned so much that her nose scrunched up. Then she turned on her side and disappeared to safety under her heather-colored blanket.

"She is quite a pretty little bundle," Arvida said. "I think we will get along."

"We'd be grateful," Riestel remarked, stiffly.

"Auntie Arvida… Well, it's certainly better than nothing," she sighed. "As it seems, motherhood isn't going to happen for me in this life."

"Please tell me if I'm asking too much. I don't wish to cause any sorrow," I urged.

"You're not," Arvida smiled brighter than I ever thought was possible with her face. "This might be my most cherished responsibility yet."

"Can you watch her for a moment?" Riestel asked and put on his coat.

"Certainly, but not for long. I have plans today."

"We will just pop out briefly," Riestel added. "If something happens, we can hear if you shout from the door."

"Alright. But afterwards we must negotiate rules for how this works and what tasks will befall on me," Arvida insisted. "And I'd like a wage."

"Obviously. Isa, a moment?" Riestel demanded and pulled me toward the door.

"Hold on, let me get my outerwear," I sighed. Riestel snatched my cape from the hook, threw it on me, and pushed me out.

I walked behind him. He stopped right at the edge of the bow, as he often did. He glanced around a moment, but when he saw there was nothing or no one close, he turned to me.

"Come closer," he said.

"Why?"

"Because I just asked."

I went to him. I could never grow tired of the scenery. The city was still blanketed in a shimmering coat of snow and frost, like a painting. I could make out outlines of new structures in some parts. Their surroundings were always lit up with fires at night to allow the rebuilding to continue despite dark evenings and a biting wind.

"I've been thinking," Riestel whispered.

"That can't be good."

"Leave the remarks. I'm trying to be helpful."

"With what?"

"Survival… Istrata, I think, is still far away. We don't even know what her form is or if she has truly managed to preserve herself."

"Why do we need to talk about this out here?"

"Have you ever heard of outlining a matter? Needle's sake. You must have been thinking about who's behind your child's fate."

"One cannot but wonder. Do you know?"

"Not for sure, but I think so."

"Don't say more."

"What? Why?"

"I have my own doubts and I will follow them. The thought vexes me too much to put into words yet."

"I'm surprised. You are finally starting to learn the ways of this city."

"I must, mustn't I, since I forced my way here?"

"Whatever you will do, I will support you."

"Miraculously, I have no doubt. I will travel with Tammaran to see if the city bears any traces of Istrata. We have to collect the suffering too. Moras will use them for tests and whatnot."

"I heard. It's risky."

"I know. But I support him. And Rime. It is their decision."

"And what if they have an effect on him?" Riestel asked, slightly shaking his head. The wind swept a few longer strands of hair to caress his cheeks.

"They are aware of the risks. As am I. But what else can be done? I want him to have a chance to exist and not just disappear when death finally comes. And I do not want the city to be filled with the suffering and eternally tormented spirits."

"Do you want any company on the journey?"

"Your daughter needs you more now. Stay here. I'm sure Tammaran is enough to guard me for the moment. I'll come to you when I know more. If I'm right, I will need your council and help."

"Isa?"

"Yes?"

"Do you want to be a part of Elona's life at all?"

"I'm not her mother. Do not attempt to pressure me into it. But… I have nothing against other roles. I care about her on some level, of you. I'm sure we can find a way to coexist."

XVIII

R ime's and Frazil's scouts had scoured the city searching for places ripe with death and events that could have, in time, resulted in twisted spirits. Moras had visited a couple of such places with us at the Peak.

A container built in the between of the worlds held some of the twisted. It could contain a vast amount, as they were so dense and shriveled. Moras was excited as all seemed to go according to his plans.

"Are they present?" I asked Tammaran, as I still couldn't see the Lighter World as easily as he could. I could sense it better than before, but not always very accurately.

"Yes. Dozens. It's not a wonder. Irinda, or her predecessors, didn't hold back on the executions."

I looked around the scaffolding. The square had a lower temperature than the surroundings. Maybe that was the wind, maybe the dead. The hanging beam and the dismantled beheading platform rested on the side. It had been easy to get rid of people here. There was no one to hold you accountable. It was hard to say if anyone had seen justice here.

When I found my way in the middle of the spirits, I closed my eyes and focused. I took hold of the nearest. It was slimy, oily, sticky, and very heavy. I burned it to soul sand. The sand the distorted turned into wasn't a starlike light substance. They became a grainy, asymmetrical mass that could sting you. There was something immensely heavy about them. They didn't seem to belong to the Lighter World nor our world. They pressed on the membrane between them as if they wanted to rip it and ooze their way home from this flowing place.

Every time we managed to clear one area, I could see black splotches on the ground or floor that seeped into the matter and out of sight. It looked like the substance I had seen trickling from the ship's walls and in my nightmares, where the whole sea around us was pure black tar.

In the Peak alone, there had been over ten places such as this filled with the viscous matter. No direct signs of Istrata among them. The amount would keep Moras busy for months, even years. Still, we went ahead to the Noble's. The first place we'd visit would be the Winter Gardens. It was the most important location of their games and had been in Irinda's favor, so it was almost impossible that it wouldn't need to be cleared.

"There's a lot I gather," I noted when we finally found our way through the maze of glass rooms and walls to the field of the Gardens. I knew it from the way it felt to walk there. It was like wading waist deep in water.

"More than enough. A thousand."

I let my hand glide through the air. I could sense the mass on the other side.

"What do you want to do?" Tammaran asked.

"To sit on a sunny meadow and drink until I fall asleep."

"Kind of hard at the end of the winter."

"I'll have to make do with this, then," I said and shifted my gaze to see both worlds. I stood in black sludge. When one touched it, it moved lazily like thick oil. Here and there were some better-preserved lives.

"Can you hold the bag? I'll take the usable ones first. After that, we'll handle Moras' business."

Tammaran nodded and held out a fabric that had been woven in the between. After traveling with Riestel in the Lighter World, I had a better understanding of its laws and the laws of these interwoven pockets. Distance was but a mere passing thought. As I focused on a spirit, it moved slowly at first and then as though it had been yanked. I had done it when feeding Rime during the battle, but it had been a violent, instinctive act. I hadn't understood how and why it had been possible.

One bag after another filled. As we had collected the least twisted, Tammaran reached into a small leather satchel and took out some metal parts. I reached for my thin drawing dagger, which I now carried in my hair everywhere I went. I opened a pocket between the worlds, between the invisible barriers separating them, and pushed my needle. I fashioned copies of the metal parts there and attached them to the membranes. I pushed my needle through the metal pipe and rings. I could feel the membrane resist and then a small prick.

I withdrew the dagger and twisted the rings. They kept the black mass from flooding out. I attached the other metal head to the membrane between this world and the pocket. Only the last shutter rings were visible at our end. I opened the previous seals. The pocket began to fill. Once the last ring would be opened, the dark ooze would flood into this world. Moras's students would come here to attach tubes to it to suck it all to their storages made from old water reservoirs. I allowed a few viscous drops to hit the ground. The thud they made on the surface of the sandy field was much louder and much harder than such a small piece of existence had any right to make.

We had discussed on many occasions if the system could operate fully in the pockets, but it was too difficult and consumed too much strength. We didn't have enough skilled consecrators or an endless room to store the matter. I had been present with Tammaran when they drained the first pocket. When most of the black tar had poured out, the between and the Lighter World had felt cleaner, flowing. It made Tammaran show a fleeting, almost hidden shadow happiness.

The red stone manor of the Maherol's quieted for the night. A few coals still burned in the guestroom's fireplace. Despite receiving all the hospitality in the world, I had slept poorly ever since giving my blessing the experiments Rime and Moras were doing. What good could come from them? A new soul, filling his void. Wonderful goals, but with this dark filth...

Was I mad not to object? I wanted desperately to find a way to give him a chance, but this path seemed wrong. The more I had to deal with the dark matter, the more worried I was. But Rime knew the risks. Moras knew them. How could I ask him to stop when it could mean a sentence of completely disappearing from the world? But if I didn't ask that, would I just be a bystander while he possibly changed to something different?

I sat up in bed after a poorly slept night. I touched the sore scar on my belly in the shy dawn light. It would last much longer than our children had. One was still somewhere but different from its original form. Not that I had any right to say that. Rime was the same, and I had no complaints about him. For now. But both of those star-bright seeds of life I had seen in the Lighter World were gone. A small, stubborn feeling tugged within. It wasn't sorrow at its purest. More anger. Anger that someone had had the audacity to decide for me and take them from me. I couldn't delay it anymore.

After getting dressed, I followed Tammaran to the carriage. He tried to diminish himself to the smallest and least annoying presence he possibly could.

"Is my mood that foul?" I asked and stared at him.

"I suspect so."

"I want to visit a healer. Someone with no ties to the Peak or any governor."

"Why?"

"To avoid gossip."

"Suspicious," Tammaran said and nodded.

"Indeed."

"Can you tell me the reason?"

"You are smart enough to figure it out for yourself, as I know you'll be there every step of the way. Provided I find out what I'm dreading."

"You won't like the suggestion. The first place I can think of that would have a person to fill those needs is the Crafter's area. If you don't want any raised eyebrows, visit the house you went to with Aravas. They are bound to feel no sympathy for the higher-ups and as you've established a link there yourself, I doubt many would suspect the call was anything but a courtesy call."

"Riestel's relatives… True. They've kept his secret for centuries. I just feel like I should ask permission for it. It is his sanctuary."

"Since when do you care what the haughty prick thinks?"

"Since I realized what I had done to him."

We installed several "taps" to the Soldier's under Samedi's watchful eye but lingered there for no more than a day. The first consecrators had arrived to train with the military under Liike's supervision. Apparently, all was going well, even without their powers.

The Soldier's had changed the most during the winter. It was fully cleared. Even old, unused buildings had been demolished to make room for all the tests to be done in spring. There were new things in the area, too. The guard towers had been reinforced, and new defenses built on the outer walls. The air smelled of molten metal and fire. It was oddly comforting to me. The hammer blows and gusts of air hissing in the smithies echoed everywhere.

The City Guard was to be swallowed by the military and retrained on Rime's command. Proper gear and weapons would be provided for them. Hostilities had to be ceased to portray a united front. Frazil had his doubts whether the former separate units could function together but had at least admitted that he would leave the decision to others, as he had less experience with the common recruits. Frazil had seemed much more at ease lately and less suspicious. It bothered me greatly, as I knew his methods.

The Crafter's didn't possess large pockets of suffering. They were spread all over. In the lower streets, you could almost feel the tarry substance form puddles. I stood at Ombra's door. Before I could knock, it opened.

"Well, now, if it isn't the mouse," she smiled and wiped her hands on the apron.

We sat down at a floury table. She took a piece of dough and started to work it in a circular motion. She nodded at another lump. I picked it up and imitated her.

"Good. We only help our own. Are you alone?"

"I'm alone here, yes."

"What can we do for you, then?"

"I want to see a healer. Not from a temple. Someone who knows their herbs and powders and such."

"Doesn't the Peak have someone for that?"

"Not one I can lean on right now. I know I'm intruding and maybe a bit rude to assume that I can weasel my way into getting help from you just because I know Riestel. But this is the level I have to stoop to."

Ombra looked at me from under her brows and grunted with a ponderous note. Once she had finished a few pastries and fixed some of mine, she called a young boy into the room and sent him out for the healer. I focused on rolling and braiding pieces of dough to keep the cold, clammy fear of being right from overtaking me as time passed. I really didn't want to know.

The healer arrived and stood at the table as everyone else cleared the room. She fixed her slightly tilted and worn glasses.

"What may I do for you?" she asked, trying to copy the manner and note of Upper's but failing at it.

I reached for the pouch inside my coat which hung on the chair's back and handed it to her with the dosage scroll.

"I've used this to… to prevent me from carrying for several years now. It is almost out, and I cannot return in the midst of my rounds to the Peak. Are you skilled enough to decipher the formula?"

"Well, I… well," she sighed and forgot her fake accent. "Maybe. Not precisely, but close enough for it to work. Can I?" she asked and took out some writing equipment.

"Certainly."

The healer opened the bag and took a little of the substance with her finger. She smelled it and wrote down a few things. Then she licked it. Her face changed to one of confusion. She tasted it again.

"Is something wrong?" I asked.

"Is this really what you've been eating?"

"Yes. Speak freely."

"Well... I... It's a wee bit odd. More of a fertility treatment to have children."

"Would taking it increase the odds of having twins?"

"In large enough doses, most certainly."

I laughed and covered my mouth. Reality seemed to distort and ripple for a moment.

"Did I say something wrong?" the healer gasped, and her posture slouched a little.

"No. You must excuse me. You just confirmed my worst fear on the matter. Please, keep this meeting to yourself. If anyone asks why we met, you can tell them, I requested the medication I told you this was," I instructed her and gave her a basket of butter and flour.

The healer nodded, a little unsure.

"Was this all you require? I feel as if I did nothing."

"Yes. You helped me more than you know. Thank you."

I said goodbye to Ombra after the healer left and stepped out of the house. Tammaran shadowed my steps. He was always there.

"And now? Should we return to the Peak? Rime should know," he urged tentatively.

"No. We will finish the rounds as planned. I need a moment to breathe before stepping under his roof again."

"Are you sure it is him?"

"I am. This was prescribed to me on his request when I first entered the Temple's service and got to spend a night with Rime with his help. It is not absolute proof, but... Oh God... I wish I was cleverer. Time and again, I trust people too much."

"You don't. You can't suspect everyone and everything," Tammaran consoled me and pulled his coat on tighter.

"No... But so many warned me about his character. I ignored them as partisan badmouthing. I didn't even stop to consider I was just someone... something of use to him."

"If you hadn't done what you did, Irinda could be the ruler at the moment. Dethroning her was right. We could be setting up for war out there instead of trying to find a way to heal this reality," Tammaran reasoned.

"Perhaps. The price is just getting to be a bit high for me."

"I don't think any one of us will make it through without a heavy toll. Rime always says you are the harbinger of chaos. You can't help that what you touch can spiral out of control. What will you do now that you know?"

"I can't say anything. I can't let on I know. It will make the situation worse. And I want to be sure he knew what I was being fed."

"How?"

"With your sweetheart."

"What?" Tammaran huffed and went red. "I don't have anyone."

"Then who left that finely folded paper rose by Arvida's door?"

"She could have other admirers."

"Other? So, you count yourself as one," I grinned.

Tammaran hurried. I ran after him and grabbed his arm.

"What?" he sighed, flinching.

"Make violets. She prefers them."

XIX

Moras was glad to receive the map and descriptions of the installed equipment. He passed them on to his students, who copied them for our records. The room was full of hissing, bubbling, and boiling. There were some many scents and smells in the air you couldn't identify any of them.

Moras gestured me into one of the back rooms. Rime was sitting on the table with no shirt, completely absent from here. He didn't react to anything in this state, nor remembered things from these sessions. I stroked his arm and the military markings burned on his skin.

"We are building a suite for your husband into the between. It is like Irinda's machine. In practice, not in size or purpose. We figured out that a mere glove won't do to keep the hunger in control and to properly master the channels. They have been torn too violently. Look here," Moras urged and walked behind Rime. His back was full of lines and symbols.

"We mapped out the strongest channels. Here are the entry points, directions, and possible sites to manifest it outward. If we install vents that utilize the natural current running in the body or, specifically, the nerves, he can open and close them on instinct. Almost like a consecrator can. We will also build another spine around his natural one. The guide pin for the whole system will be inserted from there to the nerves within."

"Sounds almost like torture," I noted. "Is it necessary?"

"Yes. Otherwise, he will lose control and consume himself. And it won't take many years. Now, the recovery will take a substantial amount of time and the whole operation is, no doubt, painful. We can ease and speed it with the soul sand. Touch here. You will feel some minor pieces already placed under his skin."

I reached out but withdrew my hand before touching him. There was no way our relationship could get more intimate, but something in examining him like this felt too much like prying.

"I believe you. Is he truly prepared to go through it all?"

"Why not?" Moras smiled content. "It is an exquisite experiment."

"An exquisite experiment... Do you care what happens to us?"

"Consecratoress... I'm sorry, of course," Moras hurried to apologize and bowed his head. "All of this is just very fascinating."

"And Governor Laukas?"

"What? I... I don't follow. I can't speak for him."

"But you fulfill his orders at the expense of our lives," I remarked and dropped the medication pouch on his table. "I was blind for a long time, but did you think me so foolish I would never find out?"

"Please, do not tell your husband," Moras squeaked as he paled. "He must be guarded from getting too anxious or stressed during all this. The suffering causes instability in him and his character. The changes might become permanent if he were to receive a shock."

"Convenient for you."

"I will not try to claim I didn't know what I was making and by whose order," Moras confessed. "I merely ask that you will allow me to continue my work without making a spectacle. I serve this city, and I thought, at least, that I was serving it when I took this task. What I didn't know was the intent behind it. Or... I knew it would increase the number of children, but I had no knowledge they would do what has been done. All this is new to me. You know that. I've spent days on end learning these things to be useful and to help. Admittedly, I may be too enthusiastic about certain things. I'm still a healer. My intent is never to harm."

I glanced at Rime. We needed Moras for him. And for many things. The healer kept his eyes fixed on the floor. His face was all wrinkled like a child's who was waiting to be punished. He didn't seem to lie, but could I trust my own judgement? No, that was too dangerous. I needed to be sure Moras would not give the slightest indication to Frazil that they had been caught.

"Let's say I believe you. It would be hasty and careless of me to act on that."

"What can I do to reassure you?" Moras asked.

"It's more about what you should not do and how I can find a way to believe you. You need a shadow that I trust."

"A shadow?"

"A shadow," Tammaran whispered right by his ear as he grabbed Moras by the neck. The healer jumped and dropped an instrument he had been holding. It chimed and spun on the floor for a moment.

"I beg you, Consecratoress. Don't harm me."

"You ask and beg a lot. Might I suggest you listen," Tammaran urged in a low voice and let go. "Shall I get her?"

"Yes, please," I replied.

Arvida stepped in before Tammaran. She pressed Moras on a chair and placed her hands on his temples.

"This may sting a little," Arvida noted, smiling, and Moras jerked. "I can feel him. Ask."

"I need to know you will not reveal that I know. If you so much as hint that we know, you are shaking the very foundation of this city, as you'd be starting a war between a father and a son. You enabled for our children to end up as they did. For both their souls to have been destroyed. I do not give a tiny wave's worth if you knew of the plan or not. I hope you didn't. I'm not going to inform Rime yet. I will heed your advice on that and not upset him more," I decided and touched Rime's neck gently. "Will you reveal to him that you were caught?"

Moras shook his head. Arvida closed her eyes and nodded.

"He speaks honestly," she affirmed.

"Why not?" I asked.

"Frazil never told me the reason for the medication," Moras replied.

"What lie did he rope you in with?"

"He merely said that he wanted for you to produce heirs as soon as possible to stabilize the family. It is a common custom among the nobles."

"True. That it is a common custom, but he is also telling the truth," Arvida said.

"So, from your point of view, there was nothing out of the ordinary in the proceedings?"

"There was," Moras groaned. "Usually, the treatment is sought by those who will take it. I know I did wrong to agree to the arrangement without conversing with the patient. If I had paused to think, I could have seen it wasn't right. I did as I was asked, as I knew you served him and I could have never made it to the main temple to see you. You have done things in his name that aren't all glorious and praiseworthy. And I didn't know you personally back then."

"I know. That's why I do understand you. Nor do I blame you. If you wouldn't have, he would have just found another person. I just needed the confirmation that it was his command."

"What happens to me now?" Moras asked, exhausted and ashamed.

"Nothing. As you noted, we need you. I do not believe you'd be so silly as to drive them even more up each other's throats. It would wound the city. I don't want that either. What I want is time. Time to find the child, a chance to get them back. Whether I'm ready for that role or not. Right now, that child is a pawn to control us. That is wrong. A life that is small and new shouldn't carry such a burden."

Moras gave a slight nod.

"I will keep this between us," he promised.

"True," Arvida confirmed and lowered her arms.

"Alright, we can remain friendly. But... I have been betrayed too many times in the name of family so remember that you may at any time have my shadow in the midst of your own," I warned Moras and glanced at Tammaran who was almost a head's worth taller than the healer when he stood in the proper posture. Moras eyed him, tugging on his collar.

"I accept that for your peace of mind with no complaint. I do wish to state that I would gain nothing by telling him. I would lose the opportunity to study all this and to invent new things. If you don't believe anything else, you know how much exploring all this means to me. I have no desire to see the world hurt."

"You will continue to supply me with the medication, but it better be the kind I have been let to believe I was eating."

"Right, of course."

Tammaran and Arvida left on my request. They kept trying to evade each other in the doorway out of courtesy so many times she started to laugh. Tammaran froze when he noticed it, stopping the dance and letting Arvida pass.

"When will you continue your work on Rime?"

"Soon. The tanks are almost full," Moras answered after clearing his throat. "We have experimented with plants a bit. The mass has its own effects on living things."

"Can you show me?"

"Yes. This way," Moras guided and assumed his normal manners as if nothing out of the ordinary had happened.

I followed Moras to a glass annex built on one of the platforms. The plants were darker, reddish, and a bit black in places. Flawed colors and the lack of symmetry were the most obvious issues. Some parts were too thick and some too thin.

"They are ugly but not poisonous as such. Not the quickly killing kind. We also keep rabbits here," he remarked and took one out of the cage. "This has been solely eating the withering plants for a few days. They don't immediately have an effect. The litter will be born in a few weeks, so we can see what the food does to the next generation who will be raised on the plants. Amazingly, the plants do seem to be quite energy dense."

The rabbit had a shiny coat, and it was a ball of content fluff, but without having to look into the Lighter World, I could feel all was not well. It munched on a leaf lopsidedly and shook its head as Moras lowered it back into the cage.

"What is it?" he asked.

"They are flawed. The offspring."

"We surmised they would be, but the exact scale and detail will be revealed once they are born. Next, if they live, we can see if the effects dissipate with clean food from generation to generation. And then we can start to experiment with dosage. The other cage over there had animals who only partly eat these plants."

"What's the current hypothesis?"

"That the change is not permanent. The most uncertainty lies in how many generations it takes to undo the damage, if it can be undone."

"Enough. Is it too much to ask that someone would deliver a summary to me whenever new things develop? I'd like to be in the know."

"Absolutely. That is one more reason to the list of things why I hope you will be able to trust me again," Moras said sternly, lowering his voice. "Our ruler to be. He does not visit. He does not ask for reports or knowledge. I send them nonetheless, but I doubt he reads them."

"Frazil's time is very limited. His focus is solely on the matters of the spring."

"I understand that, but... these experiments define the future. Whoever runs this country."

"There is no question about who it will be. No one wants to shake the balance now. But he isn't the only one who has the right to make decisions. If he doesn't have the time, I will make more time myself. Presuming our cooperation goes smoothly regarding the previous matter.

"Thank you. And I'm sorry once again."

"Don't be sorry. Be useful. Keep my husband and Elona alive, and I may forgive in time. How long will you take with him tonight?"

"To the wee hours, I'm afraid."

I would have gladly spent some time alone with Rime, but perhaps it was for the better. He would notice faster than a gale moves the curtains that I had a secret. A few days to settle my emotions would not be a bad thing. The last thing I wanted was to make things more precarious for him.

"How many weeks or months will all this take out of his life?"

"I believe we will have everything necessary done during the spring."

"Can he attend to his duties during that time?"

"As well as he has been until now."

"Fine. Tammaran, let's go. Leave the rabbit alone."

"Right," Tammaran said and blinked into view. Moras jumped a bit and took a step back. I walked in silence next to Tammaran for a while.

"Do you think that was enough?" he asked once we got away further.

"He doesn't need to think you are there all the time. Just to suspect it often enough. Visit him in surprising places or appear in corridors if you notice the opportunity. Move his things around so he knows someone has been in his study."

"Got it."

XX

I squished warm oat bread crumbs against the plate with my finger. Riestel enjoyed his tea in silence. His face was smoother and brighter these days. His manners or behavior around most hadn't improved at all, despite the rest. Not that I would have expected them to. I quite liked that he was secretly amiable only to a few people.

Elona slept. She had grown in one month almost as much as most in half a year. She was still mostly fed through the Lighter World to stabilize the body and soul connection further. Lately, she had been offered more solid food. Her growth seemed to begin to stall, but she almost walked already. The more nourishment she would get our way, the more normal her development would get.

"Since you invaded my privacy, again, would you like something else to think about for the day? I thought I'd show you a place," Riestel offered. "Arvida will be here soon."

"What place?"

"Something we made long ago. I just visited it."

"Where is it?"

"In your glasshouse. Or the door is, anyway."

"I haven't noticed any pockets there."

"Have you tried?"

"No…"

"You talentless woman… or just lazy."

"Not both surely."

"I'm considering it. Well? Or are you just planning to mosey about all day while avoiding thinking about what your husband is going through today? I am offering something interesting as a diversion."

"I'm not avoiding anything. You say it like I would be trying to be willfully blind."

"He is suffering in the experiments. You are having morning tea with me. I'm not complaining... or, well, it is a burden to be honest."

I bit my lip and looked away. I had wanted to be there during the surgery. As support. He didn't want any of it. The last time, he had escorted me out by the arm. And it hadn't been a gentle hold. I had been avoiding him a bit after that. The tar was changing him. It highlighted the unshakable parts of his character, the ones that made him such a good soldier and a strict leader. It was good for the city but painful for me. The soft moments, the moments between just us two, our own family, were gone. I knew it was temporary. I hoped it was temporary.

"And there she is. Drink your tea and I'll take mercy on your brain by distracting you."

Arvida greeted us happily and headed to Elona's bed. She took a book and sat down by her with a content expression. Her insect likeness seemed to disappear more each passing year I knew her. Riestel exchanged quick words with her and then nodded me to follow.

The snow was almost all gone from the bow. The day was a perfect spring day. Everything was shiny and the sound of dripping water was everywhere. The glasshouse sparkled as water drops slid across the panels as the sun warmed the structure. Riestel opened the door and guided me gently in.

"Feel it out," he requested.

I focused. I looked for traces of someone like me. A small vortex revealed itself like a sighing wave. It shimmered in the furthest corner. Riestel stepped in the gate and offered his hand. When I hesitated, he grabbed my wrist and pulled me through. The room was a grand mirror image of the glasshouse. Except all plants, pots, dirt, and all structures shone like the sun-kissed ocean. Like molten gold, wherever one looked.

"How did you make this?"

"Look closely," Riestel replied.

I touched a plant's leaf. They felt icy, but there was a warm flutter beneath the surface.

"The fire is inside the ice? Forever?"

"Almost forever. That corner is unraveling due to the place being unkept. Come, fix it with me."

"How?"

"I'll teach you."

Looking around, it was like being inside a crystal jewel. Flickering lights and shadows. I kneeled next to him. A strange, small machine had lost some of the flames and the ice had melted.

"See if you can command the fire now that you have most of her soul. Even though it is different, it may be enough."

I touched the flame with my index finger. It didn't burn, though it felt hot. After a moment of trying to force it, it obeyed. Riestel nodded contently.

"Can you feel what it was?"

"A cog?"

"Good. You can feel the intended design. Try molding it back. I will envelop it as soon as the shape is correct.

The flames bent and molded between my hands. Cogs and springs, one after another, found their shape again. Riestel smiled as the last one clinked into place. He attached the panel to cover them.

"What it is?"

"Just a moment," he smiled and turned the wheel on the side. The springs inside made small sharp noises as they tightened. When Riestel let go, a slow, swaying waltz played.

"I'll offer just once," he said and stretched out his hand. From a momentary lack of judgement, I took his hand. He placed his other hand on my lower back and pulled me closer. I turned my head away. The tune carried us and embraced this reality even more tightly into secrecy. I looked at his face. Riestel caught me. I turned away again. Riestel stopped and lifted his hand to my cheek, softly forcing me to face him.

"Why won't you just admit it?" he asked, stroking my cheek. "They aren't just her feelings."

I shouldn't have come here. I shouldn't spend any time with him. Why had I ever thought it appropriate? It was wrong. To both. And yet so easy. With Riestel, all problems seemed so far away. The dance flowed lightly. It was a glorious fairytale vanity which had felt better than most things in ages. It was easy to yield to in this made reality far away from the actual world.

"You are trying to seduce me again," I noted and pushed him further.

"Am I? You?" Riestel whispered with a snobbish half-smile on his face. "What of it?"

"What happened to the thought that he only has one life and you an eternity? Where did the respect for his decision to save Elona disappear to?"

"Nowhere. But would he appreciate pity?"

"So, in your logic, you are trying to steal me because you respect him? Ridiculous."

"Maybe to you. And yet... here you are," he remarked quietly and bent closer.

"Don't. Do you know what is even worse, that you'd try to tear us apart now that he needs all of my support? That you are still trying to woo me like Istrata. I have my own desires and likes. I thought you would have noticed that by now," I scolded him and stepped out of the space, hoping to have angered him enough to not follow me.

The warm sun scattered its rays through the roof. It lit up one particular spot of the glasshouse. Something small and green was poking out of the ground. I examined them. The warm ground had sprouted five bright green leaves. The red irises had germinated. Did it mean anything? I felt a small shiver inside me. Something was growing. Something that shouldn't. Riestel appeared behind me.

"She hated red," he spat and stepped closer. "You like it. I know your differences. To the smallest detail," he whispered with his lips on my neck. "Or not quite, but I would love to find out."

Before I had the possibility to react, the glasshouse's end panels shattered as Riestel was flung out. A dark, crackling cloud enveloped Rime like the tentacles of an octopus. Rime charged after Riestel with his eyes covered in black and a sickly violet glow around his iris. Moras had lost control. I ran out over the shards.

Riestel had gotten to his feet. There was blood on the ground where he had landed. They moved through the trees on the bow's garden as ghosts. Appearing and disappearing. Riestel, of course, journeyed through the pockets, but I had no idea how Rime moved as fast as he did. Each time he came back into sight, I felt the earth and air vibrate as if they had been hit by very low notes.

"Stop!" I ordered, but neither slowed down. "Riestel! You are just making this worse!"

"Me?" he scoffed as he stopped next to me. "I'm the one bleeding here."

"Stay put," I asked. "Don't annoy him more. I must get him to calm down."

Rime rushed towards Riestel. I moved between them and reached my hand toward Rime. His hunger licked each living thing on the bow. At the same time, black ooze seemed to seep out from the cracks in the world around him, just like on the ship.

"You came looking for me, right?" I asked, stepping a little closer and touching his cheek. "You came to me because you know I will help."

Rime halted but said nothing. He just stared at Riestel.

"I know you don't trust him. I'm not asking you to. I'm just asking you to breathe a little. You aren't thinking clearly right now."

Rime tilted his head and squinted. I stroked his face like that of a timid animal. The blackness subsided a little.

"Are you sure he even hears you?" Riestel pondered.

"Not a word out of you!" I snapped. Riestel crossed his arms for a second and then proceeded to comb his outgrown hair with his fingers.

"You know me," I assured and took my other hand to Rime's face. His breathing became more relaxed, but he didn't take his eyes off Riestel. He almost snarled at him.

"What happened? You were with Moras," I tried to get his attention.

Rime's face twitched with pain. He pressed the fingers of his left hand on his forehead as if he was going to try to rub a headache away.

"I know it's not comfortable, but you can't just leave. You can't stop in the middle. That might result in something much worse. We can't have that. You have promised me much, and I'm going to hold you to those promises," I scolded him, gently. His eyes dimmed. He shook his head as if to try to wake up.

"I wasn't going to leave... But I felt him near you... His hands," Rime whispered with a strange metallic twang in his voice. His eyes shifted to me. Half a smile appeared on his lips.

"I changed my mind," he said. "I want you there. I need you there."

"And I will be there," I promised.

"Are you mad?" Riestel snapped. "If he loses it even worse, is there anything to stop him from attacking you?"

"I'd never hurt my wife," Rime swore.

"That hardly seems like something you can control," Riestel remarked. "Leave her here and go fix yourself!"

Rime froze and squeezed my arm.

"Riestel, leave it. Go tend to your wound," I told him.

"I can't just leave it. You cannot be so stupid as to risk your life or the future of this world just to baby a grown man! Can't he take a bit of pain? He chose that unnatural road."

"Shut up!" I demanded.

"Stop arguing," Rime sighed. His eyes were back to normal.

"Doesn't our disagreement please you?" Riestel asked slyly.

"I will never trust you," Rime noted and waved his hand at Riestel in a dismissive gesture. Suddenly, he leaned on me as if out of breath. The black cloud and the tentacles were gone. I helped him down to the ground. A trickle of blood appeared out of the corner of his mouth.

"Get help," I ordered Riestel.

"Why? Better for everyone if his kind…"

"Do you think we will have a future of any kind if you let him die in front of me?"

Riestel's face became more serious looking, and he left muttering impolitely about pets.

Moras and his team arrived running after a while. They lifted Rime onto a stretcher. Riestel didn't return with them. I followed them to the warehouse that had been transformed into a storage of the suffering and to a temporary operating room. They placed Rime back on the table. There were all sorts of pliers, bandages, and tubes around. Just the thought of what he was trying to suffer through alone broke my heart.

"There will be risks if you are present," Moras said and wiped his chin on his sleeve while trying to strap Rime back to the restraints of the table. "We will put him to sleep the best we can to make sure there is no danger, but are you absolutely sure you want to be here?"

I sat on the floor near Rime's head.

"I'm not going anywhere. Did you hear that, you stubborn ass?" I whispered to Rime and flicked his forehead. A pleased smile passed on his face just before his consciousness faded.

Moras worked precisely and without any hurry to get everything right. The fifth metal piece was placed by his spine. The skin and tissues fed on the black tar constantly. The wounds closed and healed the moment Moras stopped cutting and stretching them.

"Should be enough for today," he yawned. "I cannot do another piece. The supports must stay in place until he awakes."

"How did he escape?" I asked while everyone cleaned the room.

"We are not sure. We were preparing the next pieces and... when we turned back around, he was gone."

"Then what good are those restraints if he can move between worlds?"

"Better than nothing," Moras replied. "Though, if he can switch planes once he has a better grasp of his abilities, I realize they won't hold him at all. But I doubt he has any conscious control over it yet, so it shouldn't happen often. We'll wash him now."

"I will. Leave us."

I took towels and a bowl of water, heated it and dipped the towel in. I wiped the dried blood from his back and picked metal shavings from his skin. His muscles twitched here and there as the nerves reattached. I touched the burn marks on his shoulder. How much was he capable of carrying on his shoulders?

"Isa..." Rime called, groggily.

"Here."

"Thank you."

"I would have been here before if you would have permitted it."

"Scolding right off the bat," Rime laughed hoarsely and swung himself to a seated position. He winced in pain.

"It just means that I love you," I said.

Rime stared at me with his mouth slightly open. Then his whole face brightened with a smile I had never seen before.

"You love me. Did you know that is the first time you've used those words?"

"You know it already."

"You can still say it now and then."

"And that means what? You yourself swore me to accept that you lie. What value can words have, then?"

"A liar can also speak the truth."

"Then tell me how you ended up attacking Riestel."

"I... During the pain, I think about us. I think about your pains and aches when you came to live with us. You endured them without complaining, mostly. I can match that. When I focused on your face, I sensed you with him. The dark shell just swallowed me, and then I was there."

"Why attack him?"

"I can only remember negative emotions. I can't make out or recall what I was thinking. It was more on instinct... Isa, do you have feelings for him? Be honest."

I sat next to Rime and laid my hand on his arm. He turned his head away.

"Of course I do," I said, and his arm tensed. "Mostly annoyance."

"Don't kid."

"I remember him. I remember how he loved Istrata and how she loved him. Some moments I can feel it. It's like an echo that some word or location brings out. It's an inseparable part of me. One could even say that I love him. But it isn't the same kind of love I feel for you. I chose you."

"You made that choice before you knew of him or remembered him."

"True. But I'd choose you even now. I'm here. I'm not comforting him," I reminded Rime. His sudden insecurity baffled me, though it was somewhat flattering.

"But I should go to him," I noted.

"Why?"

"Because Riestel is one of our most valuable weapons against Istrata. Because even if you don't trust him, besides you, he is the one person who will protect me to the end."

"Do you believe that much in him?" Rime asked gloomily.

"I do. The moments when he is an utter moron come and go. Mostly, he is tolerable, and he has a child now. He will do anything to provide a good world to her. You've seen how he looks at her."

Rime sighed and nodded.

"Go then," he agreed.

"I can't yet."

"Why not?"

"You aren't clean yet," I remarked and dropped the wet towel on his head.

XXI

I yanked the door to Riestel's apartment open. Arvida greeted me with a smile. Elona peeked from behind the couch and started to wobble towards me.

"I think she recognizes you as family," Arvida noted.

"Really?"

"I can read her. You could try to be that to her. She is a rather amusing little critter."

"I don't think that would be a good idea right now," I declined and bent down to greet her. Elona's nose scrunched a little every time she smiled.

"Where's the grouch?" I asked.

"Out somewhere. He's been rather silent the last day or so."

"Is he very annoyed?"

"No. Actually, when I heard about it, I thought he'd be unbearable for a while, but… yesterday, I kind of tried to feel him out, delicately. What I felt was hope."

"Hope?"

"Yes."

"Well, that fits, naturally, since I despair over him."

"Oh?" Arvida laughed.

"Whatever I say or do, he seems to interpret it to his benefit. I left him bleeding, and he feels hope. That's just… Gods."

"Have you told him directly, then?" Arvida asked as she guided Elona back to her snack. "She doesn't have the patience to learn how to eat. Everything else goes well, though."

"I'll go and find him."

"By the way, did you know Launea had her child?"

"No."

"A very healthy and pudgy boy."

"Good."

"I see you have no interest in the matter."

"..."

"Fine. I won't bother you with it. However, it would be well-mannered to at least say hello. You invited her here to be treated. You could accept her gratitude."

"Alright, I will," I groaned.

I might have cursed Arvida a little in my head, but she was right, and I was more than grateful that she never bowed to me. In that way, I also missed Heelis with her mule-like character. Now that time had passed, I had begun to understand that she hadn't so much chosen to betray me as much as she had chosen to hold on to her principles. I'd still never forgive her for Simew.

Greeting Launea was a chore I couldn't avoid, so it was good and well that I had people to insist that I would act according to my status. I had to learn to put my desires and comfort second, at least now and then. My actions and deeds were judged differently as a part of the ruling family.

I stopped a little ways from the glasshouse. Riestel was fixing it. His hair was open, and he had only a light linen shirt and trousers on. The shirt was casually tucked in at the front but flowed off the sides. His coat was neatly folded on the table in the glasshouse. He had draped a sheer fabric on the irises to insulate them in case of late-night frost.

"Will they survive?" I enquired.

"Yes. A few," he replied without facing me.

"And you?"

"All intact. Now new limbs lost," he answered and turned around. His countenance was bright, almost airy, and he was smiling.

"Why are you so happy? You just had the wind knocked out of you, but you look as content as a cat with a mouse."

Riestel shrugged.

"Hold the glass as I bend the supports in place," he asked. I supported the glass plate. Riestel placed the clips with the utmost care and then gently pressed them in place.

"You can let go," he said.

I lowered my hands. Riestel closed the door to the glasshouse after taking his coat.

"You can remove the fabric later, once the temperature settles."

"I thought you'd be angry at me."

"Angry? Why?" he asked, smirking, and stepped close to me. "Should I be angry that you got mad at me because you thought I can't see the real you instead of who you were? You're trying to fool yourself. You miss me."

"You are out of your mind."

Riestel tilted his head and smiled. Leaning in.

"You are hard-headed, I get that, but so am I. Even now, I bet you feel this horrendous lightness when I'm close. You want me to kiss you," he whispered. "You want it so your life would become a wonderful mess of problems, smaller and more flattering than the current ones. And precisely for that reason, I will not."

"I have no time for this nonsense," I muttered and sneaked away.

"Well, be glad that I do!" he yelled after me.

The infuriating jackass. I cursed him all the way down the halls. Riestel knew too well how to manipulate me. If I allowed it, he might even get deep enough to accomplish whatever he wanted. The feelings had a base from which to grow if I gave him any room in my thoughts.

"Isa? Arvida said you might pop around after a good talking to," Launea greeted me quietly, but cheerily, with a baby in her arms. I flinched because I had been so lost in thoughts, I hadn't even noted opening the door to her chambers. Launea was beaming. Her scars and wounds were but light memories on her skin.

"Are you well?" I asked.

"Oh, wonderful. You saved us. The healers here are such lovely people. And Rime has been very courteous. He has allowed some of his daily rations to be given to me. But that is surely no news to you," Launea accounted and fixed the baby's position. It whined in an annoying, high-pitched way.

"He doesn't need normal food right now," I stated. "Planning to stay for long? I'd imagine you'd like to return to Nissa and the rest of Simew's family soon."

"Actually, I'd like to linger still. Nissa would join me here for a moment. I want some time to talk to Heelis. I've been there a few times, but the stubborn woman won't even consider letting go of her anger. Juone is ever so frustrated. It is strange though. I thought I'd hate her more. But after the baby came, I just… I was able to forgive her on some level."

"Thank you for the effort. I wouldn't want her to hate us for all eternity."

"That wouldn't be right. She knows it. We'll keep chipping away."

"I'd like to think I'm at least a little more malleable than her."

Launea's bubbling laugh filled the room. She rocked her child and smiled with such immense joy and love that I hated her for a moment as I had when I had thought she meant more to Rime than I.

"Eilir. This is aunty Isa. She was a very good friend of your daddy," Launea chirped. I hated being called an "aunty", and I'm pretty sure Launea knew that.

"Hello," I said and waved. "He has Simew's eyes."

"I think so too," Launea sighed. Her face darkened.

"I'm a horrible person," she said suddenly and stared into a corner.

"I'm pretty sure you are one of the least horrible I know. Why say such a thing?"

"I'm falling for another. I shouldn't. Not again."

"Who?"

"I don't want to say. It is so silly. I won't let it happen."

I observed her more closely. If her feelings for Rime were being reignited, what should I do? Would I kick her out for my own insecurities? I'm sure even I wouldn't be that vile.

"Oh, for the love of the Peak! Isa, really?" Launea said, laughing, and wiped her eyes. "Oh, that face! Dear friend. I am not crazy enough to start that again," she assured and took a breath. She placed the well-fed pudgy little human in a grass-green crib. "You must keep this to yourself. Promise? I will die of shame just thinking about it," Launea whispered and came closer. "Nissa… she… reminds me so much of Simew… but it could be just my imagination."

"You are falling for her?" I had to ask, as I wasn't sure I had heard right.

"I'm horrible, aren't I? My husband's mother. Who could accept such a thing?"

"Well, it is a pretty difficult road to take."

"Should I ask her to stay away? Is it too unconventional?"

"I'm perhaps not the best person to ask that."

"We get along so well, like a family. I don't know if she feels the same, but I'm just happy I can still get these feelings. I was numb for so long!"

"Long?" I muttered since I didn't manage to stop myself. A part of me wanted to note that her recovery time between relationships seemed to be about the same length as a springfly's life. Instead, I looked her in the eyes and smiled.

"This whole world is one big mess. I don't think you will cause it any harm by acting on those feelings, should she return them."

Launea smiled and nodded. As I left, I realized that Launea probably had no actual qualms about approaching Nissa but that this was her way of telling me about their relationship, so I wouldn't be shocked and against it due to Simew's memory. The gesture was commendable.

On my desk in the Needle laid a letter. The envelope had a proud-looking seal with the squiggly and posh letters "F. L." I opened the pompous—excuse me—sophisticated, envelope. Frazil wanted to have a meeting at his quarters in the Peak. Within the envelope was a long list of issues to discuss. One item was "The rearrangement of the Peak". Riestel would have a fit if they tried to move him. He already terrorized most of the people living here with his behavior. That's why no one was ever around when he was out and about. He seemed to tolerate Moras and his students, since they had an actual purpose.

I tapped the corner of the paper against the desk. This worried me. Why such a formal invitation? To be sure, I was mad at him already for trying to run my life. But this just didn't seem right. Thankfully, it would take place tomorrow so I wouldn't have to wonder for long. I would just need to hold my tongue during the meeting. If my self-control hadn't improved over the years, the room might have suffered some damage from this announcement. Now, I just tore the letter and burned it.

XXII

I arrived to Frazil's rooms with Rime who was wearing his official clothes. He moved a bit stiffly from all the surgeries. Other than that, the healing was going well. Just before he knocked on the door, he stroked the back of my palm with his thumb.

Frazil's apartment was similarly decorated as his house in the Temple District. A servant guided us through several corridors. As I looked around, I noticed some half-unpacked luggage in a room we walked past. Women's clothing. Had Friti arrived here? Why? They had always said his wife didn't want anything to do with the administrative things. Had it been a lie? I glanced at Rime. He had noticed the same.

The pine-green room was lit more appropriately for an evening party of leisure than a meeting. Dried flowers decorated the room. Rime greeted his father, who was in a particularly elated mood. Frazil nodded to me, but with a more serious look.

Riestel was loitering by the long table with boredom oozing out of his pores. All the other guests were silently and awkwardly waiting. Riestel had likely been demanded to be here as the Temple's representative, but the use of dragging him here would be very small knowing him. He didn't greet us, though he noticed us. Frazil ordered everyone to sit. He invited Rime to sit on his left side. After the members of Rime's Black Guard and all other temporary position holders found their places, the seat on Frazil's right side remained empty.

Each guest had been granted a glass of wine and a simple but well-prepared meal. The tableware was the finest, thinnest porcelain, and they had the Laukas family's seals and gilded edges. The utensils and the glasses were covered with a layer of gold as well. All items had an inordinate amount of decorative patterns.

I recognized some of the army's lead members and superiors from my journeys. I didn't pay much attention to the greeting speech Frazil was giving, as I was battling with myself on how should I behave towards him. He was the king to be. He had been good to me, though, for his benefit. How could I just leave everything alone? The scar twinged. But how could I act as long as he had the child? Although, the child was valuable to him precisely because Frazil thought we valued her or him.

"Consecratoress Elona?" Frazil called.

"Sorry? I was in my thoughts."

"Ha, so you have some," Riestel whispered.

"I asked if you had anything to add to the report from Kymenes regarding the Temple's current condition or to Consecrator Aravas's opinions."

"No."

"I presume you have read the report?" Frazil asked, frowning.

"I have. I have nothing to add. I have talked and written to both men on every aspect of the content. I have no desire to waste my breath giving speeches when they are not needed or required," I found myself saying and bit my lip. Riestel coughed after a short laugh. Frazil's frown became deeper, but he brushed the remark off.

Frazil introduced the next subjects. Apparently, we were going to go through almost everything brick by brick. One after another, the listeners started to lose their postures. The only redeeming aspect was that we still had something to drink. Frazil was still an excellent speaker, but there was no question all of this could and should have been done in several sittings. It was silly to waste everyone's time when a written summary would have sufficed for those not directly responsible for the matter.

Frazil displayed miniatures and paintings to us to showcase his vision for the rebuilding. Riestel kept yawning at every opportunely quiet moment. Once Frazil excused himself to go and get yet another model, I heard some of his audience mutter that with the money and time spent on these small houses, we could have built some actual ones. The sluggish nature of the future ruler annoyed many and seemed to stir mistrust when it was the exact opposite of what Frazil hoped to achieve with this presentation. But amongst ruins, who but the nobles had enough interest to enthusiastically ponder the color and decorative motifs of drainage systems?

As the moon peaked from the lower left window corner, I flicked some of my drinking water on my face. Frazil was presenting a preliminary list of new governors. Rime and his guard members remained stoic. They did not comment or talk on the issue. I wasn't sure what their thoughts were on their current positions and if they wanted to keep their acquired power or not. It was difficult to discuss borderline treasonous things.

"That was all but the last two issues," Frazil announced contently as some of the more careless let out an audible sigh of relief. "I will now present my wife, Friti, or Friodora. Your queen to be. Then we shall discuss the Peak's destiny. Darling, come and join us and greet everyone," Frazil urged with a proud smile on his face. He finally sat down to his meal.

Friti arrived gracefully through a door a servant opened. She nodded to everyone with a rehearsed, virtuous look. Her wrists were heavy with bracelets chiming with her every movement. She had a dark brown simple dress on. The fabric had a sheen of gold to add just the right amount of nobility. She was perfect for her role in every way.

"Thank you, my love. My heart rejoices that all of you who have supported us on the road here are present. I can see my husband is in wonderful hands. I have remained long in the shadows, but I will partake in the government from now on to ease his burdens, especially with the Peak. All matters here belong to me. Please, approach me first. Or one of our daughters who will join us soon," Friti added, looking at Rime.

Rime's face remained unafflicted by emotion, but I could feel him darken.

"They are coming here to train before marrying," Friti added.

"Ah, yes, I forgot to share the good news," Frazil interjected. "I have in all quietness offered my eldest to the Governor of Eladion. It will help our situation and stabilize the country. As they have their own armies, it will relieve stress from my son to deal with all defense matters alone.

Rime took a deep breath and leaned back. They had lied about everything. They intended to give the crown to their children instead of Rime. I hadn't really ever liked the idea of taking the throne again, but now, as it sailed away, it bothered me. More for the lies than the power. More for the betrayal than the crown.

"We have given great thought to the new order of the city," Frazil said, picking up momentum again. "We think it best to divide the Peak among the new governors' families. Nobles would also be welcome here. We shall rule from here, so it makes sense to move most of the higher classes here."

"Wasn't the city supposed to become open to all?" Riestel asked, and the temperature dropped noticeably.

"Well, of course," Friti giggled. "But there is no reason to stop certain professions and people from forming their own communities. It is only sensible to keep the districts mostly as they are."

"Cowards," Riestel sighed, kicking his chair further from the table and putting his feet up by her plate. If it had been anyone else, eyebrows wouldn't have been the only things that were raised. No one said anything, but Friti had a sneering look of disdain for the gesture. Frazil remained silent, though gripping his napkin a bit too violently. For once, I thought Riestel's behavior perfectly acceptable.

"In any case…" Friti continued undeterred and turned to face me. "We shall divide these apartments, rooms, and premises in new ways. We will chart out the needs of each family to see what will suffice them. I hope all are willing to move in order to find the best suited rooms for everyone."

"Excuse me? Would you repeat that?" I asked. "Are you referring to the Needle and its premises?"

"Naturally," Friti confirmed, smiling. "We all understand that the Needle is emotionally important to you. But fear not, you can keep all items with you regardless of whoever should eventually hold the Needle."

I stared at the table. My hand rested upon it tremored a little. I squeezed it into a fist and glared at Frazil. How dare they? This was my world. My kingdom. Well, not my kingdom. The spoon under my hand turned partially liquid.

"The Peak, and especially the Needle… is not yours to play with," I said and stood up. I could feel beads of sweat pushing out of people's skin. Friti touched Frazil's shoulder. Riestel crossed his arms, amused. Rime tilted his head ever so slightly but made no effort to rein me in. The guard members and lower officials directed their gaze at the table, as it was customary when the Noble's talked about personal issues to give the illusion of privacy.

"Consecrator Elona, please. We all must do our part in this new world," Friti remarked with a delightfully unconcerned note. "We will do our best to find you worthy accommodation, but right now we are living more cramped than you."

"And why should that matter in a kingdom that was supposed to be based on the freedom to succeed? Surely, a king shouldn't live above everyone else and with more than everyone else just because he is the king? I have never challenged you, but there is nothing to negotiate here. The Peak is mine and the Temple's. The Needle, solely mine. There are hundreds of rooms you cannot see. Monsters you cannot imagine. The stores and halls are filled with the dead. And here, you want to establish your court? Away from all ordinary folk whom you claim to represent," I pressed them. The expressions around the table and people trying to make themselves as small as possible gave me a strange satisfaction. The side of Rime's face that was turned away from his father was decorated with a slight smirk.

"The White Needle, and all that is there, was made by me. My soul and my thoughts! You have no right to dictate to me which rooms I may and may not use. I, the Temple, or Consecrator Aravas, are not for you to command."

"I... darling. I'm lost for words," Friti sighed, looking pale, as her friendly words had fallen on deaf ears. "I realize you may not like to hear this from me as, we aren't yet as close as I hope to be..."

"A better location for a new castle for the King and his closest would be at the center of the city," Rime noted calmly. "You would see the differences in the areas and be right in the middle of all events. That remains the army's suggestion. A new center. A new government building with a door to each district to act as a heart of the city."

"It will be difficult to make people believe in change if the new king acts as the old ruler and chooses the furthest place for his residency," Samedi backed him up in his most polite tone. Many nodded.

"I understand your point of view but... Can I have a few words in private?" Frazil asked me, wiped his mouth after taking a sip of water, and guided me a little ways from the table. A talking to was exactly what I needed from him.

"Now, I realize the Peak is a sensitive matter... However, it makes the most sense for the city. We have given this much thought," Frazil whispered.

"You haven't shared any of those thoughts with us. Many here think otherwise. You merely decided and thought you'd announce it."

"My goodness, Isa. I would ask that you trust us. I presume you still agree with my goals. We will not rob you of the whole Needle, but its floors are the most suited ones to be the king's private chambers."

"Really? I see."

"Then why did you have to challenge my wife in front of everyone during her first address?"

"I said I see, not that I agree," I remarked through a persistent grin that was trying to force its way onto my lips.

"What is this? What have I done to you to deserve such treatment?"

"Excellent question," I answered and glanced at the guests. "At first, I thought you had. But you haven't, not really. That's your problem now. You may have taken our children. You had me torn open to carry on your family tradition, regardless of our wishes. That will certainly hold sway over Rime. But to me, it's nothing. You took the child before I knew it, before I became a mother. The Peak is my child, and with me it will remain unless you wish your family to wake up in a sea of flames."

Frazil gaped at me. I could almost hear how he was frantically thinking of something to say. Something to twist me back around his finger. But he had nothing he could offer, nothing to bargain with anymore.

"Does Rime know?" he asked.

"No. And I'm not about to tell him to avoid causing trouble for the city or him right now. You want your reign to have a peaceful start... I at least presume you did what you did to leash us. We had been faithful. You were the one who lost his faith, if you had ever truly meant to trust us."

I turned away and walked next to Friti at the table.

"Thank you to all for the company tonight. We have cleared the matter. The Peak belongs to the Temple now and forever. Goodnight," I told them.

"Wha...?" Friti gasped and turned to her husband. Frazil stared at the floor with a clenched jaw and just lifted his hand to signal everyone to be quiet and let the matter be. Riestel jumped up and followed me out, bowing in a very insincere manner to the ruling pair.

"Queens," Riestel sighed, amused, closing the door behind us. I covered my mouth.

"I'm going to throw up," I said and leaned on the wall as my heart kept trying to fracture my ribs.

"Aim over there if you must. I have new shoes," Riestel ordered and pulled me up by my shoulders. "Well done."

"You better appreciated it."

My hands were still shaking when I got to the White Needle. A part of me was in disbelief about actually having stood up against them. And so brazenly, with only a lie to back me up. Thankfully, I had such a hard time admitting to myself that I may have felt something for my children and a desire to have the one still alive returned to me that no one would have guessed it was all a show.

The cards were mostly out now. The future king was against me. Not that Frazil would necessarily make a bigger deal out of this or even seek to get even. Despite all, I didn't think he was an evil man. I was prepared to believe he had done such an act just because it was sensible and good for the bigger picture and that somewhere deep down, he might even regret it. But that didn't buy him a pardon.

"You could have warned me," Rime said from the door. He closed it and came to my side by the window. The night was half over.

"Well, I wasn't planning to threaten your father."

"Threaten? You went that far?"

"I might have… The words just…" I explained.

"I have placed guards at the foot of the tower."

"Is that necessary?"

"Didn't you just say you threatened the future king? I can't say it would be an exaggeration," Rime groaned but with an amused note. "My father won't do anything. He knows he needs you, but it was a big defeat in authority. Some of his supporters might be less than pleased."

"Or the wife and his daughters. I think Friti was offended more."

"Perhaps."

"Are you mad?"

"No, quite the opposite. This will force them to rearrange the city better, to shake the customs up. We have been asking them to place the palace in the center for a full moon's run, but it was starting to seem impossible to get through to them. Though, I understand why. The Peak is the most beautiful and the securest place for a ruler. Still, it would be the wrong signal to send."

"How many lies do you think he has told us of his intentions?" I whispered and leaned on Rime.

"Many. It doesn't surprise me. Kerth is full of the ambitious and power-hungry. I think he may also lie to himself about how forward-thinking and well-meaning he truly is. Besides, what better tactic to replace a regime than to paint the current administration as a failure, complain about the most minute things, and to offer an option to the disillusioned? It only needs to have a different color on the surface. If it is the only option, people will grab it."

"Do you think he will leave the Peak in peace?"

"For a moment. Depends how much Friti wants to be the noblest noble. I will try to offer them the best alternatives to solve the situation."

"You'll get to meet your sisters soon."

"It wasn't good news. But naturally, he will favor the children of his current wife. I have always been replaceable. An interchangeable cog in the machine," Rime sighed. "As any soldier. I just had hoped he'd prove me wrong. That he still might. That he would have seen some more value in me than just opportunity."

I took Rime's hand and drew on his skin with my finger.

"Are you going to do something about it?" I asked.

"No. Let him marry them off to anyone he wishes. We shall see if he can pull it off. I'm in no hurry yet. And it will create stability. He is right. It will eliminate the threat of their attack almost completely. The Governor of Eladion will have an easier path to the crown by the union. No need to lift a finger, just wait for Frazil to age."

"Yet? Would you want to sit in his place? You've always said you are happier in the shadows."

"I am," Rime replied. "But I'm horrible at forgiving people and stopping before I get all I want or the revenge that I want. And to get all I want... Well, someone would have to be a little humbler. That doesn't mean I'd place myself on the throne, though."

"Humbler? Your father?" I asked, even though I would have rather enquired what he wanted to get revenge for. Perhaps Rime already knew about the child, but I couldn't ask it without giving it away. The simplest answer, of course, was that he wanted to get back at Frazil for the way he had treated his mother.

"Him too. Did you find any clues about the Witch Queen as you toured?"

"Nothing. But I can control the nexus better... or at least it doesn't throw me out immediately. I have a theory on why we are still at peace and why nothing indicates that she would be coming."

"Tell me."

"I think she is in some sort of hibernation. Physically. The destruction of the statues wouldn't have awoken her, as they'd only prove that one of my kind had collected the soul pieces. Even getting the last one wouldn't mean that the person collecting them would survive and be different."

"What would awaken her?"

"The healing. It is the best sign that her plan is in motion. Once we gather the new crops, it will cause a ripple on all levels of existence, a flow of energy. Nature can only heal itself at a certain pace and at a certain rate. When she can feel there is more happening, she can be sure I have been created according to all her wants. At first, I thought the last statue was meant to hold the soul for her, but now I think it might have been a vessel to deliver the pieces back to their proper places for the next one to find if I perished in the fight."

"So, the moment people will have hope for the first time in ages, she will come."

"For me, for us. I just happen to be the key."

"True. A key to many things."

"What does that mean?" I asked.

"Exactly what I said, no more, no less. Have I thanked you?"

"For what?"

"Suffering through my mood changes."

"I'm just happy you caved in and let me be a part of it," I noted and snuggled up to him as he opened the window. The night carried the scent of crocus.

"I don't like that you see me in that condition," Rime complained.

"And I hate that I had to wait outside the door worrying about each noise and each silence," I complained and flicked his rib.

"I understand my mistake already," he laughed. "We are almost done."

XXIII

Flowers were poking up everywhere in the Peak. Frazil and Friti hadn't approached the subject of the Peak's rearrangement after the meeting, but they weren't preparing any accommodations anywhere else. They avoided me the best they could. The atmosphere was deceptively joyous. Servants and lower-classed nobles who flooded in and out of Friti's chambers were enthusiastic about the wedding ahead. Frazil's daughters, Ghila and Orelia, were addressed as princesses already.

I recalled Orelia from the days I had visited their home for my lessons. Now she was much taller and more subdued. I had never met Ghila before they came here, as she had been living in a boarding school at the time. I had passed her a few times in these halls already. No one could mistake who her parents were. She was almost an identical copy of Friti, just with Frazil's ears and jaw.

Wherever Ghila went, she was followed by an entourage of chatty, exuberant women in colorful outfits and hair all glossy with silky ribbons. All new things. I envied her a little. It didn't hurt to admit that. I couldn't even imagine the lightness they felt. A life without constant shadows. I groaned at myself. Was I this somber these days?

"Are you even trying?" Riestel asked and looked at me from the other side of the nexus.

"Doesn't it look like I am?"

"Oh, it looks like it, but that's never a guarantee that something is going on in that head of yours."

"Alright. You caught me," I sighed and pulled my hand out.

"I would wager that it is better to leave it alone unless you can fully focus."

"You are likely right."

"Take a break then," he suggested.

"Can it last for a few months?"

"Certainly, this whole threat of all life being destroyed is hardly a pressing matter," Riestel pondered. "You aren't the only one who'd like a break," he added. "You know, I would have thought I'd like you better now that you are old and tired like I am."

"Your complements just improve with time."

Riestel smirked brightly.

"Would you like to visit the Temple's rebuilding site? It is coming along nicely. We could spend a few days there. And yes, I know you can see it from the knot, but it is not the same thing."

"I'd like to, but there is too much to do. Moras has things to present tomorrow, and Frazil had another meeting planned for mists know what reason."

"The day after tomorrow?"

"Yes."

"I'm invited again as well. I believe it is about the arrangement concerning his daughter and the Governor of Eladion."

"Wonderful... I have no interest in the matter, but I'm glad it isn't a private talking to. I have nothing to say to him."

"I think he is so busy with the wedding that your little tantrum isn't on his mind anymore. The wife might be a different matter."

"True enough. Frazil hasn't mentioned it at all. The governors of the other cities will arrive in half a moon. I presume Ghila will wed then. Disgraceful, she hasn't even met him before."

"Frazil is spending like Irinda in her glory days for the benefit of his daughter," Riestel mused. "Do you suppose it was all a humble act? His speeches of progress."

"No, I don't. I think he is just so afraid to lose the world he has just won that he is closing his eyes to the troubles. It's not... what I was expecting, but I'm not in his shoes. Still. I hope he snaps out of it in time and remembers why he wanted the position in the first place."

"In time? For what?" Riestel asked with a sly smile. "Do you have some inkling of what your husband might be up to?"

"No, and I'm not in the mood to guess."

"Oh, you are. Just not in front of me," Riestel guessed and put his hand on my neck.

"Shush! You are not helping me concentrate."

"What an insult. But fine, whether you like it or not, I'm going to see to it that you have a day of rest. You are all tensed up."

"Let me concentrate on the nexus."

"Do concentrate, Consecratoress. Mind me not."

The knot of the worlds, the nexus, annoyed me as much as Riestel. On one day, it gave in and obeyed. On others, it almost stared at me in contempt. Or it would have had it had it eyes. The white, sun-like surface stung my fingers as Farash had when he had studied my channels and connection during my early days in the Temple. Then I felt it again. A resistance. I couldn't enter deeper and it couldn't enter me.

I saw thousands of pictures and scenes stacked and overlapping, but there was no way to concentrate on them or to pick one. I stopped forcing myself and took a breath. I looked at how my fingers united with the knot as Elona's soul had attached itself to the leash in Nameless' neck. What if this wasn't about the nexus shunning me but I it? Was I afraid of it?

I rolled my shoulders and neck. I kept gathering tension in them due to stress and poor arm positioning. After all I had seen, this little thing scared me? How had I not noticed it? I was the one that needed forcing, not the nexus.

"Riestel?" I called.

He didn't reply. I said his name again, but he just stood in place flipping through a book.

"I'm going to throw a book at you in a moment," I raised my voice.

"Right, so now I'm allowed to talk?" he asked and tilted his head towards me over his left shoulder.

"I need your help," I muttered.

"Help? My help? Mighty skies. What a blessed day."

"I can't reach it because I'm afraid."

The mocking smile disappeared from his face. He walked behind me and placed his hands on my shoulders.

"Can you calm me with a song? Not mindless, but calm. You've affected my feelings before."

"I could, but you could do with some care. The channels can get cluttered and clogged with too much tension. And it isn't good for the muscles...

Maybe..."

"Maybe... what?"

"Well, in my time, your kind had their own techniques to taking care of their body."

"What were they?"

"You might be pleasantly surprised. Well, I did promise a day off. Now, I know what we will do. Leave the knot alone for now."

"What will we do then?"

"Does the word 'surprised' mean anything to you?"

"Evidently not."

"Sit, wait. I shall return," he ordered and shoved me on a chair next to a small table.

After Riestel had gone, I eyed the pile of papers on the desk. I took the first bundle. The headline read "Cost Estimates for Repairing the Main Temple's East Wing". Further on was a list of the man hours and materials. Then pages and pages worth of drawings of the foundation and the facade. I took a pen and began to read. I crossed out dozens of unnecessary things. Decorative murals and columns could be added later. I pressed my seal on each page.

The next pile said "District Repurposing and the Local Farming Plan". Any land suitable for farming would be confiscated to the Temple as testing grounds if I approved it. Moras had listed all the usable plants, seed varieties, and earth qualities needed. Frazil wanted the Temple to take the lead on this. It was his way of supporting the Temple and dodging all the anger it would cause among people, especially if things failed.

I hesitated to approve it. If we didn't try to revive the lands, could I live a happy life without fear of Istrata? What sort of life would it be? Peaceful maybe, happy maybe, but at everyone else's expense. At the expense of the world. I buried my face in my hands for a moment. Then I pressed my seal on the pages.

As the day grew dimmer and the paper pile lessened, Riestel returned.

"Would the clerk be so kind as to follow me?" he asked from the door.

"Will I like it or regret it?"

Riestel's eyes narrowed, and his most charming smile blossomed on his face.

"I can guarantee both. Move."

"Do I need anything?"

"No, we will not venture far. I'm still quite certain you haven't been there before," Riestel added as he noticed my disappointment.

We left the Needle and followed a slope towards the fountain one of the heads had been in. The clear song of evening birds echoed from the stones. The first star appeared like a lone freckle on the wispy clouded sky. Riestel stopped at a small stone building hiding behind some trees. I hadn't paid much attention to it before. Some of the water from the mountain spring was directed into the building.

I could see the tinge of red of the stones even in the dusk. The sturdy wooden door creaked as it opened. Hot, moist air pressed on my skin the moment I stepped in. Riestel snapped his finger and pointed at the oil lamps. I was so used to being his personal fire starter I didn't even complain anymore. The soft lamp light scattered by and blurred by the moisture revealed a dome carved straight into the rock itself. The ceiling and walls were filled with carvings. Stone benches circled a heated pool.

Riestel lifted glasses on the bench and opened the wine bottle with his teeth. The sound of pouring wine already relaxed me a bit. I accepted the glass hesitantly.

"Sit over there," he told me and pointed at the last bench. He placed a few floating lanterns into the pool and sat next to me.

"Let's see if I still remember this. This is how we were taught history," Riestel explained with a smile. He leaned forward. Slowly, the low notes formed a column of water in the pool. It froze into a thousand birds all colored by the lantern fire. They flew through crystalline trees. As the animals and trees fell to the water, humans and battles took their place. A century after century played in a sparkling ice dance. Castles rose and fell. Love stories ignited and fizzled. Then everything returned to the pool.

I was so mesmerized during the show I hadn't even thought of scolding him for using his powers for something so unnecessary. And afterwards, it seemed false, so I kept my mouth shut and drew patterns into the water with my toes.

It was dark outside when Riestel poured the rest of the first bottle into my glass. A soft, cuddly mist covered my limbs and thoughts. I watched him as he got us more to drink. All was changing between us. I knew that besides Rime, there was no one in this world who wanted me to succeed as much as he. And there was the horribleness of it. I was in between. I couldn't afford to disappoint either, and I didn't want to mislead either.

I wasn't falling in love with Riestel. I had always loved him. I just hadn't remembered it. But it could never affect my marriage. And my love for him wasn't greater than my love for Rime. They were very different emotions. They had awakened and grown very differently.

"The water is quite pleasant. Are you coming or are you just going to poke your feet in all evening?" Riestel asked and pulled off his shirt. I covered my eyes as he unbuttoned his trousers.

"You know there is nothing here you haven't seen. Don't play coyer than you are," he laughed and waded into the pool. "Clothes off and get in. I can't help you otherwise."

"What do my clothes have to do with it?" I asked, feeling very suspicious.

"Do you often keep your clothes on when you get massaged then?"

Against all voices of reason in my head, I followed his order. I couldn't tell if it was the wine or a spell. I didn't even bother covering myself, as all decent courtly women should have. But what would that have helped? And Riestel wasn't even looking. He was concentrating on heating small jars on top of the candles by the pool. As the oils heated, they released wonderful flowery notes. I stepped into the pool. The water was just a little warmer than my skin. A lovely shudder went through me when I sat in deeper.

Riestel tested the oil on his skin and picked all of them onto a small tray. He glided through the water while pushing the floating tray closer to me. I could feel myself blushing while I tried to keep my gaze above the surface.

"Look all you want, no offense taken," Riestel remarked with a smirk. He passed me a glass.

"I have no intention to," I swore and took the glass, but at that very moment, my self-discipline cracked. I almost jumped back and covered myself by sitting down and pulling my legs in front of me. Riestel was laughing with a quite pleased tone.

"Liked it?"

"Don't be so... you," I objected and felt my face get redder and redder.

"I do apologize. I forgot how delicate you are these days. But yes, I do realize, this is difficult to resist," he said and brushed his wet hair back. Thin, shiny strands sparkled inside his ice arm.

"What's that light?"

"I'm growing new channels and nerves. Quite pretty," Riestel answered nonchalantly and squeezed his hand into a fist. Several of the strands gave out a small burst of light.

"Could you replace your entire body like that?"

"With time, yes. But I'm not itching to test it. There's a slightly higher platform in the middle of the pool. Sit there."

"Why?"

"Just sit."

I placed my glass on the pool's edge and pushed myself off from the edge. I glided through the water on my back watching the star-engraved dome. Riestel's hands took ahold of my forearms. Before I managed to get annoyed, he simply guided me to the platform and sat me down. He ran his fingers on my back, then moved one of his hands to my side and then from there between my breasts, all the way to my collar bone.

"This may hurt," he whispered and pressed into the side of my right blade with his other hand. Unlike in a simple massage, I could feel a power force the oil into the tissues. I would have punched him if he hadn't held me so tightly. After a moment, the sharp pain ceased. My entire body felt lighter from that side. Riestel repeated the treatment to several other spots.

Once he finished, he gently applied a mixture of the three oils to the treated muscles. I closed my eyes. There was no pain anywhere. The whole world seemed to glow.

"How does it feel?" Riestel asked quietly.

"Clean, clear, floating, happy."

"Good. Your channels should be more open now. You won't need to use so much force. If you want, I can check a few minor points. They aren't as important, but can relieve some stress as well."

I nodded. The wine and the treatment made my mind wonderfully fuzzy. A part of me, however silly, had started to trust him. Riestel took my arm, bent it into different angles to find any points that needed tending. It didn't hurt as much as it had in the back. It was more of a tickle.

He let go of my arm and took a step closer to my legs. Suddenly, the water became stiffer. It lifted me more to the surface. I covered myself a bit. Icy fingers glided to my knee. He glanced at me sideways and shook his head with a smile. I pressed my lips together when he moved to my thighs. My throat felt tight. I couldn't even seem to think of words. He bent right over my face with his clear eyes looking like a sky you could fall through for an eternity. A few wet strands of hair touched my face and dripped water on me.

Riestel licked his lower lip, coming ever closer and opening his mouth. A part of me couldn't deny that I wished for it. I knew I had kissed him during the journey, but I couldn't remember much from it. Istrata's feelings, and maybe a touch of my own, waited hungrily. I took a deep breath to give myself the resolution to stop him, but then his lips turned into a devious smirk.

"I told you. I'm not going to kiss you. Not until you beg for it," Riestel whispered. "Anyway... I better go. I wouldn't want to give your husband the wrong impression."

"My husband? What?" I panicked and fell into the water.

"Indeed. Nothing relaxes as wholly as sex. And I'm not about to stay here and be a third wheel. I have my own substitutes for you. He can entertain you for his short life. Who am I to judge you for this affair when I've had hundreds?" Riestel said as if it was perfectly clear we had always been in a relationship and always would be. He got out of the pool, took his clothes, and left before I managed to form a coherent thought.

"Isa?" Rime called a moment later.

"Here," I confessed, feeling quite nervous. I moved to a dimmer spot, as I could feel my cheeks were still red.

"Your annoying friend ordered me to appear here for something important. Not that I believed him, but it was too curious of a message to ignore," Rime explained as he stepped further in.

"I... think he... arranged us to have an evening to ourselves," I answered, as I could feel my own brain trying very hard to understand it all. Even the filled glasses by the pool weren't the same we had drunk from. I was happy to avoid an argument and a misunderstanding, but I did feel an empty spot in my chest, a squeezing tightness when I thought of Riestel walking alone into the arms of someone he cared nothing for. And no, that did not mean I would have wished to cheat on Rime or that I would have preferred to be here with Riestel. It just meant that I cared for Riestel almost more than myself and I always would.

"What exactly were you doing here?" Rime asked and looked around.

"He... opened... treated my channels. And... just before he left, he said that the best way to relax after would be to... well."

"Really? Well, I can't say that I'm disappointed with my decision to come and take a look," Rime breathed and walked closer. "You're naked."

"In what particular outfit should I be in a pool?"

Rime took his coat and boots off. Then he waded in, otherwise fully clothed.

"I suppose that is one option," I laughed. "Feeling smart?"

"Not particularly," Rime admitted and took off the rest. His whole body was a crisscrossed with scars of all types. I touched two longer incisions. I felt an urge to just press against him. My whole body ached.

"Are they still tender?" I asked.

"No," Rime answered. He still flinched a little as I placed my hand on his shoulder.

"Where in the high seas did that scoundrel get wine from? Everything should be under rationing, and I can tell you, he's already had his share."

"I don't ask when it comes to him," I sighed. "Besides, he'd never tell where, if it inconvenienced the people, he got it from."

"Then there is nothing else to do but drink it."

"I suppose not. But after," I told him and wrapped my legs around him. We were finally permitted to touch and be alone.

"You're in heat," Rime whispered wickedly.

"Then you better get to it fast before I boil you alive."

I could see the black hunger rise in him. It bit into me with an exciting but controlled sting among all the other emotions. Every touch, every moment, seemed like the first. Whatever Riestel had done made everything vibrate and echo. Time seemed to stretch out into nothingness. I felt whole and eternal, as if the sky and earth had embraced me. Everything was heightened. Then, I returned from between the worlds to my own pleasantly tired body. I laid my head on Rime's shoulder and sat quietly in his embrace in the gradually cooling water.

XXIV

T he whole Peak bustled and swarmed with life. A long chain of carriages waited in the main yard. Each and every one of any note and importance was supposed to get in one of them and head out to meet the governors of Loisto and Eladion.

Rime thought it ridiculous to put so much effort into impressing them and that it seemed like groveling. It would have been better to let them journey through the city with little fuss to give a confident impression. No one was surprised Frazil decided on the exact opposite. The only surprise had been that Rime had stopped arguing the moment the decision had been made.

I had been wrapped up in my own world since the bathhouse. Though it had been a while ago now, I couldn't stop grinning. I felt light and happy, as if I suddenly loved the entire world. That was deeply concerning. I had managed to wrangle the nexus into something that resembled control this morning. It wasn't a magnificent triumph, but it had done my small request.

The only thing making this day less than perfect was a small girl with two different colored eyes staring intently at me from the other carriage bench. Arvida didn't feel like going on a trip, so Riestel had plopped Elona into my carriage and announced brazenly as ever they would be traveling with me. She was maybe three now in human years. You could still see echoes of Rime in her, but she was clearly mine and Riestel's. It was evident from the looks on people's face who didn't know our relationship but saw us together. But as one could count on in the noble society, it was gracefully remarked on only behind our backs.

"What do you want?" I sighed as she examined my lace sleeve inching her way next to me. She giggled and looked at the world through dozens of small holes in the fabric.

"You are hopeless," Rime noted as he leaned on the carriage window. "Not that you are much better mannered," he added as Elona hid behind my arm. She took a deep breath and studied Rime with the eye that had remained brown. Then she leaped at the window as Rime had lifted a honey cinnamon stick up for her to see.

"You'd crawl over a mountain after one of these," he said softly and fluffed her hair. Elona stuffed the candy in her cheek and smiled. I couldn't understand how Rime was able to exhibit such warmth toward Elona without prejudice. It made me love him all the more.

"I came to tell you there has been a chance in plans. Each of the temporary governors will join the convoy as it passes. I will remain here to keep all things rolling," Rime explained.

"Alright. Can I stay too?"

"No, that would look too much like rebelling. Let's keep Frazil happy. Who knows what kind of mess this visit will cause? I will miss you," he whispered and kissed me before leaving.

I was feeling dangerously content. Rime's symptoms from the suffering and from most of the experiments had subsided. He hadn't lost control, and his character was returning to normal, or at least the darker side was withdrawing. On some days, he even came across as carefree.

Riestel opened the door and swung himself in.

"Daddy!" Elona squeaked and left me in peace.

The sight always stung a little, though I was happy for him. His eyes would light up whenever he got to spend time with the little critter. Riestel wanted his family to meet her.

The carriage jerked a few times before the movement settled. We'd be traveling through shortcuts and crossing districts via towers or tunnels. This meant a new carriage would be waiting on the other side of the wall each time.

It still took us more than a few days to reach the Crafter's. Riestel guided us directly to Ombra's house. She was instantly smitten with the girl who kept hiding behind her father and avoided touch. At least, she had gotten some of my character, too. At those moments, I liked her more. Incredibly selfish, I know, but I couldn't help it.

I also couldn't stop to wonder where her half-brother or half-sister might have been. I put my faith into Rime finding him or her. He'd stop at nothing to do so. And maybe it was better the child wasn't here right now, in the middle of all of this. Even if it was used to blackmail Rime, at least it wasn't at the mercy of anything worse than that. Frazil would never hurt the child. At the most, he would keep the child forever if we weren't cooperative.

"So, when are the high and mighty coming?" Ombra asked.

"A few days from now. We'll carry on to the city's main gate in the morning and wait there," I answered, as Ombra was trying to lure Elona out with some bread.

"Stop fussing," Riestel told her when Ombra tried to get Elona to give her a hug. "And you, little lady, be polite."

Elona peeked from behind her father's chair and accepted the bread. A small smile and a nod made Ombra beam. Then Elona disappeared again. After a while, she sat next to my chair. We glanced at each other.

"She looks so much like her mommy," Ombra sighed as she took more bread out of the oven. "I can see you in her too. Don't strain your face out of annoyance," she added, looking at Riestel.

"Mommy?" the girl asked as her eyes widened. "Mommy?"

"Oh my," Ombra grimaced. "Now I get why you looked at me like that."

I couldn't turn away from Elona. She bit her lip and stared at me with a very stubborn look.

"Elona, come here," Riestel ordered.

She twitched as if to move, but couldn't get her feet to agree.

"Kind of," I sighed. "But it's a secret. You get that?"

Elona tilted her head to the left and frowned. Then she nodded and hugged my arm. Riestel started laughing at my frightened expression.

"Daddy! Hush! Secret!" she snapped with such annoyance and glared at him that Riestel had no choice but to obey.

After Ombra won her over, I was left alone with Riestel.

"Are you fine with her calling you that?" he asked, avoiding eye contact.

"I will not take it back. How would you like to grow up knowing that your mother abandoned you for centuries? And it's a not a complete lie. We can't really say we look this much alike and claim to be distant relatives. Just as long as... Just teach her to refer to me like that only in private."

"I accept the terms. I just had never imagined you'd agree to anything of the sort."

"I'm responsible for Istrata's action. Why not her daughter too? It's not a chore, and it brings her comfort."

"It brings comfort to me as well. You can't imagine how difficult it is to figure out how to tell her things about her mother without saying too much or too little."

"How does she even know to ask about her?"

"There are other children in the court, you know. I don't keep her locked up, so obviously she sees what she is missing."

"I never know with you," I remarked and smelled the air. "Smoke again."

"They are burning the empty houses and apartments," Riestel said and looked out the window.

"Why? Can't they just give them to the homeless?"

Riestel gave a short laugh without amusement and looked at me, shaking his head. I couldn't keep eye contact with him because it immediately made me think of the baths.

"To the homeless," he said snidely. "You are still so endearingly clueless. Who do you think died during the winter with these shortages?"

"I… didn't think about it."

"And even if some of them are alive in some hole, those houses are of no comfort. They are filled with mold, rot, and pests. This city was already drowning in rats. There will be better places at some point, maybe even with small gardens."

Elona darted across the room after Ombra's cat. Ombra hobbled after both cursing her back and ordered Riestel to take out the root vegetables from the heat. The trio was gone as fast as they had appeared.

"This is so strange. A family," Riestel breathed. "Do you think about the others much?"

"The children? Not that often," I replied and dodged his suspicious glare. "Quite often. Everything I can't solve bothers me."

"Well, having a sibling for Elona to play with wouldn't be the worst thing."

"What? You'd let a mongrel like that play with your pure-souled daughter?"

Riestel looked genuinely angry as he dropped the vegetable tray on the table.

"You are talking about a child. I have no reason to bash such an unfortunate creature. And yes, I know where this is headed, but your brain could take into account that I have all the reasons in the world to hate your husband. If the child is trained properly, he or she may not become a similar threat," Riestel lectured me as he moved turnips into a bowl.

"You still think Rime is dangerous to us. Don't you believe in Moras?"

"I don't doubt him, but whatever he can do is temporary."

"How can you know?"

"With absolute certainty? I can't. But should I stay quiet and regret afterwards if something happens and I could have warned you?"

"No... you shouldn't," I admitted, even if I hated his words.

"Then don't demand it."

"I'm sorry."

"I will make an effort to behave, but only if you make a promise to keep your eyes open. I understand you want to believe that he could never harm you... And it may be true. I... hope it is because I wouldn't want you to suffer... too much. But it is at least as likely that there will come a day when he cannot control the hunger. What if a part of Moras' equipment breaks in battle? There are dozens of reasons something could go wrong. Do not be silly enough to rely on luck."

I smiled and promised. I wasn't relying on luck. I relied on Rime. I relied on the fact that he had thought of these things. He never left anything half way through.

"Should we go and get Elona?" I asked. "It's time to move on."

"No. Ombra will keep her here for the week. We will pick her up on the way back."

"Better that way, I guess. I have no idea what to expect from this journey."

"A lot of posturing, useless words, strutting, and insults is my guess. And colorful decorations and fireworks. Vanities on a cake of vanities."

XXV

T he stone wall had stored warmth all day. The setting sun still caressed its rugged surface. When looking at the world from the top of the outer wall, one could see a vast landscape of brown fields with a slight tinge of green. One or two houses dotted the lowlands. Even further forests and curvy roads divided the fields into a quilt. My palms became sweaty just from the thought that this world was so much larger than this city of endless consumption. But what was behind the borders of his kingdom? Would I ever get the chance to find out?

"We could just go," Riestel whispered, almost like a mind reader, and enjoyed the spring wind on his face. "I haven't often been further than Eladion," he said and wiped one of the strands tickling his face behind his ear. The sun kissed his bright, glowing skin. Riestel was so often moody and grouchy that it was easy to forget how lovely his features were.

"Could we?" I sighed and followed the long, brightly colored convoy that seemed to barely move with my gaze.

"You're becoming boring," Riestel accused me. "You could have at least pretended to like the idea."

"You aren't going anywhere either, not as long as Istrata lives."

"Only you can be this gloomy on a gorgeous day."

"Because threats heighten by contrast. How long do you think it will take them to reach us?"

"A day. They will camp once and reach the gate tomorrow in good time," Tammaran estimated as he joined us.

"Consecratoress! By a donkey's firm a– Good to see you again!" Veitso bellowed.

"You just cannot learn manners, can you? Even in office," Samedi complained.

"Damn good," I replied, smiling. Veitso stared at Samedi victoriously and poked him with his elbow, smirking.

"And you dare to take pride in dragging down a consecrator," Samedi muttered but laughed at the end. "Istrae, nice to see you. We couldn't talk at the meeting the last time. Is it true that Rime didn't come to meet them?"

"Yes. He… well, you know, is dealing with everything else."

The men nodded.

"Then we'll have a proper reunion at the Peak," Samedi pondered. "Maybe better that way. We don't want to drag your drunken behind all over the city," he added, looking at Veitso.

"I promised to remain sober until the Peak. Don't bleat like a nanny the whole way!"

It was rather wonderful to see them, but their joking did bring back many lively memories from the war. I leaned closer to Riestel.

"Tired?" he asked.

"A little. I wasn't prepared for so many people."

"We could spend the night up here. There is plenty of room to make camp on the wall."

"Really? But aren't the nights a bit cold still?"

"Asks the fire goddess," Riestel reminded.

"You know I can't waste anything."

"You know, there is this thing called a field stove the army uses. It will give enough warmth under a thick tent fabric," Riestel explained.

"There are hooks there. We could fasten the fabric to them if you wish," Veitso interjected. "Want me to scavenge the needed stuff?"

"Good skies, Veitso. Just order someone to do it," Samedi grumbled. "A governor doesn't carry around equipment."

"He does when it's for the Consecratoress," Veitso insisted and winked at me.

"Then at least accept help," Samedi demanded and followed him.

"I better go too," Tammaran noted. "Those two aren't to be left alone in public. We'll return in a moment."

"Thank you," I replied.

"Well, whatever I have to say about your husband, he does choose his friends well."

"They are quite lovely."

Riestel sighed. Twice.

"You want to say something gloomy, don't you? Even though you just admonished me for it."

"I might. I just want you to remember that they are, first and foremost, his friends. They may like you and they may respect you, but whom do they follow?"

"Why should that concern me?"

"Why shouldn't it? Are you going to go through your whole life with blindfolds on?"

"No. And I haven't for a long time now. But if I can't trust Rime, if I choose that I don't trust him and that all he does is for a good ending... What am I left with? Love won't be enough. Not forever. You, of all people, should know its limits."

Riestel stared at the softly dimming horizon and the necklace of stars that slowly appeared.

"That might have been the most painful thing you have ever said to me."

"I'm sorry."

"No... you are right. She loved me. She sacrificed me to her secret ideals and plans. If she had truly chosen me, she would have confided in me. We could have found another way. Isa..." Riestel whispered and turned to me. His blue eyes darkened to a hue of a deep forest lake with dots of starshine.

"Yes?" I breathed.

"Here comes the stove!" Veitso shouted from the stairs. "And the tent!"

Riestel remained silent and turned away. The formed guardsmen erected the tent and stove with extreme efficiency. Soon, the stove had a lively fire going whereupon a small kettle was perched, and the contents were just coming to a boil.

"It will be ruined soon," Samedi noted.

"No, it won't. It needs a bit of a kick. Otherwise, it will be just like one of your delicate perfumes," Veitso educated him. "What is the point of drinking the dreamer's bark if you don't want it to kick in the head a little?"

"What plant is that?" I asked.

"Oh, umm... a willow of some kind, I think. Definitely looks like one, a droopy-branched small tree. The bark relaxes or energizes depending on the way you prepare it," Veitso explained. "It's commonly used at the borders. The army plants them where they go. It's a little less horrible losing a hand to a field hacker when you are dreaming of a water maiden."

"Or it might make the whole world melt..." Tammaran muttered. "It isn't pleasant for all."

"And that's why you aren't getting any," Veitso noted.

"I wouldn't take it to save my life," Tammaran replied. You could see the disgust he felt.

"What about the Consecratoress? Interested?" Veitso offered.

"I don't think I need it. I have enough problems with this world. So, doesn't this count against your promise to stay sober?"

"It's not alcohol, is it?" Veitso remarked happily. "It's my sleep remedy. I can't sleep without it. Not since the border."

"Quite a few have to use it for the rest of their lives," Samedi said. "Rime is probably the only one of us that never tried it for the nightmares."

"What does it do to you?" I asked.

"Nothing nice," Samedi yawned and stretched his neck. "Let's say I become a little too much like my late aunt Yannit than anyone cares to witness."

"I see," I replied and shook my head as I remembered trying to negotiate with her during the city siege.

The scent of the drink was pleasant in the air. Light, honey-like. The thought of it fascinated me, but fear or reason won. Riestel declined the liquid before Veitso even had the chance to offer it to him. The longer I breathed in the notes of mead and violets, the sleepier I got. I leaned back and laid my head on the cushion.

"My child... My, what a long way you have traveled," a sweet voice whispered. *"Remember, the harvest comes."*

I shot up with a clammy sweat. Everyone else slept. The slightly lighter morning sky greeted me through a slit in the tent. I squeezed my hands. Had I dreamed or had Istrata talked to me again? I had thought it couldn't happen after the last statue. It would mean a part of her was conscious and waiting. The thought of the Queen in deep slumber had been much more comforting.

I got up and put my coat on. The fresh, slightly icy air banished all remnants of sleep, but not the worry they had brought.

"You're looking pale," Tammaran noted as he sat on the wall.

"Bad night."

"You slept very peacefully."

"Can you see the quality of the dreams, too?"

"Well, no. Nightmares?"

"I think so. I can't remember that much. I don't know if I want to. Can the mere smell of the bark cause people to have vivid dreams?" I asked.

"Perhaps, if you are sensitive to it. It is pretty potent, especially when Veitso brews it."

"I see the convoy is moving again. What are those carriages? They look like cages," I changed the subject.

"They are cages," Tammaran confirmed and looked down with disdain. "A wedding gift, no doubt. We are dealing with nobles."

As I squinted, a ray of sun hit the figures in the cages. A bright, piercing dot of light blinded me for a moment.

"What on earth are they wearing?" I asked as Riestel joined us.

"They are arochs," Riestel said as he stretched. "Their armor scales can be as glossy as glass."

"Arochs…" I whispered. I couldn't look away from the carriages even though the sun kept hitting my eyes. I felt oddly giddy.

"Have you met any?" I asked.

"Well, yes, I mean they are the ones we fight with at the borders," Tammaran answered. "Unfortunately."

"A few times, peacefully," Riestel replied. "Most don't talk our language. You need to communicate with images with them."

"How?" Tammaran and I asked in unison.

"I'm hardly encouraging you to kindle a friendship with the sacrifices, but I can see you are set on it already… You can talk to them by drawing in the Lighter World. Pictures, not words. I've only heard of a few arochs that can talk. Or maybe they can talk among themselves and just don't bother to try with us unless they see we have command of the different levels."

"Don't bother to… The teacher Frazil hired for me always said they are a simple rural folk. No buildings or any such signs of civilization," I recalled.

"They have their own beliefs and their own wisdom. They do not need buildings when they live as they do," Riestel noted. "It is, of course, ever so handy to paint your opponent as easy prey, but I'd like to point out that, despite all our advances, the army of this world has lost as many battles as won when facing them."

"That… is true," Tammaran chimed in. "Maybe we win a little more often.

We wouldn't have the borders we have now, if that wasn't the case, but no battle was easy. I've always found it odd that numerically there are supposed to be scattered tribes and that they are slow to carry and grow children, but we never seem to make a dent in their numbers. After a battle, there is always a new group ready. But I wonder who is dumb enough to bring them into the city, if they get loose..."

"I doubt they'd do anything," Riestel said. "Unless someone offers them a way to save their face. Their fighters and people would rather die than be captured, and if they do get captured, they do not usually fight execution, as they deem it as punishment for their lack of skill."

"I cannot understand an attitude like that..." I pondered. I didn't like that our guests were bringing prisoners into this city for toys. But I hated the subservient attitude Riestel described. If the arochs weren't going to lift a finger to help themselves, I certainly would if I could reach them and get them to trust me.

"Don't act alone," Riestel demanded.

"Why would you help?" I sneered.

"Why wouldn't I help? You are my favorite thing in this city."

Tammaran got almost startled at Riestel's words and stared at us.

"Well, that's not a lot, as you never like anything in principle," I remarked to Riestel and glared at Tammaran. Tammaran pursed his lips and then relaxed.

"I always forget how long you have known each other. I'll go and see if Frazil requires us. The convoy is getting close," Tammaran excused himself.

As Tammaran woke the rest of the Black Guard and dragged them with him, we gazed at the swaying cages.

"How are the arochs connected to Istrata?"

"She visited them. I did too. They have their own unique look on the world. I can repair my body because of the knowledge they shared. Istrata had a moment of respite with them and forged a peace for her time. I'm not sure why it shattered after her death. Might be worthwhile to look into."

XXVI

T he whole gate square was bustling with people primping and posing among brightly colored decorations. Everyone was being positioned exactly according to Frazil's wishes based on rank and presentability. He was beaming with the same enthusiasm as when he got to move his miniatures around on maps. Everything was falling into place. For a moment I wanted his victory to be a little less perfect, but I had managed to get him to back down when it came to the Peak. Perhaps that was enough of a gray cloud over this triumph for now.

The official entrance to the city didn't have a name. It was just referred to as a gate like all the other gates in the city, but it was, in fact, a massive corridor with four large consecutive gates. Cumbersomely, they began to creak open, one after the other. The hinges and cogs whined for a moment before they were drowned out by brass instruments. The last of the crafters were forced into their houses. The looks on the soldiers' faces weren't one of pride when they did so. But they did. I suppose the local residents might offend the delicate aesthetic sensibilities of the rulers should they remain seen.

Frazil postured among his bodyguards in the middle of the square. If Rime had been here, he would have complained about taking such risks. But one had to admit, despite of the state of the city, the reception was impressive. Hundreds of soldiers in uniform, the Temple's representatives in their temple clothes with a backdrop of glimmering, multicolored nobles all gathered to support Frazil gave off an image of opulence and unity.

Two gray horses with ornate feathers and bridles appeared. One had the color of red cherries, the other grassy greens. The riders directed them to the sides of the gate. Five similar pairs followed, and each took a position like the first had to form the beginning of a circle. Long lines of guards with of red or green lined jackets completed the circle before a carriage of silver and gold roses was pulled to the square. After that followed the cages, soldiers, and servants.

"The green are from Eladion, red from Loisto," Riestel whispered. "But note how similar they look otherwise."

The city's styles departed less from each other than any parts of Kerth. They were more loyal to each other than to Aderas. That was the reason this marriage was so important to Frazil. If he had sway on the other city, he had sway on them both.

An avalanche of finery and satin burst out of the silver carriage. All women had very slick costumes that emphasized every curve. They also wore trains. The men's tunics had odd lumps on their shoulders to make them look wider. All wore decorations only in the color of the city they came from, whether it was a piece of jewelry, a ribbon, or a feather. Only two of the men wore hats with feathers. The Governor of Loisto was a slightly grayed out man who leaned forward onto a cane. His eyes were dark and lively. The Governor of Eladion was years younger. His straw-colored hair drooped on his shoulders, and his pale, empty eyes revealed nothing of his character.

Frazil stepped out to meet them with open arms. Gifts and compliments were exchanged in abundance. My gaze was more drawn to the prisoners. The arochs sat with their backs to the bars so I couldn't see their faces. Their skin and metallic, scale-like bumps glistened in various hues among their clothes that were made of leather straps and metallic fastenings. The most prevalent colors were light coppers and silvers. They were clearly larger than us. Their hair looked almost like coarse bristles. I wished to go closer, but Frazil probably wouldn't have appreciated the attention that might draw.

We stood a good while as ornaments. Finally, Frazil's lengthened, eight-wheeled blue and gold carriage was driven to the square. It took twelve horses to pull it. He presented his wife and daughters to the guests. The men showered Ghila with compliments and wonder. Then they entered the carriage.

"Don't we even get an introduction?" one of the senior military personnel muttered. "Why are we here, then? The Field Marshall was right…"

Others nodded. The man who made the comment glanced at me and saluted. I acknowledged it. It was rather daunting to think Rime could challenge his father openly. That could be a mess we wouldn't be able to clear in decades. The family would be shattered and all the peace and stability in the city gone. It was still hard to ignore how much some of Frazil's actions rubbed people the wrong way after they had been promised changes.

We journeyed through the night. This time there were no shortcuts but a long, winding route to showcase the city. The roads were colored with lanterns, fabrics, and soldiers. I had no patience to sit in a carriage for days on end, so I switched at times to horseback with Riestel and the Guard. We traveled a little faster than most so we could catch up with the prisoners.

The arochs sat in almost identical postures as yesterday. They didn't move at all and ignored all curious enough to approach. Once we got closer, about a horse's length away, I could see their hair was nothing like ours. It consisted of metallic bristles or nail-like layers.

One aroch raised its head. There were odd markings in its metallic parts. Small, regularly shaped indents in the middle of beautiful, angular etchings. The yellow eyes bore into me. I lowered my gaze because I didn't know how to greet them. But I didn't manage to look away for long. Now, most of the arochs had turned to look at us.

"Why are they staring at me?" I asked Riestel.

"Well, not for your looks."

I punched him in the arm. Riestel laughed and rubbed it. Veitso, riding on our right side, was shocked.

"Maybe there's hope for you yet as you notice when others don't behave," Samedi mused and patted Veitso's shoulder. Riestel paid neither any mind.

"The arochs can sense the Lighter World. We are always connected to it. They recognize consecrators because of it," Riestel explained.

"What are those holes? They don't look natural."

"They've probably housed jewels."

"Do they grow jewels on their skin?"

"Don't be silly. They are imbedded for appearance."

"I think that was a rather justified question," I muttered and flinched. Had someone ripped them out? I felt the violation as an almost physical disgust. The slender aroch missing the jewels kept studying me. I touched my forehead as I felt uncomfortably lightheaded.

"Everything okay?" Tammaran asked.

"A stubbled man with pliers. Unclean," I mumbled. "Why am I seeing that?"

I looked at the aroch who was abused. My head filled with flames and uncertainty. I nodded slightly, though I wasn't sure the aroch would understand the gesture. At that moment, each of them turned to me with a quick jerk which didn't go unnoticed by others present. A few of Loisto's soldiers hurried their pace to catch up to the carriage and settle the prisoners down. When the slenderest of the arochs noticed them, they all returned to their sulking postures. I didn't feel or see anything else.

"I can't let them be butchered," I whispered to Riestel.

"You have no authority to order them to relinquish their prey. Frazil won't either. He is too close to take chances."

"I may not be able to demand their lives to be spared, but I can free them by force."

"Would you use your powers for them against your own people?" Riestel asked with a curious smile. "What if they fight you with weapons? Are you willing to use souls to kill people for them?"

I lowered my gaze. The questions were good and just. Why were the arochs more important than my people? And still, something within me nagged they were, at least for my future. Perhaps because of their connection to Istrata, perhaps not. Would they even know about her and the whole issue after so many years?

"I have to talk to them at least," I decided and pressed my finger on Riestel's nose. "Shut it. I remember you said they don't actually talk."

Riestel took my hand in his and moved my finger to his lips.

"I wouldn't scold you for that, would I?" he lied with a honeyed voice looking pleased with himself and let go. I stared at my hand, as I could still feel his touch on it. After a few heartbeats, I pulled my hand back. I made a fist and pressed it against my chest.

We had our first extended period of rest in the Soldier's. Frazil escorted his guests to the Governor's Palace. No one outside the immediate family had been introduced to the guests, apart from getting named and pointed at as they walked by. The military escort was happy to be relieved from their duties. Their services weren't needed, now that we had passed the Lowers.

I sat by the fire with the guard members. They had behaved much more demurely after the guests had arrived.

"Should we just go and introduce ourselves?" Samedi pondered. "It feels silly to just tag along."

"No," Tammaran replied. "Rime told us to keep out of it and let Frazil dictate the pace."

"Why?" Veitso asked. "We are governors, though temporary."

"Because that would signal that we wish to be introduced and would give him the power to grant it or refuse it," Tammaran explained. "We are playing with images."

"I'd rather be on a battlefield," Veitso grunted and went to get a drink which in his words contained so little alcohol it didn't really count.

"What else has Rime asked of you?" I enquired. Tammaran changed his position.

"Nothing else. He wants to see how Frazil behaves without any control or pressure. We are just to follow and see."

"Are you truthful?"

"I am," he answered, a little annoyed. "I'm not saying he might not have other plans. I'm simply saying, I don't know at the moment."

I wanted to push a little more, but Tammaran would never let Rime down even if there was something to share. Though I didn't appreciate being cast aside by Frazil, it would be better if everything calmed down for a while. My biggest fear was that it would be exposed that Frazil took the child to hold over us. The family was already gone, but I worried that Rime would feel such anger at his father that it would destabilize him and cause new problems with the hunger or a permanent change in his character, as Moras had warned.

It was certainly possible that Rime's people would figure it out, but then it wouldn't come as one big shock but as a ripple of clues and their conclusion, so the emotions were unlikely to boil over.

"Consecratoress," Frazil's chamberlain called. "Governor Laukas would ask you to join them for a moment."

"Fine."

"Please follow."

"Riestel, will you come?"

"I'm sorry… the invitation was only for…" the chamberlain squirmed.

"I'm not here as an individual. If an invitation is given, it is given to the Temple," I corrected him. "Coming or not?"

Riestel stood up, exaggeratedly slowly.

"Certainly, since I'm so welcome," he yawned. "Or are you the one to stop me?" he added and poked the chamberlain's forehead with his icy finger. The chamberlain's hair frosted.

We stepped in from the cool evening to an opulent library room decorated in hues of burned earth. Frazil, his family, and their guests were sipping some beverage and a polite, but not genuine, laughter punctuated their discussion. The chamberlain scampered to Frazil and gestured at us.

"Get an extra glass then," Frazil ordered. "And a chair."

"No need, I'd rather stand. I don't think we will linger," Riestel declined.

"As you wish. And the Consecratoress?"

"No, thank you, I'd rather stick to the provisions," I said, knowing full well what a double standard it was to scold them about what I had done myself. But it was one of those moments in which a little mischief was to be had. A few of the guests gazed at the floor in a show of some humility and shame.

"Such moral nonsense", the older, partly bald and grumpy looking governor spat. "You temple folk are such sourpusses."

"What my traveling companion, Governor Vuole, means…" the younger hurried to make amends, "is that I'm sure one or two little moments will hardly spoil everything. I'm sure we all take some liberties when we aren't watched. I'm Eladion's Governor Lander Edel. At your service."

"Of course, and I'm not denying such tendencies, but right now, I feel no need for indulgence. I am not here as a free individual but on duty. Why was I summoned? Hardly for company. We are not very close after all, and this gathering seems like a family matter."

Frazil frowned for a fleeting moment. It was hard to tell whether it was annoyance at my behavior or a slight tinge of guilt.

"You know why," Frazil begun. "My daughter is to fasten herself with Lander. They wish you to perform the ceremony."

"Oh, really? Why me? Why would you not insist on a consecrator that is capable of something beautiful and delicate?"

"Your position. There is no one more suited for a day of such importance," Lander assured with a smile. His sunny face was surrounded by a fluffy cloud of hair now that the hat was gone. His skin had a yellow sheen, and I could smell a pungent sweat I'd normally associate with older people.

"I understand that, but I feel I am not a proper choice."

"Trust me, you do not want her blessing," Riestel remarked as he browsed the books in the room.

"Is this still about my offense against you?" Frazil asked. "I realize we were intrusive regarding the Peak. I underestimated its meaning to you. But please do not hold a grudge for that. Not against my family. Show my daughter some good faith," he continued with a tone suitable for trying to bridle a wild horse and lowered his hand on my shoulder. "We are family, after all."

I didn't react, though I hated those words which were purely meant to manipulate me. I was sick and tired of everyone trying to sway me into doing things they needed. To guide the poorly little girl. I stared at the entourage. Humans… Was this all of them? Was there anyone who thought I wasn't just a thing to use? Riestel swatted Frazil's hand away, keeping his eyes on the book, and stepping between us. He turned his back on Frazil.

"I'm going to object on the Temple's behalf. It will cause a stir among the superstitious," Riestel said, as if he was barely aware of what had been discussed. He raised the book he had been browsing in front of me. "Studies of the Arochs." I took it from him.

"Why is that?" Lander asked. "Why would it be wrong to use her?"

"The previous couple I joined. The man ended up hanged from one of the inner walls. It is common gossip in the city," I said.

"Oh…" Lander sighed and fiddled with his necklace of Saraste. It was so quiet I could hear my own blood.

"Then… I'm sorry, my future family, but it might not be the best idea. I do not want to cause trouble right at the start, but Eladion might not accept a union blessed by a person who has caused death. Gods judge less than men."

"She isn't directly responsible for that, my goodness, it was the war!" Frazil huffed and spread his arms.

"My people might not see it like that," Lander said and looked torn. "No, it could cause much grumbling. I do not like the idea. And you, Consecrator Aravas? I understand you are the manifestation of the most holy."

Riestel glanced at the man and chortled.

"The Peak itself will fall before I wed a pair. I have even more blood on my hands," Riestel replied with a smile. "And there might be more soon."

"I know of one wonderful option," I hurried to interject before Frazil would have time to break Lander's hesitancy. "There is one Maida's consecratoress who is a sanctifier as I am. She is young but a very talented dancer and would bring with her only blessings and luck."

"Is she just a regular? Shouldn't we at least have a teacher level individual?" Lander wondered.

"She is to become a teacher. If you aren't planning on having the fasting ceremony tomorrow, we can promote her to a satisfactory level."

"Could we meet her first?" Lander asked. His future relatives and his bride remained silent but exchanging concerned looks.

"Naturally. I will arrange it when we reach the Peak. Was this all? I would like to return to my friends," I asked.

Frazil nodded toward the door. A second small victory for me. For my independence. I had helped Frazil climb to his dreams and gained much by helping him, but it felt like a thing of the past. I might not have been a queen in this life, not even the Temple's head or a teacher, but that was no reason to keep bowing to those with such titles.

In the morning, we continued among the parade. In the Merchant's, the guests were showered with gifts of all kinds. Though food was sparse, baubles were plenty. People flocked to see the slowly rolling prisoner carriages. The arochs hadn't paid much attention to me after that one time. I did still catch the slenderest sometimes looking at me.

In the Noble's, the reception was lukewarm. Simew's family didn't care to court the guests and the rest of the subjugated families followed their example obediently. There were still some performers, refreshments, and gifts left to us along the way, but knowing what the nobles were capable of, these seemed haphazard and less than impressive. I should thank the Maherols.

The Temple, on the other hand, greeted us so enthusiastically that our journey was delayed by all kinds of dance and song performances. To such an extent, that Riestel swore he'd freeze them for all eternity. We stopped to rest at the main temple. The facade had been redone and patched as well as possible. The eastern parts were still mostly rubble.

Riestel walked the ruins with me. As the birds sang, I found shards of glass from my old room.

"Did you tell Irinda to redecorate the room with a theme of irises? It seems odd that out of all the possible flowers, those were picked."

"I might have mentioned I had heard you had a penchant for them."

"Istrata had. They were blue ones."

"You do not need to keep stressing your differences. Why couldn't you enjoy beautiful things? You don't need to hate everything she held pretty or enjoyed."

"I know," I replied and picked up a shard. I looked through the violet-colored glass at Frazil's group walking further away in the garden while he was painting them a vivid picture of the battle. At least that was my guess from his gestures. A servant walked behind the ladies holding a parasol. The glass glinted. The servant's head turned to me and even from this distance, I saw Irinda's face, then mine. I jumped up and dropped the glass. A lazy, dark blood drop inched its way out of my finger. I wiped it on my mouth. As I looked at the group again, I could see the servant wasn't even a woman.

"What in the skies are you doing?" Riestel scolded me. "You are as pale as the dead."

"The glass just distorted things. I thought there was something there that wasn't."

"And you are seriously thinking I will take that explanation?"

"Well, I was hoping you'd prove a gentleman and acknowledge I have no desire to talk about it."

"You know very well I haven't an ounce of gentleman in me."

"The servant. When looking through the glass, I saw Irinda's face, then mine on him."

Riestel didn't reply right away. He nodded for us to walk into a more concealed corner of the park.

"I don't understand it. Why show herself to you? Does she still need you?" he wondered.

"To get her way peacefully, perhaps. You did say she always thinks of her people. If she can get me to agree or think like her so that I will surrender once she comes for me, there will be no need to fight and fewer people suffer."

"True. I wonder how long she's been able to reach out? Or has there always been an ounce of her present when you've spoken to the statues?"

"I think that might be true. Would you have liked to hear from her?"

"Maybe. Mostly to wish her a long journey to the bottom of the ocean. Preferably tied to a rock."

I grinned and patted Riestel's back. He gave me a sharp glance.

"What was that for?" he asked.

"For believing you. Though I have absolutely no faith in that you'd manage it with that little emotion. She is Elona's mother and the love of your life, after all."

"One of those statements is true," Riestel sighed. "The other I'm too tired to argue about. Maybe later."

"You grew up together, fell in love, knew each other…"

"You know that isn't true. All of what I've learned of her now… I was just a tool in the end."

"I told you ages ago that she loved you at the moment of her death. I wouldn't lie about it even if you'd betray me in the end because of it."

"And yet, I feel that I lost her much earlier than that. The moment she took the throne. She might have loved me, even deeply, but not as much as she loved her ideals. I was just too stupid to see that."

"Riestel…"

"This bitter old man is going to go and rest now," he scoffed and started to walk away. Then he turned and looked back. The setting sun gilded his eyes and skin.

"She must be stopped. Whatever she will offer… do not listen," he asked.

XXVII

The formed yard of the main temple and the current field with its trampled plants filled with encampment tents like mushrooms sprouting after the rain. Arochs were in the middle of their guards. Sneaking through wasn't going to be an option. Not even among all the snoring. The guards near the carriage were very alert, and there were enough to deter any too curious busybodies. And I didn't want to give any hint to Frazil that I was interested in the arochs. The timing still seemed opportune.

"Watch me," I told Rime's Black Guard. "I'm heading to the between."

I leaned on Tammaran as if I would have prepared to take a nap. I stepped into the mouse, as I didn't want the arochs to know about me right away, either. I wanted to observe them for a moment. I scurried towards them through the between. I could see the normal world from there. I would dodge boots on instinct as if they were capable of hurting me.

Once I had the carriage in my sight, I stopped. The arochs didn't have clouds of energy like us. They looked nearly as they did in the heavier world. With one exception. Sparkling strand-like currents crisscrossed between them and as far as the horizon. They carried patterns and pictures. Was that their speech?

I climbed to the top of the wheel. Some of the arochs seemed to rouse to my presence. They seemed to smell the air and turned their heads. The slender one stood up. I pressed myself flat, but the aroch locked eyes with me. They all turned to me in unison. The strands between them pulsated brighter. In the other world, the guards backed from the cage a little, wondering why their behavior changed.

The slender one came closer and pressed against the bars. She looked at me inquisitively and reached out. Pictures of broken weapons tossed on the ground filled my head. I got on her hand. When I was in the body of the mouse, I also instinctively sniffed things. It was a strange way to gather information. A rush of joy coming from the aroch surprised me. She lifted me up to her face and pointed her index finger at me. It brushed my fur like a feather. A small strand formed between us. Between me and Arid. That was her name. She nodded.

When the arochs noticed, I understood them at least a little, but the flood of images became too intense. A pulse shot out from Arid and everyone became still and mute. With pictures and gestures, Arid told me how they had been sent on a journey from their home. Here. To see the fire replica. To talk to it. That was why they had surrendered when the convoy had come upon them. Why did humans treat their prisoners so poorly? I couldn't answer that, nor many of her other questions.

After several attempts to communicate things, Arid showed me opening the cage and letting them go. It wasn't easy to answer her because I didn't know what I would do yet and that even if I were to help them, I couldn't do it now. I pointed at the guards around us and tried to imagine days changing. I showed them the Peak. It was in all scenarios the first place where I could help them without significant repercussions.

Arid squinted and looked at the Peak, then she nodded stiffly. The arochs became more at peace and sat back into their usual positions. Arid lowered me on the wheel, but before she turned away, she showed me a picture of herself. In each of the cavities in her metallic parts, there had been an extravagant jewel. They had been torn off on the way here. She wished to get them back.

On returning to my body, I had no idea what I'd do. Was saving them worth messing up the city right at the cusp of peace and restoration? I looked at them. The arochs sat hunched, looking sad and so much smaller than they were. I wouldn't be able to make any decision about them based on this kind of small visit.

Yet... this was my city, my people. How could I justify pushing it ever closer to constant chaos by defying Frazil again? My previous acts of defiance had been personal, affecting mostly his family and only known by a few people. This would be rebellion. It wasn't a decision I could make alone. But how could I tell Rime why I feared going against Frazil?

We rode at the head of the convoy for the rest of the way as I didn't want to see the arochs for the moment. I didn't want to give them too much hope before I had decided what I would do. Once the gate to the Peak opened, the convoy stopped out of surprise. There was nothing greeting us on the other side. No people, no decorations, nothing.

One guard ran to Frazil's carriage to report on the matter. Then we continued. When we had left from here, the servants had just started with the decorations on our route. In other words, they had been ordered to stop and also to undo all that had been done. My heart shivered. Would this result in an argument between Frazil and Rime? Rime couldn't win this battle if he wanted his child back, but I had kept that information from him.

I leaned on the saddle and buried my face in my hands. I needed to stop them from exacerbating the situation. Why did Rime have to constantly test his father? He had assured that he didn't wish to take the crown or to challenge it. Then why go through all this? It bothered me.

"Child, do not worry, all evil can be left behind," Istrata's voice whispered. *"Allow me to offer a road where no one needs to suffer new heartaches."*

"Leave me be!" I ordered.

Her laughter rippled around me for a moment.

"Isa?" Tammaran called. Most of the surrounding convoy stared at me.

"Spring mosquitos… I hate them…" I made an excuse and waved my hand, smiling. It seemed to placate most watching as they turned back to their own duties, muttering something about overly sensitive cuddled nobles. Tammaran certainly could tell I was lying, but he was reasonable enough not to ask.

"There we go," Riestel complimented me. "Not that anyone thought you were sane."

"And your reputation is admirable, I suppose?" I remarked.

I stayed as quiet as possible as the journey continued. Frazil had changed to horseback after the news and rode right at the front. He was anything but pleased. The Peak's planned resting stop opened in front of us. There were some tables without any particularly comfortable seats. The food served was plain, though of good quality.

Frazil spoke to his guards. One of them rode off toward the Needle. Soon, we got the order to march through the night. None of the esteemed guests wanted to sleep outside or spent an evening lacking entertainment.

Riestel spoke to, or threatened, some of the guards to get us a moment of respite in one of the carriages heated by a small brazier. I was grateful for it, as all this traveling was more taxing than I wanted to admit. Riestel leaned back and closed his eyes. My thoughts wouldn't calm down. Riestel's steady breath peeved me. I poked him.

"I can't sleep."

"Why am I punished because of it?" he muttered and opened his eyes. "Sit next to me then."

"Why?"

"I'll help you sleep."

I switched my place. Riestel took off the collar of his coat. He folded it on his lap and put his hand on my neck. With a few light touches and low notes, I fell into his lap. Riestel guided my head gently to the pillow made from his collar and stroked the arc of my ear. I closed my eyes, lulled into a perfect feeling of safety.

A quiet, hesitant group stopped at the Needle late the next morning. A few guards stood in the middle of the vast stone yard and by the doors, as usual. Nothing gave any clue that anyone expected guests. As we got out, Riestel went to another larger carriage to get Elona. She was happy to be at home. She had found all this traveling quite boring just sitting in a carriage so he had placed her with the children of the nobles to pass the time.

Frazil gave his servants all sorts of orders. They soon vanished into the building. Frazil gave me a somber look just before closing the door but didn't seem to blame me for this.

"Should we follow them to Rime?" I asked Tammaran.

"I'd certainly like to," Samedi said from behind. Tammaran and Veitso nodded. We left everything to the servants and hurried inside after Frazil and his guests. They headed towards the governmental wing.

Everyone stuffed themselves into Rime's half-circle shaped, light blue office that was furnished very similarly with dark wooden furniture as Commander Maril's in the Merchant's. The desk might have been the same, some of the objects on it definitely were. Despite all the people and sudden noise, Rime didn't look up from his papers.

"Marshall Fall," Frazil called out in a strained but polite tone. "I would urge you to salute our guests."

Rime lifted his left hand and its index finger but still didn't look at us. If I hadn't been worried about the consequences, I might have laughed.

Rime turned the last page, signed it, and sealed it, then he got up, bowed courteously and deeper than he usually did.

"I humbly and warmly welcome the representatives of Eladion and Loisto," Rime said and straightened up. He smiled with such confidence that I blushed, even though it wasn't directed at me. Frazil was almost as red as I, but for a very different reason. Still, it was difficult to admonish and lay blame on someone who, after almost snubbing them, opened his mouth with such politeness without seeming petty.

"Why have none of the arrangements been made? I'm extremely disappointed that our guests were denied the opportunity to see the Peak in all its beauty," Frazil complained.

"The Peak is impressive as it is. I made the decision after you had set out on the base of the newest cost and consumption reports. I trust our visitors to be intelligent and compassionate enough to understand Kerth's value without frivolous shows. And I have not canceled the entertainment and festivities planned here on their arrival. Just the journey. I thought it better to scale back on these things than the fasting ceremony," Rime explained. "Edel... and Vuole... Been a while," he continued and greeted them warmly.

The governors were eager to exchange a few words. It was easy to deduct that Rime had been in contact with them during his time on the Borders. Tammaran, Samedi, and Veitso also greeted them with a bit more familiarity than one would have thought suitable for their ranks.

"Let's leave this room," Rime suggested. "I have ordered tea, pastries, and welcome drinks to the salon in the apartment you shall have to your own for your visit. This way, if you please, the future king is also warmly welcome to follow us with his family. There will be plenty for all. Isa, will you join me?" he asked and offered his arm. I hurried to his side and leaned on him a little. I would have liked to embrace him, but I settled for squeezing his hand as we led the procession towards the eastern wing.

I couldn't stop myself from glancing back. Frazil and his family walked at the very back. Friti's eyes measured us with a cold anger, and she quite likely whispered fantastical curses into her husband's ear concerning us. Their daughters were in a cheerful mood. Frazil answered all questions politely, but not in his usual jovial manner.

"Alright, here we are," Rime announced and pushed the guest wing door open. We were greeted by the smell of mint tea and cinnamon. The servants made the final touches by setting the tables with painted porcelain and silver spoons. Then they disappeared into the walls. The governors all sat around the round table which was decorated with gold-threaded lace cloth. The rest of us found our places among the tables with regular white lace.

Veitso looked painfully out of place at the table. It was a smidgen too low for him and the chair a little too dainty. He was agile enough to not wreak a world of havoc, trying to inch himself to a proper position. The chair squeaked a melancholy note, residing in its fate.

A male servant cleared out the unneeded chairs and served tea. No one spoke. Everyone waited. The longer the silence lingered, the more uncomfortable Frazil's daughters looked. They fiddled with their sleeves and kept arranging their skirts. The younger's leg trembled, making the lace cloth move.

"Should the happy couple-to-be sit together?" Rime suggested.

"Yes, I would indeed like to talk to Ghila," Lander jumped at the opportunity, looking at her.

"Would that suit the bride's father?" Rime asked.

Frazil nodded, and Lander changed tables.

"Isa, I haven't seen you for a while. Take his place," Rime ordered. "We will all soon be related so we can ease up on the customs," Rime continued in a strangely warm and open manner.

We continue the game of chairs until all were seated where they wished. I forgot to eat as I kept looking at Rime's hand next to mine on the table. I liked tracing its lines and comparing the hue of his skin, which was warmer and more sun kissed, to mine.

"Wife…" he called.

"Yes?"

"I missed you," Rime said, smiled, and bent close. He gave a gentle peck on the lips in front of everyone. My face flushed. I smelled smoke and quickly put out the tablecloth. It had been a long time since I had lost control of my emotions. It was a happy thing to know I could still feel such fresh infatuation towards him. But the bubbling joy didn't mask the embarrassment that I felt wafting the curls of smoke away from the table.

"Can you come and see me tonight?" I whispered.

"I can. You won't believe it, but I'm planning to work only half days for a while."

"I didn't know that was possible."

"I know I've neglected us for a time. The night... Riestel arranged," Rime said in a hushed voice. "It made me remember that there is still more to life than this city."

"Well, if that was the result, I'm very pleased," I grinned and moved my hand to his thigh.

Rime bit his lower lip.

"You always have to choose the most awkward moments to tease me."

"I have absolutely no idea what you mean."

Frazil cleared his throat and snapped his fingers at us.

"Could I now receive a more thorough explanation of the reason for the cancellation and all the changes?" he insisted. "I should also like to know if anything of importance happened while I was away."

"Nothing that hasn't been settled already," Rime answered without looking at his father. "You are free to read all papers and reports of taken actions whenever you wish. They are on your table waiting to be filed."

"Good," Frazil replied without seeming pleased at all. "And the arrangements for the fasting ceremony?"

"I haven't laid a finger on them. They are a family matter," Rime said as he went to get a refill. "I only deal with the issues that are mine to deal with," he added and patted Loisto's ruler, Governor Vuole, on the shoulder in a familiar manner. Vuole touched his hand in response.

"Better that you don't. I should not like to see Lander and Ghila disappointed with anything," Frazil remarked and smiled coldly but politely to Lander, who nodded happily as he took his eyes off his bride for a moment. Ghila was focused on staying in a good posture, nodding, and fixing her hair whenever Lander didn't look. I had never heard Frazil's daughters speak of anything of importance or to ask questions. Was it a show or had Frazil left them uneducated apart from the basics to control them easier?

"Why would the esteemed Governor think I have any interest in meddling with his daughter's life? Someone here has to focus on ruling," Rime said. The room fell silent from the poisonous words. Frazil lowered his cup exaggeratedly slowly.

"Son, I cannot say what is spurring this attitude on, but you do not wish to pick a fight with me."

"You read too much into words. If I was picking a fight with you, I wouldn't use my words. You do remember that I'm a soldier, not a weak-wristed noble."

"Could someone tell me about the prisoners?" I almost yelped before Frazil could open his mouth. "They are fascinating. Who caught them?"

"My soldiers came upon them halfway here," Lander confessed. "That reminds me. I brought some courting gifts. Would this be a permissible moment to hand them out?"

Frazil leaned back stiffly and nodded.

"What will their fate be?" I asked. "Why did you bring them here?"

"We are descendants of the nobles of Kerth. Our traditions are quite similar. The fasting will have games," Lander explained, going through his pockets. "We thought, considering the state of things, it would be more appropriate to use prisoners of war than people of your city."

"What a lovely gesture," Friti praised him. "What a thoughtful man Ghila is fortunate enough to get."

"Here they are," Lander proclaimed and poured a bag of different colored shiny gems on the table. Friti and Ghila sighed in wonder. The feeling going through me was far from it. The shapes and colors matched those the aroch had shown me. The thought of them being dug and torn off from its skin disgusted me.

"Are they not a pleasing sight? I do realize they are a very unimaginative gift," Lander pondered with a pained look on his face.

"I wouldn't know. They are pretty," I said. "I just find myself wondering where they are from."

Lander didn't make an effort to answer.

"They are more than pretty," Friti hurried to say. "Perfect," she sighed, looking at one of them with a light source behind it and then testing it against her skin. "This yellow one would make a fine necklace. Would the smiths have time to fashion something for the ceremony of these?"

"Of course. That is what they are for," Frazil promised. "Take them with the girls and go and sketch. Our guests must surely wish to rest and have a moment to themselves after the journey."

"Well, I wouldn't mind a little peace and quiet," Vuole admitted.

"Good. Everyone out. We shall meet tomorrow at breakfast, and I shall arrange a tour of the Peak," Frazil decided. "Although I wish I could have shown it in a more festive look."

As we walked out of the room, Frazil grabbed my arm and pulled me to the side.

"You may not miss your child, so I accept that I cannot control you with it," Frazil forced the words out in a low voice. "But are you ready to gamble on his sanity? I know the delicate state he is in. Even if Moras has, for some reason, been useless as of late, he does still tell me things. If you want to shield him from a shock of a lifetime, I suggest you behave and urge him to obey. I gave you everything. I am fully prepared to take it back."

"I don't think you can. I just wish you would see that he isn't your enemy… but at this rate, you are going to make one of him or me," I replied.

XXVIII

I followed Rime to our small room in the Needle. As the door closed, he took off his jacket and sat on the bed. Frazil's threats echoed in my head. I could tell it had pained him to make that threat, but I had no doubt he would go through with it if he didn't see an option. Frazil had sought this for his entire adult life. We two meant nothing on that scale. I suppose that was the burden of those seeking the crown. People became expendable with power.

"What is it?" Rime asked, pulling his boots off.

"The gems. They were pulled from a living being," I explained, taking my clothes off.

"They were. But how would you know?"

"The aroch told me. They are here to talk to me."

Rime stared at me for a moment with his head tilted and then let out an amused sigh.

"I never know exactly what to expect when I leave you to your own devices, but I cannot say I would have ever guessed all the ways you can entangle yourself in everything."

"They prayed for their lives. They will be killed merely for customs on some stupid show of grandeur. They don't even know how cruel it will be. They think they are ordinary prisoners."

"What do they want to talk about? Is it about the Witch Queen?" Rime pondered as I slipped under the covers. He sat on the bed.

"Are you going to sleep here?" I asked.

"I thought I would. But if I'm not wanted..." he grinned and pretended to get up, but I stopped him. "Answer the question," he reminded, getting into bed. I pressed close to him and positioned my head below his chin.

"I believe it is about her."

"What will you do?"

"I don't know yet. If I help them… it will be a slap in Frazil's face on a whole different level. He wouldn't forgive that. It wouldn't be about insulting his personal honor. I'd be tampering with the glorious culmination of his plans or at least casting a long shadow on his victory day. What would your father do? Can you guess?"

"He will take it out on me. No doubt. He cannot do anything to you," Rime mused and stroked my head. "But I'm sturdy. Don't worry, whatever you do, I will weather the consequences if it benefits the city, or the world, I suppose. And if I can't… I will be of no danger to you. Not anymore. Look," he urged and showed his palms. There were small black dots in the middle.

"What are those?" I asked and touched his skin. A fear shot through me like a released bow. I pulled my hand back.

"A safety mechanism. Moras… He has partly proven his theory about a third plane. A heavy, painful world made purely out of this tar. The souls and life force are siphoned into that place when we eat. We use a certain part of the life force and then discard the rest. But as it is not a natural process, the energy or soul suffers and distorts. It gets pressed into this heavier world. The very first Knight of Saraste began it. The weight of the suffering caused it to form under all the other layers. But it is so very full these days, its spilling into this world. Now, if I think I'm losing control, I can reverse the flow and it will fill me."

"Fill you? But if it fills you, that darkness… If it charges through you…"

"The force will render me harmless," Rime said laconically. "It will make a statue of me. It will be fast. I won't suffer long."

"So… it will kill you. Eat you from the inside and spew the taint into this world through you," I specified. Rime nodded once and took my hand.

"It will do so slowly anyway," he answered. "The ritual we go through makes a forced connection to that heavy world. It began with the first knight of Saraste. It sucks in all that it can due to our equipment, but something always seeps into us as well. That is why so many of us have unstable personalities the older we get, even the ones who have eaten properly and in a controlled manner."

"All the animals he tested changed because of it…"

"I'm no rabbit," he reminded me. "And I'm not going anywhere for a long time still. I just wanted to, needed to, tell you the truth of what I can tell. And it is better that we know. Now we can try to find a way to stop it and how to turn it back to soul sand in the most efficient way."

I hid my face partly against him and the sheet. Rime held me a little tighter.

"Isa. We have years."

I nodded but within me opened a vast, hopeless chasm towards eternity and loneliness. At least we could be together now. To sleep next to each other. I had missed having the warmth of his body next to me and waking up to him staring at me or the ceiling waiting for me to wake up. The price was just too much.

I wanted to shout at him. To scold him for making a decision like this, but in the end, it was his decision to make. Not mine. Knowing this made Frazil's threats more substantial. If Rime would fear losing himself, he'd use the mechanism. He was so disciplined I had no doubt he could sacrifice himself to prevent further damage if he realized he was about to lose control.

"What will you do about your father? You antagonized him directly today."

"I can protect us from him. I just need to test one thing. I want to know if I'm completely replaceable to him. Once I have my answer, I will talk him down."

"If you will swallow your pride and make amends anyway, do you think you'll be able to do so if I help the arochs?"

"I'd rather save lives than take them," he sighed. "However talented I may be at it. If you are going to do something, do so with my blessing."

"No matter what the results?"

"I trust that if you do something, you will do it out of necessity. My life isn't worth the world, not even the city."

His answer made me even more undecided, as the responsibility was now solely mine. It would have been easier if he had just forbidden it. I wished he had. In some way, I didn't want to cause any more trouble for anyone, and in some way, I felt compelled as if anything I did would lead to it.

Rime stretched and fell asleep quickly. I held his hand and stared at the ceiling in the dim room. Fighting with myself on whether to tell Rime about Frazil. I had planned on it before he told me about the safety mechanism. It was more terrifying to me than him losing control. How worried must they have been to concoct such a method to stop him? How much Rime had to fear losing control to allow himself an option to die like that? I stroked his peaceful face. He smiled. Of course, he would choose this way. He would never give up control, unlike I often did, just floating where the current took me.

So, what would Frazil do? If we disobeyed him now, what would be the consequence? He wouldn't kill the child. He didn't have it in him, but was that a miscalculation I was willing to live with? He wouldn't kill Rime unless he would become a direct threat. Maybe not even then. I was the final item on his list. My destiny would be to be chained in some contraption built by Moras and to be used rather than killed.

I couldn't help but think of Heelis. She had sat quite a while in jail by now. It made me uncomfortable. Especially now that her warnings of Frazil came true. It irked me to no end. But was I ready to say that I would have sided with Irinda if I had known all that would happen? No. I would have ended up a well-kept pet with her.

Rime turned to his side. I rested my head against his back. Against the warm skin, I suddenly missed Simew more than anyone. Though I loved Rime above all and I knew all he did was for a better future, it didn't alleviate my loneliness. I was the outsider in many things. Simew had been my friend and mine alone. Without any goals or desires. If he had heard me now, he would have admonished me for wallowing in ridiculous melancholy and told me to behave.

When Rime woke and headed for work, I found myself wandering toward the jail after visiting the Needle's laboratory. I waved to the guard and opened the door to Heelis' cell. She sat in a corner and glared at me.

"You were right about Frazil. He is just as weasely as you told me back then."

Heelis sat up a little straighter but didn't respond.

"I'm sorry for not listening to you more, but I'm not sorry Irinda lost her throne. I will concede that Frazil seems like a better choice only by a thread's width."

"It took you long enough," Heelis scoffed. "I still won't forgive you for destroying the Temple."

"Heelis… you don't even know what we have done or decided."

"And? You know very well what a hard head I have," she sighed and her voice softened as a faint sign of amusement colored her face. "Alright, if you can admit your mistakes, I suppose I should be an adult, too. If what you said about the spirits and that they are used as fuel is true, it is all well and just that Temple is remade."

"I need your advice."

Heelis turned to me and frowned.

"Things must be much worse than I had thought to make you so humble."

"Will you listen, or shall I just leave?"

"Oh, I will listen. However, I fully reserve the right to call you an idiot if the occasion arises."

"Fine," I agreed and sat in front of her.

I explained the whole situation to Heelis. She listened without a flutter of emotion on her face, but her shoulders kept rising and became more tense.

"Well, I won't call you names," she sighed once I finished. "And... I am sorry about your friend. I didn't push him off the ledge, but I cannot say that the responsibility isn't mine. I was too angry. I didn't want to admit to being in the wrong. I did try to kill you, and I would have done so with the knowledge I had. I don't quite know what you expect from me now. I can't do anything for anyone, not even my family."

"No. Not from here."

Heelis shuddered as if a cold draft went through the room.

"What does that mean...? The last time... weeks or months ago... you said I could grow old in here. Is that why everyone constantly tries to get me to mellow in my opinions about you?"

"Yes. But at that time, I thought of you as my enemy, and you were so angry, you would have tried to kill me given the opportunity."

"Perhaps," she admitted and gave a short laugh. "I can't deny that."

"I hate people who disagree with me. You are the same. And I hate even more when people tell me I'm wrong. Yet, it is one of the most valuable things. If you sit here, you won't see how the city changes and what the world goes through, and you cannot fault me if I seem to be on the wrong path."

Heelis lowered her gaze and touched the scar on her neck.

"I will not promise to listen you or follow your guidance, but I will humble myself to give your words more weight and consideration," I offered and held out a ring that was made of two halves attached by a small hinge and spikes on the inside. I dropped it on her palm.

"What is it?"

"A way out. It was made by my researcher, Moras. He can make many a tool to handle the channels and currents in our bodies. This will stop you from using your powers towards me."

"And for something else?"

"We don't recommend using your powers for much with the world as it is."

"Right... the cycle. I have a lot to catch up on."

"Do you need to think it over?"

She nodded and weighed the ring.

"Just a little. I want to talk to Juone. I threw him out the last time," she said and closed the ring in her fist. "If he and the children will not forgive me, I don't know what I'd have to look forward to. I can admit I deserve a part of this punishment, and if they cannot be my salvation, I don't want it."

XXIX

My hand was in the nexus. It stung my skin and seemed to pout, almost as if it had a temper of its own, because I kept pushing it and myself daily. Istrata's last statue wasn't enough to break me so I certainly wasn't going to let this small, finicky piece of reality sway me from my course whether it was the one fighting me or I it.

I turned the city map around in it. It was easy to jump to familiar destinations. Locations I hadn't visited needed to be forced out. The more I connected to it, the more limitless I felt. Like a drop in an ocean that was all me. It was a horrendous, tinkly, intoxicating feeling. Then it settled into a deep feeling of peace, of purpose.

I reached to the mines Rime had spoken of. Their walls were filled with crystal shards that glistened when the workers' torches briefly illuminated them. I could see people only as black silhouettes. I meandered around the tunnels and tried to feel the light purple and blue rocks. The further down I went, the stickier everything felt. A black tar oozed from the cracks in the walls.

The third world. The heavy world. It concerned me. Everything it touched became sickly, gloomy, and twisted in some manner. What could we do with it? It was in almost everything now. Maybe the heavy world was too full and now it seeped back here. I returned to the Peak and my body.

"*Reach out in time, see my kingdom,*" Istrata whispered. "*You will see I am right, child. Do not be so stubborn.*"

But I was. I had no particular reason to not look in the past. Obviously, I was tempted to see what her reign had been like. The truth of her actions and the whole time... But what if I would see things as she did? What if I looked and saw the plan and was convinced of it? Or what if she could possess me in some manner if I allowed her room? And what if I saw her truth to be better than ours but only brought more pain as she had? Pure chaos into the world because I had the audacity to think I knew how to better arrange its laws.

A part of me lulled itself to the knowledge that all those hundreds of deaths by Riestel's hands and the suffered flawed reincarnations had molded me into something else. But was that something strong enough to resist that which had given me life? To keep me from seeking the same horrible path? I shook my head. What a silly waste of time. It didn't matter how much I was afraid or doubted myself. The only certainty was that I was going to face her one day and no amount of self-pity or complaining would help then.

And I had more pertinent things to curse about right now. The wedding between Frazil's daughter and the Governor of Eladion. The arrangements had swallowed up almost the entire area. Only the Needle was an untouched oasis of calm. Rime had managed to appease Frazil after his deeds, but there was no lingering affection between them. The meager blood tie that used to bring them together seemed to be severed beyond repair.

I wasn't fearful for my life, but for others. Frazil had drawn up a list of permanent governors to take the guard members' places after the fasting and his coronation. He'd have Kerth at his fingertips then. It would bring everyone a moment of respite whether we mended our relationship or not. It didn't matter. I just whished for it all to be over so I could focus on my life instead of these schemes and lies.

The spring wind carried a scent of freshly opened leaf buds. Maybe I imagined or wished it, but their color seemed a little brighter this spring. I needed our work to manifest at least somewhere. Certainly, the most one could hope for would be small, localized successes, but I'd take anything. It would prove the burnings of bodies and all the days and hours spent grinding soul sand were worth it.

I turned the pages of one of the darker books Istrata had written. One of the ones I had hidden at first. Eventually, most ended up in Moras' hands as they dealt with artificial creatures. The tar was suitable for their blood. If we would recycle it from one life to another, after several cycles, it could perhaps be returned to the cycle as purer and lighter. If we first discovered how to access the heavier world in a controlled manner. At this moment, the only way to accumulate the substance was to leech it out from other levels it was clogging. The only book I kept all to myself was Istrata's theory on gods, or more precisely, how to perhaps make them.

Moras' animals were mostly well, but anyone could see the corruption in them. They were more aggressive than normal ones, even the plant eaters. The plants secreted the poison into the soil which killed off ordinary plants and seedlings. There were small signs of all the negative results diminishing in time, but the calculations suggested it would take decades, even centuries, for a full recovery. The amount of the tar used in the experiments was far less than the worst affected places in the city. But at least we had some kind of road forward.

"Isa?" Arvida called from the Needle's door. After her, Elona, dressed in her finest, waltzed in. She tugged at her high-lace collar but seemed otherwise happy with her dress. She grabbed her hem and curtsied, almost like the court ladies, to show off her outfit more than to greet with respect.

"I'm almost done. I just got lost reading," I told them and straightened the sleeves of my light green silk gown. It was an improved version of my fasting dress. New fabrics had been added to emphasize the back part. The dagger's hole had been wonderfully mended out of sight.

"Did you tell the maid to jump from the Needle again before she could finish with your hair?" Arvida asked and pursed her lips. "You cannot attend the engagement festivities looking that plain."

"I like my hair down and free," I mumbled but didn't object when Arvida pressed me to sit on the chair.

"Sometimes I feel I'm watching you both," Arvida scolded me, amused. "Elona, bring your mother's jewelry from that box."

Arvida brushed my hair with her long fingers and twirled and twisted it. Elona sat next to me, swinging her feet and tilting her head to music the rest of us couldn't hear.

"What do you think?" Arvida asked her. Elona scrunched her nose in objection.

"True. Maybe the blue stone and ribbons. There's enough green in the dress."

"Yes!" she agreed and nodded. "Uncle Fall likes blue, but daddy likes green. Which do you like, Mommy?"

My ears burned. Arvida teared up, trying to hold back her laugher.

"They are both pretty," I said and turned away.

"But everyone has a favorite color," she insisted.

"I haven't given it thought. Let Arvida work in peace," I ordered. I could see through the mirror how Elona leaned on her chair and crossed her arms, staring at me with utter annoyance.

"I will think about it," I promised.

Her expression mellowed, and she began swaying her legs back and forth again.

"Right, done. Try not to poke at it," Arvida urged and slapped my hand away as I was already trying to loosen it. "If you mess it up, I will glue it the next time."

"Fine, I'll behave. No threats needed."

"What is this?" Elona asked and dipped her fingers into the nexus. "Look, Mommy. It's you sleeping."

I leaped out of the chair. The knot showed Istrata's face. I could see her breathing. Her eyelids twitched, but she didn't wake. I grabbed Elona's hand and pulled it out. Arvida and I exchanged glances. Both pale as the clouds.

"Dearest little weasel," Arvida sighed, "ask before you go about touching other people's things! It is an observation orb for the city. It will show you random and silly things if you don't know how to use it."

We hurried away from the room. As we traversed the halls, Merrie joined us with some of her guards and noble women heading the same way. We packed into the foyer of the Grand Audience Hall. My heart was still pounding from seeing Istrata. I prayed Elona hadn't woken her. The stinging in my stomach calmed when they started to summon people of lower status into the hall. They were guided to the edges of the room furthest from the throne and the family of the ruler.

Merrie swayed back and forth and hummed a tune as light as her personality. She had been quite taken with the request to officiate the marriage. Tonight, she was to perform for the couple. Despite her young age, she showed no signs of being nervous. Merrie smiled to and answered all around her. She beamed warmth and light. I glanced at the mirrored walls. Seeing her and her power so wonderfully embraced only fortified my feeling of being separated from most humans by some invisible wall.

"I'll catch up with you later," Merrie told me. "I hope to make you proud."

"I'm sure you will be wonderful," I encouraged her and conjured a smile as genuine as I could.

Merrie walked into the Grand Audience Hall with an entourage of other women from the Temple. They curtsied quickly to Frazil and the governors. Ghila's party arrived to the waiting room. They marched straight to the door, though they were above us in the ranks tonight and it would have been our turn. They were immediately announced, and the valet closed the massive doors. Arvida tilted her head and frowned.

"Did they forget about us?" she whispered.

"Like that could happen. I've been so uppity lately that I would assume this is to put me in my place."

"But we have to go. We were invited."

"Yes... but imagine how it will look if we use that door now that the event is officially under way. We will either seem impolite and tardy or they will use the moment to embarrass us publicly. Either way, it will be a hassle on their terms."

"True," Arvida sighed and frowned deeper. "What do we do?"

"By the sounds of it, they are already giving the welcome speech. What other doors lead to the Hall? The men's entrance, of course. The servant's doors. We could maybe sneak through them and slip in unnoticed. Then we'd just pretend to have been there. Though... everyone would know we were lying."

"You know, the ruler also has his own entrance," Riestel remarked behind us. Elona ran to her father and jumped as high as she could. Riestel caught her and twirled her around a few times.

"I refer to Irinda's own staircase," he specified. "It comes down directly in the middle of the Hall."

"What are you doing here?" I asked.

"Just came in to check what was going on. I can blame you for many things, but usually not tardiness. We can, of course, skulk through a side door. I'm just giving you an option if you'd like to make a statement."

This was clearly meant to be a punishment. Should I just swallow my pride and let things be? But what if it wasn't just that? What if this was to show everyone who truly ruled the Peak? Was it a sign of weakness or truce if I bowed now? These human games were starting to vex me.

I didn't believe a true truce was on offer. So, what if I behaved so badly that Frazil's attention would turn from Rime to me? What if I made him think his threats meant nothing and that he shouldn't have brought the child into this, as it was too late to control me? Perhaps then Frazil would save his leverage to discipline Rime in some other matter down the road if he thought this was a lost cause.

"Lead the way. He wants to up the ante, so let us do just that," I decided though there was a tiny part of my brain called the sensible side, sulking that it had been overruled yet again. "Are you sure you want to come through there with Elona? I can't promise they won't direct some of that hatred to you as well."

"Are you implying that I'm not capable of protecting our daughter?" Riestel asked, amused. "Besides... It has been a good while since I last pissed in the noble's tea."

"Arvida? What about you?"

"I'll tag along and mind Elona. That is my job, is it not? And those satin hens won't remember me or the little lady for long. I will make sure of that."

"This way then, ladies," Riestel gestured, and we returned to the hallway. We hurried two floors up and through several small rooms and fake walls to a dead end.

"Here?" I huffed. "But there is no way down?"

"Here," Riestel announced and hit an icy spear into a dent in the floor. The center of the room's floor collapsed down with a great ruckus drawing out and down a metallic spiral staircase. Some yelps sounded from below. The metallic railings and steps let out a distorted note as they struck the floor below. The whole structure shook for a moment. Riestel stabilized the stairs with his ice.

"Do me the honor, Consecratoress," Riestel said as he stepped on the first stair.

Too late to think this was a bad idea now. I took the hand he offered and lifted my hem a little with the other. We began to descend. Arvida and Elona followed a few steps behind. The people below us stood still. All was silent apart from the metallic echo each step sent out. I felt a strange joy, almost to the point of being giddy. Perhaps I understood Irinda's desire to the be admired a little too well.

As I came to the final step, Rime with his ribbons and a parade sword signaling his rank walked over and offered his gloved hand past Riestel. They exchanged a less-than-friendly unspoken greeting. After making his statement, Riestel stepped aside politely and allowed me to accept Rime's hand with a smile. Arvida and Elona stepped down after us. Riestel sent the stairs flying back into the ceiling. Lazy drops of water rained above the dancers all evening as the stairs thawed.

XXX

W e made our way to a quiet corner some ways away from Frazil's family. Friti kept an eye on us constantly, and if her gaze wandered away, one of her servants watched us. The family's women were adorned with all possible diamonds and jewels they could have possibly fit on themselves. All taken from the aroch. As our eyes met, I nodded politely upwards. She didn't acknowledge the gesture.

I shook my head and smiled as I moved my attention to the dancers. The engaged couple had their own space in the middle of the floor. Ghila was dressed in red silks that caressed her figure gently. Lander was also in red. No one else was allowed to use the color tonight. She tried to remain coy and gracious, but her smile widened to a vulgar glee at times. When she locked eyes with her parents, she bit her lip and returned to a demurer look. Would Ghila be the queen after Friti?

Far away, behind them, Riestel was dancing with Elona in his arms. I could hear her gentle giggle, though we were too far for it to be possible. I leaned on Rime and steadied myself. He slipped his arm around my waist. He had a false expression on his face. He smiled, yes, but his visage had a tightness to it. It was a look he had when anticipating trouble.

"Tonight then?" I whispered.

"Asked the wife who made a grand entrance through the ceiling and stole the attention of the crowd from the couple of the day while the future king was addressing the room."

"Well, they closed the door... Should I have crawled in like an uninvited guest in my home? Or are you genuinely mad that I did so?"

"No. You are my lovely seed of chaos," Rime pondered and pressed his cheek against my head. "You were made for it. Don't think I will scold you for it."

His words, though meant in a comforting way, had a bite to them. I was born for chaos? Destruction indeed. Was it always the only way with the gift of fire? My counterbalance was spending time with his daughter. His gift meant that things could last and be stable. Was all and everyone around me destined to end up in a storm? A constant change through destruction.

Launea, Uudean, Simew. Two of Rime's guards, Farash, and countless of others. Not that everything could be placed on my shoulders, but how many events were due to circumstance and how many were my doing? I squeezed the dark blue edge of Rime's jacket.

"What is it?" he asked.

"Nothing. I just like being close to you. Merrie is about to perform. If she does well, they will accept her to bless the union..."

"It is a waste of souls, the performance. You know you could have just agreed to wed them," Rime noted.

"I know. It was a selfish moment," I admitted and lowered my head.

"We are all that at times."

"You are taking everything very calmly tonight. How can you spur me on when you know I'm chipping at the very foundations of this city and when I bring such suffering?"

"You are bringing about change. I benefit from it, or have you not noticed where we reside these days?"

"Too calmly."

"Isa. When you do not change when the change is required, it will come with force and pain. There is no escape. And for many, you bring hope of a better future, a future that isn't simply waiting for this world to fall quietly into death's arms. Think of a soldier with gangrene. Cutting of the limb is no one's wish and the pain is excruciating, but without that, the person dies. You are that saw."

If I was the saw, who was the medic? Frazil? Rime? The Witch Queen? I studied his face. He nodded towards the dance floor.

A glistening, radiant Merrie, clad in a flowy silvery dress, walked to the middle. Her steps made no sound. Her face was adorned with a coy, warm smile. Her eyes had a watery sheen, and she avoided eye contact. I was guilty of her covered sorrow. She had to use life to dance and entertain because I had refused to dance to Frazil's tune and wed the couple. I was really starting to regret that decision.

A cool flute and bows conjured light, carefree notes. She danced like a pedal swirling in the wind. The light of all candles and lanterns scattered and dotted the hall as the silver dress and her crystal jewelry shone. Her sunlike hair was as pretty as any crown. Everyone stood in place, barely breathing. Only a few sighs of delight were heard with the music.

As Merrie finished, a slow wave of claps turned into a much louder cheer. There was no doubt whether she was a worthy consecrator or not. Veitso stood like a statue very close to her. Samedi nudged him to get him to join the applause. It was quite fitting that a dainty little wisp like Merrie would cast such a spell on Veitso. He was going to be ruthlessly mocked by his peers for showing his soft side.

Merrie was allowed the honor of approaching the royal family to be. She was greeted warmly and with admiration as she curtsies with all the grace in the world. Lander was perhaps a little too eager to greet her, considering his bride was right by his side. But looking at Merrie, it was hard to blame him.

People returned to their own circles and continued the festivities. Families and groups presented their engagement presents to Ghila and Lander in a long line. She let out small, enthusiastic squeaks whenever something expensive or rare was unraveled. Arvida and Tammaran were piling small pastries on Elona's plate. Riestel was out of sight.

Rime grabbed my wrist and pulled me to a wide veranda with a long empty table.

"I asked the guard members to join us here. I thought it would be nice to spend one more moment together, while we can," Rime explained.

"Right. They do need to return to their areas soon. What happens when Frazil appoints the official, permanent ones?"

"I can think of something for them to do."

"So, they will continue to serve the army?" I asked.

"Those who wish it. I won't force anyone."

The table soon filled with food as each person brought a little something from the Hall with them. The men gathered around, and the mood changed to a much more informal one. All but Samedi and Rime unbuttoned their high military collars.

Tammaran and Arvida sat at the coziest spot, under the blossoming, wonderfully scented branches of a small tree. They looked at each other with a lovely gleam in their eyes and a shy smile. Arvida waved her hand at me as a hello. I nodded. Then she turned back to Tammaran and fixed her hair with her slender white fingers. Their hands reached for each other under the table as if it was a secret even to them.

When all had arrived, we drank to the ones lost along the way. There was a brief moment of silence under the bright stars.

"Well, blast it, we've come a long way," Veitso said after emptying his mug.

"We are just beginning," Tammaran said. "At least I am looking forward to life after all of this."

"Well, you suddenly seem to have a bit more to look forward to than most of us," Marelin noted.

"Isa could set us all up with some Temple ladies," Veitso suggested.

Samedi almost choked on his brew. Marelin seemed to consider the idea. Then a new soft laugh coming from Rime confused us all.

"I can recommend it from experience," he said with an open smile. There was still an ounce of crossness and melancholy there, but that was just the way he looked. I think none of us had ever seen him so relaxed.

"Veitso has his favorite picked already," Marelin beat the others to it. "Or am I the only one who noticed?"

"You most certainly aren't," I replied. "Her name is Merrie."

"A herring's hole with you people," Veitso grunted and tried to grab his refilled mug but misjudged the distance and ended up having to grab it with both hands to keep it from knocking over completely.

"Well, I suppose it is natural for us to feel attracted to them," Rime said. "It was once a custom that all temple folk had a knight to protect them. I would wager that many of those relationships grew into much closer ones. They say the generations before us echo in us."

"Really? I never heard of that. How long ago was it?" I asked.

"I'm not sure. Maybe around the Witch Queen's era."

"Then it's almost a duty," Veitso decided and got up with a drunken determination. "By the fat fin of a whale, I'll be going now."

"Don't make a bloody fool of yourself," Samedi scoffed. "Better try your luck sober. If such a day ever comes."

"I can go and get her so the gentlemen do not need to fret about etiquette," I said, amused, and got up. "The good knights shall await just a moment and comb Veitso's hair in order, no matter the resistance."

"Mission understood," Samedi grinned and looked at his friend a little too

STRANDS OF EXISTENCE 3: KING OF NAUGHT

gleefully.

As I waded through the guests towards Merrie, a hand touched my shoulder. It squeezed it a little too much and pushed me to a quieter spot.

"Well, how is your lovely night going?" Frazil asked.

"Fine."

"Am I to assume that we are now enemies?" he whispered.

"I don't understand why you would assume that based on my action when you are the instigator of our troubles."

"I need to secure the survival of Kerth and Aderas above all else. I thought we understood each other on that."

"Certainly. How should I, in your opinion, treat you after you took our child after killing the other one?"

"It is the burden of all who marry into this line. There was no way around it. And when I see how you behave, my actions seem all the more reasonable to me. The child will have all it could want from life. The best clothes, the best... education."

"You mean an education in their abilities so they can kill me, should you command it? Is that your newest angle? Kneel before thy king or fear being slain by your progeny?"

"I wouldn't wish to imply that."

"Naturally, you wouldn't wish to, but you did. Why now? Why try to coerce me back to the fold now? I have promised to keep your dirty secrets from Rime for now."

"A man of my age doesn't have decades to seal his rule and set his family up for a future dynasty. I'm playing all my cards now because I don't want to regret anything later."

"What about regretting you played them? Isn't that a possibility? We were loyal. I did much for your revolution. All that you asked. We risked our lives. Why? For you to sit on your... throne and set up a dynasty? You were the hope of Kerth. That is how you presented yourself to me. So, if you are a false promise, then who will save us?"

"Nothing has changed about those goals?" Frazil snapped.

"No?"

"No."

"Then why are you back threatening me? If our goals are the same as before and aligned, why am I suddenly on the wrong side of your desires? Solely due to the Peak? You have no need for it, but I cannot help anyone without it or the knowledge it holds."

Frazil remained silent and turned his head away. He shook it slowly, catching a glimpse of his wife. Then he turned back to me.

"You are right. I apologize for hurting you. You aren't the one I fret over, but I see I have lost all hope of mending our relationship. I merely ask that you keep him from doing anything unadvised," Frazil pleaded with a rehearsed tone.

"Why do you fear your son so much? He sought a family with you as much as I did."

"Perhaps. But there is nothing to be done. I need him to be faithful and serve me more than I need a son. If you want to keep him, you will do your best. Once I have the crown, I promise you will have a good and luxurious life if you behave these last days."

"I'll behave just as I want to," I remarked. "Besides, the only reason for my grand entrance was that I was denied a normal one. Ghila went before me and closed the doors on me. Be the king all you want and raise your pretty princesses as you wish, but don't stoop to such petty mischief."

"I didn't order that."

"Then you have other obedience-challenged people to worry about besides me," I said and walked away as Frazil looked at his family. I dried my moist palms to my dress. It could have gone worse. He was trying to bargain with me instead of purely threatening me.

Merrie's birdsongesque laughter rang from ahead. When she noticed me, she left her company and came to me.

"Well, did it go well?" she asked and sucked on her lower lip.

"Don't play modest. You have a whole flock of admirers here. More than I ever did."

"I suppose," Merrie laughed and blushed as she took in all the nobles waiting for her. "I don't really know what to do with them."

"You don't need to do anything with them unless you want to. However, should you want a bit of respite. Come and sit with us on the veranda. Although, I have to warn you, there will be one admirer there too. He won't bother you, though."

"He won't?"

"His tongue will be too tied up before he can."

Merrie smiled all sunny and nodded.

"Maybe I could drop by for a moment," she said and waved to the others. A disappointed grumble emanated from the nobles, but none dared to object.

As we navigated the maze of rustling silks, I laid eyes on Riestel. He was chatting with a group of ladies who were complimenting Elona. I couldn't imagine Riestel talking in a civilized manner to any noble.

I turned to look again at the women, as something wasn't adding up. Their dresses were pretty but slightly outdated. They had jewels but not as detailed as ours. Of course. Riestel had managed to attract all the mistresses of the Peak to him. There was not a noble so high he wouldn't insult and not a commoner so low he wouldn't pass the time with.

It made me smile. Though he gave me awful headaches, there was a guilty pleasure in seeing and knowing his soft side. Or perhaps I should say his real side, since what I had encountered first had been a role I had forced him into. Despite his reputation and behavior, when you peeked behind the curtains, he rarely used his status for wrong.

Looking at Riestel's fine features and hair combed to an immaculate braid, it was easy to understand why Istrata had fallen for him almost at first sight. I tried to imagine what he must have been like when he had been younger, yearning to live. Unwounded by me and others. It was another life all together.

As we stepped out, Rime leaned back in his chair. He laughed with us but never quite looked like someone taking a night off despite the moment of relaxedness earlier. His other leg was crossed over the other. He looked as stern as when we had met. They were very different in many ways, but they did share something—both had the capacity for tenderness and cruelty.

I introduced all to Merrie, who greeted her pleasantly. Almost all. Veitso shot out of his chair, hit his knee on the edge of the table, knocked over his mug, and when trying to grab it, sent it rolling all over. As all others burst into laugh, he sat down looking a little defeated.

"I did say he wouldn't get a word out," I whispered to Merrie. She giggled and gave him a bright smile.

"I like the way he looks," Merrie noted. "He has a kind face but a soldier's build."

"He may even be kind, from what I know."

"This is like a small court of your own," Merrie said after observing us all for a while.

Rime's countenance darkened.

"Don't call it that," he said in a low voice. "I don't want to paint that image."

"Well, a council then," I suggested and took his hand. He nodded.

"Is something wrong?" I asked him in a hushed voice.

He shook his head, but not before looking around.

"Do not lie," I urged.

"Just a hunch about tonight," he answered confidently. "My father is in too good of a mood compared to what you pulled. I do not like it."

"Perhaps he is just genuinely happy for his daughter. It looks like Ghila and Lander could become a proper couple, not just a forced match."

Rime scoffed and leaned closer.

"You always still think everything will resolve in the best of ways. I hope that trait will never be extinguished."

XXXI

As the cool night air caressed us, Rime stood up from the table. The ruckus and merriment had turned into a soft discussion paused by yawning. Nobody wanted to be the first to leave and end this rare night where all had been well for a moment.

I took Rime's hand as he offered it. The first musicians in the Hall had ended their shift long ago. This was the third group. The music had become slower and calmer.

I swayed against Rime. A soft, mellow feeling filled my body. If I sat down, I'd fall asleep. Even if I had been a bit curious about all the happenings in the Hall, I had no regrets spending the evening in the shadows. The veranda was a reality of its own.

"Isa," Rime called. "Do you know how proud I am of how far you have come? I hope you will feel the same once all is over. Whatever happens, I want you to always follow your instinct."

I pushed him back. He was suddenly completely sober. Had he just pretended to drink?

"What do you mean? What are you going to do?" I asked and wiped my face, trying to drive the haze away.

"I've taken big chances all my life. I don't know if the results have always been worth them. But in this one, backing off isn't an option. I think I'll have the answer to all my deeds soon. I hope I'm wrong about what my father thinks of me," Rime answered and turned to the large doors. My eyes and head didn't turn as rapidly.

Rime faced the Hall. I rubbed my eyes and noticed the guests had changed into guards. Frazil walked to the veranda. His men surrounded us.

"Father," Rime greeted him. "I'd offer a drink, but there's little chance you'd accept."

"Take the soldiers away," Frazil ordered.

The guards grabbed the drunken men and pulled them to their feet. None were in any condition to fight back, though they snapped out of it much better than I.

"Thus, I release all of you from duty for a moment," Frazil announced. "I have appointed new governors for all districts. They will be sworn in after my coronation. You will have lodgings in the prison until that is over to keep you from pulling a last-minute coup. Take them."

"This isn't necessary," Rime said and stepped in their path. "You will have your crown in a few days. Are you truly this petty and fearful?"

"You are asking me to trust you and in the same breath you call me names."

"Even a stupid person can do the right thing," Rime noted. "Take me if you must, but leave my Guard alone."

"Oh no, son, you should and shall learn that if you defy me, I will go for your most prized things. Isa can await her turn, as I have use for her."

"We can go," Samedi offered and placed his free hand on Rime's shoulder. "It's only a few nights. And it would hardly be the first time I spend a night in prison in your stead," he laughed.

Rime glanced at his friend with purple-black eyes.

"Please stop. Let me talk to him before this escalates," I asked and reached my hand toward Rime. One of the guards swatted my hand away. Rime growled like a beast and hit them both in the face. They dropped dead. Life streamed from their corpses towards Rime.

"Seize them properly!" Frazil yelled and more guards came. During a horrible, messy fight where none of us were sure what to do and Rime couldn't tell us through his rage, a student of Moras jabbed a needle through Rime's clothing. His movement slowed, his eyes returned to normal, and he fell out of consciousness. I ran to him and kneeled. His skin was clammy.

Arvida squeezed Tammaran's arm to keep him, but as he shook his head, she let go. An ordinary cell wasn't going to hold him. Veitso, Samedi, and Marelin stared at their commander.

"Isa," Tammaran said. "We will go where told. Let's not make things worse. Rime is clearly not in his right mind at the moment. Get him to Moras for treatment."

"He will be taken there anyway," Frazil cut in. "And he will remain there until the coronation. You have forced me into this. I cannot trust either of you. Shall we call this an insurance of sorts? If you behave, they will be unharmed."

Arvida leaned my way and took my hand. I tried to figure out ways to defy this humiliation and to prevent them from being locked up, but each option seemed to just make everything worse.

"Take Merrie to her quarters before Frazil has you two taken as well," I requested Arvida, who nodded and returned almost unnoticed to the table to help Merrie up. They soon disappeared into the Hall without anyone being the wiser.

The Black Guard's members were escorted across an almost empty Hall. Rime was carried by three men after them. I was left alone in the crisp air with a burning desire to scorch this city. This shining jewel that I had loved before even coming here. The symbol of all of my hopes that I had only found a little goodness in. How dared Frazil toy with Rime's mind? His own son. Nothing meant anything in this city. Nothing but power.

I stroked my arms and forced myself to breathe slower before my heart would pound itself into oblivion. As much as I hated Frazil for this... we had goaded the future monarch far too long. I had half waited when Frazil would snap and put us in our place openly, not to mention Rime had been driving him to do it. Testing his limits. Why? Was this what I had given him permission to do when he requested it so cryptically?

Frazil returned to the door.

"What more do you want?" I asked with as much contempt as possible.

"I know my son will behave, as I have his Guard. I will see him walk with the family in my coronation. I will not allow them to meet again before all is done. Once they are no longer governors after my first day in office, they cannot declare me unfit and install Rime as the war counsel. Your time and means to take my future are at an end."

"I've never been after your throne," I told him. "None of us wants it."

"Are you honest with yourself about that?" Frazil quizzed and made way for me. He stopped me right by his side.

"I have given orders to take the child away from the city and educate him. Should you resist me, you will never meet him and I will make it abundantly clear to Rime this will be done based on your decision. I've sent my son to Moras and given instruction to keep him sedated by feeding him. Once he wakes, he will be more unstable than ever. Understood?"

"You've made this threat before. You have your hostages, and you've drugged your son. Fine work. Why not enjoy your last days of governorship before the entire fate of the city rests on you?"

"You will stand for me in the coronation ceremony and the wedding. You shall show everyone the unquestionable support you bestow upon me and my family. When, and only when, you do that, I am willing to negotiate a forgiveness."

"Oh, you know me," I smiled, as I knew which thread to pull. "I always pick the road which benefits me. You are the highest official to be. A future king. If you wish to coax me into good behavior, try buying me instead of threatening me."

"Perhaps it would be a better way. But I need proof I can trust you. Your insubordination paints me as weak."

"Fine, my Governor," I promised and curtsied deeply.

"Get up," Frazil ordered. He looked as if he was trying to assess whether I was mocking him or making amends, though as a practical and somewhat reasonable man, he'd realize it didn't matter as long as it was interpreted as submission in the eyes of the few people left in the Hall.

He reached out his hand and helped me up.

"Good. My mood is much improved," he said and nodded stiffly.

"Then let the Guard go."

"I said my mood has improved. I didn't say I have lost my wits," Frazil remarked. "And you will officiate them. Is that clear? Superstitious idiotism be cast aside. That shall be your gift to your King. If the strongest consecrators do not bow to the ruler, I am no ruler in the eyes of the people."

"Fine," I agreed with a bad taste in my mouth.

"Wonderful. Then you may retire for the evening."

"Can I at least visit Moras' rooms to see that I still have a husband?"

"You may, but it is hardly necessary. He will be in that state until the coronation morning," Frazil answered meekly and avoided my eyes. His jaws tensed as he swallowed. At least a hint of remorse for such stern measures.

The last drowsy nobles and other guests kept a close eye on our interaction. Their glances almost stung my skin. The Maherols seemed a little cautious, the Rosse family more than delighted. Friti and Ghila made no effort to hide their joy. Ghila whispered something to her mother, whose mouth curled with a delicious amount of ghoulish joy. The jewelry made from the aroch's stones sparkled and glistened with their movements.

Riestel leaned on the main entrance frame and absently twirled a small pocket watch attached to a chain.

"Where's Elona?" I asked as I reached him.

"Sleeping, safe."

"Why are you still here?"

"I'm going to escort you to your premises. Someone needs to… What would Elona say if I left her mother to the wolves? They are plenty hungry tonight."

My first instinct was to argue with him, but after glancing behind at the royal family and their court, his offer seemed much more pleasant. Friti hated me, as I stood in front of her dream palace. If she wanted to get rid of me, now was the moment, as Rime wasn't here.

We walked in silence for most of the way. Hallway after hallway I wanted to break it, but I had nothing to say. I turned towards Riestel's accommodation.

"It's better if you spend the night at the top of the White Needle, alone or not. No one else can get in there without your permission," Riestel reminded me.

"You can."

"Are you implying I would be dangerous to you? The lady can just count how many friends she has she can trust besides me."

"Friends?" I repeated, amazed as he pushed me toward the stairs.

"Let's call it that. Easier for now," he said.

Riestel closed the Needle's final door behind us. We hadn't been all alone for a while. I didn't believe his talk of friendship for a moment. Not after all he had done, and how I could still sense his breathing changed when he was close.

I took a blanket from the chair and wrapped myself in it. It seemed an appropriate shield. Riestel pulled the other chair closer and sat. His cold eyes measured every inch of my face.

"You really do not have a backup plan," he sighed. "I thought you would have learned by now. You cannot defy anything and everything on a whim. Not that I would mind if you suddenly managed to misplace your husband from the land of the living."

"I already agreed to perform the rites. Frazil will get his desired coronation and wedding. Things will calm down"

"Really?"

"I will not have them killed for my vanity."

"Noble."

"Not really. Mostly a selfish act. Bowing is easy when it saves someone."

"And the arochs?"

"I don't know. Rime gave me carte blanch to do as I wish."

"What do you wish, then?"

I stared into the night. The nexus and I reflected from the window.

"I want to exhume her corpse and ground her to dust so there isn't even a speck of her left. I'm so mad at her. At me."

Riestel leaned his head to the left a little and laughed quietly.

"What is wrong with you?" I asked.

"I've been waiting for that confession a long time. You've cursed me, most everyone, the whole Temple... Yet you've never shown much emotion toward your former life. Especially towards her."

"Because... when you told me what I am, I felt indebted. I was born from her. I wouldn't exist without her. It's hard to admit to hating something that gave you life. And... I know this sounds stupid, but I feel a certain gratitude she got me here, though I know there was nothing altruistic about it. It took me a while to understand that the statues did nothing for me, they just did what they had always done since they were created."

"Are you ready to face Istrata if she rises? Once she rises?"

"No," I replied. "Not in the slightest. You once said she was like a god. You've told me how she weaved reality. I've seen and felt it. How can I meet her when I can barely manufacture a body in the Lighter World?"

"That is a good question. And one we need to answer. Her plan proceeds whether we like it or not," Riestel pondered.

"She's had centuries to learn new skills. I can't possibly learn enough before the resuscitation begins to kick in."

"You're wrong. I've thought about this a lot. If we are correct, and she truly severed all connection to her soul and she only operates by her body and the worldly energy or life energy she amassed... Then has she been able to develop into anything more? Can she learn and mold new things without a soul and the fire of change?"

"The fire... Do you think she is cut off from it?" I asked, intrigued.

"She has other means to use power, I'm sure. Some new magic. She cannot do this without such powers, but what those powers are…"

"I heard her again."

"What did she say?"

"She wants me to explore her past. Her time and how much better things were so that I might realize she is worth my trust and allegiance."

Riestel stroked his chin. His eyes went from one item in the room to another.

"It could be a good idea," he mused. "I don't doubt it that she wouldn't force you to see only certain moments and scenes. But if you could wrestle her for the power even just on a few occasions, you could catch glimpses of her true plan."

"Sounds dangerous."

"Certainly. And you can't yet. You need more practice with the nexus. Come. You can rehearse on me."

"What? How?"

"Well, I was thinking about showing you, but if you can't follow a simple command like 'Come', we are in trouble," Riestel mocked with a smile. I showed by a gesture just how much I appreciated his constant ragging.

We sat face to face with the nexus between us. His icy eyes had a warm gleam in the candlelight. I lowered my gaze as I noticed my pulse change. Riestel placed his hand in the knot.

"Can you direct it?" I asked.

Riestel shook his head and smirked.

"Not the way you can. I can strengthen existing connections. I can give into them and feel them. I can seek things. I cannot unravel them or mold them like you. Place your hand. Very close to mine, but do not touch."

I lifted my left hand to mirror his. As my fingers glided into the nexus, I felt a jolt between us. Small currents, strands, twirling and flowing between us, through us. A bit like the ones between the arochs, though these were less noticeable. Light as whispers but durable as mountains.

"Pick one to follow. Some are past, some are unrealized things that still bind us or can bind us if they grow. Some may be remnants passed from Istrata. If you find them, you may find her. But pick something stronger between us for now."

As I studied the strands, I received painful reminders of how Riestel had treated me in the beginning. The injuries from the icy spears and his words echoed in my body. I wiped a bead of sweat from my nose with my free hand. It had a little blood mixed in it, but I wasn't about to give up.

I picked a different colored strand. Touching it was like wading into a warm, summery pond with a soft silt bed. I opened my eyes and stood once again in the small bathhouse. This was a memory, and it wasn't a memory. Riestel was just adjusting my channels. His hand traveled on my back, my side, and between my breasts as before. Then the memory split. I could see the strand divide into what happened and what might have happened. I followed the new option.

The strand began to gain strength when I did so. Riestel's fingers moved to my breast. His lips pressed to my neck. My body tingled. He pressed against my back and turned me to him. His ice hand slid to my neck, and he tilted my head. Small zaps of lightning arced between us.

"I knew you wanted this deep down," he whispered and kissed me.

I tore myself out of the fantasy and backed away from the nexus. Riestel stared at me and reached towards me from under the nexus. I leaned away further, but before I could avoid him, he was above me on all fours. His long, slightly luminous hair framed his face and highlighted the mischievous happiness.

"It was just a dream," Riestel whispered. "You cannot cheat in a dream," he remarked, painfully lightly.

"You are wrong," I answered.

"Only if you truly felt something," Riestel smiled, rolled away, and stood up. "Let's practice more later. Don't worry too much or you won't sleep all night."

I hugged myself in the dark. There was no denying my feelings anymore. A part of me screamed for him, and it wasn't just Istrata. I shook my head. His allure and our connection were not a reason to act. He could torture me every day from here to eternity, but I wouldn't betray Rime. I had chosen him, and I would stick to it. Two lives, and perhaps two loves entwined in me, but living just one and loving just one at a time was enough.

XXXII

O nce I evicted Riestel from my head, I still couldn't sleep, as my mind was buzzing with the possibilities the connections brought. Could I learn to handle and travel through them so delicately that I could trace Istrata and spy on her? The idea had horrible risks, but if it would work... could I even see into her thoughts and plans?

A new hope sprouted within. A hope that I could sway our future more than I thought and with less violence. A hope that I didn't just need to wait and pray that I was ready to face her once she was done waiting for the pieces to fall into place.

I touched the cold side of the bed. I had thought there would have been a chance that Frazil would have regretted his heavy-handed tactics and let his son go. Would Rime ever have the time to keep his promise and just live with me for a moment without any wars and worries? It was a bittersweet thought.

I didn't question Rime's love or what I meant to him, but his devotion to the city and the city's issues was, at times, frustrating. Then again, that unwavering determination to do as he thought right and to guide us to a better road was one of the reason's I loved him.

The wedding was to take place in two days. A visit to the prison was in order, as I wouldn't have any time to take care of my own tasks once the ceremonies started. The celebrations would go on for days. After both occasions were done, we needed to escort the governors of Eladion and Loisto all the way back to the main gate and circle around the city prancing with the new king. I had no doubt Frazil intended to drag me along to bow to him as a puppet.

The prison guards were polite, as always. The Guard was sitting in one joint cell. They seemed bored and not concerned or annoyed. They had conveniently positioned themselves so that the guards couldn't see the whole room. Apparently Tammaran was away getting them dice.

I left them to play once I saw everything was well and Tammaran returned. I headed to Heelis. She was practicing her channeling movements in the cell even though no power flowed. As she sensed me, she squinted and walked closer.

"Is it decision time?" she asked.

"If you haven't come to a decision by now, you never will."

"Possibly true. Actually, I made my mind up the same day you offered the chance."

"You could have sent word to me."

"I could have," Heelis responded and smiled mischievously. She took out the ring I had presented her.

"This is surprisingly heavy," she noted and spread the hinged ring. "I'm really not a fan of those spikes," she added, and her nose wrinkled.

After a moment of silence, Heelis clicked the ring in place on her left index finger. "Mighty ice picks these are so sharp," she cursed, but then she fell silent and looked at the metal and the few bright red drops of blood that ran down her finger. "It doesn't hurt anymore. How is that possible?"

"It has a healing spell engraved. It uses your vitality. Do not ask me to explain the mechanics. If you want to see the schematics, ask Moras. I couldn't keep in half the information he poured on me."

"And now?"

"Now we walk out."

"Is that all?" she asked, a little suspicious.

I pulled her out of the cell as she hesitated. When we exited the jail into the blinding late spring sun, she fluttered her lids and took a deep breath. Her skin was even lighter after all those months inside. She looked older and a little fragile.

"Honestly, I wasn't sure you'd ever let me out, even if I had begged. That's why I didn't want to try. Juone is very mad at me for that."

"I wasn't planning to forgive you, but I have a few other conditions than just the ring."

"And those are?"

"You and your family will live in the Peak for now, in a lightly guarded manor."

"Reasonable. What else?" she asked almost absentmindedly as she took the scenery in.

"Be as direct with me as always. I promise I will try my best to stay any urges of throwing you back in."

"Well, in that case… you should really look into the ventilation in the prison. There's this constant smell of rotten carrots," Heelis said and gave a lopsided smile. "Don't be offended, but I want to see my family now and just live a few moments without you in my head."

"I will summon your family to you. Do you see that light yellow house? That is for you."

"Were you that sure I would forgive you that you set everything up already?"

"No, but I was counting on your desire to live. You are like a weed. You always poke out from some crack in the ground."

"A weed!" Heelis scoffed and then she burst into a clear laughter. "You could have just said I'm tough."

"But that would sound like a compliment. I couldn't do that. You'd think I'd be trying to rekindle some parts of our friendship should I be nice."

"Right," she replied, amused. "Your apologies are very nicely hidden. Well, how does this weed get to her new home?"

"What do you mean how? You possess two perfectly usable legs," I teased her and suddenly heard how very much like Riestel I sounded.

"You're letting me go alone? Just like that?"

"The way I see it is if you are going to make a run for it and fight me again at some point, we better just get it over and done with."

"For Peak's sake, Isa. When did you become so cold and calculating?"

"It's not that I don't want to trust you. That I wouldn't rather call you a friend than an enemy or a past friend."

"I'm not following."

"It's simply that I've accepted the fact that I can't control others. I can't always read people right, so I'm giving you the opportunity to show me where you stand."

"I guess I'll be off then and we will see what happens," Heelis sighed and stretched a little. "See you around."

I looked after Heelis for a while. She kept stopping at trees to feel their bark and leaves and to sniff flowers. She didn't look back once. For some reason, I took that as a good omen.

I returned to the lower parts of the Needle. The red irises had grown high in the glass house. I touched one leaf. It was infuriating that I couldn't control my emotions. I didn't want to give them any space. I didn't want to feel them. I didn't want to want a future torn between the two. I wanted what I had.

I stepped into the golden room in the between that they had shaped. The music box was still in the corner. It was no use to act as if all these emotions were Istrata's. The line had been crossed and blurred ages ago. What would I feel for Riestel if I had never met Rime? If I had not married him and promised to do my best to make it a true union. Would something more have already happened?

There was only one road ahead. Being faithful. I had promised so, and I intended to keep it so. We had only this life if Riestel was right. And if he had truly slept with half of the city, he had no right to take me away yet. But at this rate, it would be difficult. Not because my feelings for Rime would have changed or subsided, but because Riestel knew perfectly well I had trouble resisting all forbidden things.

I rubbed my hands together and tore apart the golden room. It was exquisite, wonderful, and pointless. It was much more useful as a study case than as a relic. The whole city was full of mementos and graves of their love. A few less was enough.

Deconstructing the room taught me much of how Istrata created things. What she paid attention to and what she did a little less thoroughly. Perhaps if I studied more of her work like this, I could find strands that would lead to her without Riestel and me. His proposal to find Istrata was fascinating, but if I reached out for her through the strongest connections… Wouldn't that be too foolhardy? If I could find a road that still existed but was forgotten, the Witch Queen might not see me coming.

XXXIII

The door to the Needle's upper parts was tightly locked on the morning of the wedding so that no servant could bother me. I brushed my own hair and braided it. I dressed myself in the simplest temple dress I had. No embroidery, no patterns. Just a simple, off the shoulders, pale turquoise dress.

I hadn't seen Rime since the engagement evening. Moras had politely let me know that Rime was in his personal care after all that had happened. He hadn't been informed of Frazil's intentions and was quite shocked to discover a student of his agreeing to such a plan. He had sent the student away and barred him from ever entering his order again. Still, the damage had been done. Rime had been connected to the machines and fed full of the black ichor. As coming off it had to be done gently with time, he had kept Rime unconscious for the duration of the process.

It was a worry what Rime's state of mind would be when he woke up. How much hate and frustration would his mind handle? Frazil's use of power would certainly cause him to be upset. The possibility to decree Rime as the war counsel was lost, so that would further anger him. I had no wish to do anything to wind everyone up even more and to force Frazil to play his hand to rein us in.

My fingers were ice cold from being so nervous. I couldn't stop from obsessing and trying to figure out Frazil's state of mind. Rime would escort the family to the coronation. He had to be there in order for the city to believe there was no rift between the king and the army. It was for the best of the city. Moras had assured me that the rehabilitation would be ready in time, but he didn't sound as reassuring as usually.

All this for the city that sprawled under the Needle. The devout love Istrata had felt for Kerth had been peeled from me layer by layer. Was reconstruction truly the best option? What else was there to do? The surrounding areas were barren or on their way to losing all life force. What if we traveled for months, even years? If we abandoned this place altogether, would we find a place that could support us out there? Here the city was its own beast where changing the habits and customs of its people would take generations should we manage to heal it.

As I arrived to the right bow, I could see the transformation of the gray square to a sparkling forest of decorations and wonder. Everything one could hang something on had either a banner, a crystal ornament, a lantern, or a garland hanging from it. Even caged songbirds. A little ways lower from the square, the cart that held the arochs was parked. I withdrew a bit to keep them from noticing me. The fasting ceremony was to take place down on the square during the day. The coronation on this platform in the evening.

A full day of unnecessary fun and frivolity. Great. Shouldn't the coronation set the tone for the ruler's reign? And this was all he wanted to say. A beautiful story of fools and illusions of riches.

"In a fabulous mood again?" Riestel asked from behind.

"And you?"

"Surprisingly, yes. The day is fine, and I do not need to prance around like a show pony."

"Thank you for reminding me."

"Just pointing out what it will look like."

"Let it look like it. It cannot be helped. If this was up to me, none of it would take place today. Not now, not ever."

"Well, it would be a shame if your husband would lose his balance," Riestel sighed and twirled his eyes. "And yet, did you not say he told you to act exactly as you wished?"

"Don't be an ass. He wouldn't say that now with all the Black Guard in prison and he himself knocked out for days," I muttered and stopped. "Or do you think he would? Do you think he would have calculated this? That he has a plan that requires me to make the worst possible choice again?"

"I'm simply stating what I said once before: he isn't as dumb as I thought."

"Maybe... but if you are wrong and he is just a part of Frazil's plan... I'd lose him forever, and the child, too. You'd like that."

"I would. I have no qualms to admit to that. As far as I'm concerned, he can cease to exist, but it would be a loss for Kerth. And I'm hardly so heartless I would wish to see you suffer just for my benefit," Riestel answered. "After all, apart from Elona, you are one of the few creatures I can stand."

"Such a warm confession."

"Would you like one? I can make one if it pleases you," he replied, looking straight at me.

I shook my head. Riestel laughed and turned towards the square.

"Then don't beg for one," he added and jumped down.

I stared over the edge after Riestel. I could very likely survive the landing these days as well, but I rather walked to have time to gather my thoughts.

I avoided and dodged servants making final touches to the area as they ran like a line of ants from here all the way to the kitchen. Riestel's and Rime's words swirled around in my head. Rime had told me to do as I wanted, but how could he have known that Frazil would imprison them all? And there was no way that getting force fed for days could have been a plan. It was dangerous to believe Riestel.

But what if there was a plan? Which outcome would be worse? The one where I did something to ruin Frazil's day, and we'd pay for it too, or that I did nothing and all was ruined? If there was anything to ruin. I leaned on the bow's cool outer wall. If there wasn't a plan, I could lose all.

I cursed Rime for not sharing everything with me. I understood the reason well enough. If, by nature and intent, I was chaos and sowed it around me, I could destroy all plans just by knowing about them. Maybe one day I could control the nexus and my skills in the Lighter World so well I could anticipate what would befall from what action. Then I wouldn't need to be the odd one out.

"Consecratoress Elona, this way. The ceremony is about to begin," Marinone called and bowed. Her military jacket had one empty sleeve pinned to her side. I hadn't seen her since the battle.

"Alright. I didn't realize you stayed to serve Frazil. I thought you would have returned to the army."

"I'm staying for a while. Besides, the fighting military won't have me now," she said and glanced at the sleeve and its decorations. "But I have a desk job waiting in the Soldier's."

"Are you going to miss all this?"

"A little. But being one handed is a little too noticeable of a trait for a spy. I carry no grudge about it. It was my arm or my life. I appreciate the latter more."

"I am still sorry I couldn't think of another way."

"Let's leave it at that. They are waiting."

Marinone walked just half a step ahead of me as she escorted me. She was more stoic than before. Her wild, frizzy hair had been wrangled into a braid that looked ready to explode at any minute. The curious and confident outer shell had a few cracks. A hard breeze made our clothes flutter and her face frown. The stub must have been quite sensitive still.

Was my effect on people always the same sooner or later? Was it something I could learn to control? If not, it was clear who was meant to curb my powers in the world. I looked at Riestel, who had claimed a shady spot under a tree for himself. We would never be rid of each other, even if we fixed all of Istrata's doings.

"Up here, please," Marinone guided me onto a stage filled with yellow flowers and fabrics shining against the bright blue sky. From the stage began a path of petals and confetti for the pair to walk upon. Musicians tuned their instruments under the relentless sun. Soon, a joyous tune echoed all around the Needle. The square filled with guests. They danced, laughed, and took their places infuriatingly slowly. All dressed in honey-yellows.

Beads of sweat broke out on my forehead and my impatience grew as people kept debating about their places. Servants brought them cool drinks with ice shavings, but not for anyone else. Finally, at the end of the path, walked Frazil with his family. Behind them an absent-looking Rime with Moras. After them came the guard of the Governor of Loisto. Rime's face showed no emotions. Was he drugged into obedience? The thought strangled my throat.

Frazil ascended to the stage with his daughter and her groom. Dozens of stolen jewels shone on her bosom and in her hair. Their glow scolded me. I could hear them sighing for help as Frazil spoke and the sun reached its zenith.

The midday heat wrapped itself around me more and more. All fell silent. Ghila and Lander approached the center of the stage. They kneeled down on fluffy cushions and joined hands. I worked without words as I placed the fasting ribbon and sealed their hands with the sun rune.

Frazil inched his way to me.

"Aren't you going to speak at all?" he urged.

I turned to him and then the couple.

"A union can begin for many reasons, I should know, and none of them define the strength of it or how your feelings will grow if they grow," I said. "To you who have been sold as guarantees for peace, I pray for a true union. For that is something all who take this step with a pure heart deserve. My power is the power of ruin, destruction, and change. My path will not pardon any, but before the price you will pay for choosing my blessing falls on you to pay, I sincerely hope you will find the comfort without which the world rings empty from each other."

The audience was quite wide-eyed and didn't know what to make of the words. Riestel hid his smirk with the back of his palm, but his shoulders revealed he laughed. Rime stared into a void still.

"Be happy. The seal—blessing or a curse—you chose by turning to me has now been cast. May your lives be at a constant flow and renewal. Lean on each other and follow the waves together without fighting them so that your trials will not break you but strengthen you," I added and gestured them to exchange their tokens.

For once Frazil was lost for words. He looked as if he was trying to squeeze out and estimate all possible meanings of the words but couldn't decipher whether I had cursed the union or blessed it against harm. There was enough to interpret positively that he could get everyone to cheer and clap for the new couple. Whatever his personal doubts, he was more than capable of selling my words as pure golden grace.

Friti and the rest of the family got up to congratulate them. The newly wed governor stepped closer to me when everyone embraced Ghila.

"Will this end in tragedy now?" he asked with a pale countenance. "I had no desire to force you into this. I have always honored the gods. How can I fix this?"

"It will end as you want it to end. My gods, as all gods, are gone. You have only us to guide you. If you truly care for Ghila, remember our worth. My worth."

Lander nodded, frowning, and joined his wife.

I left the stage. Moras, Rime, and the guards had gone, so I found myself heading to Riestel. He was under a tree again. I slid down with my back against the silky white bark. There was a lightness about now that my part was done. I placed my palms against the earth and listened. From deep within echoed a lovely voice. A beautiful, bubbling, and humming voice that carried meaning with no words.

"Emissary of Fire, I beseech thee. Save my firstborn."

The sound of the request traveled as a wave through me and startled me awake. Riestel had just kneeled in front of me and touched my shoulder with an icy drink.

"I thought you could use some refreshments before the tediousness."

"Something just asked me to help the arochs. Someone just spoke to me like Istrata, but it wasn't her. And none of them."

"Are you sure the sudden heat wave didn't boil your brain?"

"Please, you know it's long gone," I muttered and took the drink. "Thank you. I'm sure I heard it."

I tried to listen to it once more with closed eyes but couldn't perceive anything out of the ordinary. The sound of horses and a steady creek of wheels meant the arochs were being presented.

The prison carriage was opened by the stage. Each aroch had a colored ribbon on both their arms. One around their neck. Riestel explained with an appropriate tone of dislike that they were to be released and hunted. The hunter only needed to bring a ribbon. The bodies could be discarded. Each limb counted towards the points. Whoever got the most would win a piece of jewelry made from their stones.

I jumped up and drew Riestel with me.

"I guess we have made our mind up," he noted.

"Long ago. Now be useful."

The arochs stood surrounded by Frazil's guards. They held on to each other and smelled the air nervously. Frazil had just stopped his explanation on the point system and declared the hunt on. The guards tore the arochs apart and began to shove them to get them to move and run. Then someone fired a gun, the arochs took off.

Frazil took out his pocket watch and raised his arm. Once he lowered it, all guests who wanted to take part would move out. I tried to keep an eye on the directions the arochs headed, but most importantly, on where Arid ran. She was always the one they protected.

"Take the ribbons and keep them safe," I ordered.

"Why the ribbons wouldn't it be easier to just..." Riestel started.

"You aren't always that smart, either. The rules of the game did not state a person had to obtain the ribbons by crippling or killing them. If we collect them and win, Frazil cannot make a number out of it publicly."

Riestel looked content despite the insult.

Arid had disappeared from sight, but I followed some of the nobles and their servants to the direction she had headed. When Maherols noticed I was taking part, they put their weapons away and withdrew back to the celebration area. Many of the lower nobles followed their lead.

Out of breath, I reached a small clearing. I noticed some of the contenders looking through bushes. My toes tickles as if a wave had splashed over them. I touched the ground and felt slight tremors coming from a few larger boulders. Once I got closer, I could see her. Her skin had taken on the tone and color of the surroundings. Not perfectly but enough to fool someone in a hurry.

I raised my hands and showed her my palms while I walked to her. She was agitated and not too happy with me. I tried my best to explain that I needed her ribbon and that she should follow me to save the others. The answer was a very snappy, stinging wave of complaints about leaving them to wait for rescue for days and pressure to keep my promise. Almost like getting a slap across the face.

"Can you?" Arid asked in our tongue without much variation in pitch.

"I'm sorry my assistance is late. But I'm here. I will do all that I must. Please. The sooner we find the others, the faster I can get you into a safe place."

Arid raised her hand as if she was reaching for something in a tree. Her fingers tensed and spread apart a little. The air around them rippled like a pond when dropping a stone. Then she pointed East.

"Cliffd," she said.

"One of your guards?" I asked.

"Yes. Hand, take," Arid demanded and reached her delicate fingers towards me.

I did as she requested. She yanked me into the Lighter World. She ran through it as Tammaran did but pulled me along like a kite. The landing was anything but pleasant. Being dragged in whole trough the lighter plane twisted and turned my innards and almost made me throw up on entry back to the regular world.

Arid looked puzzled at my poor condition. Then she pointed to a group of men. The nobles had surrounded one of the arochs.

"Hey! Leave him be!" I ordered.

The men of the Rosse line turned to us, laughing. Their excitement turned sour when they recognized me.

"Why is the Temple meddling in this? This is our prey. You have one of yours already."

"That is the wrong question," I replied. "What you should be asking is how many breaths you have time to breathe before you burn like a silk skirt in a smithy's forge," I instructed them and lit a ring of fire between them and the aroch. The nobles withdrew, grumbling, and headed back.

Arid hurried to the other aroch and embraced him. Their metallic hairs entwined for a moment as if they checked the other one for injuries and traumas. It was such a gentle gesture that I felt their connection must have been something more.

Arid felt the air again and grabbed my wrist. Cliffd took my other hand. The jump was still unpleasant but with two of them holding me, I felt more stable and less pulling on my body. As we came out, Riestel was taking a ribbon of one exhausted aroch. There were two more behind him.

I turned to Arid and tried to ask how many were left. We hadn't taken much time, but some nobles had been carrying guns. Riestel handed me his ribbon. The sound of shots rang in the air.

Arid told me three were still missing. She and the others grabbed us and we flew. Riestel came out without any signs of nausea. One aroch was close to us on his knees. He was bleeding. Two others stood looking around nervously. A wall of rocks towered before them as a cover.

"I noticed you were looking for these, so I thought I would lend a hand," Heelis said and handed me several ribbons. Her smile was warmer than ever before. The glow of her hair and eyes slowly dimmed as she released the channeled powers used to make the stone wall.

"Thank you. Truly," I said.

"Just paying my debts."

"You have no debts standing with me. We have said all that was needed."

"I do. My marriage. I lied to Juone for years. Now, he knows what happened to our first child, and he stayed. For the first time, I feel like that wound can heal."

After confirming with Arid that we had found all her escorts and that the injured one would survive, we walked back to the ceremony stage. There were dozens of nobles complaining about us. Frazil and Lander were being bombarded with demands. As I climbed up the stairs, I kicked large flames towards the crowd. They quickly clammed up and withdrew to a more suitable distance.

"I'm getting fairly tired of constantly demanding an explanation from you," Frazil said. "We shall begin again. A noble's wedding must contain a hunt to please the crowds. It is almost a sacred tradition."

"Give me the ribbons!" Friti insisted and tried to snatch them.

"Lander," I called. "They are your prisoners and your tribute to the marriage. Nowhere was it stated that we must kill them for the ribbons. And nowhere was it stated that we cannot participate. These are my trophies, and as the owner of the prisoners, I beseech you to honor the rules as they were told. We did not break them."

Lander swayed uncomfortably. He squeezed his hands and rubbed them.

"I knew she would try to ruin Ghila's wedding!" Friti fumed. "I told you, but no! You had to drag her here instead of chaining her!" she scolded the king to be.

"That was not my intention. I'm merely trying to lead us to a new era where sacrifices like this are no longer welcome. No wedding of a king's daughter or a king himself is worth the life of another. Only the Temple can save or damn souls and lives. Should you have come to seek advice before organizing this empty and cruel display, I would have helped you to find something to replace it. Something to truly honor this new age."

Frazil's face twitched, but he remained silent. Perhaps to try to figure out how to turn the tide and calm things down. But it was hard to speak for slaughter and come off as noble. Lander straightened himself.

"Consecratoress," he began with a surprisingly committed tone. "I accept your victory. Let this gift be my declaration to the Temple that Eladion understands the severity of our plight. Ghila, let us celebrate this union with a decision to honor life instead of death. Would that not be a better way?"

Ghila looked at her parents then as a surprise to all, I suspect, she reached for her husband's hand and nodded.

"Father, please, I don't want anyone to die for us, not even those things," she backed her husband with a wispy voice.

"We cannot just unleash the brutes," Friti grumbled.

"They aren't free. They are mine," I stated and glanced at Arid. She fell to her knees without hesitation and the rest followed.

"See? Isn't it better to enslave them than to kill them? If we can negotiate with them, they can be conquered with trade," I suggested to cover my true intentions.

"Fine. I see no reason to force myself into this decision," Frazil declared. "The nobles, however, are quite unlikely to approve."

"Is there any other reason than the fact they cannot get their rewards?" I asked. "You have baskets full of gifts and guns to give. Let them have them. Let all of them have them. Why would I need them?"

Lander gestured to the servants to do as I suggested. The unsatisfied murmurs stopped once the nobles realized they were getting their baubles for no effort. Only Friti and Frazil stood surrounded by a cloud of gloom. I said nothing to them, just nodded, and left with the arochs.

We took the arochs towards the Needle. Heelis left us to join her family. Riestel walked behind us. His icy presence ensured no one tried anything.

"Show them to the Needle's top floor and lock the door," I asked. "I can't follow you until the coronation and whatever festivities take place once it is over."

"Alright," Riestel promised and opened the door to the tower. The arochs studied the building with awe and suspicion. After a moment, they calmed and stepped in. Arid stopped at the door and turned to me.

"You come to talk?" she asked.

"Tonight," I assured. "Riestel?"

"What might your humblest servant do now?"

"Keep them safe, whatever the price. Istrata had a deal with them. I have to know about it. I think they want to renegotiate it with me."

"Whatever the price... well, since you asked so nicely," Riestel agreed and transferred a kiss from his lips to my forehead with two fingers.

The door to the Needle froze shut after him.

XXXIV

Frazil's family headed to the bow. As the future king walked past me, he lifted his hand to his forehead to greet me, but this was no greeting as his hand was covered with his metal glove and the number of guards had doubled since the wedding. I found my way to Rime. He was still mostly out of it and constantly under observation. Moras pulled me aside for a moment.

"This treatment is monstrous," he sighed and wiped sweat from his brow, glancing at Frazil. "But he is doing well, considering the circumstances. They talked alone earlier. Frazil promised this was just for today. Then he will loosen the reins."

"Right. Can I talk to him? Can he hear me if I try?"

Moras nodded and stepped aside. He managed to get the nearest guards to give us a little more breathing room. Rime sat staring into the distance. He kept twirling grains of sand between his thumb and index finger as if saying a mechanical prayer. I sat right next to him and touched his face. Rime looked at me sideways. His eyes were darker than normal but not pitch black.

"Are the arochs safe?" Rime asked, continuing to play with the sand and returning to look straight ahead. His voice was quite monotone, and his mouth moved only the bare minimum necessary to form the words.

"Yes, for now," I told him, a little confused. That was the first thing he asked about?

"Riestel is guarding them. How are you?" I asked.

"Fine. All is said and done. The future of the city will be stable."

"Did you two settle your differences or come to some agreement?"

"In a way. We talked, and we both agree he should take the throne. No more arguments."

I stroked Rime's hand. It was lovely to hear they wouldn't be butting heads anymore. But why had we gone through all this? Why had he insisted on pushing Frazil and made himself a target for all his father's wrath just to make amends a little later? It was bizarre to me that both of them could change their attitudes and opinions so fast. At least now, I had time on my side to tell him all that he needed to know.

"And your status?" I asked. "Will you have to give it up? Do you want to?"

"He promised to let the Guard out as soon as he has his crown. That is what matters to me more than my title. The wellbeing of this city and the world is more important than any of us. I can't only consider what is beneficial for me. Besides… I had the honor of being a field marshal. I'm sure I will find suitable work again," he mused and flicked the sand off his fingers. He leaned back and looked at the sky and his old self shone right through. He brushed his forehead and smiled with the taste of freedom on his lips.

"For the first time in my life, I'm not sure whether tomorrow will pour or shine," he said. "But let's jump. I'm happy that you are with me."

"Let's jump? What does that mean?"

Rime took my hand and pressed a kiss on it. Then he fell back into a stiff and absent look, got up, and walked to the coronation platform like the most polite and obedient son in the world. A performance indeed.

Soldiers and guards in finely starched uniforms began to encircle the Needle's square. They formed a winding alley for Frazil to walk through once he was ready. All nobles and other important quests had been guided in front of a marble and gold podium that held the ceremonial throne. It was a simple wooden stool to signify the modesty of the king and to emphasize his role as a servant to the city. Hundreds of silken ruffles brushed the earth as the nobles took their places. Each marked spot had a small gift parcel in front of it.

When I had been crowned, there had been only a few people present. Then the city could have afforded all this. It could have celebrated for weeks with no repercussions. For a moment, I could feel the metal press on my head. It was a wonderful feeling not having to wear it anymore, but it was terrible to watch as others tried to steer history to their liking.

The two governors from outside the city kneeled on the first step of the platform. Rime and Kymenes did the same by their side. Frazil's family wasn't present anymore. They had gone to change their clothing for the evening. I could see the soldiers begin to lift their blades. The wave of metal progressed much quicker than the man it honored.

I kneeled next to the Maherols. Frazil walked past me in clothes that were of the same deep dark blue as late fall nights. They were embroidered with a warm-colored brass thread. His face was adorned by a rehearsed smile that almost made it to his eyes but lacked strength right at the crucial moment. He raised his hands towards the city. I could hear the familiar clicking of the noble's nails as they gossiped.

Looking around, it was easy to notice they were more interested in chatting than their king. Same was true for the men. They might not have had the same language and means, but not many seemed to give this coronation their undivided attention. Further down, the merchants and other representatives of the Lower's were the exact opposite. They had their arms raised up to the sky like they would be praying for rain.

"My friends and countrymen," Frazil began, pleased with himself. "This day is truly an important one for me, but also for our fair city. Let us seek unification under the same goals and consider ourselves more as Kerthians than just nobles or merchants. It has been the custom for many generations that the Temple anoints the new ruler. We are breaking these old ways, so I call on my son to crown me. As the head of the army, he has all the right to do so with their might equaling that of the Temple. But I would like to enquire from the Temple if this will please them as well."

"We do not object," Kymenes answered. We didn't. What difference did it make who laid the crown on his head? I cared not, and the more independence the Temple had from the city, the better. There was no room for spirituality in politics. The only thing that galled me was that Frazil was making a point of stepping on the military's leader.

"Will our sister cities accept me?" Frazil asked.

"Loisto will accept you! Our loyalty is yours until you harm the country."

"Eladion will accept you! Our loyalty is yours until you harm the country."

Frazil nodded and spread his arms towards the crowds.

"And I ask you, representatives of the city, will you accept me? Stand up to give your consent."

Each row, beginning from the humblest, begun to get up. The nobles in a slightly unorganized manner, sighing at the task. Rime frowned at me and gestured me to get up. I jumped to my feet as I had completely forgotten to do so while staring at all the others.

"Good," Frazil said with an annoyed note and sat on the throne. "My son."

Rime took the box from behind the seat and opened it. The crown shone beautifully. Frazil had chosen a model that looked more like a headband than a high crown. There were several polished stones, but the decorations were very subtle. Rime picked the crown up slowly and walked to his father's feet.

"The military salutes you. I offer you this city and the loyalty of our troops until you harm the country," Rime said, then he kneeled and raised the crown to his father. Frazil accepted it. For a moment, before lowering it on to his head, he admired it against the sky. Frazil closed his eyes, looking as if he enjoyed the weight of it together with the rays of the setting sun.

The representatives of the Merchant's and the rest of Lower's burst into cheers. The nobles gave a short, lukewarm applause. The rows of soldiers stayed in place. Frazil got up. He looked picture perfect as the king. There was a self-righteous smile lurking in his eyes when he ordered Rime to make way and walked past him to the edge of the platform, almost stepping on his son's fingers.

"I thank you all for your time," Frazil said. "And I invite you to make merry and celebrate the new era with me. You are all welcome. Even the temporary governors…" he continued and chuckled to himself. "If they will kiss my feet. You have proven to be quite a nuisance, so I demand this sign of humility," he demanded as the members of the Black Guard were brought out.

Their hands were tied behind their backs. Rime looked surprised but returned to his kneeled posture after a quick look without a show of emotion.

"Well?" Frazil pressed.

The soldiers holding the Guard let them go and shoved them towards the throne. They walked a little uneasily to Frazil and kneeled one by one and bowing down as low as possible.

"Field Marshal," Frazil called. "You too. Unless you wish your sins to keep them as my guests for an even longer period."

Rime lifted himself a little. The men looked very uncomfortable. Veitso especially looked as if he would have rather been at the border fighting than groveling and being used against Rime.

"If it brings you peace of mind," Rime finally answered and bent down to his father's feet as the guard members before him. A darkness returned to his eyes.

After obeying his father, he got up and walked to the Guard after they had been excused, too. Frazil gave the rest of his speech and told people where to go for the festivities. Because, gods forbid, the different classes should mingle in the same hall at the beginning of this new and improved era.

I hurried to take Rime's arm. He had a slight smile on his face, despite everything. Public humiliation hadn't been in Frazil's arsenal before.

"We will see…" Rime whispered, "… how long the crown stays."

"Have you plans for it?"

"Of course, I will do my best to keep it on him to the end," Rime laughed as we headed indoors. "He is the king."

XXXV

T he Grand Audience Hall had been redecorated after the engagement celebrations with, if possible, even grander things. As there weren't enough real flowers to pick, the servants had crafted and sown roses and lilies from expensive fabrics. Among the silken pedals laid jeweled anthers. The walls had huge hand-painted maps with promises and plans for the city on display, new plans for buildings to replace all the destroyed ones.

Each wall and corner were guarded by a chain of men in the colors of the new king. The modest coronation chair burned in the massive central fireplace. The official throne was just being installed on the eight-stepped dais. It had blue velvet cushioning, a silver-plated seat with red and yellow stones in the armrests. At the top of the back was a large engraved, blue-painted snake. Their sigil as a family line of the Knights of Saraste.

Once the throne was ceremonially blessed and Frazil sat on it, waves of salutes echoed around. Rime's men sat below the platform to the left. Their hands were still bound behind their backs. To the right side, sat the rest of the family and the governors on smaller but almost equally glamorous chairs.

Rime touched my shoulder and offered me a glass of wine.

"For the duration of this celebration, I am solely at your disposal," he said.

"And the Guard? Aren't you going to demand their release? Your father promised to let them go once he had the crown?"

"Isa. Do you think I have the status or standing to demand that from a just-crowned king? I am a servant among many. Maybe even one of the less favored," Rime noted and took a drink. "The Guard knows it. They agreed to this foolishness so I could know what my father thinks. It would have been nice to prove my mother wrong and to prove my father was more interested in getting a son than utility, but one cannot have all."

"Have you spoken to Enna after you sent her to sober up? You haven't talked of her for a long time."

"I have. She has mostly stopped. I take some pride in that, but there isn't a place for her here yet."

"Is she mad at me?"

"No," Rime answered with a smile. "On the contrary. The first thing she said after being sober for a longer time was that I should be grateful to possess a woman that will stand up to a mother when she is wrong. She knows what you'd do for me, so why should she fault you when you were scared for my life?"

I pressed the cool glass on my warm cheek.

"Would you rather have had a talking to?"

"Kind of," I muttered. "I don't know how I can face her."

"You can, but not for a moment still."

After touring the Hall, we sat in a small nook with a table. It felt odd to think that everything was settled. Kerth and Aderas had a new king. The Temple's rebuilding was progressing fast. Only our fate was open. I took Rime's hand. It wasn't as coarse as before. Still as strong.

"What happened to your house in the Merchant's?" I asked. "Does it still exist, or did you sell it?"

"Would you like to move back there?"

I nodded absentmindedly.

"If I have roots anywhere in this city, it is your house."

"It's still ours. I haven't yet given thought to what we should do with it. Or should I plead for my old position back? We could return and live a normal life for a moment," Rime pondered and glanced at the throne.

"I could make and bring you lunch every day," I mused. "You could take me to the tavern to dance and we could walk the rainy streets and share a quilt by the fire."

"I'm not saying I wouldn't love to do that, but it has to be some other life, Isa."

I withdrew my hand and lowered my gaze from his warm eyes. I knew that.

"Our family is already larger than just us. Would you like the same life added with a child?" he asked.

I tilted my head and bit my lip. I didn't want to bring the real world into this conversation.

"Your mother can take care of them. She will meddle anyway."

Rime laughed and nodded. His forehead frowned a moment before the smile and a curious look.

"I suppose that would be impossible to prevent."

"Have you any new information on the child?" I asked reluctantly.

"I don't know where the child is right now, but I know where it was held. I can't say more yet. I don't want to speculate," Rime replied and stretched back, looking tired. "I've watched you with Elona. You like her more than you'd like to admit," Rime noted, leaning against the table again. "I'm happy we chose to save her."

"It was your choice more than mine. I'm grateful for it. I couldn't have made it in time or had the heart suggest it. You are far too rehearsed at making tough decisions. Although, perhaps with me, it is unavoidable."

"I can't deny that," he breathed and looked at the Guard and the new royals.

"What are you thinking?" I wondered.

"I'm merely trying to guess how much longer this night will last and when the Guard will be freed. When my father settles down from this temper tantrum and his family will revert back to all the normal interests of nobles, I want you to start training for Istrata. I will do the same, Riestel will do the same. We may not know what she is capable of, but we must reach our potentials before the enemy is at our gates. We can do this. Together."

"You mean you'd spar with me?"

"Yes. I must learn to control these forced channels, especially against you. And you against me. Isa, don't pout," he asked, amused, as he saw my face and pulled me closer to his side of the table. "The world isn't going to break any faster if we talk about true things."

I sighed, curling up to his side. His loving gaze studied me.

"Are you planning on fidgeting all evening trying to find a comfortable position?" he asked.

"Well, it is a very precise job. If I'm in a slightly wrong angle, my hand will go numb or my foot. You'll just have to wait until I'm done," I replied and shook my shoulders to get into an even cozier position. I closed my eyes and enjoyed the peace I always felt in his arms.

"So, what would our actual future entail?" I asked. "What do you think is possible?"

"You want to be here, in the Needle, I know that much. No matter how many stories of our life in the Merchant's you'd weave. As long as your place is here, we are not going anywhere. You supported me during all the promotion hassles, waiting for me to return from the border, trusted me, and stayed with me once you knew what I was. I don't know if I care about this career path anymore. I wouldn't complain if I had no other agency than to protect you. Not that I haven't earned each brand and ribbon…"

"Then it's more important to you that you have something meaningful to do?"

"Yes. And the most vital thing to this city is to keep you here, studying the steps of your ancient self and fixing the issues she caused. That is the only goal that matters."

"Not that I don't appreciate your support or know that I have it… that can't be all," I complained. "What do you want for yourself? When we were taking the city and you thought I was sleeping, I heard you say that I'm your witch and that every king has one."

Rime tilted his head.

"It was a fleeting idea. A crown will make a person a target, it complicates things. A title isn't the only way to power."

"You are dancing around my question."

"I'm not. I'm just waiting for the opportune moment," Rime whispered. "And I'm doing so in the best company."

We admired the dancers and took in the whole evening talking hours on end about all the things we had never said. Then the Hall went quiet. Frazil had hit a booming bell to signal he had something to say. Perhaps his first official speech of too many. At least, that's what I thought until he ordered the Guard to stand and bring them forth.

"Return them to the cells," he ordered. "This parading will do."

Rime jumped up. He gritted his teeth.

"I'm sorry. It is time I ruined his evening," Rime said as his eyes darkened.

Rime marched towards the line of soldiers and Frazil's guards. I ran after him. I knew he couldn't leave the Guard to face poor treatment, but why wait this long? Had he still held out, hoping for a conciliatory gesture from his father? Whatever Rime intended, the timing was a mystery to me. All had been done, and the new king was anointed.

Rime lifted his hand in front of the first guard to halt him.

"What is this?" Rime asked Frazil, keeping his eyes firmly on the guard who gripped Samedi a little tighter. "Will you betray your words on the first night you hold the throne?"

"I am sorry, should you believe it or not. No matter. I cannot keep fighting this seemingly endless quarrel about all decisions I make. I must be allowed to act freely as the king."

"And that freedom entails breaking you promises?" Rime pressed.

"I'm hardly executing them," Frazil jeered. "I'm taking this road for my safety, and for Isa's sake, so I do not have to use her against you."

"What in high skies did that mean?" I demanded to know. Frazil chose his words with poisonous precision.

"Our admirable King," Loisto's Governor Vuole cut in from his chair. "Would it not be a better evening for forgiveness?" he suggested in earnest with a warmer tone than I had ever heard him use. "They have all kneeled to you. I believe these young men are an asset to your city and all of Aderas. Let us not waste them in jail."

"NO!" Friti yelled, getting up from her seat. "This is what I mean! Something unravels every time you listen to them and let them be," she complained.

Frazil looked at them both.

"My wife, your Queen, is correct. As soon as all calms, they will be let out."

"But how can he take your word for it?" Vuole asked as his face dimmed with disappointment. "First you said only until the coronation. Then you gave your word they'd not suffer another night as prisoners after you had your crown. Twice now you have broken the promise. This game isn't worthy of you, my friend."

"Keep your moral lectures to yourself," Friti scoffed and hung herself on her husband's arm. "You have betrayed as many as a governor as anyone else. It is not the King's place to make amends to the offenders."

Vuole looked dismayed at her words. The old man mumbled something to himself and got off the platform. He walked to us. As he reached Rime, he laid his hand on Rime's shoulder. Vuole's whole being oozed disappointment and worry.

"Alright, I believe you," Vuole whispered to Rime. "He has shown his character, so I will yield this back to you."

A wicked, content smile spread on Rime's face as Vuole handed him a roll of paper with multiple different colored ribbons.

"Clear the Hall!" Rime growled and hit the floor with a seething black pole axe that appeared in his hand out of thin air. Even the people on the farther side of the Hall, who had been blissfully unaware on the argument, stopped in their tracks.

"The festivities are at an end. Leave! We have family matters to discuss!" Rime insisted. Those who knew him better headed to the doors, but many stood in place awaiting Frazil to confirm or deny the order.

"Son, do not test me this evening," Frazil asked with a cold tone while gesturing the guards to keep going. "Be at ease, dear guests. A small family squabble, we may continue with the entertainment in just a moment," he announced to all in the Hall with a soothing smile. Some of the guests still left while others returned happily to their conversations.

"Out!" Rime yelled with a voice carrying a foreign animal echo as his eyes fell under the black shroud. "NOW!" he demanded, and black spear-headed swirls of the darkest night rushed towards Frazil's guards. Vuole stepped sideways partially behind me as if I was meant to be there to shield him.

Before anyone could object, all the men fell lifeless to the floor. A thick cloud of blackness swarmed around Rime, and his steps marked the floor with a black mud-like ichor. The members of his guard ran to chase people out. Dozens of guards positioned themselves between us and Frazil. Soon the Hall filled with soldiers to save their king. Friti's face had a poisonous sneer. Ghila and Lander had hidden in a corner with Ghila's younger sister, Orelia. They were trying to melt into the wall.

"You want me to order your execution?" Frazil asked. "There is no way I can pardon you for an attempt on my life."

"You are wrong, again," Rime responded with an echoey, rough voice. "The only thing I want is for you to read this paper," he insisted and broke the seal to the scroll with his thumb. "Read and commit to memory. But before that, send all that do not need to be here away."

"And what would stop you from trying to take my life if I send my soldiers away?"

"What do you think is stopping me now? These men? Your glove and skill? Fine. Let us see," Rime suggested as his eyes bled oily streaks. I grabbed Samedi's sleeve and pulled him towards one of the side doors. The others followed.

"Shouldn't we stay to help?" Samedi whispered.

"This is between them," I answered quietly.

"Well, don't let him get himself killed," Veitso grumbled.

"I won't," I promised. "I will step in if need be."

Tammaran entered the door last and turned around for a moment. His face was all wrinkled, and he glanced around looking uncomfortable in his skin.

"What is it? You aren't yourself." I asked.

"I remembered something of that day. The smell that wafted into the room when your child was taken. I think I noticed it again. It was a sweet..."

"Tell me once this evening is passed. Take yourselves to safety first," I talked over him and shoved him out the door. I stayed there for a moment with my back against the door. Rime was surrounded by forty men with long spears. Frazil lowered his hand on the back on his throne. A few clicks later, a part of the throne had attached itself to his hand as a familiar glove.

Rime was standing in an almost relaxed posture, leaning on his poleaxe and waiting. I wanted to slap them both on the back of the head and drag them out to cool off in the river. But if this wasn't dealt with, it would just fester and rot.

"Shall we?" Rime asked and tilted his head from right to left like a heavy pendulum.

Frazil finally ordered his family to vacate the room. Vuole, Lander, and Friti refused. All guns and weapons were pointed at Rime. When Frazil turned fully to us, the first line of guards took a step forward in unison and gripped their spears more firmly. Then they jabbed them forward. Rime lifted his poleaxe towards the ceiling. A back curtain covered him. The spears sunk into the darkness and couldn't be pulled out. Soon the weapons fell on the floor, eaten through from where they had sunk into the mass.

Rime appeared from the shield. It tore into dozens of silky strings that grabbed and twisted around the necks of Frazil's troops. They bit like a barbed wire, tearing them apart bit by bit like swarming ants. Frazil stopped in his tracks and hesitated. I would have too. This was their power unchained.

"Stop or you will never see your child again!" Friti threatened with a squeaky voice. At that moment my brain processed Tammaran's last words. "Sweet rowan liquor." My head swirled in an ocean of relief and bottomless despair. I walked towards Rime.

"Never ever will you lay eyes on the child!" Friti stressed.

"Do not make empty threats. You do not possess the child," I replied. "You never held the child. Where is your mother keeping him? Where is Enna? Tell me!" I insisted.

Rime yanked the black strings from the soldiers, who collapsed empty to the ground. His gaze focused only partly on me.

"Safe," a hollow voice said. I wasn't sure if he even knew it was me asking. His reaction certainly didn't seem like it.

"What are you talking about?" Frazil asked nervously. "The child has been with my people from the day he was born."

A grim, content smile spread on Rime's face.

"Each report you have received of him was delivered on a yellowed paper with a flaw in etiquette in the opening paragraph," Rime said. Frazil wiped his forehead and look at his wife, who nodded.

"Stop wasting time. Come and read!" Rime pressed. "Or see how your soldiers fall from him to the last," he threatened and shot out more of the dark wires towards the next line of soldiers. One was charging toward Friti. Frazil's face paled.

"Stop! Fine. Send it to me, and I will read it," Frazil said impatiently.

"No," Rime replied and the rest of the soldiers fell dead. Friti took a step back, looking shaken. Frazil lifted his hand as a soothing gesture and took off the glove.

"I will come and read your ridiculous scroll!" Frazil promised. "Leave her be."

Frazil stepped down from the platform and walked to his son. Rime stretched his hand out towards his father, dangling the scroll. As Frazil tried to take it, he yanked it back.

"I didn't say you could touch it," Rime remarked and lifted it to his father's face.

Frazil skimmed through the paper, his face filled with mistrust. Then his brows furrowed deeper than ever before. He looked decades older and more bitter than ever.

"I should have known better than to trust you. As your father, I wanted to believe in a different outcome," Frazil said and spat at Rime's feet.

"You should have known?" Rime asked. "You do realize that I still am not, after all this, taking your precious crown away from you? I would have worn your family crest with honor and pride forever should you have been capable of trusting me," he continued in a low voice and charged forth. Frazil fell unceremoniously on his back.

"Enjoy your reign," Rime said and placed the scroll into his jacket pocket.

"When did you orchestrate all this? When did you manage to talk them into making you a war counsel?" Frazil muttered and got up. "What do you want from me?"

"Nothing anymore. A year ago, a father," Rime answered and the dark substance withdrew. "What I want now is for you to move to the center of the city and to rule according to my orders. I am, after all, letting you keep your head and your crown. They are the perfect front. None will know about this. Is it clear?"

Frazil gave a tired laugh and glanced at the Governor of Loisto.

"Why?" Frazil asked. "What else did I need to offer you? What did he offer that I couldn't?"

The older governor lowered his head a little and shook it. "I am sorry, my King. At first, I fought it. But then Rime suggested that I merely give the needed stamp and my ribbons and I can keep all of them, the original and the copies, until I see proof. I didn't want to believe it. But if you are prepared to go back on your word to your son… what would await us once we disagree?" he explained. "He gave you ample opportunity to trust him. I witnessed them. My people reported them. At least with Rime, I know what I'm getting thanks to his years at the border and his visits to us," Vuole added and stepped further away.

"Now, if you play nice, you may keep that shiny crown, your throne, and above all, your precious honor. I will declare this arrangement public only if you fail to recognize the good of your family and yourself. You will stand as the head of the city, mighty and trustworthy. I will make you one of the greatest kings as long as you remember that in reality, you're a king of naught. Funnily enough, the same applies to me. As your first deed after tonight, you will pack up and head to the center and leave the Peak to those whom it belongs."

Rime yanked Frazil to his feet and shoved him towards the door his family had fled through.

"Remember to look as if all your dreams have been fulfilled," Rime ordered with a smile.

"Do you think he will obey?" I asked, counting the bodies.

"Yes. And if for no other reason, to save his family from the humiliation.

They have their status as the royals and they can live in opulence compared to most."

"Right… Well, I should go. The arochs are waiting in the Needle.

"Go. I will clean up."

XXXVI

T he corridors of the palace were silent and still. I walked slowly towards the staircase of the Needle. Right now, the world had no place I would have felt comfortable in or that I would have missed or wanted to see. I didn't have the strength to be angry or even surprised. I was just tired. I knew all the decisions he made were for the city. I knew I had given him free rein when we had talked of the paths before us. Still, their deed was hard to come to terms with.

An ice-casing covered the staircase's door. It was as thick as my arm and cooled the air many steps around it. I stared at my distorted image in the ice and touched it. It was full of Riestel's clear and pure power. Hot tears ran down my face. I sat on the floor.

The ice resided, and Riestel bent down next to me faster than I could have asked. He helped me up without a word. I leaned on him floor after floor.

"I will move the arochs to the lower room to give you some privacy," Riestel said as he guided me past the baffled guests.

I sat by the nexus and looked at the night sky when Riestel returned. He sat next to me and took my hand.

"You may cry aloud should you want to," he whispered.

"Take me away. Far away. So far that this tower's shadow doesn't reach there."

"I'm not sure we should."

"Rime knew. He has had the child all along. His mother," I said and touched my stomach.

"What?" Riestel asked, genuinely surprised, and started to get up. I grasped his sleeve and pulled him back.

"I don't mean he did it. Not the worst thing, but all that Tammaran recalled and told me means they knew of the plan to take the child and let it happen."

Riestel sighed and stroked my head. I went over every moment again and again. Certainly, I knew I wouldn't have died then, but something inside me broke more and more. This cursed city was so important to Rime that even my wellbeing came in second. Then again… it was only right. What did any one person mean against so many others? I had just hoped that he'd be a little more selfish when it came to me.

"I'm sorry. I cannot whisk you away forever yet. I did, however, have a conversation with the arochs. From what I understood, they want you to come and speak to their ruler. I can escort you there if you want a break. Istrata was summoned there in her days."

"Yes. Now. Let's go immediately."

"You know I'd do much for you, but I cannot just up and leave without letting at least Arvida know so Elona won't be frightened and alone. I will make the arrangements; you will rest for the darkest hour. Once I return, we will disappear for a while."

As Riestel closed the door, I thought I would feel more anger and sorrow for what Rime had kept from me. But it was just so ridiculous. Despite everything darkening, my life just kept rolling along and pushing me further and further. I was at the very top of Kerth in all the possible meanings. It was mine again. Ours. The horizon wasn't. I wanted it. To explore it.

I already knew all the reasons Rime would give me for his actions. And from his perspective, they were all acceptable and noble even. It would be a tough debate to have if I wanted to scold him and his mother. But as much as I excused them, my heart was raw and hurting.

"*You see?*" Istrata asked. "*No one can truly love the fire. That is why I wish to remove it from the world. Without it, there is not so much suffering, losses. There is no endless dance of life and death to grind us up and spit us out.*"

"Your timing is immaculate," I sighed. "How exactly do you spy on me? There has to be some little thread you use to climb into my head like a spider," I asked and stuck my hand into the nexus.

"*You could save so many from unnecessary pain and fear if you give yourself to me. Losing the fire will not hurt. I will win in the end, anyway.*"

"The thing is, I like the fire. I'm selfish, unlike you. I don't know if I care how much your people suffer," I taunted her while pocketing the small morsel of knowledge that she knew what giving up the fire felt like. The Queen had given her creation powers in favor of another road. My first reaction was to end the conversation and run to tell Rime, but I stayed myself.

"Would you judge the world just to spite me?"

"Ask Riestel that. He can give a more trustworthy answer about my character," I smirked. Though I didn't see her face, I felt her annoyance.

"Why fight it so? Do you honestly think you may have an effect on my plans? The future I have planned for centuries?"

"Why? That... is a remarkably silly question from the person who created me as I am. Forced me to be what I am. I think about things so differently than you. I value different things. You made me selfish and stubborn. Cruel even. You made sure all these lives I lived and died under Riestel's boot distanced me from other living people. Do I care about your people? Some of them, but not them as a whole."

The Queen said nothing more. I tried to feel where the connection was, but there were too many strands and ways to follow. I couldn't isolate which her consciousness used.

Riestel's hand brushed my shoulder.

"Are you sure about this?" he asked as I got up.

"No, but I feel this is the right path."

"We can still wait a moment if you want to talk to him or say something to him."

"Are you of all people trying to mend my marriage?" I asked with a sullen amusement.

"I don't have any tissues with me and I hardly want you to use my sleeves again," Riestel explained and picked imaginary lint off his coat. I threw my notetaking pen at him. He froze it in the air and dropped it down.

"Mind your manners, Consecratoress," he demanded happily. I bit my lip because I didn't want to ruin my perfectly good start to becoming depressed again.

"He won't share his decisions with me, even if they affect my life. I know he does so with good intentions for the whole of Aderas. I don't blame him for that. But I am petty enough to give him a taste of his own medicine," I explained.

"I would call it nothing but reasonable," Riestel pondered and looked around. "Do you need anything?"

"I don't know. Do I?" I asked Arid as she peaked into the room. She shook her head and promised all our needs would be taken care of.

"Can I still take something if I wish to?" I checked. Arid nodded. I drew out Istrata's notebook from under the nexus. It was the one I had never shown anyone else. It was a journal of a different experiments. Achieving godhood and the many ways towards that goal. It was her goal—then she would reign all. The smooth cover hid many tantalizing secrets. Istrata had forsaken her natural route towards higher powers and looked for another one, perhaps an easier one, perhaps a harder one. She did so because she despised the fire, but I loved the flames. I hid it in my clothes.

"Do we travel with horses or...?" I asked, trailing off. "I do not want them to track me right away. Not that they necessarily would in this situation. Rime will be busy with the city's affairs. But I want to be sure I have some peace and quiet."

Arid dismissed the idea about horses and showed how we would jump the city's walls. Riestel shrugged.

"It can't be worse than before," he said. "And no one can trace us, should we travel like that."

"Tammaran might be able to, but I don't think I would object to talking to him. Arid? How far can we get with your way? You home must be weeks away on horseback. Do we need to walk long distances? I wouldn't like to be gone for the entire summer."

"Travel fast," Arid promised. "We know way home, always. Here walk because not know place. Home few jumps," she explained. "Must rest in between them. Maybe five days. We have two to carry."

"Efficient, aren't they?" Riestel remarked. "We shall entrust our wellbeing to you."

Arid nodded in a good mood. Her metallic hair made almost bell-like sounds. She took our hands, joined them, and made us promise not to let go. We needed to think of our own shape and the shape of the other. The rest of the arochs came in from the stairs. They formed a circle around us and each laid a hand on me or Riestel. I felt an electric vibration crisscross my body. They memorized us down to each flaw so we would not break while traveling in the Lighter World for longer periods.

It felt as if we would have been lifted up by the wind, like a dandelion seed. Then the breeze grabbed us and pushed us through the city. As there were so many arochs helping us, my nausea was much improved from traveling with her alone. I saw lines, colors that didn't exist, and frozen still pictures of familiar places. Kerth and the White Needle were left behind looking like small dots on the horizon without meaning. As we stopped, the last wavy fields with well-doing plants were between us and the city.

In the other direction, the green color reached far, but not so far the eye couldn't see where the poorer lands begin. The scenery turned to a dry yellow and then a brown, barren land. Well, the holiday location might not be the most idyllic, but right now, it was good enough.

Arid announced that we'd travel by foot for a moment then sleep and jump again. I felt a certain joy wandering around, almost free of thought around new lands. I glanced back at the Needle. I could feel Rime at the door. I felt his surprise when he realized the quarters were empty and I was nowhere to be found. My body ached from that knowledge. The nexus told me all of it without focusing. I apologized to Rime in my mind for leaving so abruptly. He'd likely understand, but the return wasn't going to be easy for either of us.

Riestel walked beside me humming contently. He picked a flower here, another there. Once the evening darkened a bit, he sat beside me, took my hand, and wrapped a bracelet on my wrist he had crafted from blushing pink-meadow anemones and blue-sky anemones. Their little balls of pollen shone against the petals as grains of sugar held against the sun.

"What for?" I asked.

"If you don't like it, give it back," Riestel said and reached for it. I pulled my hand to safety.

"It wasn't a complaint. It's pretty."

"Do I always and forever need a reason to be nice?"

"Nice? You started coming on to me the moment we crossed over the walls."

"Coming on to you? Me? Heavenly stars above, what is it in that small head of yours that turns every polite gesture into courtship? The world doesn't always revolve around your behind, lovely as it is."

I was just about to respond to Riestel when I realized all the arochs were looking at us like a flock of curious birds with their heads tilted. Arid moved closer.

"All good?" she asked. "Fighting all time, even with gift. Curious. You express love?"

"Indeed," Riestel grinned and nodded. "She likes so much she wants to kill me."

A wave of amusement emanated from Arid, though she didn't laugh. Her metallic hair curled a little. I went red. I had never considered what we looked like to outsiders. In Riestel's company, I was always allowed to be my annoying self.

Riestel stretched out, lying on his back in the meadow. The orange glow from the horizon dusted his skin with golden hues. Each white tip of his eyelashes shone like a torch as the light hit them. I shook my head and looked away. I cooled my cheeks with my fingers. The bracelet's scent became stronger as the night drew closer. The arochs were making a small hut out of earth and branches to shelter us for the night. But before I even noticed, I was again staring at a pair of crystal-like, winter sky-blue eyes. It was not a good sign.

Riestel grabbed my wrist and pulled me over to his side. My nose almost touched his cheek. He turned his head and looked at me with half-shut eyes.

"On this journey, I am nothing more than a friend," he whispered. "Nothing else. As long as you are hurting over him, I will not pursue anything."

"Noble," I muttered with a partially icy arm as my pillow.

"I thought so. But I do mean it. I am here to support and help as one of your family, not a rival. That would help no one."

"Quit being so sweet."

"Why? What's the harm in that?" he asked, eyes closed and smiling. The sun's last sliver disappeared and made room for a turquoise evening.

XXXVII

I woke in the meadow to a surprisingly chilly morning. The others slept. Arochs sitting, Riestel on his side, curved like a crescent moon. I missed Rime despite everything, but in all honesty, I felt something deep for Riestel. Something very different.

Rime had pulled me to him right from the start, like a current. No matter how hard I swam and told myself I could get out, there was never a way out. I hadn't even known I was capable of such strong emotions. Amusingly so, as he was the one who could kill me, all of me. A chill went through me. Had a part of the current that pulled me to him been my desire to end my life, to escape this ever-repeating chain of lives? It was an uneasy thought, but not one easily dismissed.

Riestel. Under all that attitude and coldness, he was gentle and considerate. At least to people he liked. I felt so at ease with him. He didn't care how I acted, what I did. He didn't consider my status or any etiquette rules. My feelings for him were a mixture of delicate silence and a bottomless ocean. Grief and sympathy. A desire to hold his hand and heal what was broken. I stopped in my tracks when I realized I really did have a thing for fixing men.

"Continue," Arid called.

We traveled for several days like this. First a jump, then a walk to stabilize the body, then a nightly rest. Each stop was gloomier than the previous. The sky's beauty didn't wane even in the harshest places. Quite the contrary, the stars shined so brightly, it almost felt they were both mocking this dying land and crying for it.

"We shall reach the border of Aderas soon," Riestel whispered.

"One more leap," Arid said. "Then home. Better place, even if getting small."

"I can't feel anything here. No life." I sighed. "Is this the world she wished to bring about?"

"I'm sorry," Riestel replied. "There's nothing else I can say. I've been thinking many nights now, especially after I got Elona back. I helped Istrata into this cycle when I killed her according to her instructions. If I had just waited a moment, the Knights of Saraste would have come and none of this would have happened."

"How can you think like that?"

"It's true."

"No, it is not, you moron. You loved her. You didn't know she was lying that one time."

"Didn't I? Can I say I didn't wonder even back then if the plan she told me made sense or if it could backfire in the most horrendous way? I'm not sure, not anymore. I've played out that scene so many times in my head that I cannot tell if the memory rings true."

"Then believe in yourself," I urged and touched his arm. "I'm not going to say you are always pleasant, but deep down, you are better than most of us. I can't know how you were then, before all this suffering was placed on you, but I can see the beauty and the lightness you carried yourself with. It's not gone, no matter how damaged you think you are. Just polish yourself a bit and it will get better," I teased him and tried to rub his shoulder like polishing a pot.

"You are carrying her most cherished notes with you. Is that a road you are taking?"

"May the sea salt your eyes, must you notice everything?" I agonized and took the booklet out. "Do you think it is possible? To become a god?"

"Suppose that depends on how you define a god. Is it the silent beginning or is it someone who is more powerful than anyone else, or is it someone who can change the world according to their will? Is it any of those or all?"

"I don't know. I can sense something behind all of this. I don't know what. I don't think we can be that."

"I feel it too."

"But... I suppose it would be enough to be ageless, almost eternal and powerful. Something else than a limited, fragile man."

"Do you want to be that? Why? I can tell you that a long age isn't always a blessing."

"And yet, you did not wish to relinquish it when I offered a way."

Riestel laughed and grinned.

"True. As there are still things in this world that are new to me or give me joy," he admitted.

"Would you become one if offered to you?"

"Who on earth would be stupid enough to offer me such status?" he mused and gave me a sly look.

I shrugged.

"Let's just pretend there was a person that dumb," I suggested.

"I would take the offer in a heartbeat."

"In a heartbeat? That is a big statement."

"As long as you exist, I want to exist. If you become what you secretly seek, I must follow. If for no other reason than to balance the world."

"Who said I was? I'm just poking about."

Riestel's sparkling laugh filled the air. Sometimes, when he forgot his duties and the world, he seemed to get younger right in front of me. Especially around Elona.

"We do not rest today, second leap soon," Arid told us. "Not long, we make it," she pondered. "Fine with you?"

"Yes, this place isn't exactly welcoming," Riestel answered for us.

The last jump felt like a routine thing already. There was no nausea, and the arochs didn't need to guard me so closely. As we appeared through the world's membrane to the arochs' home, I was speechless. Even Riestel was silent, though he knew the place.

In the middle of the barren lands was a pocket plane, woven with more gracefulness than anything else I had ever witnessed. There were radiant trees as though made of jewels. They chimed and sparkled in the wind, which wasn't supposed to blow in here. The pocket was so seamlessly a part of the world that you couldn't separate any plane. The hairs of the arochs rang like tiny bells as they announced their return. No one came to greet us, but everyone knew we were there.

Arid took us to a cavern hidden by bright ferns. She picked two leaves, and they expanded into beds of sort. We were brought water and fruit.

"Rest a little, walk a little, explore a little," Arid said. "The Head meets you once it knows you."

"What does that mean?" I asked.

"It means we are being observed," Riestel told me.

"Yes, the Head sees and feels you. Please share honestly," Arid encouraged me with a smile.

"Share what?"

"Anything that comes to the surface," Arid said and yawned. "I need rest too. I may see you again."

I sat on the fern bed. It was lovely and soft with a scent of a rainy forest. Riestel already laid on his eating a small green fruit.

"Raspberries and oranges. Not at all like I remembered it should have tasted," he said. "Have some."

"I'm more interested in their Head. This seems like a waste of time. Just sitting," I complained and took a bite. The fruit tasted like a blend of pears and blueberries. Did it change according to the person's taste? This place was enchantingly real and unreal at the same time.

"She did say to explore a little so we can do that if you feel up to it. But if you want to move things along, try speaking the truth about things that are important to you. They are trying to estimate how much to trust us, so the more open you are, the better they can judge you."

"Really? I don't know what to talk about."

"Anything. Or should I pick a subject?"

"Please don't, you'll just ask something that makes me look horrible and complicates my life."

"You can ask me things, too. If you dare."

"Right... as you are so known for your honesty," I remarked. "But alright. You say you love me. You loved Istrata too. I'm hardly as nice as she was. I'm hardly a shining beacon of light. I'm a jealous creature, and I tend to be wary of people. I probably have more negative traits than good ones. Why do you love me so willingly? I can't understand the reason."

Riestel coughed and threw the pit out of the cavern. He had a curious look about him. Like he was going to tell me a secret I didn't want to know.

"Why?" he said, tasting the question. "Because you try. You go on when I know you don't want to, but you still do. You hide everything behind that paradoxically cold surface, and yet the only thing you ever want from anyone is to take your hand and show you that you aren't alone. That someone cares. That someone would be willing to love you despite all your attempts at being unlovable. That's why you grabbed his offer so ferociously. He promised to try to love you and wanted to make your marriage real. I, on the other hand, I'm promising to follow you to the ends of existence and beyond until you can admit to yourself that all you ever wanted was for people to like you, love you as you wanted to love them but didn't dare."

"Shut up."

"I see how bitter you can be because so many fail your expectations. Small things, big betrayals, they all eventually do something you can use to excuse pushing them away. You even fail your own expectations, which is the worst. Despite that, you have faith that someday, somewhere, you will find someone who can prove you can be loved. And I intend to be there once it gets through your thick head, no matter how many decades it will take. You can test me all you want, but you will not get rid of me. My turn. Why did you need to know that?"

"I... I... don't know. I just wanted to... I wanted to because I find it preposterous that you could. You do realize you shouldn't?"

"But I must. Who else can heal you once you are willing to be healed?"

"I need to sleep."

"You aren't being very cooperative," Riestel noted, a little too amused and annoyingly unflustered with having been asked to be truthful of the extent of his feelings.

"I know."

"I won't ask if you return my feelings at this moment in time, but I do want to know if you think you ever could after all that I did to you," Riestel said.

I stared at the mossy cavern walls. To be honest or to lie? Might as well.

"I do," I answered.

"Think it or love me?"

"Love you."

"You do?" he asked in an almost sad tone. "Then my future is set," he added quietly.

"But it changes nothing. I'm still married. And I won't let him go. I will find a way to heal him."

"That's quite alright," Riestel replied and closed his eyes, smiling. "A fool thrives on hope."

XXXVIII

T he next day, if there was such a thing in this peculiar pocket, we wandered about. All things were heightened. Though not as much as in the true Lighter World. Suddenly, the sky lit up with four back-to-back shooting stars. The streaks were all of different color, and whatever they carried hit the ground a little ways from us.

"What in the skies was that?" I asked Riestel.

"Go and see. It is an interesting feature of the arochs. It explains why you rarely see children and why their numbers hardly diminish or grow."

"Do you know the answer to that? You know and haven't told the people in our city?"

"I don't think that would have changed much. They would have still attacked and we would have still attacked. They, because they made a pact, and we because of greed."

The place where the stars landed looked like barren sand wastes. But when I stepped on the sand, it felt like there was water underneath. I could see the glow of a soul coming through the grains and through the water. I pushed the floating grains aside. I could see a body forming.

"Do their souls cycle back here on death? Right away? To a new body?"

"To the same body. A copy," Riestel specified.

"So... this is where Istrata got the idea of recycling me to change her soul? This is where she learned how to create a copy of herself over and over again."

"Yes. I don't think she was told how, but she figured it out well enough."

"The arochs are then all copies of copies of the originally created... Like me."

"Yes."

"I felt so alone being the only one created like this. I'm still the only one of my kind, but… It's a natural mechanism? I'm not just some strange artificially made abomination. I'm actually a part of the world. That's… I…"

"Makes you a little less sad on the inside, right?" Riestel asked.

"It does."

"The Head will meet you," Arid announced happily from behind with a flood of emotions, pictures, and a great deal of relief.

As we walked, Arid expressed to us the proper way to behave and greet their leader. She excitedly told us how uncertain this assignment had been considered and that many had assumed that I would not be interested in meeting them or that they would ever reach me alive due to the years of conflict.

"You did well," I said. "I hope we find a way to help each other."

Arid stopped and gestured us to take the path framed by silver trees. Riestel offered his arm. I was nervous, so I took it. An image of us walking this path once before flashed in the air. Istrata's dark plum-colored train brushed the earth before our feet. Her posture was impeccable and defiant.

"This is like a huge nexus," I whispered. "Or not exactly, but… do you feel it?"

"Yes. There is something very ancient and holy here. You'll meet it soon."

As we reached a dazzlingly bright spring surrounded by beds of moss, we kneeled at the sides. The water mirrored all perfectly. I poked the greener than any green piece of moss. Riestel picked one small bronze flower from it and placed it on his tongue. He reminded me to do the same. It spread a metallic, wild strawberry-like taste. It was pleasant, but I could feel the substance spread through my body. It relaxed me.

I fell into the moss, feeling light as a feather. Riestel landed a little more gracefully. My mind and body traveled in a thousand directions between shiny particles.

"*Emissary of Fire and the Lord of Ice,*" a soft voice greeted us. The glistening specs united into grains and soon, in front of us, in the middle of the darkest womb where stars were born, was a creature I had never seen before. It had features and qualities from both humans and arochs in perfect symmetry. But they changed, as if turning a kaleidoscope. None were its true form, and yet all were. In one moment, it grew several pairs of bird's wings, and in another it had the mane of a beast.

"*I am grateful for your attention and for saving my first children. Momentarily anyway. I am the eldest,"* the creature said. *"I am called the Source. I let your fore-mother here once, and she promised me many things. My task here is done, apart from one thing. Thus, I am stuck in this world instead of building anew. Now, I will tell you what I promised her and she me and my first. Promised, but apparently betrayed us."*

I wanted to ask a thousand things, but Arid had demanded for us to be silent and not interrupt, as the flower could only be eaten when the creature allowed and no one knew how long it affected each person.

"I help to create worlds," the creature said. *"And it is my duty to find them a caretaker. She was my choice. All was well. But I cannot read minds or souls unless they volunteer it. I taught her of structures, I showed her how to mold it and life. You may recall, Lord of Ice, the dreams you also saw."*

Riestel nodded politely.

"Instead of honoring the laws I have laid," Source said with a sorrowful voice. *"She began to create her own. The world only existed in this plane and the one you inhabit, and the places they mixed in. Now, a third dimension has been forced into it. One of suffering for all that encounter it. That she intends to pull over all the others and make the only one. A frozen, stuck world. I do not understand this desire and I cannot reach her. The black ichor, the heavy stains that she forced to bring about through your... knights, must be removed,"* the creature said, and raised its hand to keep me from speaking. *"I know of your experiments. I am pleased. They show you understand the plague unleashed on this world. But it is not enough. She has amassed it for a long time, even from my perspective. There are three oceans of it waiting to flood into your world."*

Source smiled as it sensed how I struggled to keep quiet.

"I know your question. Why do you not help? Why do you not do anything? I cannot. I am a builder. Once I build a world and lay its rules, I have no more power over it. I exist and I do not exist here. I know all the structures of this world, but I can no longer rewrite them nor affect physical things, for I only exist in the weave. A will, an echo, a source. Thus, I cannot give you anything but knowledge. And I will give it to you, all that I gave her. And I will pray that you use it for something better, something more precious. You, Lord of Ice, would have been more merciful than her, but alone you cannot be enough. I hope this time the fire will not burn you."

Riestel flickered and disappeared.

"Stay awhile with the arochs. Live here in my house and sleep here. Each day you

will wake from a dream I visit. Go, Emissary of Fire. We will meet."

With a small nudge, the Source sent me back into my body. I stared up at the dusky, striped sky. I turned my head to Riestel. His face was adorned with a relaxed, happy expression. As if he had finally rested enough to heal.

"So, I'm going to have to stand you for a few more centuries," he said. "I'm not sure I've deserved such a cruel fate."

"I'm sure you've done something during your long life to deserve it."

HI THERE!

Thank you for reading my book! It means a lot to me. Please consider leaving a review or a star rating if you liked the story as it will encourage me to get the next book in the series out sooner rather than later.

ACKNOWLEDGEMENT

Colton Allen – for proofreading and editing this book and the two previous books in the SoE series, as well as leaving small notes about the story in the manuscript.

Aava L. – for making me understand life from another perspective and how precious time is.

STRANDS OF EXISTENCE

This series is a four-part fantasy series chronicling Istrae Elona's life and how she acts as a catalyst to bring about change and sometimes chaos. After this book, there will be one more.

Island Girl

First book in the series.

Sea Of Shadows

Second book in the series.

Printed in Great Britain
by Amazon

12717601R00164